Riptide

Also by Catherine Coulter

RIPTIDE

Catherine Coulter

ORION

First published in Great Britain in 2001 by Orion,
an imprint of the Orion Publishing Group Ltd.

A CIP catalogue record for this book is
available from the British Library.

ISBN 075284 609 4 (hardback)
ISBN 075284 610 8 (trade paperback)

Set in Bembo

Printed in Great Britain by
Clays Ltd, St Ives plc

The Orion Publishing Group Ltd
Orion House
5 Upper Saint Martin's Lane
London, WC2H 9EA

My ongoing love and thanks to
Iris Johansen and Kay Hooper,
and a big special hug
to Linda Howard
for a terrific twist.

—CC

Riptide

Chapter 1

New York City

June 15
Present

*B*ecca was watching an afternoon soap opera she'd seen off and on since she was a kid. She found herself wondering if she would ever have a child who needed a heart transplant one month and a new kidney the next, or a husband who wouldn't be faithful to her for longer than it took a new woman to look in his direction.

Then the phone rang.

She jumped to her feet, then stopped dead still and stared over at the phone. She heard a guy on TV whining about how life wasn't fair. He didn't know what fair was.

She made no move to answer the phone. She just stood there and listened, watching it as it rang three more times. Then, finally, because her mother was lying in a coma in Lenox Hill Hospital, because she just plain couldn't stand the ringing ringing ringing, she watched her hand reach out and pick up the receiver.

She forced her mouth to form the single word. "Hello?"

"Hi, Rebecca. It's your boyfriend. I've got you so scared you have to force yourself to pick up the phone. Isn't that right?"

She closed her eyes as that hated voice, low and deep, swept over her, into her, making her so afraid she was shaking. No hint of an Atlanta drawl, no sharp New York vowels, no dropped R's from Boston. A voice that was well educated, with smooth, clear diction, perhaps even a touch of the Brit in it. Old? Young? She didn't know, couldn't tell. She had to keep it together. She had to listen carefully, to remember how he spoke, what he said. *You can do it. Keep it together. Make him talk, make him say something, you never know what will pop out.* That was what the police psychologist in Albany had told her to do when the man had first started calling her. Listen carefully. Don't let him scare you. Take control. You guide him, not the other way around. Becca licked her lips, chapped from the hot, dry air in Manhattan that week, an anomaly, the weather forecaster had said. And so Becca repeated her litany of questions, trying to keep her voice calm, cool, in charge, yes, that was her. "Won't you tell me who you are? I really want to know. Maybe we can talk about why you keep calling me. Can we do that?"

"Can't you come up with some new questions, Rebecca? After all, I've called you a good dozen times now. And you always say the same things. Ah, they're from a shrink, aren't they? They told you to ask those questions, to try to distract me, to get me to spill my guts to you. Sorry, it won't work."

She'd never really thought it would work, that stratagem. No, this guy knew what he was doing, and he knew how to do it. She wanted to plead with him to leave her alone, but she didn't. Instead, she snapped. She simply lost it, the long-buried anger cutting through her bone-grinding fear. She gripped the phone, knuckles white, and yelled, "Listen to me, you little prick. Stop saying you're my boyfriend. You're nothing but a sick jerk. Now, how about this for a question? Why don't you go to hell where you belong? Why don't you go kill yourself, you're sure not worth anything to the human race. Don't call me anymore, you pathetic bastard. The cops are on to you. The phone is tapped, do you hear me? They're going to get you and fry you."

She'd caught him off guard, she knew it, and an adrenaline rush sent her sky-high, but only for a moment. After a slight pause, he recovered. In a calm, reasonable voice, he said, "Now, Rebecca sweetheart, you know as well as I do that the cops now don't believe you're being stalked, that some weird guy is calling you at all hours, trying to scare you. You had the phone tap put in yourself because you couldn't get them to do it. And I'll never talk long enough for that old, low-tech equipment of yours to get a trace. Oh yes, Rebecca, because you insulted me, you'll have to pay for it, big-time."

She slammed down the receiver. She held it there, hard, as if trying to stanch the bleeding of a wound, as if holding it down would keep him from dialing her again, keep him away from her. Slowly, finally, she backed away from the phone. She heard a wife on the TV soap plead with her husband not to leave her for her younger sister. She walked out onto her small balcony and looked over Central Park, then turned a bit to the right to look at the Metropolitan Museum. Hordes of people, most in shorts, most of them tourists, sat on the steps, reading, laughing, talking, eating hot dogs from the vendor Teodolpho, some of them probably smoking dope, picking pockets, and there were two cops on horseback nearby, their horses' heads pumping up and down, nervous for some reason. The sun blazed down. It was only mid-June, yet the unseasonable heat wave continued unabated. Inside the apartment it was twenty-five degrees cooler. Too cold, at least for her, but she couldn't get the thermostat to move either up or down.

The phone rang again. She heard it clearly through the half-closed glass door.

She jerked around and nearly fell over the railing. Not that it was unexpected. No, never that, it was just so incongruous set against the normalcy of the scene outside.

She forced herself to look back into her mother's lovely pastel living room, to the glass table beside the sofa, at the white phone that sat atop that table, ringing, ringing.

She let it ring six more times. Then she knew she had to answer it. It might be about her mother, her very sick mother, who might be dying. But of course she knew it was him. It didn't matter. Did he know why she even had the phone turned on in the first place? He seemed to know everything else, but he hadn't said anything about her mother. She knew she had no choice at all. She picked it up on the tenth ring.

"Rebecca, I want you to go out onto your balcony again. Look to where those cops are sitting on their horses. Do it now, Rebecca."

She laid down the receiver and walked back out onto the balcony, leaving the glass door open behind her. She looked down at the cops. She kept looking. She knew something horrible was going to happen, she just knew it, and there was nothing she could do about it but watch and wait. She waited for three minutes. Just when she was beginning to convince herself that the man was trying new and different ways to terrorize her, there was a loud explosion.

She watched both horses rear up wildly. One of the cops went flying. He landed in a bush as thick smoke billowed up, obscuring the scene.

When the smoke cleared a bit, she saw an old bag lady lying on the sidewalk, her market cart in twisted pieces beside her, her few

4

belongings strewn around her. Pieces of paper fluttered down to the sidewalk, now rutted with deep pockmarks. A large bottle of ginger ale was broken, liquid flowing over the old woman's sneakers. Time seemed to have stopped, then suddenly there was chaos as everyone in view exploded into action. Some people who'd been loitering on the steps of the museum ran toward the old lady.

The cops got there first; the one who'd been thrown from his horse was limping as he ran. They were yelling, waving their arms—at the carnage or the onrushing people, Becca didn't know. She saw the horses throwing their heads from side to side, their eyes rolling at the smoke, the smell of the explosive. Becca stood there frozen, watching. The old woman didn't move.

Becca knew she was dead. Her stalker had detonated a bomb and killed that poor old woman. Why? Just to terrorize her more? She was already so terrified she could hardly function. What did he want now? She'd left Albany, left the governor's staff with no warning, had not even called to check in.

She walked slowly back inside the living room, firmly closing the glass door behind her. She looked at the phone, heard him saying her name, over and over. *Rebecca, Rebecca.* Very slowly, she hung up. She fell to her knees and jerked the connector out of the wall jack. The phone in the bedroom rang, and kept ringing.

She pressed herself close to the wall, her palms slammed against her ears. She had to do something. She had to talk to the cops. Again. Surely now that someone was dead, they would believe that some maniac was terrorizing her, stalking her, murdering someone to show her he meant business.

This time they had to believe her.

Six Days Later

Riptide, Maine

She pulled into the Texaco gas station, waved to the guy inside the small glass booth, then pumped some regular into her gas tank. She was on the outskirts of Riptide, a quaint town that sprawled north to south, hugging a small harbor filled with sailboats, motorboats, and many fishing boats. Lobster, she thought, and breathed in deeply, air redolent of brine, seaweed, and fish, plus a faint hint of wildflowers, their sweetness riding lightly on the breeze from the sea.

Riptide, Maine.

She was in the sticks, the boondocks, a place nobody knew about, except for a few tourists in the summer. She was sixty-four miles north of Christmas Cove, a beautiful small coastal town she'd visited once as a child, with her mother.

For the first time in two and a half weeks, she felt safe. She felt the salty air tingling on her skin, let the warm breeze flutter her hair against her cheek.

She was in control of her life again.

But what about Governor Bledsoe? He would be all right, he had to be. He had cops everywhere, brushing his teeth for him, sleeping under his bed—no matter who he was sleeping with—hiding in his washroom off his big square office with its huge mahogany power desk. He would be all right. The crazy guy who had terrorized her until six days ago wouldn't be able to get near him.

The main street in Riptide was West Hemlock. There wasn't an East Hemlock unless someone wanted to drive into the ocean. She drove nearly to the end of the street to an old Victorian bed-and-breakfast called Errol Flynn's Hammock. There was a widow's walk on top, railed in black. She counted at least five colors on the exterior. It was perfect.

"I like the name," she said to the old man behind the rich mahogany counter.

"Yep," he said, and pushed the guest book toward her. "I like it, too. Been Scottie all my life. Sign in and I'll beam you right up."

She smiled and signed Becca Powell. She'd always admired Colin Powell. Surely he wouldn't mind if she borrowed his name for a while. For a while, Becca Matlock would cease to exist.

She was safe.

But why, she wondered yet again, why hadn't the police believed her? Still they were providing the governor extra protection, so that was something.

Why?

Chapter 2

New York City

June 15

They had Becca sit in an uncomfortable chair with uneven legs. She laid one hand on the scarred table, looking at the woman and two men, and knew they thought she was a nut or, very likely, something far worse.

There were three other men in the room, lined up against the wall next to the door. No one introduced them. She wondered if they were FBI. Probably, since she'd reported the threat on the governor, and they were dressed in dark suits, white shirts, blue ties. She'd never seen so many wing tips in one room before.

Detective Morales, slight, black-eyed, handsome, said quietly, "Ms. Matlock, we are trying to understand this. You say he blew up this old woman just to get your attention? For what reason? Why you? What does he want? Who is he?"

She repeated it all again, more slowly this time, nearly word for word. Finally, seeing their stone faces, she tried yet again, leaning forward, clasping her hands on the wooden table, avoiding the clump of long-ago-dried food. "Listen, I have no idea who he is. I know it's a man, but I can't tell if he's old or if he's young. I told you that I've heard him many times on the phone. He started calling me in Albany and then he followed me here to New York. I never saw him in Albany, but I've seen him here, stalking me, not close enough to identify, but I'm sure it was him I saw three different times. I reported this eight days ago to you, Detective Morales."

"Yes," said Detective McDonnell, a man who looked like he sliced and diced criminal suspects for breakfast. His body was long and thin, his suit rumpled and loose, his voice cold. "We know all about it. We acted on it. I spoke to the police in Albany when we didn't see anything of him here in New York. We all compared notes, discussed everything thoroughly."

"What else can I tell you?"

"You said he calls you Rebecca, never shortens your name."

"Yes, Detective Morales. He always says Rebecca and he always identifies himself as my boyfriend."

A look went between the two men. Did they think it was a vengeful ex-boyfriend?

"I've told you that I don't recognize his voice. I have never known this man, never. I'm certain of it."

Detective Letitia Gordon, the only other woman in the room, was tall, wide-mouthed, with hair cut very short, and she carried a big chip on her shoulder. She said in a voice colder than McDonnell's, "You could try for the truth. I'm tired of all this bullshit. You're a liar, Ms. Matlock. Sure, Hector did everything he could. We all tried to believe you, at first, but there wasn't anyone around you. Not a soul. We wasted three days tagging you, and all for nothing. We spent another two days following up on everything you told us, but again, nothing.

"What is it with you? Are you on coke?" She tapped the side of her head with two long fingers. "You need attention? Daddy didn't give you enough when you were a little girl? That's why you have this made-up guy call himself your boyfriend?"

Becca wanted to punch out Detective Gordon. She imagined the woman could pulverize her, so that wouldn't be smart. She had to be calm, logical. She had to be the sane adult here. She cocked her head at the woman and said, "Why are you angry at me? I haven't done anything. I'm just trying to get some help. Now he's killed this old woman. You've got to stop him. Don't you?"

The two male detectives again darted glances back and forth. The woman shook her head in disgust. Then she pushed back her chair and rose. She leaned over and splayed her hands on the wooden tabletop, right next to the clump of dried food. Her face was right in Becca's. Her breath smelled of fresh oranges. "You made it all up, didn't you? There wasn't any guy calling you and telling you to look outside your window. When that bag lady got blown up by some nutcase, you just pulled in your fantasy guy again to be responsible for the bomb. No more. We want you to see our psychiatrist, Ms. Matlock. Right now. You've had your fifteen minutes of fame, now it's time to give it up."

"Of course I won't see any shrink, that's—"

"You either see the psychiatrist or we arrest you."

A nightmare, she thought. *Here I am at the police station, telling them everything I know, and they think I'm crazy.* She said slowly, staring right at Detective Gordon, "For what?"

"You're a public nuisance. You're filing false complaints, telling lies that waste manpower. I don't like you, Ms. Matlock. I'd like to throw you in jail for all the grief you've dished out, but I won't if you go see our shrink. Maybe he can straighten you out. God knows someone needs to."

Becca rose slowly to her feet. She looked at each of them in turn. "I have told you the truth. There is a madman out there and I don't know who he is. I've told you everything I can think of. He has threatened the governor. He murdered that poor old woman in front of the museum. I'm not making anything up. I'm not nuts and I'm not on drugs."

It did no good. They didn't believe her.

The three men lined up along the wall of the interrogation room didn't say a word. One of them simply nodded to Detective Gordon as Becca walked out of the room.

Thirty minutes later, Becca Matlock was seated in a very comfortable chair in a small office that had only two narrow windows that looked across at two other narrow windows. Across the desk sat Dr. Burnett, a man somewhere in his forties, nearly bald, wearing designer glasses. He looked intense and tired.

"What I don't understand," Becca said, sitting forward, "is why the police won't believe me."

"We'll get to that. Now, you didn't want to speak with me?"

"I'm sure you're a very nice man, but no, I don't need to speak to you, at least not professionally."

"The police officers aren't certain about that, Ms. Matlock. Now, why don't you tell me, in your own words, a bit about yourself and exactly when this stalker first came to your attention."

Yet again, she thought. Her voice was flat because she'd said the same words so many times. Hard to feel anything saying them now. "I'm a senior speech writer for Governor Bledsoe. I live in a very nice condominium on Oak Street in Albany. Two and a half weeks ago, I got the first phone call. No heavy breathing, no profanity, nothing like that. He just said he'd seen me running in the park, and he wanted to get to know me. He wouldn't tell me who he was. He said I would come to know him very well. He said he wanted to be my boyfriend. I told him to leave me alone and hung up."

"Did you tell any friends or the governor about the call?"

"Not until after he called me another two times. That's when he told me to stop sleeping with the governor. He said he was my boyfriend, and I wasn't going to sleep with any other man. In a very calm voice, he said that if I didn't stop sleeping with the governor, he'd just have to kill him. Naturally, when I told the governor about this, everyone licensed to carry a gun within a ten-mile radius was on it."

He didn't even crack a smile, just kept staring at her.

Becca found she really didn't care. She said, "They tapped my phone immediately, but somehow he knew they had. They couldn't find him. They said he was using some sort of electronic scrambler that kept giving out fake locations."

"And are you sleeping with Governor Bledsoe, Ms. Matlock?"

She'd heard that question a good dozen times, too, over and over, especially from Detective Gordon. She even managed a smile. "Actually, no. I don't suppose you've noticed, but he is old enough to be my father."

"We had a president old enough to be your father and a woman even younger than you are and neither of them had a problem with that concept."

She wondered if Governor Bledsoe could ever survive a Monica and almost smiled. She just shrugged.

"So, Ms. Matlock, are you sleeping with the governor?"

She'd discovered that at the mention of sex, everyone—media folk, cops, friends—homed right in on it. It still offended her, but she had answered the question so often the edge was off now. She shrugged again, seeing that it bothered him, and said, "No, I haven't slept with Governor Bledsoe. I have never wanted to sleep with Governor Bledsoe. I write speeches for him, really fine speeches. I don't sleep with him. I even occasionally write speeches for Mrs. Bledsoe. I don't sleep with her, either.

"Now, I have no clue why the man believes that I am having sex with the governor. I have no clue why he would care if I were. Why did he pull the governor, of all people, out of the hat? Because I spend time with him? Because he's powerful? I just don't know. The Albany police haven't found out anything about this man yet. However, they didn't think I was a liar, not like the police here in New York. I even met with a police psychologist, who gave me advice on how to handle him when he called."

"Actually, Ms. Matlock, the Albany police do believe you are a liar. At first they didn't, but that's what they believe now. But do go on."

Just like that? He said everyone believed she was a liar and she was just to go on? "What do you mean?" she said slowly. "They never gave me that impression."

"That's why our detectives finally sent you to me. They spoke to their counterparts in Albany. No one could discover any stalker. They believed you were disturbed about something. Perhaps you had a crush on the governor and this was your way of getting him to acknowledge you."

"Ah, I see. I have, perhaps, a fatal attraction."

"No, certainly not. You shouldn't have referred to it like that. It's much too soon."

"Too soon for what? I'm still trying to get the hang of it?"

Anger flashed in his eyes. It made her feel good. "Just go on, Ms. Matlock. No, don't argue with me yet. First tell me more. I need to understand. Then we can determine what's going on, together."

In his dreams, she thought. A crush on the governor? Yeah, right. What a joke that was. Bledsoe was a man who would sleep with a nun if he could get under her habit. He made Bill Clinton look as upstanding as Eisenhower, or had Ike had a mistress, too? Men and power—the two always seemed to go with illicit sex. As for Bledsoe, he'd been very lucky thus far, he hadn't yet run into an intern as voracious as Monica, one who wouldn't just fade into the woodwork when he was done with her.

"Very well," she said. "I came to New York to escape that maniac. I was—I am—terrified of him and what he'll do. Also, my mother lives here and she's very ill. I wanted to be with her."

"You're staying in her apartment, is that right?"

"Yes. She's in Lenox Hill Hospital."

"What's wrong with her?"

Becca looked at him and tried to say the words. They wouldn't come out. She cleared her throat and finally managed to say, "She's dying of uterine cancer."

"I'm sorry. You say this man followed you here to New York?"

Becca nodded. "I saw him here for the first time just after I arrived in New York, on Madison near Fiftieth, weaving in and out of people to my right. He was wearing a blue windbreaker and a baseball cap. How do I know it was him? I can't be specific about that. I just know. Deep down, I recognized that it was him. He knew I saw him, I'm sure of that. Unfortunately I couldn't see him clearly enough to give more than a general impression of what he looks like."

"And that is?"

"He's tall, slender. Is he young? I just don't know. The baseball cap covered his hair and he was wearing aviator glasses, very dark, opaque. He was wearing generic jeans and that blue windbreaker that was very loose." She paused a moment. "I've told the police all of this, many times. Why do you care?"

His look said it all. He wanted to see just how specific, just how detailed her descriptions were, how much she'd embellished her fantasy man. And all of the marvelous particulars were from her imagination, her very sick imagination.

She kept it together. When he hesitated, she said mildly, "He ducked away when I turned toward him. Then the phone calls started again. I know he's keeping close tabs on me. He seems to know exactly where I am and what I'm doing. I can feel him, you know?"

"You told the officers that he wouldn't tell you what he wanted."

"No, not really, other than to tell me if I didn't stop having sex with the governor, he would kill him. I asked him why he'd do that and he just said he didn't want me to have sex with any other man, that he was my boyfriend. But it sounded funny, like it was just something he was saying, not something he really meant. So why is he doing this, really? I don't know. I will be frank with you, Dr. Burnett. I'm not crazy, I'm terrified. If that's his aim, he's certainly succeeded. I simply don't understand why the police think I'm the bad guy here, that I'm making all of this up for some crazy reason. Perhaps you could believe me now?"

He was a shrink; he hedged well. "Tell me why you believe this man is stalking you and making these phone calls to you, why you don't believe that he wants to be your boyfriend, that it really all just boils down to an obsession and his possession of you?"

She closed her eyes. She'd thought and thought about why, but there wasn't anything. Nothing at all. He'd targeted her, but why? She shook her head. "At first he said he wanted to know me. What does that mean? If he wanted that, why wouldn't he just come over and introduce himself? If the cops wanted a nutcase to send to you, they should find him. What does he really want? I just don't know. If I even had a supposition about it, I'd throw it out there, believe me. But the boyfriend thing? No, I don't believe that."

He sat forward, his fingertips pressed together, studying her. What did he see? What was he thinking? Did she sound insane? Evidently so, because when he said very quietly, gently even, "You and I need to talk about you, Ms. Matlock," she knew he didn't believe her, probably hadn't believed her for a minute. He continued in that same gentle voice, "There's a big problem here. Without intervention, it will continue to get bigger and that worries me. Perhaps you're already seeing a psychiatrist?"

She had a big problem? She rose slowly and placed her hands on his desktop. "You're right about that, doctor. I do have a big problem. You just don't know where the problem really is. That, or you refuse to recognize it. That makes it easier, I guess."

She grabbed up her purse and walked toward the door. He called after her, "You need me, Ms. Matlock. You need my help. I don't like the direction you're going. Come back and let me talk to you."

She said over her shoulder, "You're a fool, sir," and kept walking. "As for your objectivity, perhaps you should consult your ethics about that, Doctor."

She heard him coming after her. She slammed the door and took off running down the long dingy hallway.

Chapter 3

*B*ecca kept walking, her head down, out the front doors, staring at her Bally flats. From the corner of her eye, she saw a man turn away from her, quickly, too quickly. She was at One Police Plaza. There were a million people, all of them hurrying, like all New Yorkers, focused on where they were going, wasting not an instant. But this man, he was watching her, she knew it. It was him, it had to be. If only she could get close enough, she could describe him. Where was he now?

Over there, by a city trash can. He was wearing sunglasses, the same opaque aviator glasses, and a red Braves baseball cap, this time backward. He was the bad guy in all of this, not her. Something hit her hard at that moment, and she felt pure rage pump through her. She yelled, "Wait! Don't you run away from me, you coward!" Then she started pushing her way through the crowds of people to where she'd last seen him. Over there, by that building, wearing a sweatshirt, dark blue, long-sleeved, no windbreaker this time. She headed that way. She was cursed, someone elbowed her, but she didn't care. She would become an instant New Yorker—utterly focused, rude if anyone dared to get in her way. She made it to the corner of the building, but she didn't see any dark blue sweatshirt. No baseball cap. She stood there panting.

Why didn't the cops believe her? What had she ever done to make them believe she was a liar? What had made the Albany cops believe she'd lied? And now, he'd murdered that poor old woman

19

by the museum. She wasn't some crazy figment in her mind, she was very real and in the morgue.

She stopped. She'd lost him. She stood there, a long time, breathing hard, feeling scores of people part and go around her on either side. Just two steps beyond her, the seas closed again.

Forty-five minutes later, Becca was at Lenox Hill Hospital, sitting beside her mother's bed. Her mother, who was now in a near-coma, was so drugged she didn't recognize her daughter. Becca sat there, holding her hand, not speaking about the stalker, but talking about the speech she'd written for the governor on gun control, something she wasn't so certain about now. "In all five boroughs, handgun laws are the same and are very strict. Do you know that one gun store owner told me that 'to buy a gun in New York City, you have to stand in a corner on one leg and beg.'"

She paused a moment. For the first time in her life, she desperately wanted a handgun. But there was just no way she could get one in time to help. She'd need a permit, have to wait fifteen days after she'd bought the gun, and then hang around for probably another six months for them to do a background check on her. And then stand on one leg and beg. She said to her silent mother, "I've never before even thought about owning a gun, Mom, but who knows? Crime is everywhere." Yes, she wanted to buy a gun, but if she did finally manage to get one, the stalker would have long since killed her. She felt like a victim waiting to happen and there was nothing she could do about it. No one would help her. She was all she had, and in terms of getting a hold of a gun, she'd have to go to the street. And the thought of going up to street guys and asking them to sell her a gun scared her to her toes.

"It was a great speech, Mom. I had to let the governor straddle the fence, no way around that, but I did have him say that he didn't want guns forbidden, just didn't want them in the hands of criminals. I did pros and cons on whether the proposed federal one-handgun-a-month law will work. You know, the NRA's opinions, then the HCI's—they're Handgun Control, Inc."

She kept talking, patting her mother's hands, lightly stroking her fingers over her forearm, careful not to hit any of the IV lines.

"So many of your friends have been here. All of them are very worried. They all love you."

Her mother was dying, she knew it as a god-awful fact, as something that couldn't be changed, but she just couldn't accept it down deep inside her where her mother had always been from her earliest memories, always there for her, always. She thought of the years ahead without her, but she simply couldn't see it at all. Tears stung her eyes and she sniffed them back. "Mom," she said, and laid her cheek against her mother's arm. "I don't want you to die, but I know the cancer is bad and you couldn't bear the pain if you stayed with me." There, she'd said the words aloud. She slowly raised her head. "I love you, Mom. I love you more than you can imagine. If you can somehow hear me, somehow understand, please know that you have always been the most important person in my life. Thank you for being my mother." She had no more words. She sat there another half hour, looking at her mother's beloved face, so full of life just a few weeks ago, a face made for myriad expressions, each of which Becca knew. It was almost over, and there was simply nothing she could do. She said then, "I'll be back soon, Mom. Please rest and don't feel any pain. I love you."

She knew that she should run, that this man, whoever he was, would end up killing her and there was nothing she could do to stop him. If she stayed here. Certainly the police weren't going to do anything. But no, she wasn't about to leave her mother.

She rose, leaned down, and kissed her mother's soft, pale cheek. She lightly patted her mother's hair, so very thin now, her scalp showing here and there. It was the drugs, a nurse had told her. It happened. Such a beautiful woman, her mother had been, tall and fair, her hair that unusual pale blond that had no other colors in it. Her mother was still beautiful, but she was so still now, almost as if she were already gone. No, Becca wouldn't leave her. The guy would have to kill her to make her leave her mother.

She didn't realize she was crying again until a nurse pressed a Kleenex into her hand. "Thank you," she said, not looking away from her mother.

"Go home and get some sleep, Becca," the nurse said, her voice quiet and calm. "I'll keep watch. Go get some sleep."

There's no one else in the world for me, Becca thought, as she walked away from Lenox Hill Hospital. *I'll be alone when Mom dies.*

Her mother died that night. She just drifted away, the doctor told her, no pain, no awareness of death. An easy passing. Ten minutes after the call, the phone rang again.

This time she didn't pick it up. She put her mother's apartment on the market the following day, spent the night in a hotel under an assumed name, and made all the funeral arrangements from there. She called her mother's friends to invite them to the small, private service.

A day and a half later, Becca threw the first clot of rich, dark earth over her mother's coffin. She watched as the black dirt mixed with the deep red roses on top of the coffin. She didn't cry, but all of her mother's friends were quietly weeping. She accepted a hug from each of them. It was still very hot in New York, too hot for the middle of June.

When she returned to her hotel room the phone was ringing. Without thinking, she picked it up.

"You tried to get away from me, Rebecca. I don't like that."

She'd had it. She'd been pushed too hard. Her mother was dead, there was nothing to stay her hand. "I nearly caught you the other day, at One Police Plaza, you pathetic coward. You jerk, did you wonder what I was doing there? I was blowing the whistle on you, you murderer. Yeah, I saw you, all right. You had on that ridiculous baseball cap and that dark blue sweatshirt. Next time I'll get you and then I'll shoot you right between your crazy eyes."

"It's you the cops think is crazy. I'm not even a blip on their radar. Hey, I don't even exist." His voice grew deeper, harder. "Stop sleeping with the governor or I'll kill him just like I did that stupid old bag lady. I've told you that over and over but you haven't listened to me. I know he's visited you in New York. Everyone knows it. Stop sleeping with him."

She started laughing and couldn't seem to stop. She did only when he began yelling at her, calling her a whore, a stupid bitch, and more curses, some of them extraordinarily vicious.

She hiccuped. "Sleep with the governor? Are you nuts? He's married. He has three children, two of them older than I am." And then, because it no longer mattered, because he might not really exist anyway, she said, "The governor sleeps with every woman he can talk into that private room off his office. I'd have to take a number. You want them all to stop sleeping with him? It'll keep you busy until the next century and that's a very long time away."

"It's just you, Rebecca. You've got to stop sleeping with him."

"Listen to me, you stupid jerk. I would only sleep with the governor if world peace were in the balance. Even then it would be a very close call."

The creep actually sighed. "Don't lie, Rebecca. Just stop, do you hear me?"

"I can't stop something I've never even done."

"It's a shame," he said, and for the first time, he hung up on her.

That night the governor was shot through the neck outside the Hilton Hotel, where he was attending a fundraiser for cancer research. He was lucky. There were more than a hundred doctors around. They managed to save his life. It was reported that the bullet was fired from a great distance, by a marksman with remarkable skill. They had no leads as yet.

When she heard that, she said to the Superman cartoon character playing soundlessly on the television, "He was supposed to go to a fundraiser on endangered species."

That's when she ran. Her mother was dead and there was nothing more holding her here.

To Maine, to find sanctuary.

Riptide, Maine

June 22

Becca said, "I'll take it."

The real estate broker, Rachel Ryan, beamed at her, then almost immediately backpedaled. "Perhaps you're making this decision too quickly, Ms. Powell. Would you like to think about this for a bit? I will have everything cleaned, but the house is old and that includes all the appliances and the bathrooms. It's furnished, of course, but the furniture isn't all that remarkable. The house has been empty for four years, since Mr. Marley's death."

"You told me all that, Mrs. Ryan. I see that it's an old house. I still like it, it's charming. And it's quite large. I like a lot of space. Also it's here at the end of the lane all by itself. I do like my privacy." Now, that was an understatement but nonetheless the truth. "A Mr. Marley lived here?"

"Mr. Jacob Marley. Yes, the same name as in *A Christmas Carol.*

He was eighty-seven years when he passed away in his sleep. He kept to himself for the last thirty years or so of his life. His daddy started the town back in 1907, after several of his businesses in Boston were burned to the ground one hot summer night. It was said his enemies were responsible. Mr. Marley Senior wasn't a popular man. He was one of those infamous robber barons. But he wasn't stupid. He decided it was healthier to just leave Boston and so he did, and came here. There was already a small fishing village here, and he just took it over and renamed it."

Becca patted the woman's shoulder. "It's all right. I've thought about it, Mrs. Ryan. I'll give you a money order since I don't have a bank account here. Could it be cleaned today so I can move in tomorrow afternoon?"

"It will be ready if I have to clean it myself. Actually, since it's summer, I can round up a dozen high-schoolers and get them right over here. Don't you worry about a thing. Oh yes, there's the most adorable little boy who lives not far from here, over on Gum Shoe Lane. I'm not really his aunt but that's what he calls me. His name is Sam and I watched him come into this world. His mother was my best friend and I—"

Becca raised her brow, listening politely, but evidently Rachel Ryan was through talking.

"All right, Ms. Powell, I will see you in a couple of days. Call me if there are any problems."

And it was done. Becca was the proud renter of a very old Victorian jewel that featured eight bedrooms, three spacious bathrooms, a kitchen that surely must have been a showplace before 1910, and a total of ten fireplaces. And as she'd told Rachel Ryan, it was very private, at the end of Belladonna Drive, no prying neighbors anywhere near, and that's what she wanted. The nearest house was a good half mile away. The property was bordered on three sides by thick maple and pine trees, and the view of the ocean from the widow's walk was spectacular.

She hummed when she moved in on Thursday afternoon. She even managed to work up a sweat. Even though she wouldn't use them, she cleaned the bedrooms just because she wanted to. She wallowed in all the space. She never wanted to live in an apartment again.

She'd bought a gun from a guy she met in a restaurant in Rockland, Maine. She'd taken a big chance, but it had, thank God, worked out. The gun was a beauty—a Coonan .357 Magnum automatic, and the guy had taken her just next door, where there was a sports shop with an indoor range, and taught her how to shoot. He'd then asked her to go to a motel with him. He was child's play to deal with after the maniac in New York. All she'd had to do was say no very firmly. No need to draw her new gun on the guy.

She gently laid the Coonan in the top drawer of her bedside table, a very old mahogany piece with rusted hinges. As she closed the drawer she realized that she hadn't cried when her mother died. She hadn't cried at her funeral. But now, as she gently placed a photograph of her mother on top of the bedside table, she felt the tears roll down her cheeks. She stood there staring down at her mother's picture, taken nearly twenty years before, showing a beautiful young woman, so fair and fine-boned, laughing, hugging Becca against her side. Becca couldn't remember where they were, maybe in upstate New York. They'd stayed up there for a while when Becca was six and seven years old. "Oh, Mom, I'm so sorry. If only you hadn't locked your heart away with a dead man, maybe there could have been another man to love, couldn't there? You had so much to offer, so much love to give. Oh God, I miss you so much."

She lay down on the bed, held a pillow against her chest, and cried until there were no more tears. She got up and wiped the light sheen of dust off the photo, then carefully set it down again. "I'm safe now, Mom. I don't know what's going on, but at least I'm safe for the time being. That man won't find me here. How could he? I know no one followed me."

She realized, as she was speaking to her mother's photo, that she also ached for the father she'd never known, Thomas Matlock, shot and killed in Vietnam so long ago, when she was just a baby. A war hero. But her mother hadn't forgotten, ever. And it was his name that her mother had whispered before she'd fallen into the drug-induced coma. "Thomas, Thomas."

He'd been dead for over twenty-five years. So long ago. A different world, but the people were the same—both good and evil, as always—mauling one another to get the lion's share of the spoils. He'd seen her before he'd gone, her mother had told her, seen her and hugged her and loved her. But Becca couldn't remember him.

She finished hanging up her clothes and arranging her toiletries in the old-fashioned bathroom with its claw-footed bathtub. The teenagers had even scrubbed between the claws. Good job.

There was a knock on the door. Becca dropped the towel she was holding and froze.

Another knock.

It wasn't him. He had no idea where she was. There was no way he could find her. It was probably the guy to check the one air-conditioning unit in the living room window. Or the garbage man, or—

"Don't be paranoid," she said aloud to the blue towel as she picked it up and hung it on the very old wooden bar. "Do you also realize you've been talking out loud a whole lot recently? Another thing, you don't sound particularly bright." But who cared if she sang to the towel rack, she thought, as she walked down the old creaking stairs to the front entrance hall.

She could only stare at the tall man who stood in the doorway. It was Tyler, the boy she'd known in college. She'd been one of his few friends. He'd been a geek loner and hadn't managed to make more than a few non-geek friends. Only he wasn't a geek anymore. No more heavy-rimmed glasses and pen protector on his shirt pocket. No more stooped shoulders and pants worn too high, his ankles showing his white socks. He was wearing tight jeans that fit him very well indeed, his hair was long, and his shoulders were wide enough to make a woman blink. He was buff, in very good shape. Yes, he was a good-looking man. It was amazing. She had to blink at him a couple of times to get her bearings.

"Tyler? Tyler McBride? Is it really you? I'm sorry I'm gawking. You look so very different, but it's still you. Actually, to be perfectly honest about this, you're very sexy."

He gave her a huge grin and gripped her hands between his. "Becca Matlock, it's good to see you. I came over to see my new neighbor, never dreaming it could be you. Is Powell your married name? I can't imagine why you're here of all places, the end of the world. But whatever. Welcome to Riptide."

Chapter 4

She laughed and squeezed his hands and said, "Goodness, you're not a nerd anymore. Listen, Tyler, it's because of you that I'm here. I would have called you. I just haven't gotten to it yet. Can I really be so lucky to have you for a neighbor?"

He gave her a very nice smile and just stood there, waiting. Had he had braces? She couldn't remember. It didn't matter, he had gorgeous teeth now. What a difference. Incredible.

"Oh, yes, everyone's a neighbor in Riptide, but yes, I live just one street over, on Gum Shoe Lane."

She let go of his hands although she didn't want to, and stepped back. "Do come in. Everything, including the furnishings, is ancient, but there aren't any springs sticking up in the sofa, and it's fairly comfortable. Mrs. Ryan sent an army of teenagers here to clean the place. They did a pretty decent job. Come in, Tyler, come in."

She managed to make two cups of tea on the ancient stove while Tyler sat at the kitchen table watching her. "What do you mean you came here because of me?"

She dipped a tea bag in and out of the cups of hot water. "I remembered your talking about your hometown, Riptide. You called it your haven." She paused a moment and stared down into her teacup. "I'll never forget your saying that Riptide was in the boondocks, near nothing at all, so private you nearly forgot that you were even here. Just out on the edge of the world, nearly falling into the ocean, and nobody knew where it was, or cared. You also said that Riptide was the place where the sun first rose in the U.S. You said for those moments, the sky was an orange ball and the water was a cauldron of fire."

"I said that? I didn't know I was such a poet."

"That's nearly word for word, and, as I told you, that's why I came. Goodness, I can't get over how you've changed, Tyler."

"Everyone changes, Becca. Even you. You're prettier now than you were back in college." He frowned a moment, as if trying to remember. "Your hair's darker and I don't remember you having brown eyes or wearing glasses, but otherwise, I'd know you anywhere." Well damn, she thought, that wasn't good. She pushed the glasses higher on her nose.

He accepted the cup of tea, not speaking until she sat down at the table across from him. Then he smiled at her and said, "Why do you need a haven?"

What to tell him?

That the governor had been shot in the neck because of her? No, no, she couldn't feel responsible. That madman shot the governor. She stalled.

He backed off and said, "You went to New York, didn't you? You were a writer, I remember. What were you doing in New York?"

"I was writing speeches," she said easily, "for bigwigs in various companies. I can't believe you remember that I went to New York."

"I remember nearly everything about people I like. Why do you need a haven? No, wait, if it isn't any of my business, forget it. It's just that I'm worried about you."

She wasn't a very good liar, but she had to try. "No, it's okay. I'm getting away from a very bad relationship."

"Your husband?"

No choice. "Yes, my husband. He's very possessive. I wanted out and he didn't want to let me go. I thought of Riptide and what you'd said." She didn't want to tell him about her mother dying. To mix that with a lie was just too much. She managed to shrug and raise her teacup to click it against his. "Thanks, Tyler, for being at Dartmouth and talking about your hometown to me."

"I'm glad you're here," he said, his eyes serious upon her face. "If your husband is after you, how do you know he didn't follow you to the airport? I know New York traffic is nuts, but it's not all that hard to follow someone, if you really want to."

"It's a good thing I've read a lot of spy novels and seen lots of police shows." She told him how she'd changed taxis three times on the way to Kennedy. "When I got out at the United terminal, I was sure no one had followed me. My last driver was one of a vanishing breed—a native New Yorker cabbie. He knew Queens as well as he knew his ex-wife's lover, he told me. No one followed me, he was sure of it. I flew to Boston, then on to Portland, and bought myself a used Toyota from Big Frank's. I drove up here to your haven, and he'll never find me."

She had no idea whether or not he believed her. Well, all that about her escape from New York was the truth. She'd only lied about who she was running from.

"I sure hope you're right. But I plan to keep an eye on you, Becca Powell."

She managed to get him to talk about himself. He told her he was a computer consultant, a troubleshooter of sorts, and he designed software programs for major accounting and brokerage firms, "to track clients and money and how the two come together. I'm successful, Becca, and it feels good. You know, you were the only girl in college who didn't look at me and giggle at what a jerk I was. You called me a nerd and a geek, but that was okay, it was the truth. Do you know we've got a gym in Riptide? I'm there three days a week. I find that if I don't work out regularly, I get all skinny again, lose my energy, and want to wear a pocket protector."

"You're sure not skinny now, Tyler."

"No," he said, grinning at her, "I'm not."

When she showed him out some fifteen minutes later, she wondered again if he'd believed her reason for coming to Riptide. He was a nice guy; she'd hated to lie to him. She was glad he was here. She wasn't completely alone. She watched him get into his Jeep. He looked up and waved at her, then executed a sharp U-turn. He lived just one street over, on Gum Shoe Lane, but it was a good distance away.

Her house. That felt good. She slowly closed the front door and turned to look at her ancient furnishings. Her mother, the antiques nut, would have shuddered. When Marley Senior had furnished this house, she wondered if he'd ordered anything out of the turn-of-the-century Sears catalogue.

Now that she was settled in, her two suitcases emptied and tucked in the back of her bedroom closet, she decided to explore the town. She locked up the house and got into her car and drove down West Hemlock past one of Riptide's half-dozen white-spired churches. It was a charming town, isolated, and unspoiled. Just being in such a quaint village made her feel safe.

When she turned her Toyota onto Poison Oak Circle ten minutes later, she spotted the Food Fort. Everyone there was friendly, including the produce woman, who handed her the best head of romaine lettuce in the bin. Since it was a fishing town, there was lots of fresh fish available, mainly lobster. Becca was eager to give everything a try.

Her evening was peaceful. She spent the twilight time leaning over the railing of the widow's walk, staring out at the ocean. The water was calm; waves crested gently against pine-covered rocks that she could barely make out from where she stood. But Marley Senior had named the town Riptide. Was there a vicious tide that pulled people out to sea? She'd have to ask. It was a scary thought. She'd been caught in a riptide once when she was about ten years old. A lifeguard the size of Godzilla had managed to save her, telling her to swim parallel to shore until she was free of the strong current.

She wasn't being sucked out now, dragged under to die a horrible death. She'd escaped, just as she had when she was ten. Only this time she'd saved herself. Like the ocean on this beautiful evening, her life was calm again. She was safe.

She looked to the left at the dozen or so fishing boats coming back into the harbor. Since it was summer, some tourists were out in their white-sailed boats, enjoying the last bit of the day. The deep scent of brine settled around her. She quite liked it. Yes, she was going to be safe here.

The phone installers were coming the next day. She'd changed her mind at least a dozen times as to whether or not she would even have a phone. In the end, she'd decided in favor of getting connected, perhaps as a gesture of confidence that her stalker would fail to track her down.

The next morning just after nine o'clock, Tyler appeared again at her door, a little boy at his side, holding his hand.

"Hi, Becca. This is my son, Sam."

His son? Becca looked down at the solemn little face looking up at her. He didn't look a thing like Tyler. He was sturdy, compact, with a head of very dark hair and eyes a beautiful light blue. Sort of like hers, she thought, and smiled. He looked all boy. He didn't seem happy to be there. She opened the screen door and stood back. "Do come in, Tyler, Sam."

He was so wary, she thought. Distrustful. Or was it more than that? Was there something wrong with this precious little boy? Was this Rachel Ryan's Sam, the little boy she obviously adored? She smiled down at him, then slowly came down on her knees. "I'm Becca. It's a pleasure to meet you, Sam." She held out her hand.

"Sam, say hello to Becca."

There was a slight edge to his voice. Why was that? She said quickly, "It's all right, Tyler. Sam can do what he wants. I don't think I was all that talkative, either, when I was his age."

"It's not that," Tyler said, frowning down at his son.

The child just stared up at her, unmoving, so very still. She didn't stop smiling. "Would you like a glass of lemonade, Sam? Mine's just about the best east of the Rockies."

"All right." His voice was small and wary. Thank goodness she'd bought some cookies. Even wary little boys had to like cookies.

She sat him at the kitchen table, saying, "Do you have an aunt Rachel, Sam?"

"Rachel," Sam repeated, and he gave her a huge smile. "My aunt Rachel."

Sam said nothing more after that, but he ate three cookies and drank nearly two glasses of lemonade. Then he wiped the back of his hand over his mouth. All boy, she thought, but what was wrong? Why didn't he speak? And he looked so blank, as if his mind wasn't focused on the here and now.

"Do come back, Sam. I'll make sure there are always cookies here for you."

"When?" Sam said.

"Tomorrow," she said, giving him a big grin. "I'll be here all morning."

"What are you doing tomorrow afternoon?" Tyler said as he took his son's small hand.

"I'm going to *The Riptide Independent* to see if they need a reporter."

"Then you'll be seeing Bernie Bradstreet, he's the owner and the main contributor. A really nice older guy who has his finger in every pie in this town. He'll probably be very impressed with you. Hey, it seems like you're going to stay for a while."

"Yes, I just might."

"Ah, maybe I'll see you later when Sam's with his aunt Rachel. She's not really his aunt, she's just a really good friend and his baby-sitter."

Chapter 5

*B*ecca pulled the brush through her brown hair. It was long now, to her shoulders. She pulled it back in a ponytail, then stared at herself in the mirror. She hadn't worn a ponytail since she was thirteen years old. Then she hadn't known what evil was. *No, don't think about him*. He would never find her. She looked back at herself. The glasses changed her looks quite a bit, as did her darkened eyebrows.

She looked over at her small portable television and knew that during the news they'd soon show another photo of her. They did. It was from her driver's license. She was grateful they hadn't gotten a more up-to-date shot. She didn't much resemble that photo, except maybe on an excruciatingly bad day. With the slight alterations she'd made to her looks just before coming to Riptide, she felt reasonably sure that none of the townspeople would find her out. Only Tyler would make the connection, and she felt she could trust him. Now that her story was being flashed on CNN, she'd have to tell him the truth. She should have told him right away, but she couldn't, just couldn't, not then, not at first. Now there was no choice.

But Tyler beat her to the punch. Not fifteen minutes after her story aired, her doorbell rang.

"You lied to me." It was Tyler. He stood on the front porch, stiff all over, so angry he nearly stuttered.

"Yes, I know. I'm sorry, Tyler. Please come in. I need to throw myself on your mercy."

She told him the whole story, and was amazed at how relieved she was to confide in him. "I still don't know why the cops didn't believe me. But I'm not hiding because of them. I'm hiding because of the madman who's been terrorizing me. Maybe he wants to kill me now, I don't know." She kept shaking her head, saying over and over, "I can't believe he actually shot the governor. He really shot him."

"The cops could protect you." Tyler wasn't standing so stiffly now, thank God, and his eyes had calmed. Just a minute before they'd been flat and very dark.

"Yes, probably, but they would have to believe I was in danger first. They would have to believe there really was a stalker. There's the rub."

Tyler fell silent. He pulled a small wooden carving of a pyramid out of his pants pocket and began fiddling with it. "This isn't good, Becca."

"No. Is that Ramses the Second's tomb?"

"What? Oh this. No, I won it in a geometry competition when I was a senior in high school. You changed your name to Powell."

"Yes. You're the only one who knows the truth, about everything. Do you think you can keep it quiet?"

"You're not married, then?"

She shook her head. "No. Also, I would have run sooner but I couldn't leave my mother. She was dying of cancer. After she died, there was nothing holding me back."

"I'm very sorry, Becca. My mom died when I was sixteen. I remember what it was like."

"Thank you." She wasn't going to cry, she wasn't. She looked toward an ancient humidor that sat in the corner and jumped to her feet. She just realized what she'd done. "Oh God, I can't believe this. I'm a jerk. This is a big mistake. Listen, Tyler, you've got to forget all of this. I don't know what's going to happen. I don't want you in harm's way. And I just thought of Sam. I can't take a chance on anything happening to him. It's too risky. Whoever this maniac is, he'll do anything, I'm convinced of it. Then there's the cops. I don't want them to arrest you for keeping quiet about me. I'll just go somewhere else that isn't on the map. Jesus, I'm so sorry I spilled my guts to you."

He stood, taller than she by a good five inches. No more anger in him, just determination. It calmed her. "Forget it. It's a done deal. I'm now up to my neck in this with you. Don't worry, Becca. I don't think they'll ever find you." He paused a moment and looked down at the pyramid lying in the palm of his left hand. "Actually, I've already told a few folks in town that my old college friend Becca Powell has come to live here. Even if someone thinks you look like this Rebecca Matlock they saw on TV, they won't make the connection. I've already vouched for you, and that makes a difference. Also those glasses really alter your looks. You don't wear them usually, do you? And your eyes aren't really brown."

"You're right on both counts. I'm wearing brown contacts. The glasses are just window dressing; they're not prescription, just plain glass. I also darkened my hair and my eyebrows."

He nodded, then suddenly he grinned. "Yeah. I remember you as a blonde. All the guys wanted to go out with you, but you weren't really interested."

"I was only a freshman, too young to know what I wanted, particularly in guys."

"I remember there were some bets in the frat houses on who would get you in the sack first."

"I never heard about that." She shook her head, wanting to

laugh and surprised by it. "Guys are immensely focused, aren't they?"

"Oh, yeah. I was, too, only it never did me any good, at least not then. I remember wishing somehow that it would be me you'd go out with, but I was too chicken ever to ask. Now, we'll get through this, Becca. You're not alone anymore."

She couldn't believe he'd do this for her. She threw her arms around him and hugged him tight. "Thank you, Tyler. Thank you very much." She felt his arms tighten around her back. She felt safe for the first time in a very long time. No, not safe. She didn't feel alone anymore. That was it.

When she finally stepped back, he said, "It might even help if you go out with me, be seen with me around town. You know, lull any suspicions, if there are any. You'll fit in if you're seen with me, since I'm a native. I'll always call you Becca, too. That's a very different name from Rebecca. I believe that's the only name the media has used."

"To the best of my knowledge it is."

Tyler slid the wooden pyramid back into his jeans pocket and hugged her once more. He said against her left ear, "I wish you'd trusted me right away, but I understand. I think it'll be over soon. A three-day news hit and then it's gone."

As she pulled away from him, she devoutly prayed he was right. But how could it be? The man had tried to murder the governor of New York. He was still at large. They couldn't just forget about it. The thing was, there was simply nothing more she could tell the authorities. What if she called Detective Morales and told him she didn't know anything more, that she'd already told them every-thing? Immediately after Tyler left, she went back into the living room and picked up the phone before she could second-guess her-self. She had to try to make him believe her. She didn't know the sophistication of their tracing equipment. Well, she'd just have to get it over with, quickly, before they could get a lock on her location. She got through very quickly to Morales, which had to be a miracle in itself. "Detective Morales, this is Becca Matlock. I want you to listen to me now. I'm well hidden. No one's going to find me, nor is there any reason for anyone to find me. I'm not hiding from you, I'm hiding from the stalker who terrorized me and then shot the governor. You do believe me now, don't you? After all, I'm sure not the one who shot him."

"Look, Ms. Matlock, why don't you come in and let's talk about it? Nothing's for sure right now, but we need you here. We have a lead you could help us with—"

She unclenched her teeth and spoke very slowly. "I can't tell you anything more than I already did. I told you the truth. I still don't have any idea why none of you ever believed me, but it was the truth, all of it. I can't help you with any so-called lead. Oh, that's a lie, isn't it? Anything to get me back. But why?" She paused for a moment. Time was passing, he didn't answer her. She said, "Listen, you still don't believe me, do you? You believe I shot the governor?"

"Not you yourself, no. Ms. Matlock—Rebecca—let's talk about it. We can all sit down and work this out. If you don't want to come back to New York, I can come wherever you are to talk."

"I don't think so. Now, I don't want you to be able to trace this call. I will say it once more: The madman who shot the governor is out there and I've told you everything I know about him. Everything. I never lied to you. Never. Goodbye."

"Ms. Matlock, wait—"

She hung up the phone, aware that her heart was pounding deep and hard. She'd done her duty. There was nothing more she could do to help them.

Why didn't they believe her?

She had dinner that night with Tyler McBride at Pollyanna's Restaurant nearly at the end of West Hemlock, on a small curved cul-de-sac called Black Cabbage Court.

She said over their appetizer, "What's with the names in this town?"

He laughed as he speared a cold shrimp, dipped it in horseradish, and forked it into his mouth. "Are you ready for this? Okay, there was this rumor that began floating around in 1912 that Jacob Marley Senior found out his wife was sleeping with the local dry-goods merchant. He was so upset that he poisoned her, and that's why he renamed all the central streets after plants that are toxic."

"That's amazing. Any proof of it?"

"Nope, but hey, it makes for a good tale. Maybe he was a closet Borgia, who knows? I think my favorite is Foxglove Avenue. It runs parallel to West Hemlock."

"What are some more?"

"There's Venus Fly Trap Boulevard, which runs parallel to West Hemlock to the north, Night Shade Alley, that's where my gym is, and Poison Ivy Lane, just to the south of us."

"Wait, isn't the Food Fort on Poison Oak Circle?"

"Yes. Since I live outside the center of town, it's just Gum Shoe Lane for the likes of me. However, since you're in Marley's house, you get his pièce de résistance—Belladonna Drive. Even better, you're not in a big house next to all the peasants, no, you're out there all by yourself, surrounded by all those beautiful trees and just that narrow driveway to get to you."

She was laughing as she said, "Why did he name his own street Belladonna Way?"

"That's supposedly what Marley Senior used to poison his un-faithful wife. Pollyanna's Restaurant is on Black Cabbage Court.

That's the name for this plant in Indonesia that'll kill you with a single lick. It evidently has this sugary-sweet smell and taste, and that's how it gets its victims."

She was laughing when a man came up to their table and said, "Hello, Tyler. Who's this?"

Becca looked up at the older man, who had lots of white hair, a good-sized belly, and a big smile. He said, frowning down at her, "Hey, you look familiar, you—"

"I've known Becca for nearly ten years, Bernie. We were at Dartmouth together. She got tired of the rat race in New York City and decided to move here. She's a journalist. You want to hire her for the *Independent?*"

She hadn't gone to see Bernie Bradstreet for the simple reason that it had dawned on her that she didn't have any legitimate ID and now her face was plastered all over TV. She just sat there, smiling stupidly, not knowing what to say. She'd forgotten to say anything to Tyler. She was a fool.

Very sharp gray eyes focused on her. He held out his hand, with large, blunt fingers. "I'm Bernie Bradstreet."

"Becca Powell."

"You write what? Crime coverage? Weddings? Local charities? Obits?"

"None of those things. I mainly write human interest articles about strange and wonderful things that are all around us. I try to amuse people and perhaps give them a different perspective on things. I'm a luxury for a newspaper, Mr. Bradstreet, not a necessity. I'm the last sort of frill a small newspaper needs."

She'd whetted his appetite. Just great. He said, a brow arched, "Like what, Ms. Powell?"

"Why feta cheese and glazed pecans taste so delicious in a spinach salad."

"I suppose you went into all sorts of folklore, nutrition information, stuff like that?"

"That's right. For example, with the feta, pecans, and spinach, it all has to do with a chemical reaction that zings the taste buds."

Bernie Bradstreet looked too interested. She drew back, lowered her eyes to the napkin Tyler had tossed beside his plate.

Tyler said, "Dessert, Becca?"

She said, grinning up at Mr. Bradstreet, "Yep, that's what I am, dessert for a newspaper. I'm low on a priority list, very low."

"No," Tyler said. "I mean real dessert. Coffee and dessert for you, Bernie?"

Bernie couldn't stay. His wife was at the far table with one of their grandkids. "They make special hot dogs for kids here," he said; then, "Why don't you drop by with some of the articles you've written, Ms. Powell? Actually, bring me the feta cheese article."

"I didn't bring any of them with me, sir, sorry."

Tyler gave her a look but didn't say anything. But his eyes had widened just a bit. He'd finally realized that this was the last thing she needed. Good, she thought, she was out of it. But no, he just ruminated awhile, looking at her, then said, "All right, write me up one— whatever topic you like—not over five hundred words, and we'll see."

She nodded, wishing the guy was more hard-nosed. She watched him walk back to his table, stopping at three more tables on the way. She looked at Tyler and raised her hand to stop him. "No, I can't work for him. I don't have any ID I can use. I doubt he'd want to pay me in cash."

"Damn," he said. "I didn't think of that. I just finally realized that the more he saw you, he just might put you together with the Rebecca on TV."

"It's okay. I'll write up an article or two and give them to him, tell him to see how the readers like them, then we can talk. He shouldn't get suspicious then. I don't need the money. I'm not going to starve. It's just that I do need something to keep my mind busy."

"Are you any good with computers?"

"I guess I'm what you'd call a functional genius, but a technological moron."

"Too bad. Since I'm a small-time consultant, I don't need any frills, either."

The night was clear and warm, with just a slight breeze off the Atlantic. The stars were brilliant overhead. Becca stood by Tyler's Jeep, staring up at the sky. "Nothing like this in New York City. I could get used to this real fast, Tyler. Too bad you can barely hear the ocean from here. The briny smell is fainter, too."

"Yeah, I found I missed it so much I had to move back, and so I did just a couple of years after I finished my master's degree. But you know, more and more young people leave and stay gone. I wonder if Riptide will still be here in another twenty years or so."

"There are lots of tourists to boost the economy, aren't there?"

"Yes, but the entire flavor of the town has changed over the past twenty, thirty years. I guess that's progress, huh?" He paused a moment, staring up at the Milky Way. "After Ann went away, I thought I wanted to leave Riptide and never come back—you know, all the memories—but I realized that all of Sam's friends are here, all the people who knew Ann are here, and memories aren't bad. I can work anywhere, and so I stayed. I haven't regretted it. I'm glad you're here, Becca. Things will work out, you'll see. The only thing is winter. It's not much fun here in January."

"It's not much fun in New York, either. We'll see what's happening by January. I don't understand about your wife, Tyler. Did she die?"

She wanted to take it back at the look of pain that etched lines around his mouth, made his eyes look blank and dead. "I'm sorry, I shouldn't have asked."

"No, it's all right. Of course you're curious. Everyone else in town is."

"What do you mean?"

"My wife didn't die. She just up and left me. She was here one day, gone the next. No word, no message, nothing at all. That was fifteen months, two weeks, and three days ago. She's listed as a Missing Person."

"I'm very sorry, Tyler."

"Yeah, so am I. So is her son." He shrugged. "We're getting by. It gets better as the time passes."

What an odd way to put it. Wasn't Sam his son, too?

"The townspeople are like folk everywhere. They don't want to believe that Ann just up and left Riptide. They'd rather think I did her in."

"That's ridiculous."

"I agree. Now, Becca, don't worry. Things will get better. I'm an expert at things eventually getting better, particularly when they can't possibly get any worse."

She sure hoped he was right. They made a date to go to the gym together the following day. His wife had just walked out—on him and on her own little boy? That had to be incredibly tough for both of them. Why did folks want to believe he'd kill her?

Three nights later, on June 26, Becca was watching TV, not to see if she was still a footnote in Governor Bledsoe's ongoing story, but to check in on the weather again. The most violent storm to hit the Maine coast in nearly fifteen years was surging relentlessly toward them, bringing with it forecasts of fifty-mile-per-hour winds, torrential rains, and the probability of immense property damage. Everyone was warned to go to shelters, which Becca considered doing for about three minutes. No, she wasn't about to leave. Being with other people up close and personal as one would be in a shelter would put her at greater risk of being recognized. She didn't think many of the Mainers would even consider leaving their homes. They were incredibly tough, only nodding philosophically when discussing the incoming storm.

Becca paced the widow's walk as the storm approached, watching the skies, the now disappearing stars as clouds blanketed them, the boats in the harbor, bobbing about in the rising waves. Then the winds suddenly increased and tore through the trees. The air turned as cold as a morning in January. When the rain finally hit, crashing down hard and fast, she was driven inside. It was just before ten o'clock at night.

The lights flickered. Becca had bought candles and matches and she set them on her bedside table. She paused to listen as the storm bludgeoned the shoreline. She heard a newscaster predict great destruction of lobster boats and pleasure craft if they hadn't been thoroughly secured. She could imagine what the harbor looked like now, waves frothing high, whipping against the sides of the boats, probably sending water crashing over the sides.

She shivered as she pulled on a sweater and snuggled down into her bed. She kept the TV on nonstop weather coverage and looked at the light show outside her bedroom window. The thunder was deafening. The house rattled with the force of it.

The meteorologist on channel 7 said that the winds were strengthening, nearly up to sixty miles per hour now. He said people should go to official shelters away from the coast for protection. Oddly, he sounded excited. Becca still had no intention of leaving. This old house had doubtless seen its share of comparably violent storms in its hundred-year history just as the Piper Lighthouse had up the road. Both had survived. Both would survive another storm, she didn't doubt that, although she couldn't help but cringe as the house groaned and creaked.

Suddenly, with no warning, thunder boomed, lightning streaked through the sky, and the lights went out.

Chapter 6

*I*t wasn't dark for long. The lightning and thunder kept the sky lit up for a good five minutes, without a break. She could easily read her clock. It was just after one in the morning. She finally couldn't stand it any longer and reached for the phone, to call Tyler, but the line was dead. She stared at the receiver, then looked out her bedroom window as a huge streak of lightning lit up the sky. She felt the thunder deep in her eardrums as it boomed, almost simultaneous with the flash. It would be all right. It was only a storm. Storms in Maine were just another part of life, like the hordes of mosquitoes that occasionally blanketed a town. This was nothing to get alarmed about.

As Becca lay in the darkness, looking out the bedroom window, she swore that the winds were growing even stronger as they ravaged the land. She felt the house literally shudder around her. It shook so hard, she briefly worried that it would pull free of its foundation. A loud wrenching sound had her bolt upright in bed. No, it wasn't anything, really. Had she come here just to be killed in a ferocious summer storm? She had wished earlier that she was closer to the ocean, listening to the waves hurling themselves against the high cliffs covered with pine trees bowed and bent from the winter winds, or beating against the clustering speared black rocks that lined the narrow cluttered beach at the end of Black Lane, a narrow, snaking little dirt road that went all the way to the ocean.

But not now. It was just as well that crashing angry waves weren't added to the mix. She watched the lightning continue to tear through the sky, making it bright as day for long moments at a time. She felt the scoring of the thunder to her toes. It was impressive, utterly dramatic, and she was getting scared.

Finally she couldn't stand it any longer. She lit the three precious candles, stuck them in the bottom of coffee mugs, and picked up the Steve Martini thriller she'd been reading until the storm had really gotten serious.

Was the storm easing up? She read a few words, then realized that she couldn't remember the story line. This wasn't good. She put the novel back on her nightstand and picked up the *New York Times,* carried only by a small tobacco shop off Poison Ivy Lane. She didn't want to read about the attempted assassination, but she did, naturally. Page after page was devoted to the governor's attempted murder. She was mentioned too many times.

Thunder rolled loud and deep over the house as she read: *There is a manhunt for Rebecca Matlock, former speech writer for the governor, who, the FBI says, has information about the attempt on the governor's life.*

Former speech writer now, was she? Well, since she'd left without a word or any warning, she supposed that was fair enough.

It was nearly two o'clock in the morning.

Suddenly, with no warning at all, the wind gave a howl that made the hair bristle on the back of her neck and set her teeth on edge. A flash of lightning exploded, filling the sky with a bluish light, and a crack of thunder seemed to lift the house right into the air. She nearly bit her tongue as she stared out her bedroom window. She watched the proud hemlock weave once, then heard a loud snap. The old tree wavered a moment, then went crashing to the ground. It didn't hit the house, thank God, but some upper branches crashed into the window, loud and so scary that she leapt from the bed and ran to the closet. She crouched between a yellow knit top and a pair of blue jeans, waiting, waiting, but there was nothing more. What had happened was over with. She walked slowly back into the bedroom. Tree branches were still quivering as they settled just above a pale blue rag rug on the floor. The window was shattered, rain slithered in around the beautiful green leaves, dripping onto the floor. She stood there, staring at the huge tree branch in her bedroom, listening to another loud belt of thunder, and thought enough is enough. She didn't want to be alone, not anymore.

She dressed and ran downstairs. She had to find something to block up the window. But there wasn't anything except half a dozen dish towels with lighthouses on them. She ended up stuffing all her pillows around the tree branch. It worked.

She closed the front door behind her and stepped into the howling wind. She was wet clear through before she'd taken three breaths. No hope for it. She ran through the heavy rain to the Toyota and fumbled with the lock even as her hair was plastered to her head. Finally she got the door open and climbed in behind the wheel. When she turned the key in the ignition, the car growled at her, then stopped. She didn't want to flood it so she didn't turn the ignition again. No, give it a rest for a moment. Again, finally, she turned the key, and Lord be praised, the engine turned over, started. Tyler's house was just about a half-mile down the road, the first street to the right, Gum Shoe Lane.

At a loud crack of thunder, she looked back at Jacob Marley's house. It looked like an old Gothic manor in the English countryside, hunkered down in the rain filled with lost and ancient spirits. It looked menacing even without billowing fog to shadow it in more gloom. A sharp lightning flash streaked down like a silver knife. The house seemed to shudder, as if from a mortal wound. It

51

looked like the gods wanted to rip it apart. She was very glad she was leaving. Maybe Jacob Marley Senior really had poisoned his wife and God was just now getting around to some punishment. "Thanks a lot for waiting until I was here," she yelled heavenward. She waved her fist. "I come here and you decide, finally, to mete out divine justice. You're a little bloody late!"

The huge hemlock that could have so easily smashed right into the side of the house lay on its side nearly parallel to the west wall. That one very full and long branch that had crashed through her bedroom window looked like a hand that had managed to reach into the house. She shuddered at the image. Everything suddenly seemed alive and malevolent, closing in on her, like the man who had called her and stalked her and murdered that old woman and shot the governor. He was near, she felt him.

Just stop it. She drove very slowly down the long narrow drive, no choice there. Debris filled the road, wind bent trees nearly to the ground. The boughs glanced off her windshield. Branches whipped toward her, rain hammered against the windshield, pounded against the car, making her wonder if she'd come to Maine only to be done in by a wretched storm. She had to get out of the car twice to pull fallen branches out of the way. The wind and rain slammed hard into her, making it impossible to stand straight and nearly impossible to walk. She knew there had to be dents in the car fenders. The insurance company was going to love this. Oh dear, she'd forgotten, she didn't have any insurance. That required being a real person with real ID.

Suddenly headlights cut through the thick, swirling sheets of rain, not twenty feet from her. They were coming toward her, fast, too fast. Damnation, to get killed on Belladonna Way. There had to be some irony in that, but she couldn't appreciate it right then.

She'd come to hide herself and be safe, a tree branch came into her bedroom, and now she was going to die because she couldn't bear to stay in that old house, knowing it would collapse on her, swallow her alive. She smashed down on the horn, jerked the steering wheel to the left, but these headlights kept coming inexorably, relentlessly toward her, so fast, so very fast. She threw the car into reverse but knew that was no good. There was so much debris behind her that it was bound to stall her out. She slammed on the brakes and turned off the engine. She jumped out of the car and ran to the side of the road, feeling those damned headlights crawl over her, so close she wondered if the stalker hadn't found her and was now going to kill her. Why had she ever left the house? So there was a tree branch in her bedroom dripping on a rag rug. It was still safe, but not out here, in the middle of a wind that was whirling around her like a mad dervish, ready to hurl her into the air, and a car that was coming after her, a madman at the wheel.

Then, suddenly, miraculously, the headlights stopped about eight feet from her car. Rain and lightning battered down, blurring the headlights, turning them a sickly yellow. She stood there, the wind beating at her, breathing in hard, soaked to her bones, waiting. Who was going to get out of that car? Could he see her, huddled next to some trees that were nearly folding themselves around her from the force of the wind? Did he want to kill her with his own hands? Why? Why?

It was Tyler McBride and he was yelling, "Becca! For God's sake, is that you?" He had a flashlight and he pinned her with it, the light diffused from all the rain, pale, blue-rimmed, and it was right in her eyes. She brought up her hand.

She opened her mouth to yell back at him and nearly drowned. She ran to him and clutched his arms. "It's me," she said, "it's me. I was coming to your house. A tree branch crashed through the bed-room window and it sounded like the house was going to col-lapse."

If he wanted to smack her because she was teetering on the edge of hysteria, he didn't let on, just gripped her shoulders in his big wet hands and said very slowly, very calmly, "I thought I saw some car lights but I couldn't be sure. All I thought about was getting to you. It's okay. That old house won't fall down. There's nothing to be afraid of. Now, follow me back home. I left Sam alone. He's asleep but I can't count on him staying that way. I don't want him to wake up and be scared."

She got herself together. She wasn't helpless, not like Sam was. The wind tore at their clothes, the rain was coming down so hard it hurt where it struck. Her jeans felt stiff and hard and heavy. But she didn't care. She wasn't alone. Tyler wasn't the crazy man from New York. She took a deep breath and watched as he drove at a snail's pace back to his house on Gum Shoe Lane. It took another ten minutes to get to the small clapboard house that sat back in a lovely lawn that was planted heavily with spruce and hemlock. She jumped out of the car and yelled as she ran to the front door, "Gum Shoe, what a wonderful name." She began to laugh. "Gum Shoe Lane!"

"It's okay, Becca, we're home now. We made it. Jesus, this is one of the worst storms I can remember. As bad as the one back in '78, they said on the radio. I remember that one, I was a little kid and it scared me shitless. I've got to say that your timing is wild, Becca, coming to Riptide just before this mother of all storms hits." He gave her another look, then added, slowly, his voice calm and low, "It's sort of like the Mancini virus that came along last year and crashed every computer in this small software company called Tiffany's. They called me in to fix it. That was a job, I'll tell you."

Becca stood dripping in the small entrance hall, staring at him. He was trying to talk her down and doing a good job of it. "Computer humor," she said, and laughed after him when he fetched some towels from the bathroom. A slash of lightning came through the window and lit up the pile of newspapers on the floor beside the sofa. "I'm okay," she said when Tyler began to lightly rub his palm over her wet back. He drew back, smiling down at her. "I know. You're tough."

Sam was still asleep, curled on his side, his left hand under his cheek. The world was exploding not ten feet away and Sam was probably dreaming about his morning cartoons. She pulled the blanket over him, paused a moment, and said quietly to Tyler, who was standing just behind her, "He is precious."

"Yes," he said.

She wanted to ask him why Sam didn't talk much, was so very wary, but she heard something in his voice that made her go still and keep her question to herself. There was anger there, bitterness. Because his wife had left him? Walked away without a word? With not a single regret? Well, it made sense to her. Her own mother had left her, and she felt sick with rage at being left alone. Not her mother's fault, of course, but the pain of it. She looked down at Sam one last time, then turned and left the small bedroom, Tyler on her heels. He gave her one of his wife's robes, pink and thick and on the tatty side, well worn, and she wondered what sort of woman Ann McBride had been. Why hadn't she taken her robe? She couldn't ask Tyler now. The robe fit her very well. It was warm, comfy. She and Ann McBride were of a size.

They drank coffee heated on a Coleman stove Tyler got out of the basement. It was the best coffee she'd ever tasted and she told him so. She fell asleep on the old chintz sofa, wrapped in blankets.

The sun was harshly bright, too bright, as if the storm had

scrubbed off a thick layer of dust from all the trees and streets and houses, even given the sky a thorough shower. Becca's jeans were soft, hot from the drier, and so tight she had barely been able to zip them up when Tyler had tossed them to her.

Sam said, his small voice unexpected, startling her, "Did you bring cookies, Becca?"

An entire sentence. Maybe he was just very frightened and wary of strangers. Maybe he didn't think of her as a stranger anymore. She hoped so. She smiled at him. "Sorry, kiddo, no cookies this time." She'd awakened with a start, frightened, tingling, to see Sam standing beside the sofa, holding a blanket against his side, his thumb in his mouth, just staring at her, saying nothing at all.

Sam said now, "Haunted house."

Tyler was pouring cereal into a small bowl for his son. He looked over at Becca.

She said, "You could be right, Sam. It was a bad storm and that old house shook and groaned. I was scared to my toes."

Sam began eating his Cap'n Crunch cereal his father put in front of him.

Tyler said, "Sam's too young to be scared."

Sam didn't look up from his cereal bowl.

It was nearly eleven o'clock that morning when Becca drove back to Jacob Marley's house. It no longer looked frightening and menacing. It looked bedraggled, very clean, and the hemlock with its branch sticking through her second-floor window no longer looked like a ghostly apparition, but like a tree that was dead now, nothing more. She smiled as she walked around the house, assessing damage. Not much, really, just the branch in the window. They'd have to haul the tree away.

She called the real estate agent, Mrs. Ryan, from a working public phone in front of Food Fort, who told Becca she would notify the insurance company and the tree-removal people and not to worry about a thing, everything was covered.

Becca went back to the house and toured for the next twenty minutes, not seeing any damage anywhere inside. The electricity flickered on, then off again. Finally, when it was nearly noon, the lights came on strong and bright. The refrigerator hummed loudly. Everything was back to normal. Then, with no warning, the hall and living room lights went off. The circuit breaker, she thought, and wondered where the devil the box would be. The basement, that was the most likely place. She had to check down there anyway. She lit one of her candles and unlatched the basement door, which was at the back of the kitchen. Steep wooden stairs disappeared into the darkness. *Great,* she thought, *now to top it all off, maybe I can fall and break my neck on these rickety stairs.* They were wide and felt sturdy and strong, not so dangerous after all, a relief. There were a dozen steps. The floor was uneven, cold and damp concrete. She raised the candle and looked around. There was a string hanging down and she gave it a pull. The bulb switch clicked but nothing happened. *This light must be on the same circuit.* She began at the right of the stairs, lifting the candle to light up the wall. It was dank down there, and she smelled mildew. Her toes sloshed in a bit of water. Yep, leaks from the storm. On the wall facing the stairs she finally found the circuit breaker box. Beside it were stacks of old boxes, everything dirty and damp. She flipped the downed circuit breaker switch and the bulb overhead blossomed into one-hundred-watt light. Stacks of old furniture, most of it from the forties, perhaps some even earlier, were piled against the far wall. So many boxes, all of them very large, labeled with faded and smeared spidery handwriting.

She started forward to look at the writing on one of the labels when there was a low rumbling noise. She stopped cold, fear spiking

57

through her. Where was it coming from? Where? All the night-mares from the night before tore through her. Sam's words—"haunted house." Shadows, the damned basement was filled with shadows and damp and rot.

She whipped around at the crash not thirty feet away from her, in the far corner of the basement. She watched as the wall heaved and groaned and spewed brick outward onto the basement floor, leaving a jagged black hole.

She stood there a moment longer, staring at the hole in the wall. She was surprised. The house was very old, sturdy. Why, suddenly, would this happen? The storms over the years must have gradually weakened this particular wall and now, finally, the one last night was the final blow. Perhaps all the damp contributed, as well.

She walked to the corner, dodging crates and a huge steamer trunk that looked to be from the nineteen twenties. The light didn't reach quite that far. She raised her candle high and looked into the black hole.

And screamed.

Chapter 7

*T*hat black gash in the basement wall had vomited out a skeleton mixed with shards of cement, whole and broken bricks, and thick dust that flew through the air to settle slowly, thickly, on the basement floor.

The skeleton's outstretched hand nearly touched her foot. She dropped the candle and jumped back, wrapping her arms around herself. She stared at that thing not more than three feet from her. A dead person, long dead. It—no, it wasn't an it, it was a woman and she couldn't hurt anybody. Not now.

White jeans and a skimpy pink tank top covered the bones, many of which would have been flung all over the basement floor were it not for the once-tight jeans holding them together. One sneaker was hanging off her left foot, the white sock damp and moldy. The left arm was still attached, but barely. The head had broken off and rolled about six inches from the neck.

Becca stood there, staring down at that thing, knowing that at one time, whoever she was, she'd breathed and laughed and wondered what the future would bring. She was young, Becca realized. Who was she? What was she doing inside a wall in Jacob Marley's basement?

Someone had put her there, on purpose, to hide her forever. And now she was just shattered bones, some of them covered with moldy white jeans and a pink tank top.

Slowly Becca walked back upstairs, covered with dust, her heart still pounding. In her mind's eye the skeleton's skull was still vivid, would probably remain terrifyingly vivid for the rest of her life. Those eye sockets were so empty. Becca knew she had no choice. She phoned the sheriff's office on West Hemlock and asked to speak with the sheriff.

"This is Mrs. Ella," came a voice that was deep as a man's, and harsh—a smoker's voice. "Tell me who you are and what you want and I'll tell you whether or not you need Edgar."

Becca stared at the phone. It certainly wasn't New York City.

She cleared her throat. "Actually, my name is Becca Powell and I moved into Jacob Marley's house about a week ago."

"I know all about you, Miss Powell. I saw you at the Pollyanna with Tyler McBride. What'd you do with little Sam while you two were gallivanting around, enjoying yourselves at one of Riptide's finest restaurants?"

Becca laughed, she couldn't help herself, but it soon dissolved into a hiccup. She felt tears pool in her eyes. This was crazy. Still, she said only, "We left him with Mrs. Ryan. He's very fond of her."

"Well, that's all right, then. Rachel and Ann—she's the dead Mrs. McBride—well, they were best friends, now weren't they? And Sam dearly loves Rachel, and she him, thank God, since his mama is dead, now isn't she?"

"I thought that Ann McBride disappeared, that she just walked away from her family and from Riptide."

"So he says, but nobody believes that. What do you want, Miss Powell? Be alert now, and concise, no more going off on tangents or feeding me gossip. This is an official office of the law."

"There's a skeleton in my basement."

For the first time in this very strange conversation, Mrs. Ella was silent, but not for long. "This skeleton you're telling me is in your basement, how did it get there?"

"It fell out of the wall in the middle of a whole lot of rubble when the wall collapsed just a while ago, probably weakened by the big storm last night."

"I believe I will transfer you to Edgar now. That's Sheriff Gaffney to you. He's been very busy, a lot of storm damage, you know, a lot of people demanding his time, but a skeleton can't be put off until tomorrow, now can it?"

"You're right about that," Becca said, and had an insane desire to laugh her head off. She wiped the tears out of her eyes. She realized she was shaking. It was the oddest thing.

A man came on the line and said, "Ella tells me you've got a skeleton in the basement. This don't happen every day. Are you sure it's a skeleton?"

"Yes, quite sure, although, to be honest, I've never seen one before, at least lying at my feet on the basement floor."

"I'll be right there, then. You stay put, ma'am."

Becca was staring down at the phone when Mrs. Ella came back. "Edgar said I was to keep talking to you, not let you go all hysterical. Edgar tends to get tetchy around women who are crying and wailing and carrying on. I'm surprised that you fell apart on him, given the way you were talking to me about this and that."

"I appreciate that, Mrs. Ella. I'm not really hysterical, at least not yet, but how could the sheriff have possibly known that I was wavering on the edge? I never said a word to him."

"Edgar just knows these things," Mrs. Ella said comfortably. "He's very intuitive, now isn't he? That's why I'll keep talking to you until he gets there, Miss Powell. I'm to help you keep your wits together."

Becca didn't mind a bit. For the next ten minutes, she heard how Ann McBride disappeared between one day and the next, no explanation at all, just as Tyler had told her. She learned that Tyler wasn't Sam's father but his stepfather. Sam's real father had just up and disappeared from one day to the next, too. Odd, now wasn't it, the both of them, just up and out of here? Of course, Sam's father had been a rotter, whining and bitching about how hard life was, and he didn't want to stay here, so his leaving made some sense, now didn't it? But not Ann's, no, she couldn't have just up and left, not without Sam.

Then Mrs. Ella began with all her pets, and there were a bunch of them, since she was sixty-five years old. Finally, Becca heard a car pull up.

"The sheriff just arrived, Mrs. Ella. I promise I won't fall apart." She hung up the phone before Mrs. Ella could give her own mother's tried-and-true recipe for stretched nerves. And she wouldn't fall apart, either, because by Mrs. Ella's fifth dog, a terrier named Butch, there were no more tears in her eyes and the bubbling, liquid laughter was long dried up.

Sheriff Gaffney had seen the Powell girl around town, but he hadn't met her. She looked harmless enough, he thought, remembering how she was squeezing a cantaloupe in the produce department at Food Fort when he first saw her. She was pretty enough, but right then, she was as white as his shirtfront last night before he'd eaten spaghetti. She'd opened the front door of the old Marley place and was standing there staring at him.

"I'm the law," he said, and took his sheriff's hat off. There was something odd about her, something that wasn't quite right, and it wasn't her too-pale face. Well, finding a skeleton could put a person off in a whole lot of ways. He wished she'd stop gaping at him like she didn't have a brain or, God forbid, was hysterical. He was afraid she would burst into tears and he was ready to do just about anything to prevent that. He threw back his shoulders and stuck out a huge hand. "Sheriff Gaffney, ma'am. What's this about a skeleton in your basement?"

"It's a woman, Sheriff."

He shook her hand, pleased and relieved that now she appeared reasonably under control and her lower lip wasn't trembling. Her eyes looked perfectly dry to him, from what he could tell through her glasses. "Show me this skeleton who you believe with your un-trained eye is a woman, ma'am," he said, "and we'll see if you're guessing right."

I'm in never-never land, Becca thought as she showed Sheriff Gaffney down to Jacob Marley's basement.

She walked behind him. He was nearing sixty years old, and was a walking heart attack. He was a good thirty pounds overweight, the buttons of his sheriff shirt gaping over his belly. The wide black leather belt tight beneath his belly carried a gun holster and a billy club, and nearly disappeared in the front because his stomach was so big. He had a circle of gray hair around his head and very light gray eyes. She nearly ran into him when he suddenly stopped on the bottom step, stood there, and sniffed.

"That's good, Ms. Powell. No smell. Gotta be old."

She nearly gagged.

She kept back when he went down on his knees to examine the bones.

"I thought it was a woman, maybe even a girl, since she's wear-ing a pink tank top."

"A good deduction, ma'am. Yep, the remains look pretty old, or maybe not. I read that a dead person can become a skeleton in as little as two weeks or it can take as long as ten years depending on where the body's put. It's a shame that it wasn't airtight, you know, a vacuum back behind that wall. If it had been, then maybe something would have been left of her. But critters can get in most places and they were looking at a whole bunch of really good meals with her. Lookee here, the person who put her down here hit her on the head." He looked up at her, expecting her to see what he'd found. Becca forced herself to look at the skull that had snapped, probably during the upheaval, and rolled away from the neck.

Sheriff Gaffney picked up the skull and slowly turned it in his hands. "Look at this. Someone bashed her but good, not in the back of the head but in the front. Now, that's mean, really vicious. Yep, violent, real violent. Whoever did this was mad as hell, hit her as hard as he could, right in the face. I wonder who she was, poor thing. First thing is to see if any of our own young people went missing a while ago. Thing is, I've been here nearly all my life and I don't remember a single kid just up and disappearing. But I'll ask around. Folk don't forget that. Well, we'll find out soon enough. I think she was probably a runaway. Old Jacob didn't like strangers— male, female, it didn't matter. Probably found her poking around in the garage or maybe even trying to break in, and he didn't ask any questions, just whacked her over the head. Actually, he didn't like people who weren't strangers, either."

"You said the blow looks violent, and it's in the front. Why would Jacob Marley be enraged if she was a runaway, or a local kid, just hanging around his property?"

"I don't know. Maybe she back-mouthed him. Old Jacob hated back talk."

"The white jeans are Calvin Klein, Sheriff."

"You're saying this is a guy now?"

"No, that's the designer. The jeans are expensive. I don't think they'd go real well on a runaway."

"You know, ma'am, many runaways are middle-class," Sheriff

Gaffney said, and heaved himself to his feet. "Strange how most folk don't know that. Very few of 'em are poor, you know. Yep, the storm must have knocked something loose," he said, bending over to examine the wall closely. "Looks like old Jacob stuffed her in there pretty good. Not such a good job with the concrete and bricks, though. It shouldn't have collapsed like that, nothing else in here did."

"Old Jacob was a homicidal maniac?"

"Eh?" He spun around. "Oh no, Ms. Powell. He just didn't like nobody hanging around his place. He was a real loner, once Miranda up and died on him."

"Who was Miranda? His wife?"

"Oh no. She was his golden retriever. He buried his wife so long ago I can't even remember her. Yep, she lived to be thirteen, just keeled over one day."

"His wife was only thirteen?"

"No, his golden retriever, Miranda. She just up and died. Old Jacob was never the same after that. Losing someone you love, so I hear, can be real hard on a man. My Maude promised me a long time ago that she'd outlive me, so maybe I'd never have to know what it's like."

Becca followed the sheriff back up the basement stairs. She looked back once at the ghastly pile of white bones wearing Calvin Klein jeans and a sexy pink tank top. Poor girl. She thought of the Edgar Allan Poe tale *The Telltale Heart* and prayed that this girl had been dead before she was stuffed in that wall.

Sheriff Gaffney had laid the skull on top of the skeleton's chest.

An hour and a half later, Tyler stood next to her, off to the side of the front porch. Dr. Baines, shorter than Becca, whiplash thin, big glasses, came out nearly at a run, followed by two young men in white coats carrying the skeleton carefully on a gurney.

65

"I never thought Mr. Marley could murder anyone," Dr. Baines said, his voice fast and low. "Funny how things happen, isn't it? All this time, no one knew, no one even guessed." He pushed his glasses up on his nose, nodded to Becca and to Tyler, then spoke briefly to the men as they gently lifted the gurney into the back of the van.

The unmarked white van pulled away, followed by Dr. Baines's car. "Dr. Baines is our local physician. He got on the phone to the medical examiner in Augusta after I called him about the skeleton. The ME told him what to do, which is kind of dumb, since he's a doctor and I'm an officer of the law, and of course I'd be really careful around the skeleton and take pictures from all angles and be careful not to mess up the crime scene."

Becca remembered him carefully setting the skull on the skeleton's chest. But he was right, with a skeleton, who cared?

Sheriff Gaffney said on a shrug, "In any case, Dr. Baines will take the skeleton into Augusta to the medical examiner and then we'll see."

Sheriff Gaffney looked out at the two dozen people who were hovering about and shook his head and waved them away. Of course no one moved. They continued talking, pointing at the house, maybe even at her.

Sheriff Gaffney said, "They'll go on home in a bit. Just natural human curiosity, that's all. Now, Ms. Powell, I know you're upset and all, being a female with fine sensibilities, just like my Maude, but I ask that you keep yourself calm for just a while longer."

He had to be about the same age as her father would have been had he lived, Becca thought, and smiled at him then, because he meant well. "I'll try, Sheriff. You don't have any daughters, do you?"

"No, ma'am, just a bunch of boys, all hard-noses, always back-talking me, and covered with mud and sweat half the time. Not at

all the same thing for little girls. My Maude would have given anything for a little girl, but God didn't send us one, just all them dirty
boys.

"Now, Ms. Powell, Dr. Baines will be talking to the folk in the
medical examiner's office in Augusta—that's our capital, you
know—once he gets there. They'll do an autopsy, or whatever it is
they do on a mess of bones. The folk up there have lots of formal
training, so they'll know what they're doing. Like I told you, they'll
document that old Jacob or somebody hit her right in the forehead, smashed her head in. They'll determine that it was real mean,
vicious, that blow. In the meantime we gotta find out who she is.
There wasn't any ID on her. You got any more ideas about it?"

"Calvin Klein jeans have been popular since the early to mid-
eighties. That means that she wasn't murdered and sealed behind
that wall before 1980."

Sheriff Gaffney carefully wrote that down. He hummed softly
while he wrote. He looked up then and stared at her. "You sure do
look familiar, Ms. Powell."

"Maybe you saw me in a fashion magazine, Sheriff. No, don't
even consider that, I'm just joking with you. I'm not a model. I'm
sure I would have remembered you, sir, if I'd ever met you before."

"Well, that's likely enough," he said, nodding. "Tyler, you got any
thoughts about this?"

Tyler shook his head.

Sheriff Gaffney looked as if he would say something else, then
he shut his mouth. However, he gave Tyler another long look. "I'll
be in touch," he said, snapped out a sharp salute, and walked to his
car, a brown Ford with a light bar over the top. At the last moment,
he looked back at them, and he was frowning. Then he managed to
squeeze his bulk into the driver's side. He hadn't been interested in
her background, a blessing. Evidently, he realized that she could

have had nothing to do with this and so who she was, where she was from, and what she did for a living simply did not matter.

"He's amazing," Becca said as he drove away. "Too bad he didn't have a daughter to go with all those dirty boys."

She looked to see that Tyler was staring down at his feet. She lightly touched her fingers to his arm. "What's wrong? You're afraid I really am going to be hysterical about finding that poor girl?"

"No, it's not that. You saw the sheriff. Even though he didn't really say anything, it was clear enough what he was thinking."

"I don't know what you mean. What's wrong, Tyler?"

"I realize it occurred to him, just before he got into his car, that the skeleton might well be Ann."

Becca looked at him blankly, slowly shaking her head back and forth.

"My wife. She wore Calvin Klein jeans."

Chapter 8

Becca walked into the Riptide Pharmacy in the middle of Foxglove Avenue the next morning and found, to her horror, that she was the center of attention. For someone who wanted to fade into the woodwork, she wasn't doing it very well. Everywhere she went, she was stared at, questioned, introduced to relatives. She was the girl who'd found the skeleton. She was even given special treatment at the Union 76 gas station at the end of Poison Oak Circle. The Food Fort manager, Mrs. Dobbs, wanted her autograph. Three people told her she looked familiar.

It was too late to dye her hair black. She went home and stayed there. She got at least twenty phone calls that day. She didn't see Tyler, but he'd been right about what the sheriff had thought, because everybody else was thinking it, too, and was talking about it over coffee, to their neighbors, and not all that quietly. Tyler knew it, too, of course, but he didn't say anything when he came over later that evening. He looked stoic. She had wanted to yell at everyone that they were wrong, that Tyler was an excellent man, that no way could he have hurt anyone, much less his wife, but she knew she couldn't take the chance, couldn't call attention to herself anymore. It was too dangerous for her, and so she listened to everyone talk about Ann, Tyler's wife and Sam's mother, who had supposedly disappeared fifteen months before without a word to anybody, not her husband, not her son. Ann had had a mother until two years before, but Mildred Kendred had died and left Ann all alone with Tyler. She'd had no other relatives to hassle Tyler about where his wife had supposedly gone. And just look at poor little Sam, so quiet, so withdrawn, he'd probably seen something, everyone was sure of that. That he wasn't at all afraid of his step-father just meant that the poor little boy had blocked the worst of it out.

Oh, yes, it all made sense now to everyone. Tyler had bashed his wife on the head—she probably wanted to leave him, that was it—and then he'd bricked her in the wall in Jacob Marley's basement. And little Sam knew something, because he'd changed right after his mother disappeared.

Tyler remained stoic during the following days, saying nothing about all the speculation, ignoring the sidelong looks from people who were supposedly his friends. He went about his business, seemingly oblivious of the stares.

He was in misery, Becca knew that, but there was nothing she could do except say over and over, "Tyler, I know it isn't Ann. They'll prove it was someone else, you'll see."

"How?"

"If they can't figure out who she was, then they'll check for run-aways. There are DNA tests. They'll find out. Then there are going to be a whole lot of folk apologizing to you on their hands and knees."

He looked at her and said nothing at all.

Becca went shopping at Food Fort at eight o'clock the next night, hoping the store would be nearly empty. She moved quickly down the aisles. The last item on her list was peanut butter, crunchy. She found it and picked up a small jar, saw that it had a web of mirrored cracks in it, and started to call out to one of the clerks, only to have it break apart in her hands. She yelped and dropped it. It splattered all over jars of jams and jellies before smashing onto the floor at her feet. She stood there staring down at the mess.

"I see you buy natural, not sugar-added. That's the only kind I'll eat."

She whirled around so fast she slid on the peanut butter and nearly careened into the soup. The man caught her arm and pulled her upright.

"Sorry, I didn't mean to startle you. Let me get you another jar. Here comes a young fellow with a mop. Better let him wipe off the bottom of your sneaker."

"Yes, of course." The man not two feet from her was a stranger, which didn't mean all that much since she hadn't met everyone in town. He was wearing a black windbreaker, dark jeans, and Nike running shoes. He was careful not to step into the peanut butter. Her first impression was that he was big and he looked really hard and his hair was on the long side, and as dark as his eyes.

"The only thing," he continued after a moment, "it's a real pain to have to stir the peanut butter before you put it in the refrigerator. The oil always spills over the sides and on your hands." He smiled, but his eyes still looked hard, as if he looked at people and saw all the bad things they were trying to hide, and was used to it, maybe even philosophical about it. She didn't want him looking at her that way, seeing deep into her. She didn't want to talk to him. She just wanted to get out of there.

"Yes, I know," she said, and took a step back.

"Once I got used to it, though, I found I couldn't eat the other peanut butter, too much sugar."

"That's true." She took another step away from him. Who was he? Why was he trying to be so nice?

"Miss Powell, I'm Young Jeff. Ah, Old Jeff is my pop, he's the assistant manager. Just hold still and I'll clean off your sneaker." He picked up her foot, nearly sending her over backward. The man held her up while Young Jeff wiped a wet paper towel over the bottom of her sneaker. He was very strong, she could feel it since his hands were in her armpits. "I'm sure glad you're here, ma'am. I wanted to know if that poor dead skeleton was Mrs. McBride. Everyone is talking about how it can't be anybody else, what with Mrs. McBride just up and disappearing like she did not all that long ago. Everyone says you know it's Mrs. McBride, too, that you were sure, but how could you be? Did you meet Mrs. McBride?"

He finally released her foot. She pulled away from Young Jeff and the man, a good two feet. She felt cold, very cold. She rubbed her hands over her crossed arms. "No, Jeff, I never met Ann McBride. I didn't know anything about her. No one said a single word to me about her. Also, everybody is being premature. Now, I'll just bet that we'll be hearing very soon that the poor woman I found can't be Ann McBride. You tell everyone I said that."

"I will, Ms. Powell, but that's not what Mrs. Ella says. She thinks it's Ann McBride, too."

"Believe me, Jeff, I was there, and I saw the skeleton; Mrs. Ella didn't. Hey, I'm sorry about the mess. Thanks for cleaning off my shoe."

The man stuck out his arm and helped her over the shards of glass. "Young Jeff is a teenage boy with raging hormones," he said, very aware that she had pulled away from him again. "I'm afraid you're now the object of his affection."

She shuddered. "No, I'm the object of everyone's curiosity, nothing more, including poor Young Jeff." She stopped. The man couldn't help it that she was spooked. She drew a deep breath, gave him a nice big smile, and said, "I've got a few more things to buy, Mr.—?"

"Carruthers. Adam Carruthers." He stuck out his hand and she

automatically shook it. Big hand, hard, just like the rest of him.
She'd bet the last dime in the bottom of her purse that even the
soles of his feet were hard. She knew without being told that he
was very disciplined, very focused, like soldiers or bad guys were
focused, and that made her so afraid she nearly ran out right that
minute. Which was silly. Only one thing she really knew for sure—
she didn't ever want to have to tangle with him. Actually, if she
never saw him again, it would be just fine by her. "I haven't seen
you around town before, Mr. Carruthers."

"No, I just got here yesterday. The first thing I heard about was
your finding that skeleton. The second thing I heard was it was the
missing wife of your neighbor, Tyler McBride, and that you were
seeing him and now wasn't that interesting?"

A reporter, she thought. Oh God, maybe he was a reporter or a
paparazzo, and they'd found her. Her brave new world in the
boondocks was going to be over just as it was beginning. It wasn't
fair. She began backing away from him.

"Are you all right?"

"Yes, of course. I'm very busy. It was a pleasure to meet you.
Goodbye." And she was nearly running down the aisle lined with
different kinds of breads, hamburger buns, and English muffins.

He stared after her. She was taller than he'd expected, and too
thin. Well, he'd be skinny, too, if he'd been under as much pressure
as she was. What mattered was that he had found her. Amateurs, he
thought, even very smart ones, couldn't easily disappear. He
thought about how he had managed to misdirect the FBI, and
grinned at the jars of low-fat jams and jellies. They had more procedures, more requirements, more delays built into the system, a
system that could have been designed by a criminal to give himself
the best shot at escaping. Another thing they didn't have was *his*
contacts. He was whistling when he carried his can of French roast

drip coffee to the checkout counter. He watched her climb into her dark green Toyota and drive out of the parking lot.

He went back to his second-floor corner room at Errol Flynn's Hammock, booted up his laptop, and wrote a quick e-mail:

I met her over a broken jar of peanut butter in Food Fort. She's fine, but nervous as hell. Understandable. You won't believe this, but now she's embroiled in a mess here in Riptide. A skeleton fell out of her basement wall. Everyone in town believes it's a neighbor's wife who disappeared over a year ago. Who the hell knows? Will keep you informed. Adam

He sat back in his chair and smelled the coffee perking in the Mr. Coffee machine he'd bought at Goose's Hardware when he'd gotten into town.

She was wary of him, maybe even afraid. Well, he couldn't blame her, a big guy trying to pick her up in Food Fort after she'd found a skeleton in her basement, while already on the run from the FBI, the NYPD, and a murderous madman. He didn't think she'd been amused by his peanut butter wit, which meant she wasn't a dolt.

He poured a cup of coffee, sipped it, and sighed with bone-deep satisfaction. He leaned back in the dark-brown nubby chair, which was surprisingly comfortable. The TV played quietly on its stand against a far wall, providing background noise. He closed his eyes, seeing Becca Matlock again.

No, now she was Becca Powell. Under that name she'd quickly rented the Jacob Marley place and promptly had a skeleton fall out of her basement wall after that incredible storm that had battered the Maine coast.

The woman had pretty sucky luck.

Now all he had to do was make her come to trust him.

Then, just maybe, he would have a very big surprise for her.

But first he had some reconnaissance to do. It never paid to rush into things.

So Adam kept his distance the next day, watched her house during the morning and saw Tyler McBride and his little boy, Sam, pay her a visit around eleven o'clock. The kid was really cute, but he didn't yell and jump around like other kids his age. Was everyone right? Had the son witnessed McBride killing his mother, or was it just talk?

Adam wondered what was going on between Tyler McBride and Becca Matlock/Powell. He watched Sheriff Gaffney pay her a visit, even overheard the sheriff speaking to her outside the front door, on the big wraparound porch. He heard them clearly.

"Nothing yet from the medical examiner's office, Sheriff?"

"They say hopefully tomorrow. I just wanted to go over the basement again, see what I could sniff out. My boys didn't find any fingerprints, but just maybe there's something there that we all missed. Oh, and another thing, Rachel Ryan asked me to tell you that some boys would be arriving to remove the tree and fix the window for you."

The sheriff left after an hour, a chocolate chip cookie in his hand. Adam knew it was chocolate chip. He could smell the chocolate from twenty yards and was salivating.

He sent an e-mail after lunch and within an hour knew all about how Becca Matlock had met Tyler McBride at Dartmouth College. Had the two of them been college sweethearts? Lovers? Perhaps. It was interesting. And now everyone believed the skeleton was Tyler McBride's missing wife, Ann. He'd find out everything he could about Tyler McBride. He supposed there was a certain possible irony at play here. What if she'd managed to get away from one stalker only to stumble upon a man who'd done away with his wife?

Yep, her luck sucked, big-time.

He still wasn't ready to approach her, she was too spooked. So he kept an eye on her that evening as well. She didn't leave the house. Since it stayed light so late in Maine during the summer months, five guys, all armed with chain saws, came to take care of the old fallen hemlock that lay along the west side of the house. They pulled the limb out of the upstairs window and sawed it up. They cut off and sawed up the branches from the tree, then wrapped thick chains around the trunk and dragged the tree away.

Through all of this, Becca read outside on the wraparound porch, sitting in an old glider, rocking back and forth until he was nearly nauseated watching that slow back and forth, that never-ending back and forth, and hearing the small creaking sounds that went with every movement in between the loud grating bursts from the chain saws.

She went to bed early.

Around noon the next day, Becca was thanking the window-pane guy for replacing the glass in her bedroom window. Not half an hour later, Tyler and Sam were there, eating tuna fish sandwiches at her kitchen table. She said, "We should be hearing from Sheriff Gaffney soon, Tyler. It should be today, that's what he said when he came yesterday. They're sure taking their time. Then all this non-sense will be over."

He was silent for the longest time, chewing his sandwich, helping Sam eat his, then said finally, some anger in his voice, which surprised her, "You're quite the optimist, Becca."

But she wasn't thinking about the skeleton at that moment. She was wondering why that man—Adam Carruthers—was watching her house. He was standing motionless just to the right, in amongst the spruce trees, not twenty feet away. He wasn't the stalker. It wasn't his voice, she was sure of that. The stalker's voice was not old, not young, but unnervingly smooth. She knew she would recognize that voice from hell anywhere. Carruthers's voice was different. But who was he? And why was he so interested in her?

Adam stretched. He went through a few relaxing tae kwon do moves to ease his muscles. He was just in the process of slowly raising his left leg, his left arm extended fully, when she said from behind him, "Your arm is a bit too high. Lower your elbow at least an inch and extend your wrist, yeah, and pull your fingers back a bit more. That's better. Now, don't even twitch or I'll shoot your head off."

He was faster than she could have imagined. She was a good six feet behind him. She had her Coonan .357 Magnum automatic, chambered with seven bullets, aimed right at him, and in the very next instant, his whole body was in motion, moving so fast it was a blur, at least until his right foot lightly and gracefully clipped the gun from her hand, and his left hand smacked her hard enough in the shoulder to send her flying backward. She landed on her back.

Becca grabbed the gun, which lay on the ground two feet to her left, and brought it up only to have him kick it out of her hand again. Her wrist stung for a moment, then went numb.

"Sorry," he said, standing over her now. "I don't react well to folks holding guns on me. I hope I didn't hurt you." He actually had the gall to reach out his hand to help her up. She was breathing hard, her shoulder was aching and her wrist was useless. She scooted backward, turned, and tried to run. She wasn't fast enough.

He grabbed her and hauled her back against him. "No, just hold it a minute. I'm not going to hurt you."

She stopped cold and became very, very still. Her head fell forward and he knew in that moment that she had simply given up.

He knew her shoulder had to hurt, that her wrist was now probably hanging numb. "It'll be all right. You'll get feeling back in your wrist soon. It'll burn a bit but then it'll be okay again."

Still drawn in on herself, she said, "I didn't think he could be you—your voice is all wrong, I would have sworn to that—but I obviously was wrong."

She thought he was the stalker, the man who had murdered that poor old woman in front of the museum, and then shot Governor Bledsoe. Automatically, he let her go. "Look, I'm sorry—" He was speaking to the back of her head. She'd taken off the second he'd let her go. She was off at a dead run, through the spruce trees, back toward her house.

He caught her within ten yards, grabbed her left arm, and jerked her around. She moved quickly. Her fist hit him solidly on the jaw. His head snapped back with the force of her sharp-knuckled blow. She was strong. He grabbed both her arms, only to feel her knee come up. His fast reflexes saved him, just barely, thank God, and her knee got him in the thigh. It still hurt, but not as bad as if she'd gotten him in the crotch. That would have sent him to the ground, sobbing his guts out. He whirled her around and brought her back against his chest. He clamped her arms at her sides and simply held her against him. She was breathing hard, her muscles tensing, relaxing, then tensing again. She was very afraid but he knew she'd act again if he gave her the opening. He was impressed. But now he had her.

"I don't know how you found me," she said, still panting. "I did everything I could think of to hide my trail. How did you track me down?"

"It did take me two and a half days to track you to Portland, actually longer than I'd expected."

She twisted her head to look at him. "You bastard. Let me go."

"Not just yet. I want to hang on to my body parts. Hey, you didn't do too badly for an amateur."

"Let me go."

"Will you stop with the violence? I can't stand violence. It makes me nervous."

Her look was incredulous as she chewed her bottom lip. Finally, she nodded. "All right."

He let her go and took a quick step back, his eyes on her right knee.

She was off and running in a flash. This time, he let her go. She was fast, but he knew that from her dossier. She'd spotted him watching her house. It amazed him. He was always so very careful, so patient, as still as one of the spruce trees. In the past, his life had depended on it more times than he cared to remember. But she'd cottoned on to the fact that someone was out there, with her in his sights.

Well, the stalker had been after her for more than three weeks in New York. That had sharpened her senses, kept her alert. There was no doubt she was afraid, but it hadn't mattered. She'd come out and confronted him anyway. He whistled as he walked over and bent down to pick up her Coonan automatic. It was a nice gun. It had a closed breech that gave it very high velocity. His brother had one of these babies, was always bragging about it. It was steady, reliable, deadly, and not all that common. He wondered how she handled the recoil. He dumped the seven rimmed cartridges into his hand, then dropped them into his pocket. He paused a moment, wondering if he shouldn't leave the gun in her mailbox or slip it just inside her front door.

He imagined she wouldn't feel safe without it.

He saw Tyler McBride and his son leave about ten minutes later. He saw her wave from the front porch. He saw her looking over toward where he quietly stood, surely not visible through the trees. She went back into the house after Tyler McBride and his son drove off. He waited.

Not three minutes later she was back, standing on the front porch, looking toward him. He saw her thinking, weighing, assessing. Finally, she trotted toward him.

She had guts.

He didn't move, just waited, watching her. He realized when she was only about ten feet from him that she had a big kitchen butcher knife clutched in her hand.

He smiled. She was her father's daughter.

Chapter 9

Slowly, he pulled her gun out of his pants pocket and aimed it in her general direction. "Even that big honker knife can't compete with this Coonan you managed to get off that guy you met at the restaurant in Rockland. He was, however, pissed that you wouldn't go to bed with him." He grinned at her. "Hey, you got what you needed. You did good."

"How did you know about that? Oh, never mind. My knife can certainly compete with the Coonan now. I watched you take the bullets out."

He grinned at her again, he just couldn't help it, and held the automatic out to her, butt first.

"What good is it? You've got the bullets. Give them to me now."

He scooped the seven bullets out of his pocket and handed them and the automatic to her.

She eyed the gun and the bullets, then backed up another step. "No, you want me to come a bit closer and then you can kick my knife away. You're fast, too fast. I'm not stupid."

"All right," Adam said, and he thought, Smart woman. He laid the bullets and the gun down on the ground and took a good half dozen steps back.

He said easily, "It's an effective weapon, that Coonan, but if I have to carry one of those things, I prefer my Colt Delta Elite."

"It sounds like some western debutante."

He laughed. "Aren't you going to pick up the gun?"

She shook her head at him and didn't move. She was holding the butcher knife like a mad killer in a slasher movie, her arm pulled back, the point out and arched. The sucker looked really sharp. He could get it from her, but one of them could easily get sliced up. He stayed put. Besides, he wanted to see what she'd do.

"Tell me what you're doing here. Why did you come up to me at Food Fort? Why are you watching me?"

"I'd really rather not tell you just yet. I hadn't expected you to see me. When I've wanted to stay hidden in the past, I've managed it quite well." He suddenly looked pissed off, not at her but at himself. She almost smiled, then tightened her grip on the knife.

"Tell me, now."

"All right, then. I'm here to do research on why women dye their hair."

She very nearly ran at him with the knife. She was so mad she nearly forgot the bone-grinding fear. "All right, you jerk, I want you to lie on the ground and fold your hands underneath you. Do it now."

"No," he said. "The windbreaker is new. It looks good on me, hey, maybe it even looks dangerous and sexy. What do you think? Women like black, I've heard. Nope, I don't want it to get dirty."

"I called Sheriff Gaffney. He should be here any minute."

"Nah, you can't bluff me on that. The last person you want here is the sheriff. If I spilled the beans, he'd have to call the New York cops and the FBI."

She was so pale he thought she'd pass out. Her hand trembled a bit, but then she got ahold of herself. "So you know," she said. "I don't think you're the stalker—your voice is all wrong and you're too big—but you know all about him, don't you?"

"Yes. Now listen to me, Becca. I'm not here to hurt you. I'm here to— Think of me as your own personal guardian angel."

"You're so dark, you look more like the devil, but you're taller than I think the devil is. What's more, unlike the devil, I'll bet you don't have a lick of charm. The last thing you are is a guardian angel. You're a reporter or a paparazzo, aren't you?"

"Now you've offended me." She nearly laughed. But she had to remember that he was dangerous, fast and dangerous. No, she couldn't afford to forget that, not for an instant. She would still have laughed if her gut hadn't been frozen with fear for nearly as long as she could remember. He was trying to disarm her, at least figuratively this time. Thank God he didn't have use of her gun. And he was too far away to kick out at her. But he was fast. He had long legs. She took another step back, as insurance.

She waved the knife at him. "I've had it. Tell me who you are. Tell me now or I might have to hurt you. Don't underestimate me, I'm strong. No, it's more than that. I'm beyond frightened. I've got nothing to lose now."

He looked at her—too pale, her flesh drawn tightly over her bones, too thin, so stressed out he could nearly see her insides quivering. He said slowly, his voice as unthreatening as he could make it, "To hurt me you'd have to come closer. You know better than to do that. Yeah, you're strong, maybe I wouldn't even want to run into you in a dark alley. But there's a big something you're wrong about. Everyone has something to lose, including you. Things have just gotten a bit out of hand for you, that's all."

"A bit out of hand," she repeated slowly, then laughed, an ugly, raw sound. "You have no idea what you're talking about." She waited, just stood there, the knife up and arched, her hand starting to cramp, her muscles starting to protest, staring at him, wondering what to do, wondering if she could believe him and knowing she'd be a fool even to consider it.

"Actually, I do. What I wanted to say was that the media and the press are after you in full force, that's a fact, but you should be safe here."

"You found me."

"Yeah, but I'm so good I occasionally even surprise myself."

She raised the knife even higher. She felt the sun warm between her shoulder blades. It was a beautiful day and everything was a mess. He was her guardian angel? Her arm muscles were burning.

He started to say something more, then stopped. It was the look on her face that kept him quiet. It was like they were both frozen in time and place. Then she surprised the hell out of him. She dropped the knife to the ground and walked straight up to him. She stopped a foot short, looked up at him thoughtfully, then stuck out her hand. He shook hers, bemused, as she said, "If you're my guardian angel, then get on the phone to the medical examiner's office in Augusta and find out how long that poor woman who fell out of my basement wall was buried in there."

He didn't release her hand. She was tall. He didn't have to look down that far. "All right."

She snapped her fingers in front of his nose. "Just like that? You're so powerful you can find out something just that fast?"

"In this case, yes, I can. You don't look much like your mother."

The hand stiffened, but she didn't jerk free. She said calmly, "No, I don't. Mom always told me that I'm the picture of my dad. My dad—his name was Thomas—he died in Vietnam. He was a hero. My mother loved him very much, probably too much."

"Yes," he said. "I know all about that."

"How?"

"It's not important right now. Believe me."

She didn't, of course, but she was willing to put it on hold for the moment because she said then, "I saw a really old snapshot of him. He looked so young, so happy. He was very handsome, so tall and straight." She paused a moment, and he heard the hitch in her voice. "I was too young to remember him when he died, but my mom said he'd seen me born, held me and loved me. And then he left and didn't come back."

"I know."

She cocked her head to one side, and again she let it go, saying, "When I first saw you in Food Fort, I thought you looked hard, like you didn't smile very often, like you ate nails and hot salsa for snacks. I thought you could be mean if you had to, maybe even cruel. You still look mean. I can sense that you're dangerous; actually, I just know it, so don't even bother trying to deny it. Who are you, really?"

"I'm Adam Carruthers. I told you that at Food Fort. That really is my name. Now, take me to your house and I'll get on the phone. We won't find out who the skeleton is, but we'll find out at least how long she was in that wall. They'll have to do DNA tests; that takes a while. First things first."

He watched her pick up her Coonan and stuff the bullets in her jeans pocket. He picked up her kitchen knife and followed her back to Jacob Marley's house.

It took him eleven minutes and two phone calls. When he laid down the phone the second time, he looked over at her and smiled. "It shouldn't take long." In no more than three seconds, the phone rang. He motioned her away and picked it up. "Carruthers here."

He listened, wrote something down on a sheet of paper. "Thanks a lot, Jarvis, I owe you. Yeah, yeah, you know I always pay up. It just might not be tomorrow. You know how to reach me. Okay, thanks. Bye."

He carefully laid the phone back into the cradle. "It isn't Ann McBride, if that's what you're worried about."

"No, of course it's not Tyler's missing wife. I never thought it was. I've known him since I was eighteen. I've never met a more decent man. Really." But she was nearly shaking with relief, and he saw it. However, it was his turn to let it go.

But then she said, "I couldn't have stood it if Tyler had been a monster instead of a really nice guy. I guess I would have just hung it up."

"Yeah, your boyfriend is off the hook. The skeleton was buried inside that wall for at least ten years, possibly more. She was probably in her late teens when she was killed by a hard blow right in the face, the forehead actually. Whoever did it was really pissed, enraged, totally out of control. Jarvis said it was a vicious blow, killed her instantly."

"It looks like Jacob Marley really might have killed her, then."

He shrugged. "Who knows? It's not our problem, thank God."

"It's certainly mine, since she tumbled out of the wall onto my basement floor. I can't believe anyone would kill a teenager for wandering across his yard, and with such viciousness."

A second later the phone rang. It was Bernie Bradstreet, owner of *The Riptide Independent,* wanting to know what she could tell him. "I know the sheriff wants to keep a lid on this, but—"

She told him everything, omitting only what Adam Carruthers had just found out from the medical examiner's office. She didn't think the sheriff would like to be cut out of that particular loop. Then Bernie Bradstreet asked her to dinner, with his wife, he hastened to add when she didn't say anything. She put him off. When she hung up the phone, Adam said, "Newspaper? You handled it well. Now you need to call the sheriff. Don't tell him you already know the answers, just encourage him to call the medical examiner's office. Jarvis told me they're not ready to release the information yet, but if the sheriff calls, he might be able to pry it out of them.

Oh, yeah, when the sheriff comes, tell him I'm your cousin from Baltimore come to visit. Okay?"

"Cousins? We don't look anything alike."

He gave her a crooked grin. "Thank heaven for that."

Sheriff Gaffney didn't like the news from Augusta. He liked tidy conclusions, puzzles where all the pieces finally locked cleanly into place, not this: an old skeleton, identity unknown, that had been bricked inside Jacob Marley's basement wall after her gruesome murder. He didn't really want Ann McBride to be dead, but it would have made things so much cleaner, so nice and straightforward. He glanced at Tyler McBride. The guy looked calm, but relieved? He just couldn't tell. Tyler had always managed to keep what he was feeling close to his vest. He was good at poker, nobody liked to play against him. Funny thing, though, the sheriff would have sworn that Tyler had killed his wife. He still kept his eye on Tyler, hoping to see him do something strange, like visit an unmarked grave or something. Well, he'd been wrong before. He guessed maybe he was wrong again. He hated it, it wasn't pleasant, but sometimes it happened, even to a man like him.

Sheriff Gaffney looked over at Ms. Powell's cousin, a big, tough-looking guy who looked like he could take care of himself. His body was hard and in good shape, but he seemed like a man who could be patient, as if he was used to waiting in the shadows, like a predator stalking its prey. Gaffney shook his head. He had to stop reading those suspense novels he liked so much.

He looked over at Becca Powell, a nice young woman who wasn't, thank God, so pale now, or on the verge of hysteria. Hopefully her cousin would keep her that way. After finding that skeleton, just maybe she would be glad to have him around for a while. He found himself studying Carruthers again. The guy was dark, from his black hair—too long, in the sheriff's opinion—to his eyes, nearly black in the dim late-afternoon light in Jacob Marley's living room. He had big feet in scuffed black boots, soft-looking boots that looked like he'd worn them for a good decade and waited in the shadows with those boots on his feet, not making a whisper of a sound. He wondered what the hell the man did for a living. Nothing normal and expected, he'd bet his next meal on that. Just maybe he didn't want to know.

The sheriff looked around the living room. Jesus, the place looked like a museum or a tomb. It felt old and musty, although it smelled like lemons, just like at home.

He knew, of course, that everyone was looking at him, waiting. He liked that. It built suspense. He was holding them in the palm of his hand. Only thing was, they didn't look all that scared or worried or ready to gnaw off their fingernails. A real cool bunch.

Becca said finally, "Sheriff, won't you be seated? Now, you have news for us?"

He took the old chair she was waving at, eased down slowly, then cleared his throat. He was ready to make his big announcement. "Well now, it does appear that this skeleton isn't your wife, Tyler."

There was a sharp moment of silence, but not the surprise he'd expected, that he'd wanted, truth be told.

"Thank you for telling me so quickly, Sheriff. I'm pleased that it wasn't, because that would have meant that someone had killed her and it wasn't me. I hope that wherever Ann is, she's very much alive and well and happy."

But Tyler hadn't acted surprised. He acted like he already knew. Well, damn, if Tyler hadn't killed Ann, then he would certainly know that the skeleton wasn't her, or if it was, then someone else had put her there. That logic made the sheriff's head ache. "Humph, I wouldn't know about that. I've contacted all the local authorities and they're going to check on runaways from between ten and fifteen years ago. There's a good chance we'll find out who she is. She was young, probably late teens. That makes it even more likely that she was a runaway. She was murdered, though. Now, that makes it a big problem, my big problem."

"It's not possible that it's a local teenager, Sheriff?" Becca asked.

The sheriff shook his head. "Nobody just up and disappeared in the town's memory, Ms. Powell. Something like that, folk just wouldn't forget. Nope, it's got to be a runaway."

Adam Carruthers sat forward, his hands clasped between his knees. "You think this old man, Jacob Marley, did it?" He was sitting in a deep leather chair that old Jacob had liked. He looked like he was the one in charge and that burned the sheriff a bit. Fellow was too young to be in charge, not too much beyond thirty, about the same age as Maude's nephew, Frank, who was currently in prison out in Folsom, California, for writing bad checks. Frank had always had soggy morals, even as a boy. Maybe the fellow was shiftless, like Frank. But hell, the last thing this guy looked was shiftless.

"Sheriff?"

"Yeah? Oh, it's possible. Like I told Ms. Powell here, old Jacob didn't like people poking around. He had a mean streak in him and no patience to speak of. He could have bashed her."

Adam said, a dark eyebrow raised a bit, "Mean streak or not, you believe he actually bashed a young girl in the face with a blunt instrument and walled her in his basement because he was pissed to see her trotting across his backyard?"

Sheriff Gaffney said, "A blunt instrument, you say. Well, the ME didn't know what the murderer struck her with, maybe a heavy pot, maybe a bookend, something like that. Did Jacob do it? We'll just have to see about that."

"Nothing else makes much sense," Tyler said, jumping to his feet. He began pacing the room. His whole body was vibrating with tension. He had good muscle tone, the sheriff thought, remembering his own buffed self that the ladies had stared at when he was that young. Tyler whirled around, came to a stop, nearly knocking over a floor lamp. "Don't you see? Whoever killed her had to have access to Jacob's basement. Surely Jacob would have heard someone knocking away bricks, then putting them back up. The killer had to have cement to do that. Also, he had to haul the body into the house and down the basement steps. That would be quite an undertaking. It had to be Jacob. Nothing else makes sense."

Adam said, leaning back in that old leather chair now, his legs crossed at his ankles, his fingers steepled, the tips lightly tapping together, "Now, wait a minute. You're saying that Jacob Marley never left his house?"

"Not that I remember," Tyler said. "He even had his groceries delivered. Of course, I was gone four years when I was in college. Maybe he used to be different, went out more."

"Two things were always true about old Jacob," Sheriff Gaffney said slowly. "Two things you could always count on. He was here and he was mean." He heaved himself from his seat. He froze when the button right above his wide leather belt up and popped off. He watched, paralyzed, as the damned button rolled across the polished oak floor to stop at the big toe of Carruthers's right boot. He sucked in his belly, but he still felt that wide leather belt of his continue to cut him something fierce. He didn't say anything, just held out his hand.

Adam Carruthers tossed him the button. He didn't smile. The

sheriff clutched that damned button close. Jesus, maybe he should think about that diet Maude was always nagging him about.

Becca pretended not to see anything. She rose and stuck out her hand to the sheriff. "Thank you for coming and telling us in person. Please let us know when you find out who that poor girl is."

"Was, ma'am, was. I will. I'm glad I called them. I had to worm it out of them, but I finally got to speak to the main guy, a hard-nose named Jarvis, and he finally coughed up the info." He nodded to Tyler McBride, who looked hollow-cheeked, as if he'd been put through a wringer, and then to Adam Carruthers, a cocky bastard who hadn't laughed when his button had popped off.

"I'll see you out, Sheriff," Becca said and walked beside him out of the living room.

Adam said to Tyler, "Becca told me what was going on. I'm glad I was nearby and could get here to help."

Tyler eyed the man. There hadn't been time to question him before the sheriff had arrived. He said slowly, suspicion a sharp thread in his voice, "I didn't know Becca had a cousin. Who the hell are you?"

Chapter 10

*A*dam said easily, "Becca's mom was my aunt. She died of cancer, you know, very recently. My mom lives in Baltimore with my step-dad. A great guy, loves to fish for bass."

Thank God she heard that before she came back into the living room. The man was quick and smooth. He was a very good liar. She would have believed him herself if she hadn't known better. Actually, her mother was an only child, both her parents long dead. Her father had been an only child as well. His parents were also dead. Who was Adam, anyway?

Tyler turned toward Becca and said in a warm voice that was far too intimate, "Well, just maybe Sam can have a stepmom, just like you got yourself a stepdad, Adam."

Becca felt a jolt that landed a lump in her throat. She couldn't breathe for a minute. Tyler was looking at her like that? A future stepmom for Sam? She cleared her throat twice before she could speak. Well, she'd known him forever and he hadn't killed his wife, but he was a friend, nothing more than a very good friend, which was quite enough, given what her life was right now. "It's getting late. Adam, how about—"

He interrupted her smoothly, standing, stretching a bit. "I know, Becca. I'll be back over in a little while. I've got to get my stuff from the Errol Flynn Hammock. It's a great B-and-B. That guy Scottie is a hoot. You want to eat out tonight?"

"Becca and I were going to go to Errol Flynn's Barbecue this evening," Tyler said, and now he was standing perfectly still, his shoulders back, his chin up, ready for a fight, Adam thought, like a cock ready to defend the henhouse against the fox.

Adam grinned. "Sounds good to me. I like barbecue. You bringing Sam? I'd like to meet him."

"Of course Sam's coming," Becca said, her voice firm as that of a den mother faced with a dozen misbehaving ten-year-olds. "What street is Errol Flynn's Barbecue on, Tyler?"

"Foxglove Avenue, just across from Sherry's Lingerie Boutique. I hear that Mrs. Ella loves Sherry's lingerie, always in there on her lunch hour." He shook his head. "It's rather a scary thought."

"I haven't met Mrs. Ella yet," Becca said, then to Adam, "She's the sheriff's dispatcher, assistant, protector, screener, whatever—but I know about every one of her pets for the last fifty years. Her job was to save me from hysteria while I was waiting for the sheriff to come."

"Did it work?" Adam said.

"Yes, it did. All I could think about was the beagle named Turnip who died by running right off a cliff when he missed the corner chasing a car."

Both men laughed, and the male pissing contest that had nearly made her take a kitchen knife to both of them was out of sight, at least for the moment. She would have to speak to Tyler if it turned out he was getting the wrong idea, and evidently he was. But didn't he realize that being her first cousin meant that Adam was no threat? She didn't need this. She could eat barbecue with them, she supposed. Thank God Sam would be there.

Sam didn't have much testosterone yet.

It was just after midnight. Tyler McBride was still hanging about at the front door, and Sam was asleep in the car, his bright-blue

T-shirt and black kid jeans covered with the sauce from the pork barbecue spareribs. The kid hadn't said much—shy, Adam supposed—but he'd eaten his share. He'd finally said Adam's name when he'd taken a big bite of potato salad, then nothing more.

Would the guy never give it up and leave? Adam took a step closer to get him out of there when he overheard Tyler saying quietly to Becca at the front door, "I don't like him staying here with you, alone. I don't trust him."

And then Becca's voice, calm and soothing, and he could practically see her lightly touch her fingers to Tyler's arm as she said, "He's my first cousin, Tyler. I never did like him growing up. He was a bully and a know-it-all, always pushing me around just because I was a girl. He's grown up into a real sexist. But hey, he's here and he is big. He's also had some training, something like army special forces, I think, so he'd be useful if someone came around."

"I still don't like it."

"Look, if something happens, he's an extra pair of hands. He's harmless. Hey, I heard from his stepdad that he is probably gay."

Adam nearly lost it then. The laughter bubbled up. He practically had to slap his hand over his mouth to contain it. The laugher dried up in less than a second. He wanted to leap on her, close his hands around her skinny neck, and perhaps strangle her.

"Yeah, right, sure," Tyler said. "A guy like that? Gay? I don't believe it for a minute. You should stay with me and Sam, to be on the safe side."

She said very gently, "No, you know I couldn't do that, Tyler."

Even after that, it took her another couple of minutes to get Tyler out of the house. She was locking the door when he said from behind her, "I'm not a sexist."

She turned around to grin at him. "Aha! So you were eavesdropping. I thought you were probably lurking back there. I was afraid that you were going to try to throw Tyler out of the house."

"Maybe I would have if you hadn't finally gotten a grip and pushed him out. I wasn't a bully or a know-it-all, either, when I was growing up. I never tortured you."

"Don't become part of your own script, Adam. I can also write whatever I want to on that script, since it involves me."

"I'm not gay, either."

She just laughed at him.

He grabbed her by the shoulders, jerked her against him, and kissed her fast and hard. He said against her mouth, "I'm not gay, damn you."

She pulled away from him, stood stock-still, and stared at him. She wiped the back of her hand over her mouth.

He streaked his fingers through his hair, standing it on end. "I'm sorry. I don't know why I did that. I didn't mean to do that. I'm not gay."

She started shaking her head, then, just as suddenly, unexpectedly, she threw back her head and laughed and laughed, wrapping her arms around herself.

It was a nice sound. He bet she hadn't laughed much lately. She hiccuped. "You're forgiven for trying to enforce your manhood. Got you on that one, hmmm?"

He realized he'd leapt for the bait. How could that have happened? He looked down at his fingernails, then buffed them lightly against his shirtsleeve. "Actually, what I should have said is I'm not at all certain yet that I'm gay. I'm still thinking about it. Kissing you was a test. Yeah, I'm still not certain one way or the other. You didn't give me much data." Not much of a return hit, but it was something.

She walked past him into the kitchen. She started measuring out coffee. When she finished, she turned the machine on and stood there, staring at the coffee dripping into the pot. Finally she turned and said, "I want to know who you are. Now. Don't lie to me. I can't take any more lies. Really, I just can't."

"All right. Pour me that coffee and I'll tell you who I am and what I'm doing here."

While she poured, he said, leaning back in his chair, balancing it on its two back legs, "Because you're an amateur I looked at the problem very differently. But like I already told you, you didn't do badly. Your only really big mistake was your try at misdirection with the flight from Dulles to Boston, then another flight on to Portland. Another thing: I reviewed all your credit card invoices. The only airline you use is United. Since you're an amateur, it wouldn't occur to you to change."

She said, "Trying another airline flicked through my brain, but I wanted out as fast as I could get out and I feel comfortable dealing with United. I never thought, never realized—"

"I know. It makes excellent sense, just not in this sort of situation. I didn't even bother checking any of the other airlines."

"However did you get ahold of my credit card invoices?"

"No problem. Access to any private records is a piece of cake, for anyone. Thankfully, law enforcement has to convince judges to get warrants and that takes time, a good thing for you. Also, I've got a dynamite staff who are so fast and creative that it sometimes surprises even me.

"No, don't stiffen up like a poker. We're talking absolute discretion here. Now, there were only sixty-eight tickets issued to women traveling alone within six hours of the flight you took to Washington, D.C. I believed it would be three hours, but we all wanted to be thorough. It turned out you called the airline to make reservations only two hours and fifty-four minutes before the flight, as a matter of fact. You moved very quickly once you made up your mind to get the hell out of Dodge. Then you had to buy a ticket to Boston, then on to Portland, Maine, when you arrived at Dulles in Washington, D.C. You didn't want to buy it in New York, for obvious reasons. You ran up to the ticket counter, knowing full well that the next flight to Boston was in a scant twelve minutes. You wanted out of the line of fire and to get where you were going as quickly as you could. There was a flight from Dulles to Boston leaving only forty-five minutes after you landed in Dulles, but you turned it down. You didn't have any checked luggage, too big a risk with that, which was smart of you. The woman at the check-in counter recognized your photo, said she realized you might miss that plane, but you insisted even though she tried to talk you out of it. She didn't understand at the time, since there was another flight so soon. She told you the chances were very high that you'd miss the first plane to Boston."

"I nearly did miss it. I had to run like mad to catch it. They'd already closed the gate but I talked my head off until they opened it."

"I know. I spoke to the flight attendant who greeted you at the door when you came rushing onto the plane. She said you looked somewhat desperate."

She sighed, but didn't say anything, just crossed her arms over her chest and stared at him, still as a stone. "Come on, let's hear the rest of it."

"It didn't take long to find you on that flight to Portland. Your fake ID was pretty amateur. I'll bet they were really busy at the check-in counters in New York and Dulles for you to get passed on through. At least you were smart enough not to use that driver's license again to get yourself a rental car. You waited an hour for a flight from Boston to Portland, then you took a taxi into Portland—yes, one of my people found the driver and verified that it was you—and went to Big Frank's Previously Owned Cars on Blake Street. You wanted your own car. That told me that you had a definite destination in mind, a place where you were going to burrow in for the long haul. I got all the particulars out of Big Frank, including your license plate number, the make, model, and color of your Toyota. I called a friend in the Portland PD to put out an APB on you and it didn't take more than a day and a half to net you. Remember when you got gas at the Union 76 station when you were first coming into town?"

She'd paid cash. No trail. No record. "I didn't make any mistakes."

"No, but it turns out that the guy who pumped your gas is a police radio buff with an excellent memory for numbers. He heard the APB, remembered your car and license plate, and phoned it in. It got to me really fast. Don't worry, I canceled the APB. Needless to say, I owe a good-sized favor to Chief Aronson of the Portland PD. Also I spoke to the kid who pumped your gas, told him it had all been a mistake, thanked him, and slipped him a fifty. Oh yes, I got a good laugh over the name on the fake ID—Martha Clinton—a nice mix of presidential names."

"I did, too," Becca said, wondering why she'd bothered at all.

"At least Martha was young and had blondish hair. Did you buy it off a street kid in New York?"

"Yes. I had to try six of them before I could find an ID that looked anything remotely like me. I liked the name. When did you get here to Riptide?"

"Two days ago. I went immediately to the only bed-and-breakfast in town and of course you had stayed there for one night. Scottie told me you'd taken the old Marley place." He splayed his fingers. "Nothing to it."

"Why didn't you come to see me right away?"

"I wanted to get the lay of the land, watch you awhile, see what was happening, who you spoke to, things like that. It's an approach I've always used. I've never believed in rushing into things, if I have a choice."

"It was so easy for you." She sighed, her arms still crossed over her chest. "That means that the FBI should be ringing the doorbell at any minute."

"Nah, they're not as smart as I am."

She threw her empty coffee cup at him.

He snagged the cup out of the air and set it back on the table. His reflexes were good. He was very fast. She said, "I'm awfully glad I didn't come any nearer to you. You could have nailed me in a flash, couldn't you?"

"Probably, but that's not the point. I'm not here to hurt you. I'm here to protect you."

"My guardian angel."

"That's right."

"Why don't you think the cops and FBI will be here any moment?"

"They have to follow all sorts of legal procedures to get to the goodies." He paused a moment, grinning at her. "And I also sent them on a wild-goose chase. I'll tell you about it later."

"All right. Let's cut to the chase. If you're not a cop, then who are you and who hired you to help me?"

He shook his head. "For the time being I'm not at liberty to tell you that. But someone wants me to clean up this mess you've gotten yourself into."

"I didn't do anything at all. It was that demented man stalking me who's responsible. Oh, maybe like the cops in New York and Albany, you don't believe me, either?"

"I believe you. Would you like to know why the cops in New

York and Albany didn't believe you? Thought you were a screwed-up fruitcake?"

She nearly fell out of her chair. "I don't believe this. You know something the cops don't? They thought I was crazy or malicious or infatuated with the governor. Come on, what do you know?"

"They believed you were a fake because someone close to the governor told them that it was all a sick sexual fantasy. When the cops called from New York, that's what the Albany police told them. However, the threat to the governor was quite real, no question about that, since someone shot him. They had to refocus, think things over again."

"Who in the governor's office said that about me? Don't you dare just sit there staring at me. Damn you, I deserve to know who betrayed me."

"Of course you do. I'm sorry, Becca. It was Dick McCallum, the governor's senior aide."

She nearly fell over in shock. "Oh, no, not Dick McCallum. Oh, no, it doesn't make any sense. Not Dick." She looked stricken and he was sorry for it.

She was shaking her head at him, not wanting to believe him but afraid not to. "But why? Dick has never said anything mean to me or acted like he had it in for me. He never asked me out, so there wouldn't be any sort of rejection involved. I didn't threaten him in any way. I was sure he liked me. I wrote most of the governor's speeches, for God's sake. I didn't head up strategy sessions or conduct policy meetings or have anything to do with spin or scheduling or anything that would be in his bailiwick. Why would he do it?"

"That I don't know yet. But to be realistic about it, it will probably come down to money. Someone paid him a lot of money to do it. Now, one of the cops in Albany told me he'd come to them, supposedly feeling all sorts of guilty, but swearing he had no choice because he was afraid you'd go after the governor. I promise you I will find out why he did it. He's got to be the key to this." Actually, he thought, Thomas Matlock was going over everything in McCallum's background, including where he got the small knife tattoo on the back of his right shoulder blade.

She said slowly, thinking aloud really, "If Dick McCallum said those things about me, then he must know about the stalker, maybe even who he is and why he picked me to terrorize. Maybe Dick even knows who is trying to kill the governor."

"Yes, all of that is possible. We'll see."

"Do you mean 'we' as in you and me?"

"No."

"Let me call the cops again. I'll tell them I know about what Dick McCallum told them. I can tell them he's lying. Won't they have to question him more thoroughly?"

"No, Becca, it's too late. I'm really sorry about this."

"What do you mean, it's too late? I know I can get ahold of Detective Morales."

"We'll have to go another route to find out why Dick McCallum did what he did, and who probably paid him a whole lot of money to do it."

She became very still. She shook her head. He said very gently, "I'm sorry, Becca, but someone ran Dick McCallum down in front of his apartment building in Albany. He's dead."

There wasn't a single thought in her mind, just numbing horror.

"They think you could be involved. Everyone's gone nuts. Actually, they were nuts the moment the governor was shot. No one could believe the distance on that shot. Now they're very serious about finding you and finding out what you know, if you're involved in any way. I planted information for them to find and got them off on a wrong track, so you're safe for a while."

He sat back in his chair and cradled his head against his arms. He gave her a big fat smile. "They're not going to find you anytime soon, trust me on that."

Chapter 11

She could only stare at him. "All right, you're the greatest. Now, tell me how you fooled them."

"Thank you. Actually, I had nearly everything in place before Dick McCallum was killed. To be very precise, I did it right after the governor was shot. I had to shut the spigot off before they had the chance to really turn it on.

"They immediately mounted quite a manhunt. FBI offices all over the country are on the lookout for you. They were just beginning to track you from New York, just like I did, but then—a wonderful thing happened. They became convinced that you'd climbed on a Greyhound bus and had gone all the way down to North Carolina, probably disguised in a black wig, maybe even brown contacts. All they had to work on was your driver's license and that was pretty scary. They searched your mom's apartment, but you'd cleaned it out really well. They're still looking for a storage facility for more information about you, photos and stuff like that. I assume you rented a storage locker. Where?"

"In the Bronx. Under an assumed name. To be honest, I didn't have time to go through my mother's stuff. I just piled everything into boxes and hauled the stuff to the Bronx. Now, Adam, where would they come up with the idea that I'd be in North Carolina?"

He smiled sweetly at her. "Fiddling. I enjoy it and I'm good at it."

"By 'fiddling' you mean you scammed them?"

"Right. Sometimes con men use it to express that they got something over on their marks. Ah, sometimes law enforcement uses it, too."

She shook her head at him. "I don't want to know which you are. You're kidding about this, right? You yourself didn't feed them that information, did you?"

"No. I got one of their best snitches to feed it to them. That way they wouldn't have any doubts at all. I even planted some evidence in your apartment in Albany to show that you knew all about North Carolina, that you'd even vacationed on the Outer Banks, your favorite town, Duck. Agents were swarming all over Duck within four hours of the FBI getting the information."

"I have been to Duck. I've stayed at the Sanderling Inn."

"I know, that's why I selected it."

"But I don't think I kept any souvenirs or books or anything like that."

"Oh yeah, sure you had souvenirs. There were a couple of T-shirts, some shells with 'Duck' etched on them, a couple of Duck pens, and a cute little candy dish showing ducks marching. Now the Feebs will scour the Outer Banks all the way down to Ocracoke. Did you hear about the Cape Hatteras lighthouse being moved?"

"Yes. Do you want more coffee?"

"Please. Oh, yes, Becca, give me the name of the storage locker and the assumed name. I'll get all your stuff out of there and to a safe place."

She snapped her fingers at him. "You can get things accomplished just like that?"

"I can but try." He tried to look modest, maybe even humble, but he couldn't pull it off. "What's the name you used and what's the storage locker name?"

"P and F Storage in the Bronx, and the name is Connie Pearl."

"I don't think I want to know where you got that name."

He watched her walk to the sink with the empty coffeepot and rinse it out. When she turned to reach for the coffee, her head slanted in a certain way. He blinked. He knew that certain set of the head very well. He'd seen her father do that not six days before. He watched her closely and saw that her movements were economical, graceful. He liked the way she moved. She'd inherited that from her father, too, one of the smoothest, most elegant men Adam had ever known. He clasped his hands behind his head, closed his eyes for a moment, picturing Thomas Matlock clearly in his mind's eye, and thought back to that meeting between the two of them on June 24.

Washington, D.C.

The Sutter Building

"**S**he still believes you're dead."

He nodded. "Of course. Even when Allison knew she was dying, we decided not to tell Becca about me, it was just too dangerous."

At least, Adam thought, Thomas had been in close contact with his wife since e-mail had come along. They were online every night, until his wife had gone into the hospital. Adam said, "I don't agree with that, Thomas. You should have contacted her when her mother fell into a coma. She needed you then, and the good Lord knows, she needs you now."

"You know it's still too risky. I haven't known where Krimakov is since right after I shot his wife. I realized soon enough that I would have to kill him to protect my family, but he simply disappeared, with the help of the KGB, no doubt. No, I can't take the risk that Krimakov could find out about her. He would slit her throat and laugh and then call me and laugh some more. No. I've been dead to her for twenty-four years. It stays that way. Allison agreed with me that until I know for certain that Krimakov is dead, I stay dead to my daughter." Thomas sighed deeply. "It was very hard for both of us, I'll be honest with you. I think if Allison hadn't slipped into that drugged coma, she might have told Becca, so that she'd know she wasn't really alone."

The pain in his voice made Adam silent for a long time. Then he said, all practical again, "You can't stay dead to her now and you know it. Or haven't you been watching CNN?"

"That's why you're here. Stop frowning down at me. Pour yourself a cup of coffee and sit down. I've done a lot of thinking. I've got a favor to ask."

Adam Carruthers poured himself some coffee so strong it could bring down a rhino. He stretched out in the chair opposite the huge mahogany desk. A computer, a printer, a fax, and a big leather desk pad sat in their designated spots on top of the desk. No free papers stacked anywhere, no slips or notes, just technology. He knew that on this specific computer there were no deep, dark secrets, just camouflage. Even he would have a hard time getting through all the safeguards installed to protect any hidden files on the machine, if there had been any, which there weren't. Thomas Matlock had stayed at the top of his game by being careful and smart.

Adam said, "The governor of New York was shot in the neck two nights ago. The man was lucky to be surrounded by doctors and that he'd promised more big state bucks for heart research, otherwise they might have let him bleed to death."

"You're cynical."

"Yeah, well, you've known that for ten years, haven't you?" Adam took a drink of the high-test coffee and felt a jolt all the way to his feet. "Everyone is after her now, particularly the Feebs. She's gone to ground. They've pulled out all the stops, but no sign of her yet. Smart girl. To fool everyone isn't easy. She's your daughter, all right. Cunning and sneakiness are in her genes."

Thomas Matlock opened a desk drawer and pulled out a 5x7 color photo set in a simple silver frame. "There are only three people alive who know she's my daughter, and you're one of them. Now, her mother got this to me just eight months ago. Her name's Becca, as you know, short for Rebecca—that was my mother's name. She's about five feet eight inches tall, and she's on the lean side, not more than one hundred twenty pounds. You can see that she's in good shape. She's athletic, a whiz at tennis and racquetball. Her mother told me she loves football, not college but professional. She'd kill for the Giants, even in their worst season.

"You've got to find her, Adam. I don't know if Krimakov will connect her to me. It's very probable he's known all along that I had a wife and a daughter, no way to bury that, and we didn't want to do the witness protection program. But you know something? I still don't have a clue where he is or what he's been doing the past twenty years. I've got tentacles all over the world but no definite leads on his whereabouts. Now I've upped the ante, but still nothing.

"But you know he's on top of American news, all of it. The instant he hears the name 'Matlock,' he'll go *en pointe*. She's in deep trouble. She doesn't even realize how deep, that the cops and the FBI are the least of her worries."

"Don't worry, Thomas. I'll find her and I'll protect her, from both the stalker and Krimakov, if either of them shows up."

"That's just it." Thomas sighed. "This stalker bothers me. What

109

are the odds that a stalker would go after Becca? Too great, I think. What I'm thinking is that just maybe Krimakov already found her, just maybe he's the stalker."

"Jesus, Thomas," Adam said. "I guess it's possible, but unlikely, I think. If he's the stalker, then that means he found her even before your wife died."

"Yes, it scares me to my toes."

"But there's no proof at all that it's Krimakov. Now, first things first. I've got to get the locals and the Feds off her trail once and for all."

"You've already begun to track her, then?"

"Sure. The minute I heard her name, I got all my people working on it. What would you expect? You're the one who always has to look at the big picture. I don't. Let me make a phone call right now, let Hatch know you've approved everything, get all my people on this."

"And if I hadn't called you?"

"I'd have taken care of her anyway." Adam turned to pick up the phone. "She's your daughter."

Adam knew that Thomas Matlock was looking at him as he lifted the receiver of the black phone and punched in some numbers. He knew, too, that Thomas had worried and worried, tried to figure out the odds, determine the best thing to do, but Adam had simply stepped in and begun protecting his daughter from a stalker who could be, truth be told, Krimakov, although to Adam the odds were that Krimakov was long gone. But it was a lead. It was something, the only thing they had.

Thomas should have known that he didn't have to even ask. Adam also imagined that Thomas Matlock felt a goodly amount of relief.

As he spoke quietly on the phone, he saw the jolt of pain cross

Thomas Matlock's face, and he knew it was because Thomas would never again see Allison. And more than that. Thomas Matlock hadn't been with his wife when she died. He'd wanted to be, but Becca was there, always there, and he couldn't take the chance. The pain and guilt of that had to be tearing him up inside.

Oh yeah, he'd try to save Thomas's daughter.

Only one mistake in the seventies, and Thomas Matlock had lost any chance at the promising life he'd begun. He'd had to hold himself private. He'd kept his position in the intelligence community so he would know if Krimakov ever surfaced. But he'd had to remain alone.

Jacob Marley's House

Adam slowly opened his eyes. He was in the same room with Allison and Thomas Matlock's daughter, and she was looking at him with an odd combination of helplessness and wariness. Damn, she looked so very much like her father. He couldn't tell her yet. No, not yet. He said on a yawn, "I'm sorry, I guess I just sort of flashed out for a while."

"It's late. You're probably exhausted what with all your skulking around spying on me. I'm going to bed. There's a guest room at the end of the hall upstairs. The bed might be awful, I don't know. Come on and I'll help you make it up."

The bed was hard as a rock, which was fine with Adam. His feet didn't hang off the end, another nice thing. He watched her trail off down the hall, pause for just a moment, and look back at him. She raised her hand. Then he watched her close the door to her bedroom.

He'd wondered about Becca Matlock for a very long time, won-

111

dered what she was like, how much she'd inherited from her father, wondered if she was happy, maybe even in love with a guy and ready to get married. He discovered he was still wondering about her as he lay on his back and stared up at the black ceiling. All he knew for sure was that someone had put her in the center of his game and was doing his best to bring her down. Kill her? He didn't know.

Was it Vasili Krimakov? He didn't know, but maybe it was time to consider anything that put even a shadow on the radar.

He woke up at about four A.M. and couldn't go back to sleep. Finally, he booted up his laptop and wrote an e-mail: *I told her about McCallum. She really doesn't know anything. I don't either, yet. You know, just maybe you're right. Just maybe Krimakov is the stalker and the one who shot the governor.*

He turned off the compact and stretched out again, pillowing his head on his arms. To him, Krimakov was like the bogeyman, a monster trotted out to scare children. To Adam, the man had never had any substance, even though he'd seen classified material about him, been briefed about his kills. But hell, that was over twenty-five years ago. Nothing, not even a whiff of the man since then.

Twenty-five years since Thomas Matlock had accidentally killed his wife. So long ago and in a place that was no longer even part of the Soviet Union—Belarus, the smallest of the Slavic republics independent since 1991.

He knew the story because once, just once, Thomas Matlock had gotten drunk—it was his anniversary—and told him about how he'd been playing cat and mouse back in the seventies with a Russian agent, Vasili Krimakov, and in the midst of a firefight that never should have happened, he'd accidentally shot Krimakov's wife. They'd been on the top of Dzerzhinskaya Mountain, not much of a mountain at all, but the highest peak Belarus had to offer. And she'd died and Krimakov had sworn he would kill him, kill his wife, kill anyone he loved, and he'd cursed him to hell and beyond. And Thomas Matlock knew he meant it.

The next morning, Thomas Matlock had simply looked at Adam and said, "Only two other people in the world know the whole of it, and one of them is my wife." If there was more to the tale, Thomas Matlock hadn't told him.

Adam had always wondered who the other person was who knew the whole story, but he hadn't asked. He wondered now what Thomas Matlock was doing at this precise moment, if he, like Adam, was lying awake, wondering what the hell was going on.

Chevy Chase, Maryland

It was raining deep in the night, a slow, warm rain that would soak into the ground and be good for all the summer flowers. There was no moon to speak of to shine in through the window of the dimly lit study. Thomas Matlock was hunched over his computer, aware of the soft sounds of the rain but not really hearing it. He had just gotten an e-mail from a former double agent, now living in Istanbul, telling him that he'd just picked it up from a Greek smuggler that Vasili Krimakov had died in an auto accident near Agios Nikolaos, a small fishing village on the northeast coast of Crete.

Krimakov had lived all this time in Crete? Since Thomas had found out about his daughter's stalker, after the man had murdered that old bag lady, he'd put everyone on finding Krimakov. Scour the damned world for him, Thomas had said. He's got to be somewhere. Hell, he's probably right here.

Now after all this time, all these bloody years, he'd finally found him? Only he was dead. It was hard to accept. His implacable enemy, finally dead. Gone, only it was too late, because Allison was dead, too. Far too late.

Was it really an accident?

Thomas knew that Krimakov had to have enemies. He'd had years to make them, just as Thomas had. He'd gotten messages from Krimakov back in the early years, telling him he would never forget, never. Telling him he would find his damned wife and daughter—yes, he knew all about them and he would find them, no matter how well Thomas had hidden them. And then it would be judgment day.

Thomas had been terrified. And he'd done something unconscionable. He escorted a very pretty young woman, one of the assistants in his office, to an Italian embassy function, then to a Smithsonian exhibit. The third time he was with her, he was simply walking her to her car from the office because the skies had suddenly opened up and rain was pouring down and he had a big umbrella.

A man had jumped out of an alley and shot her between the eyes, not more than six feet away. Thomas hadn't caught him. He knew it was Krimakov even before he'd received that letter written in Vasili's stark, elegant hand: "Your mistress is dead. Enjoy yourself. When I discover your wife and child, they will be next."

That had been seventeen years before.

Thomas had considered seeing Allison that weekend. He had canceled, and she'd known why, of course. He sat back in his chair, pillowing his head on his arms. He read the e-mail from Adam. *Consider Krimakov.*

But Krimakov was finally dead. The irony of it didn't escape him. Krimakov was gone, out of his life, forever. It was all over. He could have finally been with Allison. But it was too late, just too late. But now someone was terrorizing Becca. He just didn't understand what was going on. He wished he could learn about Dick McCallum, but as of yet, no one had seen anything out of the ordinary. No big deposits, no new accounts, no big expenditures on his credit cards, no strangers reported near him, nothing suspicious or unexpected in his apartment. Simply nothing.

Thomas remembered telling Adam how there were only two other people—besides Adam—who knew the real story. His wife and Buck Savich, both dead now. Buck had died of a heart attack some six years before. But there was Buck's son, and he was very much alive, and Thomas realized now that he needed him, needed him very much.

The man knew all about monsters. He knew how to find them.

Georgetown
Washington, D.C.

Dillon Savich, head of the Criminal Apprehension Unit of the FBI, booted up his laptop MAX and saw there was an e-mail from someone he didn't know. He shifted his six-month-old son, Sean, to his other shoulder and punched up the message.

Sean burped. "Good one," Savich said, and rubbed his son's back in slow circles. He heard him begin to suck his fingers, felt his small body relax into his shoulder. He read:

Your father was an excellent friend and a fine man. I trusted him implicitly. He believed you would change the course of criminal investigations. He was very proud of you. I desperately need your help. Thomas Matlock.

115

Sean reared back suddenly and patted his father's whiskered cheek with his wet fingers. Savich stroked his son's small fingers and dried them on his cotton shirt. "We've got a neat mystery here, Sean. Who the hell is Thomas Matlock? How did he know my father? He was an excellent friend? I don't remember ever hearing my father mention his name.

"MAX, let me get you started on this. Find out about this man for me." He punched in a series of keys, then sat back, Sean bouncing from foot to foot on his stomach, watching MAX do his thing.

Savich reached up and flicked the drool off Sean's chin. "You're teething, champ. It's not going to be a pretty sight for the next several months, so that book says. You don't seem like you're feeling any pain. Believe me, that's a relief for both of us."

Sean gurgled very close to Savich's ear.

He held his son back and smiled into that splendid little face that looked more like him than Sherlock. Sean had his dark hair, not Sherlock's curly red hair. As for his eyes, they were as dark as his father's, not that sweet, soft blue of his mother's. "You want to know something? It's four o'clock in the morning and here we are wide awake. Your mama's going to think we're both nuts."

Sean yawned then and stuck three fingers into his mouth. Savich kissed his forehead and stood, gently laying his son over his shoulder. "Let's see if you're ready to pack it in again."

He went to his son's room and dimmed the light. He laid him on his back and pulled a yellow baby blanket over his light diaper shirt.

"You go to sleep now, hear? I'm even going to sing you one of my favorite songs. Your mama always laughs her head off when I sing her this one." He sang a country-and-western song about a man who loved his Chevy truck so much that he was buried with the engine and all four hubcaps, special edition, all silver. Sean

looked mesmerized by his father's deep, rich voice. He was out after just two verses. One good thing about country-and-western
music—there was always another verse. Savich paused a moment,
smiled down at the precious human being that still jolted him
when he realized that he was, indeed, his very own child, part of
him. Just as Savich had been his father's child. He felt a sharp pull
somewhere in the region of his heart. He missed his dad, always
would.

Who was this Thomas Matlock, who claimed to have known his
father?

He went back to his study.

MAX beeped as he walked in. "Good for you," Savich said, sitting back down. "What have we got on this Thomas Matlock
guy?"

Chapter 12

*A*dam said, "You mean they're giving up trying to find her on the Outer Banks?"

Adam knew that Hatch, his right hand, was sitting crouched in a phone booth somewhere, his dark sunglasses pressed so close to his eyes that his eyelashes got tangled, got into his eyes, and sometimes caused eye infections. "Yeah, boss. Since they have no leads at all, they're counting on Becca knowing something, maybe even knowing this guy who shot the governor. That's why they're searching high and low for her. Agent Ezra John is the SAC running the show down there. I hear he's cursing up a blue streak, wondering where she could have hidden herself. Says they looked everywhere for her and she just ain't anywhere, just like smoke, he says, and the others grin behind their hands. Oh yeah, you'll love this, boss. Old Ezra believes that Ms. Matlock is a lot smarter than anyone gave her credit for, keeping out of sight like she is. If he knew it was you that duped him, he'd want to put your head on a pike and find some bridge to stick it on."

"Thanks for sharing that, Hatch."

"Knew you'd like it. You and old Ezra go back a long ways, don't you?"

That wasn't the half of it, Adam thought, and said only, "Something like that. Okay now. In other words, Ezra's finally come to the conclusion that she conned him? That she isn't anywhere near the Outer Banks?"

"That's it."

"I don't think I need to fiddle them anymore. Too much time has passed for them to find her now. I think we're home free—well, at least for the moment."

Silence.

"Hatch, I know you're lighting a cigarette in a closed phone booth. Put it out right now or I'll fire you."

Silence.

"Is it out?"

"Yeah, boss. I swear it's out. I didn't even get one decent puff."

"Swell news for your lungs. Now, what about the NYPD?"

"They're talking to their counterparts all over the country, just like the Feebs are. But hey—nothing, nada, zippo. This Detective Morales is a wreck, probably hasn't slept for three days. All he can talk about is how she called him, repeated to him that she'd told him everything, and he wasn't able to talk her in. There's this other detective, a woman name of Letitia Gordon, who evidently hates Ms. Matlock's guts. Claims she's a liar, a nutcase, and probably a murderer. Old Letitia really wants to bring her down. She's pushing everyone to charge her with the murder of that old bag lady outside the Metropolitan Museum. You know, the murder Ms. Matlock reported? The one the stalker did to get her attention?"

"Yeah, I know."

"Well, they told Detective Gordon to pull her head out of her armpit and try for a bit of objectivity. The woman's really got it in for our gal."

Adam made a rude noise. "Let Detective Gordon get hives over it for all we care. Neither Thomas nor I ever believed they were going to charge her with murder. But a material witness? That's possible. And you know as well as I do that the cops couldn't protect her from this stalker. Nope, that's our job. Now, what do you have on Mc-Callum?"

Adam wasn't expecting anything, so he wasn't disappointed when Hatch sighed and said, "Not a thing as of yet. A real pro spearheaded this operation, boss, just like you thought."

"Unfortunately, it can't be Krimakov because Thomas finally got him tracked down. He was living on Crete, and as of a week ago, he's dead. I'm not sure of the exact date. But it was before McCallum was run down in Albany. I guess Krimakov could have been involved, but he certainly wasn't running the show, and that's not his MO. Anything Krimakov was involved in, he was the Big Leader. Thomas is willing to bet his ascot on that. But if Krimakov was somehow involved, it means he knew about Becca being Matlock's daughter. Jesus, it makes me crazy."

"Nah, the guy's dead. This is a new nutcase, fresh out of the woodwork, and he's picked Becca."

Adam scratched his head and added, "No, I don't think so, Hatch. It's got to be some sort of conspiracy, there's just no other answer. Lots of folk involved. But why did they focus on Ms. Matlock? Why put her in the middle? I keep coming back to Krimakov, but I know, logically, that it just can't be. Someone, something else, is driving this. How's the governor?"

"I hear his neck is a bit sore, but he'll live. He doesn't know a thing, that's what he claims. He's very upset about McCallum."

Adam sat there and thought and thought. The same questions over and over again. No answers.

Silence.

"Put out the cigarette, Hatch. I know about your girlfriend. She loves silk lingerie and expensive steaks. You can't afford to lose your job."

"Okay, boss."

Adam heard some papers shuffling, heard some mild curses, and smiled. "Anything else?"

"Yeah, of course there's no positive ID on that skeleton that popped out of Ms. Matlock's basement wall. For sure it was a teenage girl who got her head bashed in some ten or more years ago. I did find out something sort of neat, though."

"Yeah?"

"It turns out there was an eighteen-year-old girl who just up and disappeared from Riptide, Maine. Now ain't that a neat coincidence?"

"I'll say. When?"

"Twelve years ago."

"No one's heard from her since?"

"I'm not completely sure about that. If she's still unaccounted for and they decide she's a good bet, then they'll do DNA tests on the bones."

Adam said, "They'll need something from her—like hair on a brush, an old envelope that would have her saliva, barring that, then a family member would have to give up some blood."

"Yeah. Thing is, though, it wouldn't be admissible in court if it ever came to it. It'll take some time, a couple of weeks. No one sees any big rush on it."

"I don't like the feel of this, Hatch. We've got this other mess and now this damned skeleton falling out of Becca's basement wall. It's enough to make a man give up football."

"Nah, you've always told me that God created the fall just for football. You'll be watching football when you throw that last pigskin into the end zone in the sky, if they still have the sport that many aeons from now. You'll probably lobby God to have pro football in Heaven. Stop whining, boss. You'll figure everything out.

You usually do. Hey, I hear that Maine's one beautiful place. That true?"

Adam stared at the phone for a moment. He had been whining. He said, "Yeah. I just wish I had some time to enjoy it." He suddenly yelled into the receiver, "No smoking, Hatch. If you even think about it, I'll know it. Now, call me tomorrow at this same time."

"You got it, boss."

"No smoking."

Silence.

Becca said very quietly, "Who is Krimakov?"

Adam turned around very slowly to face her. She was standing in the doorway of the moldy-smelling guest room where he'd spent his first night in Jacob Marley's house. She'd opened the door and he hadn't heard a thing. He was losing it.

"Who is Krimakov?"

He said easily, "He's a drug dealer who used to be involved with the Medellin cartel in Colombia. He's dead now."

"What does this Krimakov have to do with all this craziness?"

"I don't know. Why did you open the door without knocking, Becca?"

"I heard you on the phone. I wanted to know what was going on. I knew you wouldn't tell me. I also came up to get you for breakfast. It's ready downstairs. You're still lying. This doesn't have anything to do with drug dealing."

He had the gall to shrug.

"If I had my kitchen knife, I'd run at you, right this minute."

"And what? Slice me up? Come on, Becca, why can't you just accept that I'm here to do a job and that job is to make sure that you don't get wiped out? Get off your high horse."

He stood up then and she backed up a step. She was afraid of him still. Hell, after seeing him all civilized that entire evening with four-year-old Sam, it surprised him. "I told you I wouldn't hurt you," he said patiently. He realized at that moment that he didn't have a shirt on. She was afraid he might attack her? Well, after his teenage attempt last night to prove to her he wasn't gay, he supposed he couldn't blame her. He moved slowly, deliberately, and picked up his shirt from where it was hanging over a chair back, then turned his back to put it on. He faced her again as he buttoned it up.

"Who are you?"

He sighed and tucked in his shirt. Then he flipped the sheet and blanket over the bed. He straightened the single too-soft pillow that smelled, unexpectedly, of violets.

When he finally turned to face her again, she was gone. She'd heard Krimakov's name. It didn't matter. She'd never hear it again. The bastard was dead. Finally dead, and Thomas Matlock was free. To come and finally meet his daughter. Why hadn't Thomas said anything about that? He combed his hair, brushed his teeth, and headed downstairs.

She fed him pancakes with blueberry syrup and crispy bacon, just the way he liked it. The coffee was strong, black as Hatch's fantasies, the fresh cantaloupe she'd sliced, ripe and sweet.

Neither of them said a word. She ate a slice of dry toast and had a cup of tea. It looked like she was having trouble getting that much down.

He said, a dark eyebrow arched, his mouth full of bacon, "What is this? No questions right in my face? No bitching at me? By God, could it be that you're sulking?"

That got her, just as he hoped it would.

"How would you like that nice sticky syrup down the back of your neck?"

He grinned at her and saluted with his coffee cup. "I wouldn't like that at all. At least you're speaking to me again. Look, Becca, I'm just trying to find out what's going on. Everyone is floating a lot of ideas, a lot of names. Now we have this skeleton."

He was so slippery, she'd bet if he were a pig in a greased pig contest, no one could hold him down, but she was tenacious.

"Who were you telling not to smoke?"

"Hatch. He's my main assistant. He has more contacts than a centipede has legs, speaks six languages, and is real smart except when it comes to cigarettes and loose women. That's the way I can control his smoking. I pay him very well and threaten to fire him if he lights up."

"But I heard you tell him to put out the cigarette. Obviously he's still smoking. And he knew you were on the other end of the line."

"Yeah. It's more a game now than anything else. He lights up just to hear me blow."

"Did he find out anything about the skeleton? What's this about DNA testing? They think they know who that poor girl was?"

He stretched, drank down the last of his coffee, carefully set the cup on the table, then stood up.

She was on her feet in the next instant. Two fast steps and she was in his face. She was fast, he'd give her that, and she was mad. He was grinning down at her when she slammed her fist in his belly. Becca felt her face turning red. "Damn you, you will not treat me like a cipher, like I'm a moron who isn't even important enough to talk to. Who are you?"

He grabbed her wrist. "That was a good shot. No, don't hit me again or I'll have to do something. I want to keep those pancakes happy."

"Yeah, what?" She just didn't care anymore. She smashed her other fist into his left kidney.

He held both her wrists now. He knew she'd bring up her knee next so he jerked her around so her back was pressed against his chest. He held her arms pressed to her sides. "You'd look better as a blonde. Usually a woman's roots are darker than her hair. In your case, you've got all this baby-light hair at the roots."

She kicked back, grazing his shin. He grunted. He sat back down on the chair, holding her on his lap. She was pinned against him and couldn't move. "Now," he said, "I'm sorry that we're playing only by my rules, but that's the way it's got to be unless I'm told otherwise."

"You need to shave. You look like a convict."

"How do you know? You've got the back of your head to me."

"You've got as much hair on your face as you do on your chest."

"Oh yeah? Well, you did get an eyeful in the bedroom."

"Go to hell."

Adam's cell phone rang. "Well, shit. Will you let me answer this without attacking me again?"

"Actually, I don't want to be anywhere near you."

"Good." He dropped his arms and she jumped off his lap.

He flipped open the small narrow phone. "Carruthers here."

"Adam, it's Thomas Matlock. Is Becca there with you?"

"As a matter of fact, yes."

"All right, then, just listen. I sent an e-mail to Dillon Savich, a computer expert here at FBI headquarters in Washington. I knew his father very well. Actually, Buck Savich was the only other person who knew about all the mess with Krimakov. He's been dead for a while. I e-mailed his son for help. His job is finding maniacs using computer programs. He's good. He managed to track me down before I could even get back to him. That's beyond good. He's agreed to a meeting. I'm going to see him. We need all the help we can get."

"I think that's a mistake," Adam said, thinking of the logistics. "I don't think we need anyone else in on this. I'm worried about maintaining control here."

"Trust me on this, Adam. We do need him. He's got lots of contacts and is very, very smart. Don't worry that he'll talk and expose Becca's whereabouts if he comes on board. He won't. Have you learned anything more of value?"

"There's nothing at all to be found in any of McCallum's records. The governor says he doesn't know a thing. I assume you've come up dry as well?"

"Yes, but I think that Dillon Savich will be able to help us there as well. Word is he's magic with a computer and gathering information."

Adam said, "We don't need anyone else, Thomas." The instant the name was out of his mouth, Adam jerked his head up. Becca was looking at him, her eyes narrowed, intent. He cleared his throat. "We don't want more hands stirring this pot. It's too dangerous. Too much chance of cracks and leaks. It could lead to Becca."

"You slipped, Adam. Is she listening?"

"No, it's okay." At least he hoped it was. She was now simply looking wary and interested, both at the same time.

Adam said again, "Maybe you could just have this guy do some specific searches for you."

"That, too, but he's a specialist just like you are. All right. We'll see. I'm meeting with him to see what he has to say. Maybe he won't want to join up with us, or maybe he won't have the time. I just wanted you to know. Keep her safe, Adam."

"Yeah."

Becca shook her head at him when he closed his cell phone. She knew there'd be downright lies or at the very least evasions out of his mouth. She was furious, frustrated, but, surprisingly, she felt safer than she had in weeks. When he looked like he would say something, she smiled at him and said, "No, don't bother."

The Egret Bar & Grill
Washington, D.C.

Thomas Matlock rose very slowly from his chair. He didn't know what to say but he didn't like what he saw. Damnation, Savich wasn't alone.

Savich smiled at the man he'd never heard of before receiving the e-mail at four A.M. that morning. He extended his hand. "Mr. Matlock?"

"Yes. Thomas Matlock."

"This is my wife and my partner, Lacy Sherlock Savich, but everyone calls her Sherlock. She's also FBI and one of the best."

Thomas found himself shaking the hand of a very pretty young woman, on the small side, with thick, curling red hair, the sweetest smile he'd ever seen, and he knew in his gut, knew without even hearing her speak or act or argue, that she was tough, probably as tough as her hard-faced husband, a man about Adam's age, who looked stronger than a bull. Meaner, too. He didn't look like a computer nerd. Whatever that was supposed to mean nowadays.

"So," Thomas said, "you're Buck's son."

"Yes," Savich said and grinned. "I know what you're thinking. My dad was all blond and fair, a regular aristocrat with a thin straight nose and high cheekbones. I look like my mom. You can bet that my dad was always pissed about that. I never had my dad's smart-ass mouth, either. That pissed him as well."

"Your dad could charm the widow's peak off a fascist general and outwit a Mafia don. He was an excellent man and friend," Thomas said, eyeing the man. "I wasn't expecting you to bring anyone else." He found himself clearing his throat when Savich didn't immediately respond. "This is all rather confidential, Mr. Savich. Actually, it's all extremely confidential, there's a life at stake and—"

Savich said easily, "Where I go Sherlock goes, sir. We're a package deal. Shall we continue or would you like to call this off?"

The young woman didn't say a word. She didn't even change expressions. She just cocked her head to one side and waited, very quietly, silent. A professional to her toes, Thomas thought, just like her husband.

Thomas said then, "Is your name really Sherlock?"

She laughed. "Yes. My father's a federal judge in San Francisco. Can you imagine what the crooks are feeling when they're hauled in front of him—Judge Sherlock?"

"Please sit down, both of you. I'm grateful that you came, Mr. Savich."

"Just Savich will do fine."

"All right. I understand you head up the CAU—the Criminal Apprehension Unit—at the FBI. I know you use computers and protocols you yourself designed and programmed. And with some success. Naturally, I really don't fully understand what it is that happens."

Savich ordered iced tea from the hovering waiter, waited for the others to order as well, then leaned forward. "Like the Profiling Unit, or ISU, we also deal with local agencies who think an outside eye just might see something they missed on a local crime. Normally murder cases. Also like the ISU, we only go in when we're asked.

"Unlike the ISU, we're entirely computer-based. We use special programs to help us look at crimes from many different angles. The programs correlate all the data from two or more crimes that seem to have been committed by the same person. We call the main program PAP, the Predictive Analogue Program. Of course, what an agent feeds into the program will determine what comes out. Nothing new in that at all."

Sherlock said, "All of it is Dillon's brainchild. He worked on all the protocols. It's amazing how the computer can turn up patterns, weird correlations, ways of looking at things that we wouldn't have considered. Of course, like Dillon said, we have to put the data in there in order to get the patterns, the correlations, the anomalies that can point a finger in the right direction.

"Then we look at the possible outcomes and alternatives the computer gives us, act on many of them. You said Buck Savich was an excellent friend. How did you know Buck Savich, sir?"

"Thank you for the explanation. It's fascinating, and about time, I say. Technology should catch crooks, not let the crooks diddle society with the technology. Yes, Buck Savich was an incredible man. I knew him professionally. Tough, smart, fearless. The practical jokes he used to pull had the higher-ups in the Bureau screaming and laughing at the same time. I was very sorry to hear about his death."

Savich nodded, waiting.

Thomas Matlock sipped his iced tea. He needed to know more about these two. He said easily, "I remember the String Killer case. That was an amazing bit of work."

"It wasn't at all typical," Savich said. "We got the guy. He's dead. It's over." Then he looked at his wife, and Thomas saw something that suddenly made him aware of the extraordinary bond between them. There was a flash of incredible fear in Savich's eyes, followed by a wash of relief and so much gratitude that it went all the way to Thomas's gut. He should have had that bond with Allison, but one stray bullet in a woman's head had put an end to that possibility forever.

Thomas cleared his throat, his mind made up. These two were bright, young, dedicated. He needed them. "Thank you for explaining more about your unit. I guess there's nothing more to do except tell you exactly what's going on. My only favor—and I must have your agreement on this—if you don't choose to help me, you will not inform your colleagues about any of this conversation. It all remains right here, in this booth."

"Is it illegal?"

"No, Savich. I've always believed that being a crook requires too much work and energy. I'd rather race my sailboat on the Chesapeake than worry about evading the cops. The FBI is, however, involved, and that does make for some conflict of interest."

Savich said slowly, "You're a very powerful man, Mr. Matlock. It took MAX nearly fourteen minutes to even find out that you're a very well-protected high-ranking member of the intelligence community. It took him another hour and two phone calls from me to discover that you are one of the Shadow Men. I don't trust you."

Sherlock cocked her head to the side and said, "What are the Shadow Men?"

Thomas said, "It's a name coined back in the early seventies by the CIA for those of us who have high security clearance, work very quietly, very discreetly, always out of sight, always in the background, and frankly, do things that aren't sanctioned or publicized or even recognized. Results are seen, but not any of us."

"You mean like the 'Mission Impossible' team?"

"Nothing so perfectly orchestrated as all that. No, I've never burned a tape in my life." He smiled then and it was an attractive smile, Sherlock thought. He was a handsome man, well built, took care of himself. A bit younger than her father, but not much. Ah, but his eyes. They were filled with bleak, dark shadows, with secrets huddled deep, and there was pain there as well, pain there for so very long that it was now a part of him, burrowed deep. He was a complex man, but most important, he was alone, so very alone— now she saw that clearly—and he was afraid of something that went as deep as his soul. She didn't think that being a Shadow Man was the reason for all that bleakness in his eyes.

She said, "It sounds like cloak-and-dagger stuff, sir, like it should have gone out of business when the Cold War ended."

Thomas said, "Perhaps there's a bit of cloak-and-dagger still in the mix. Actually, before the end of the Cold War things were a lot simpler. We knew the enemy. We knew exactly how the enemy operated, what to expect. However, now the projects we're in-volved in are rarely so clean, so splendidly satisfying and clear-cut as that 'Mission Impossible' TV show.

"In my area, there is rarely an obvious and clean line between us and the bad guys, although Saddam and Qaddafi look like they're going to be long-timers. An enemy of yesterday is a confederate of today. Unfortunately, the opposite is also true.

"This is more true today, of course. So many petty tyrants and greedy despots who want to rule, if not the world, then a larger portion of it than they do currently. China is the giant fist, more frightening than the USSR ever was. So many people, so many natural resources, such endless potential. Somehow we have to deal with all of them."

Thomas looked off over Sherlock's left shoulder, seeing into the past, into the future, she didn't know. Then he said quietly, "There are always failures, mistakes, lives lost needlessly. But we try, Mrs. Savich. More often than not, thank God, we do succeed and per-haps make the world a bit safer. For the most part we're not al-lowed to be nice people, so your husband is smart not to trust me.

However, this is something entirely different. This isn't business. This is entirely personal. I need help badly."

She lowered her head and began weaving a packet of Equal through her fingers. Finally, she looked straight at him, picked up her iced tea glass, raised it toward him, and said, "Why don't you call me Sherlock."

Thomas clicked his glass to hers. Somehow, he knew, she and her husband had communicated, had agreed to hear him out. "Sherlock. It is a charming name. It goes very well with Savich."

Savich sat forward then. "Let's cut to the chase, Mr. Matlock. We give you our word that nothing you tell us today will go beyond this booth. We will accept the possibility of a conflict of interest, at least for the moment."

Thomas felt the same sort of loosening in his gut that he'd felt when Adam had told him he'd already begun to protect Becca. He smiled at the two of them and said, "Why don't you call me Thomas."

Chapter 13

Sheriff Gaffney said, "Well now, what we got was an anonymous tip, Mr. Carruthers."

"That's rather odd, don't you think, Sheriff?" Adam had his arms folded over his chest and was leaning against Jacob Marley's screened front porch. Sheriff Gaffney looked tired, he thought, a bit pasty in the face. He wanted to tell the sheriff to lose fifty pounds and start walking the treadmill.

"No, sir, not odd at all. Folk don't like to get involved. They'd rather tattle in secret than come smartly forward and tell you what they know. Sometimes, truth be told, folk are just shits, Mr. Carruthers."

That was true enough, Adam thought. "You said the girl's name is Melissa Katzen?"

"That's right. It was a woman with a real whispery voice who said it was Melissa. She didn't want to tell who she was. She said everyone believed at the time that Melissa was going to elope right after high school graduation. So when she up and was just gone, everyone figured she'd done it. But she thinks now, what with the skeleton, that Melissa didn't go anywhere."

"Who was the boyfriend?" Adam asked.

"No one knew, since Melissa wouldn't tell anyone. Her folks didn't know what to think after she was gone. They didn't know about any elopement talk, came as a shock to them. I'm thinking that maybe one of Melissa's family called in this tip, or a friend and that friend is afraid she's in danger if she tells us who she is. Now, if that skeleton is Melissa Katzen, then she didn't elope. She stayed right here and got herself murdered."

"Maybe," Becca said, "she decided she didn't want to elope after all and the boy killed her."

"Could be," said Sheriff Gaffney, shaking his head. "A bad way to end up."

He got no argument.

The sheriff adjusted his thick leather belt that was digging into his belly and said on a sigh, "As the years passed, most folk just forgot about her, figured she was in another state with six kids now. And maybe she is. We'll find out. We're talking to all the people who remember her, went to school with her, things like that."

"You don't have any idea who called this in, Sheriff?"

"Nope. Mrs. Ella took the call, said it sounded like someone with a doughnut in her mouth. Mrs. Ella believes it's a relative, or a chicken-shit friend."

"You'll do DNA tests now?"

"As soon as we can locate Melissa's parents and see if they have anything of hers we could use to get her DNA to match against what they have in the bones. It's going to take a while. Science—all this newfangled stuff—it's all iffy as far as I'm concerned. Just look at how poor O.J. was nearly sent away because of all that flaky so-called DNA evidence. But the jury was smart. They didn't believe any of that stuff for a minute. Well, it's something to do. We'll know in a couple of weeks."

"Sheriff," Becca said mildly, "DNA is the most scientifically solid tool that law enforcement has going for it today. It's not flaky at all. It will clear innocent people and, hopefully, in most cases, put monsters in jail."

"So you think, Ms. Powell, but you force me to tell you that

yours is an Uninformed Opinion. Mrs. Ella doesn't like all this
fancy stuff, either. But she thinks it's real possible that the skeleton
is poor little Melissa, even though she remembers Melissa as being
all sorts of shy and sweet and so quiet you'd have thought her a little ghost. Who'd want to kill a sweet kid like that? Even old Jacob
Marley, who didn't like anybody."

Adam shook his head. "I don't know, Sheriff. I go for the
boyfriend. Hey, at least there's something to go on now. Won't you
come in?"

"Nah. I just wanted to fill in you and Ms. Powell. I gotta go talk
to the power company, hear they accidentally cut a sewage pipe.
That'd be no good. You pray the wind doesn't blow in this direction. Now, Mr. Carruthers, you going to hang around with Ms.
Powell much longer?"

"Oh yeah," Adam said easily, looking over at Becca, who hadn't
said a single word since Sheriff Gaffney, button sewn back on, be-
moaned poor O.J.'s treatment. "She's still real jittery, Sheriff, jumps
whenever there's a sound in this old house. You know how women
are—so sensitive it makes a man want to coddle them until the
sun's shining again."

"That was well said, Mr. Carruthers. We got us one of our perfect summer days. Just smell the air. All salty ocean and wildflowers, and that sun smell. Nothing like it.

"Ah, here's Tyler and little Sam. Good morning. Just running
down possibilities on Ms. Powell's skeleton. Could have been
Melissa Katzen. Don't suppose you disguised your voice like a
woman's and called in the tip?"

"Not me, Sheriff," Tyler said, raising an eyebrow. "Who did you
say? Melissa Katzen?"

"Yep, that's right. You remember her, Tyler? Didn't you go to
school with her? Your ages are about right."

Tyler slowly lowered Sam to the porch and watched him wander over to a low table that held a stack of books, some of them very old indeed.

"Melissa Katzen." Tyler frowned. "Yes, I remember her. A real sweet kid. I think she might have been in my high school class, or maybe a year behind me. I'm just not sure. She wasn't really pretty, but she was nice, never said a bad thing about anybody, as I remember. You really think she could be the skeleton?"

"Don't know. Got an anonymous call about her."

Tyler frowned a bit. "I think I remember hearing that she was going to elope, yeah, that was it. She eloped and no one ever heard from her again."

Sheriff Gaffney said, "Yep, that's the story. Now DNA will tell us, at least if what those labs claim is true. Well, it's time for me to see the power company. Then I'll call that Jarvis guy in Augusta, see what they're doing."

Sam was holding a small, thick paperback in his hands.

Adam dropped down to his knees and looked at the little book with a fancy attack helicopter on the cover. He said, "It's *Jane's Aircraft Recognition Guide*. I wonder what Jacob Marley was doing with one of Jane's publications?"

"Jane?" Sam said.

"Yeah, I know, that's a girl's name. Hey, they're Brits, Sam. You've got to expect them to do weird things."

Becca said, "Hey, Sam, you want a glass of lemonade? I just made some this morning."

Sam looked up at her, didn't say anything, but finally nodded.

Tyler said, his chin up, a hint of the aggressor in his voice, "Sam loves Becca's lemonade."

"I do, too," Adam said. "Now, I'm out of here. I'll be back tonight, Becca."

She wanted to ask him where he was going, who he was going to talk to, but she couldn't say a blasted thing in front of Tyler. "Take care," she called out after him. She saw Adam pause just a moment, but he didn't turn back.

"I don't like him, Becca," Tyler said in a low voice a few minutes later in the kitchen, one eye on Sam, who was drinking his lemonade and looking for the goody in the box of Cracker Jack Becca had handed him.

"He's harmless," she said easily. "Really harmless. I'm sure he's gay. So you knew this Melissa Katzen?"

Tyler nodded and took another drink of his lemonade. "Like I told the sheriff, she was a nice kid. Not real popular, not real smart, but nice. She also played soccer. I remember once she beat me in poker." Tyler grinned at some memory. "Yeah, it was strip poker. I think I was the first guy she'd ever seen in boxer shorts."

"Rachel makes good lemonade," Sam said, and both adults looked at him with admiration. He'd said four whole words, strung them all together.

Becca patted his face. "I'll bet Rachel does lots of really good things. She rented me this house, you know."

Sam nodded and drank more lemonade.

After they'd left ten minutes later to go grocery shopping, Becca cleaned up the kitchen and headed upstairs. She made her bed and straightened the bedroom. She didn't want to have anything to do with Adam Carruthers, but she sighed and walked down to his bedroom. The bed was neatly made. Nothing was out in plain sight. She walked over to the dresser and pulled out the top drawer. Underwear, T-shirts, and a couple of folded cotton shirts. Nothing else. She pulled his dark blue carryall out from under the bed. She lifted it on top of the bed and slowly started to pull back the long zipper.

The phone rang. She nearly leapt three feet in the air. The phone rang again.

She had to run downstairs, as that was the only phone in the house. Her cell phone had run out of power and was recharging. She picked it up on the sixth ring. "Hello."

Breathing. Slow, deep breathing.

"Hello? Who's there?"

"Hello, Rebecca. It's your boyfriend."

Her brain nearly shut down on her. She stared at the phone, not believing, not wanting to believe, but it was him, the stalker, the man who murdered that poor old woman, the man who shot the governor in the neck.

He'd found her. Somehow he'd found her. She said, "The governor's alive. You're not so great after all, are you? You didn't kill him. You were so ill informed, you didn't even know there would be a bunch of doctors around him."

"Maybe I didn't want to kill him."

"Yeah, right."

"All right, so the bastard is still breathing. At least he won't be climbing into your bed anytime soon. Hear he's having a tough time talking and eating. He needed to lose a few pounds anyway."

"You killed Dick McCallum. You made him tell those lies about me and then you killed him. How much did you pay him? Or did you threaten to kill him if he didn't do as you asked?"

"Where did you get all this information, Becca?"

"It's true."

Silence.

"Nobody could have found me. The FBI, the NYPD, nobody. How did you find me?"

He laughed, a rich, mellow laugh that made her want to vomit. How old was he? She couldn't tell. Think, she told herself, listen and think. Keep him talking. Use your brain. Is he young or old? Accent? Listen for clues. Make him admit to murdering Dick.

"I'll tell you when I see you, Becca."

She said very deliberately, very slowly, "I don't want to see you. I want you to go someplace and die. That or turn yourself in to the cops. They'll fry you. That's what you deserve. Why did you run down Dick McCallum?"

"And just what do you think you deserve?"

"Not this bullshit from you. Are you going to try to kill the governor again?"

"I haven't made up my mind just yet. I know now that he isn't sleeping with you, but only because he doesn't know where you are. An old man like that. You should be ashamed of yourself, Rebecca. Remember Rockefeller croaking when he was with his mistress? That could be you and the governor. Best not do him again. But you're a little slut, aren't you? Yeah, you'll probably call him so he can come sleep with you some more."

Why hadn't she had the phone tapped? Because neither she nor Adam dreamed he'd find her here in Riptide and call her.

"You murdered Dick McCallum, didn't you? Why?"

"You're all confident again, aren't you? You've been away from me for only a couple of weeks, but you're all pissy again. Too confident, Rebecca. I'm coming for you very soon now."

"Listen, you bastard. You come anywhere near me and I'll blow your head off."

He laughed, throaty, deep laughter, indulgent laughter. Was he young? Maybe, but she couldn't be sure. "You can try, certainly. It'll add some spice to the chase. I'll see to you soon. Real soon, count on it."

He hung up before she could say anything more. She stood there, staring blankly at the old-fashioned black phone, staring and knowing, knowing deep inside her that it was all over. Or it soon would be. How could anyone protect her from a madman? She'd done the best she could and yet he'd found her, nearly as easily as Adam had.

How had he found her? Did he have as many contacts as Adam? Evidently so. No, she wasn't going to give up and let him come to kill her. No, she would fight.

She laid the phone into the cradle and walked slowly from the living room. She was tired, infinitely tired. She couldn't just stand there in the middle of Jacob Marley's house, she just couldn't. She felt itchy from the inside out, and cold, very cold. Nearly numb.

She loaded her Coonan .357 Magnum automatic, slipped it in the pocket of her jacket, and walked to the woods where she'd confronted Adam two days before. Had it really been only two days? She sat down in front of the tree where he'd been doing his tae kwon do exercise. She looked at the spot where she'd stood, pointing her gun at him, so afraid she'd thought she'd choke on it. But she hadn't had time to shoot or to choke. He'd kicked the gun out of her hand before she could draw two breaths. She closed her eyes and leaned back against the tree. Would the stalker have just as easy a time with her as Adam? Probably so.

She closed her eyes and let her mind shut down. She saw her mother, laughing down at her—she couldn't have been more than seven years old and she was trying to do a cheerleading chant. Then her mom had showed her how to do it and it had been so wonderful, so perfect. Her mother's laughter, so sweet, filling her, making her warm and happy. She rubbed her wrist where Adam had kicked the gun out of her hand. It didn't hurt, but there was memory of the cold numbness that had lasted for a good five minutes. Where was he? Why had he left?

Adam was back at Jacob Marley's house and he was so scared for a moment he couldn't think. She was gone. The door was open but she was gone. There were even two lights on but she was gone. The stalker had gotten her. No, no, that was ridiculous. He was the only one who had found her.

He searched every damned room in the house. He saw his carryall lying on top of his bed. It looked like she'd started unzipping it and then, for whatever reason, had just walked out of the room, leaving it there for him to see.

Why? Where had she gone?

Don't panic. She'd gotten a call, something of an emergency. She'd gone to Tyler's house. It had to do with Sam. The kid was sick, yeah, that was it.

But she wasn't there, no one was home. He drove by the Food Fort, the gas station, the hospital. Jesus, he could drive all over this dammed town and not find her.

He drove slowly back to the house. He cut the engine and sat in his black Jeep, his forehead against the leather-wrapped steering wheel.

Where are you, Becca?

He didn't know why he raised his head and twisted around to look toward the woods. He just did it. And in that instant he knew she was there. But why? It took him three minutes to find her.

She was asleep. He came up on her very quietly. She didn't stir. She was leaning against the tree trunk, her right hand in her lap. She was holding the Coonan, its polished silver stock gleaming from the slashes of sun through the tree branches.

Had he seen that flash of silver? He didn't know how he could have, yet he'd known she was there. Why couldn't he have had this marvelous intuition before he'd scared himself spitless?

He came down on his haunches. He looked at her, wondering what had made her come out here. He saw dried tear streaks down her cheeks. Everything had gotten to be too much for her, and no wonder. She looked pale, too thin. He looked at her fingers curled around the trigger of the Coonan, at her nails, short and ragged. He touched his fingertips to her cheek. Her flesh was soft to the touch. He lightly stroked her cheek. Then, slowly, he shook her shoulder.

"Becca. Come on, wake up."

She came awake instantly at the sound of a man's voice, the Coonan up and ready to fire. She heard him curse, then felt the gun fly out of her hand. Her wrist was instantly numb. "Not again."

"Shit, you nearly shot me."

It was Adam. She looked up at him and smiled. "I thought it was him. Sorry."

His heart began to slow. He eased down beside her. "What's up?"

"What time is it?"

"Nearly four o'clock in the afternoon and I couldn't find you and I nearly lost my mind trying to figure out where you were. You scared me, Becca. I thought he'd taken you."

"No, I'm here. I'm sorry. I didn't think. So how'd you find me?"

He shrugged. He didn't want to tell her that he just knew very suddenly exactly where she was. He would sound nuts. She didn't need anyone else around her sounding nuts.

"How long will my wrist be numb this time?"

"Not more than five minutes. Don't whine. Did you expect me to let you shoot me?"

"No, I guess not."

"You look tired. Better if you'd taken a nap in your bed than come out here to snore beneath the tree. It just might not be all that safe." That was one of the best understatements out of his mouth yet.

"Why? The only one who was ever lurking outside here was you, and you're not lurking out here anymore. You've moved right into the house." She sighed. "I don't know why I came out here. I just couldn't stand to stay in the house alone anymore."

He said again, "You scared me, Becca. Please don't take off again without leaving me a note."

She looked up at him, her face so pale now it was nearly as white as winter sleet, and said in a dead voice, "He's found me. He called."

"He?" But he knew. Oh yeah, the stalker had found her and he hated it, had dreaded it, but he'd known it would happen. This guy was good. Too good. He had contacts. Whoever he was, he knew people, knew how to use them to get what he wanted. Adam was sure he'd been on her the minute she'd left New York. Still, it surprised him. More than that it scared him to his soul. He hated that surge of fear, deep and corroding. He could almost smell the flames. The fire was coming closer.

"All right, so he called. Get a grip." He stopped, grinned at her. "Oh yeah, I'm talking to myself, not you. Now, what did he say? Did he tell you how he found you? Did he say anything that would help us pinpoint him?"

He'd said "us." She had felt utterly frozen inside, then he'd said "us." Slowly, she began to feel a shift deep inside her. She wasn't alone anymore.

She looked up at him and smiled. "I'm glad you're here, Adam."

"Yeah," he said. "Me, too."

"Even though you're gay?"

He looked at her mouth, then jumped fast to his feet. A man did better when temptation wasn't one inch from his face. He looked down at her, then offered his hand. "Yeah, right. Now come on back to the house. I want you to write down everything you can remember him saying. Okay?"

She got a look on her face that was hard and cold and determined. Good, he thought, she wasn't going to lie down and let this guy kick her like a dog.

"Let's do it, Adam."

They walked side by side up the steps to the veranda. They were nearly to the front door, and he was thinking that he needed to show her again that he wasn't gay, when a shot rang out, and a knife-sharp chunk of wood flew off the door frame not two inches from Becca's head and slammed into Adam's bare arm.

Chapter 14

*A*dam twisted the doorknob, pushed the door in, and shoved Becca into the entrance hall in an instant, and still it seemed too slow. Another bullet struck the lintel right over his head, spewing splinters in all directions. None struck him this time. He twisted about and slammed the front door, then grabbed Becca's arm and dragged her out of the line of fire.

He came down on his knees beside her. "Sorry to throw you around. Are you okay?"

"Yeah, I'm okay. That bastard, that horrible man. He's a monster, crazy. It's got to stop, Adam. It's got to." He watched her jerk her Coonan out of her jacket pocket and crawl to one of the front windows. He was right behind her. "Becca, no, wait a minute. I want you to stay down. This is my job."

"He's after me, not you," she said calmly and, slowly, very cautiously, leaned up to look out of the corner of the window. He thought he'd collapse of fright right then.

Another two shots came at heart level through the front door, spewing shards of wood into the entrance hall. Another shot. Becca saw the flash of light. She didn't hesitate, just fired off all seven rounds. He heard the *click click click* when there were no more bullets in the clip.

There was dead silence. Adam was on his knees right behind her, furious with himself because his Delta Elite was in his carryall in the guest bedroom. "Becca? I want you to stay right here. Don't move. I've got to get my gun. Stay down."

She gave him a quick look. "Go ahead and don't worry. We're not helpless. I hit him, I know it, Adam."

"Just stay down."

"It's okay." He watched her pull another magazine out of her jacket pocket. He stared at her as she slowly, calmly shoved it into the Coonan.

"Go get your gun," she said, looking out the window, her back to him. "If I didn't hit him, I can at least keep him away from the house."

He couldn't think of anything else to say. He was up the stairs and to the bedroom in three seconds flat. When he came back downstairs, his pistol in his hand, Becca hadn't moved. "I haven't seen a thing," she called out. "Do you think maybe I was lucky enough to hit him?"

"I plan to find out. Keep a sharp lookout. And don't shoot me."

And then he was gone before she could draw a breath. She heard him walk quickly through the kitchen, then the back door opened and closed very quietly. She prayed she'd hit him. Maybe right in his throat, where he'd hit the governor. Or in the gut. He deserved that for killing that poor old bag lady. She waited, waited, not moving, watching for Adam, for his shadow, anything to show her he was all right.

Time passed so slowly she thought it would become night before anything more happened. Suddenly, she heard a shout.

"Come on out, Becca!"

Adam. It was Adam and he sounded all right. She was through the front door like a shot, her hair tangling in her face, realizing only then that she was sweating and cold at the same time, and laughing. Yes, she was laughing because they were safe. They'd beaten the monster. This time.

Adam was standing at the edge of the woods, waving toward her. It was in the exact same direction where she'd fired off all seven rounds. He waited until she was right in front of him. He smiled down at her, then wrapped his arms around her and squeezed her hard. "You got the bastard, Becca. Come take a look."

Blood on fallen leaves. Like Christmas decorations—rich dark red on deep green.

"I got him," she whispered. "I really got him."

"You sure did. I've looked but I can't find a trail because once he realized he was out of the game, he stanched the wound and carefully brushed ground cover over his tracks so he wouldn't leave any kind of a trail."

"I got him," she said again, and she was smiling. "Oh God, Adam, no!"

"What is it?"

"Your arm." She dropped her Coonan back into her jacket pocket and grabbed his hand. "Don't move. Look, this splinter of wood is stuck in you like a knife. Come back to the house and let me get it out. Oh God, does it hurt really bad?"

He looked down at the shard of wood sticking like a crude knife out of his upper arm. He hadn't even felt it. "It didn't hurt before I knew about it. Now it hurts like the very devil. Well, shit."

Thirty minutes later, they were arguing. "No, I'm not going to a doctor. The first thing the doctor would do is call Sheriff Gaffney. You don't want that, Becca. I'm fine. You've disinfected me and bandaged me up. You did a great job. No problem. Let it go. You even pushed three aspirin down my gullet. Now, how about a big jigger of brandy and I'll be ready to sing opera."

She thought of Sheriff Gaffney coming here and asking questions about a guy who shot at them. *"My my, who'd want to do that, folks?"*

She gave him another aspirin for good measure, and since she had no brandy, she gave him a diet Dr Pepper.

"Close," he said and downed a huge drink.

They both froze when there was a knock on the front door.

Then they heard the front door slam open, voices low and muffled.

Becca grabbed her Coonan and crept toward the kitchen door. "Stay put, Adam. I don't want you to get hurt again."

"Becca, I'll be all right. Just hold it a second." Adam was right on her heels, his voice low, his hand on her gun arm.

"Who is it?" he called out.

A man yelled out, "You guys all right? This door looks like an army tried to shoot its way in."

"I don't know who it is," Adam said. "Do you recognize his voice?"

She shook her head.

"Who the hell is out there? What are your damned names? Tell me or I'll blow your heads off. We're a bit on the cautious side here."

"I'm Savich."

"I'm Sherlock. Thomas sent us. Said we needed to meet Adam and Becca, talk to them, get all the facts straight and together. Then maybe we can nail this stalker."

"I told him not to," Adam said and slipped his gun back onto the kitchen table and walked out into the hallway. A big man stood there, a 9mm SIG pistol held snug in his hand. A woman stood just behind him, as if shoved there for protection. She stepped around the man and said, "Don't be alarmed. We're the good guys. As Dillon said, Thomas sent us. I'm Sherlock and this is my husband, Dillon Savich. We're FBI."

It was the man Thomas wanted to save his daughter's butt. His friend's son, the computer hotshot at the Bureau. Adam didn't like it, any of it. He stood there frowning at the two of them. A man brought his wife to a possible dangerous situation? What kind of an idiot was he?

Becca stepped forward. "You've got a neat name, Sherlock. You're Mr. Savich? Hello. Now, I don't know who this Thomas is, but he's probably Adam's boss, only Adam refuses to tell me anything about who hired him and why. I'm Becca Matlock. The man who's been stalking me and shot the governor, he was just here. He called me and then he tried to kill us. I hit him, I know it. Adam found some blood, but he's gone, covered his trail, and I had to bandage Adam up and so—"

"Now we understand everything," Sherlock said and smiled at the young woman facing her. Sherlock thought she was pretty, but she looked like she'd been ground under for a long time now. She'd been pushed over the line. She said to the big man, Adam, who was standing beside Becca, "Dillon here is great with wounds. Do you want to have him look at your arm?"

Adam was pissed and he felt like a jerk for feeling pissed. If the guy really was a genius with computer tracking programs, or whatever it was he did, maybe it could help. He shook his head. "No, I'm fine. I hope to heaven the sheriff doesn't show up here, what with all that gunfire."

"This place is set way back from its neighbors," Savich said. "And all those thick trees, it's doubtful anyone heard the shots unless he was real close."

Becca blinked up at him, then said, "I hope you're right. This is Adam Carruthers. He's here as my cousin. He's here to help clean up this mess, and to protect me. As I said, I guess he works for this Thomas character. I told the guy down the street that he's gay because I'm afraid he's jealous of Adam, but he's really not."

Sherlock said, "He's really not jealous?"

"No, Adam really isn't gay."

Savich, that big guy who'd been standing very still until this instant, looking solemn and mean, began to laugh. And laugh.

The woman with the beautiful bright red curly hair looked up at her husband, cocked her head to one side, sending all that hair to bouncing around her head, and began laughing herself.

"I'm glad you're not gay," Savich said. "What? You really think this other guy is jealous of Adam here?"

Becca nodded. "Yes, and it's so stupid really. This is a life-and-death situation. Who would ever think of jealousy or sex at a time like this? That's just nuts."

"That's right," Sherlock said. "No one would. Right, Dillon?"

"That's exactly what I would have said," Savich said.

Adam watched Savich slip the SIG back into its shoulder holster. Well, shit. All right, maybe the two of them could help. He'd wait and see what they did before he said anything more.

Becca said, "Adam is drinking a diet Dr Pepper since I don't have any brandy to help him get over the shock of being wounded. Ice or lime in yours?"

Savich grinned at her. "Give me a goodly amount of lime and then Sherlock and I will go out and buy some brandy." He then looked long at her. He wanted to tell her that her father was worried sick about her, that she looked a lot like him, that, when this was all over, he would come into her life for the very first time. But for now, Savich couldn't say anything at all. They'd promised Thomas Matlock that they'd keep him in the shadows until the mess was all cleared up. Thomas had said, "Until I can be certain that Krimakov is really dead, I just can't take the chance. And for me to believe that, really believe it all the way to my gut, I've got to see a photo of him lying on a slab in a Greek morgue."

Sherlock had said, "But if he's not dead, sir, and he is orchestrating all this, then he already knows about Becca and is trying to terrorize her with the ultimate goal of getting to you through her."

Thomas had said, "I know only enough to scare myself spitless, Sherlock. I just want to keep a lid on all of this until I'm certain. In the meantime, I want to keep her hidden from all the cops and the FBI because I'm certain that they can't protect her from this stalker."

Becca said over her shoulder as she led them into the kitchen, "Before anyone comes over, you've got to tell me who you are and why you're here. As I told you, Adam's cover is that he's my gay cousin."

Adam said as he cocked the soda can at Savich, "You want to be her other gay cousin?"

"Then what would that make me?" Sherlock said. "I can't keep my hands off him. That would blow the cover right off."

"Maybe we'll be your friends, Adam. I know quite a bit about you and your background. You and I went to school together, how about that?" Savich said.

"Then what the hell are you doing in Riptide, Maine?"

Sherlock took a glass of soda from Becca, sipped it, and said, "We're here because of that skeleton that fell out of your basement wall, Becca. You guys wanted some help, and since we live in Portsmouth, it wasn't tough for us to get up here."

"How do you know where I went to school?" Adam said, his eyes dark and hard on Savich's face.

"MAX gave me most of your particulars. It took him a while longer to find out about all your other activities. You went to Yale. No problem. Did we crew?"

Well, damn, Adam thought, it was a good idea. "Yeah," he said. "We did crew. We also beat Harvard, that bunch of pissy little wimps."

Sherlock wondered why Adam Carruthers didn't want her or Dillon there. Didn't he realize that they could help? The stalker was here in Riptide, he'd tried to kill them.

Sherlock gave Adam a sunny smile. "Why don't we go look in the woods and try to uncover a trail for this guy?"

"Yeah," Savich said, rising. "Then we need to figure out why he would want to kill Becca like this. It doesn't make sense. He's into terrorizing her. Why just shoot her and end it all? He'd have no more fun."

"Good question," Becca said. "We haven't had time to think about anything since it happened. Me, I don't think he wanted to kill either of us, just scare us real bad, just announce that he was here and ready to play again."

Becca sucked in her breath. "Oh dear, we need to get the front door repaired before our neighbor, Tyler McBride, or the sheriff come to visit. I don't want to try to explain bullet holes in the door."

"Let's check for a trail first," Sherlock said. "Then, Becca, you can tell us what the stalker said to you this time while we all repair the door."

"You're good," Savich said some thirty minutes later to Adam. "You said there was no trail and there isn't."

Adam grunted. "Let's go out a bit farther. Maybe we'll see some tire tracks."

"No way," Sherlock said. "The stalker is a pro, which means that he isn't really a stalker. That's just a cover. A misdirection."

Savich nodded. "I agree. He isn't a stalker."

Becca said, "What do you mean, exactly?"

Adam said, as he slowly lifted leaves some ten feet away, "It doesn't make sense, Becca. Usually stalkers are sick guys who, for whatever strange reason, latch on to someone. It's an obsession. They're not pros. This guy's a pro. This was well thought out."

And Savich thought: *If Krimakov is alive, then it's a terror campaign, and Becca's just the means to the end. Thomas Matlock is right to be afraid.* And the ending Krimakov planned wasn't good for either father or daughter.

Becca was shaking her head. "But he sounds nuts whenever he's called me. He called a couple of hours ago. He said much of the same things. He sounded all sorts of excited, very pleased with himself, like he couldn't wait. I know he's toying with me, getting a real kick out of my fear, my anger, my helplessness." She stopped a moment, looked at Adam, and added, "The thing is, I can't help but feel that inside, he's just dead."

Sherlock said, "Maybe he's dead on the inside, but it's the outside we've got to worry about. On thing we know for sure is that he's clever; he knows what he needs to do and he does it. He found you, didn't he? Now, could we go back to the house and Becca can tell us everything? You said he called you again. Tell us exactly what he said. Then we can put all our brainpower together and solve this mess."

"Another thing," Savich said as he brushed his black slacks off, "I don't want us out in the open like this. It isn't smart."

And Sherlock, her brilliant red hair shining brightly in the fading afternoon light, led them back to Jacob Marley's house.

They found caulk, an electric sander that worked, and some wood stain in the basement, on some shelves near the hole in the brick wall.

They took the front door off its hinges and brought it inside. While Savich sanded it down and Adam caulked in the bullet holes, Becca and Sherlock kept watch, their guns in their hands, watchful. Very soon, Sherlock had Becca talking and talking. ". . . and when he called me just a while ago, he said the same sorts of things, like I would contact the governor as soon as he was well enough again and have him come to me."

"You know," Adam said, "he doesn't believe you've slept with the governor. It's just part of a script. He needed something so that he could claim you needed punishment."

"You're right," Sherlock said, giving Adam his first look of approval, for which he didn't know whether to be pleased or snarl. "Yes, you're perfectly right. Go ahead, Becca, what else did he say?"

"When I asked him about Dick McCallum, he wouldn't admit that he killed him, but I know that he did. He said I'd gotten all pissy, that I'd gotten too confident, that he was coming for me soon. I tell you, when I hung up, I was ready to throw in the towel. He calls himself my boyfriend. It's beyond creepy."

"Yeah," Adam said, raising his head to look at her, "she was ready to throw in the towel for about three minutes." Then he said toward Savich, "Then she put her Coonan in her pocket and went out into the woods. Why'd you go out there, Becca? It wasn't real smart, you know."

She looked inward for a moment, all of them saw it—and the sanding and caulking stopped. Not one of them was surprised when she shrugged. "I don't know, really. I just wanted to go there, alone, and sit under the sunlight against that tree. Jacob Marley's house was getting to me. There are ghosts here, the air is filled with remnants of the people who lived here, residue, maybe, not all of it good."

"Before I finally found her, I nearly croaked," Adam said, realizing he was grinning at Savich. Well, hell, why not? He was here and he did seem competent, at least so far. Maybe he'd still fall flat on his face.

"Listen, I've got to contact my men," Adam said. "The stalker—or whatever he is—is here. He tried to kill us, or maybe he was just after me—that's more likely. We've got to close this town down. And we need to finish with this damned door before he just walks right up and shoots us."

"He won't even get close," Becca said and raised her Coonan.

"Agreed," Savich said. He winked at Sherlock. "You want to tell Adam about how we've got everything covered?"

"Yep. A half dozen guys from Thomas are on their way here." She looked down at her wristwatch. "In about an hour, I'd estimate. And here we were worried that there wouldn't be enough for them to do. We were really wrong on that one."

"The timing's perfect," Savich said as he wiped all the sawdust off his hands. "Don't anyone fret that they'll all be piling into town and staying at Errol Flynn's Hammock. Nope, they won't stick out at all, but they'll have this place well covered. Now, we need to get busy as soon as we're done with this door. We need to bug the phone. He'll probably call again, soon. Also, we need protection around the house. The guys will be calling in and we'll set up a guard rotation. Also, Adam, you can show them where the blood is and they can get it analyzed. We'll at least verify that it's human."

"I know I hit him."

Savich nodded to Becca. "Yes, I'm sure you did. We'll see if anything interesting shows up in the blood work. Now, it would probably be a smart thing if you stayed inside, Becca."

Sherlock said, "If he was trying to kill Adam, to make things easier for him, then that makes all of us open season. It would be wise if this Tyler McBride kept himself and his kid away from here. It isn't safe."

And Adam thought, *Where's my brain? I should have thought and said all of that.*

Becca said, looking Sherlock straight in the eye, "No, I don't want Tyler or Sam in any danger, either. Now, who's this Thomas?"

"He's Adam's boss," Savich said, well aware that Adam was on full alert, "or he used to be. Now Adam is on his own. Actually, as I understand it, Adam is doing Thomas a favor. Hey, don't worry about it, Becca, you don't know him. Adam, you did a good job of filling in all the holes. A bit of stain and the door will look perfect again."

Becca jumped up. "I left it in the kitchen."

"I'll go with you," Sherlock said. "I think I'd like to look at that gash in the basement wall again."

"Of course he was after you," Savich said easily, once Becca was out of hearing. "He wanted you out of the way, wounded or dead, it didn't matter to him. It still doesn't."

"Yeah, I know."

"He wants her. He wants to take her so he figured he'd have to knock you out of the way."

"That's what I figure."

Chapter 15

*B*ecca held the can of stain in front of her.

Adam, instead of taking the can, found himself just standing there staring down at the too thin, formerly pale young woman who was now flushed red to her eyebrows.

"I'm really mad now," she said, and he believed her, and smiled. "He shot up Jacob Marley's damned door. That's beyond the line." He couldn't cut off his smile, because her eyes were glowing. Her soft blue eyes were hard and pulsing with rage. Her dyed hair was nearly standing on end. "I heard the two of you talking. He tried to kill you, Adam, to get to me. That's beyond the line, too." She was panting now. She was major-league pissed, and she wanted to protect him. He took her face between his big hands. His mouth was nearly touching hers. He immediately straightened and took the damned can of stain. He didn't want this, but he couldn't help it. An enraged Becca Matlock who still wanted to protect him did something to him, something strange and wonderful that seared him to the soles of his scuffed boots.

He looked at her mouth again, but instead of kissing her, he started to laugh. And he kept on laughing, he wanted to kiss her that bad.

She blinked at him and then took a step back. "Don't get stain on your clothes. I'm not going to wash them for you."

"When it's necessary, I'll wash my own clothes," Adam said, then added on a grin, "if you'll show me how to work the washing machine."

"Mechanical things defeat you, do they? No, don't say it, only mechanical things that involve work could defeat a guy."

Adam eyed Savich's outstretched hand, grunted, and handed him the stain. His arm burned and ached and Savich knew it, the damned interloper. He said, "You know something? I'd really like to rearrange your pretty face when this is all over."

Savich stared at him, then laughed. "If you think my face is pretty, then you've got a big problem, because that's what I think about yours."

"Bullshit."

Savich shook his head. "You want to play at the gym? Fine by me."

Becca stood by the front window as Savich stained the front door, her Coonan held loosely in her right hand, looking all around, just like a pro. After a bit, Adam couldn't stand it and took the brush from Savich.

Savich grinned at him. Sherlock said, "I love to see a real macho guy in action."

Adam brushed on the stain, slowly, carefully, gritting his teeth because his arm hurt. But he wasn't about to whine. He whistled low, between his teeth, hoping Savich heard it.

Tyler showed up with Sam an hour later. "Hey, what's that smell? Who are these people?"

Becca went blank for a moment, then said, "I didn't like the stain on the front door. It was looking tatty and old. I just finished re-staining it." She waited to see if Tyler would say anything about hearing bullets, but he didn't.

Sam stared up at her, sniffing, but as usual he didn't say anything.

"Smells weird, huh, Sam? Hey, here are some friends of Adam's. This is Sherlock and her husband, Savich."

Sherlock went down on her knees in front of the little boy. She made no move at all toward him, just said after he'd studied her for a bit, "Hi, do you like my name?"

Sam didn't step back, but he did lean his head back a bit. He gave Sherlock a bit of a smile and eyed her hair. He reached out two fingers and patted the top of her head.

Savich came down beside her. "We've got a little kid, Sam, a lot younger than you are. His name is Sean and he's only six months old. He can't pat the top of his mama's head yet. He doesn't even talk yet. But he is growing teeth."

"Teeth are good," Sherlock said, "but all that drool is a pain."

That drew Adam up really fast. These two had a kid? Well, why was he so surprised? Most men his age were married and had children. He'd been married once, and he'd wanted a kid, lots of them as a matter of fact, but Vivie hadn't been ready yet. A long time ago now, five years, nearly long enough to forget her damned name, if it hadn't sounded like a song out of *Cabaret*.

Becca said easily, "Sam doesn't talk much, Sherlock. I think it's because he's always thinking so hard."

"I like a kid who thinks a lot," Savich said. "Do you want to come to the kitchen with me and we'll find you a goody to eat?"

Sam didn't hesitate, just lifted his arms. Savich scooped him up and carried him away on his shoulders. "I don't think I'll even have to burp you, Sam. I'm really good at that. Sean likes to burp a lot."

Sam grabbed Savich's hair, and Becca saw the smile on his face. Then he turned his head and looked at Adam, at his bandaged arm. He shook his head, frowning, looking confused, then afraid.

Adam said, "It's okay, Sam. I didn't hurt my arm bad, just a little bit. Becca fixed me right up."

"Yep, and I did a good job, Sam, don't worry." Then Sam and Savich were gone, and Tyler said, "What the hell happened here? No, Becca, don't try to lie to me."

She thought of Tyler and Sam and the two of them accidentally being in the line of that madman's fire, and said, "The stalker found me. He fired at me and Adam. I shot him, but he got away. We're okay, but I'm worried about you and Sam coming here. It's not a good idea, Tyler."

He shook his head at her and said, "He shot the door?"

"He fired through it a couple of times, really messed it up. I don't want the sheriff to see it. He'd ask too many questions."

"Don't worry, Mr. McBride," Sherlock said. "Things will be under control, but you know Becca's right. It's best if you keep Sam away from here until we bring this guy down. It could be dangerous until we catch him."

Tyler looked both angry and determined. "Yeah, I'll go but I want Becca to come with me and Sam, either to my house or away, maybe to California. I want her kept safe."

"No, Tyler," Becca said, lightly touching her fingertips to his arm. "We've got to clean it up. There are lots of people here now to help me."

Tyler turned to Adam. "Who the hell are you, really? And you?" he added to Sherlock.

"Savich and I are FBI, Mr. McBride. Adam here is on special assignment to protect Becca." That sounded like he was with the Bureau as well, Adam thought, which was probably for the best. An independent security consultant didn't sound like he'd know what to do with a madman. FBI did.

"You never told me," Tyler said to Becca, his voice low. "You didn't trust me. You let me think he was your cousin. Why the hell did you do that?"

Becca couldn't think of a thing to say that wouldn't make everything worse. She hadn't meant to hurt him, to keep him in the dark, to make him feel unimportant to her, but—

"Get over it, Tyler," Adam said. "This isn't fun and games. It's serious business. You're not trained to do this sort of thing. We are. Besides, you've got Sam. He's got to be your first priority."

"You bastard," Tyler said, his hands fisted at his sides. "You're not gay, are you?"

"No, not any more than you are."

"You want to seduce her, to take advantage of her. She's scared and you just want her to depend only on you. You're afraid to have me here."

"Look, McBride—"

But Adam didn't have time to calm the man down. Tyler leapt at him, knocking him over on his back in the entryway. Adam landed on his hurt arm, grunted, then bounded back up. He wasn't seeing red this time, he was seeing a very sharp and clear target—right in the middle of Tyler's kidney. Hellfire, no, he couldn't. It wouldn't be fair. He could seriously hurt the guy. Well, damn.

Tyler, breathing hard, out of control, was about to jump at him again when Sherlock calmly tapped him lightly on the shoulder, and when he turned, distracted, she clipped his jaw. His head flew back and he stumbled. He regained his balance and stood there, feeling his jaw. He looked at her, stupefied, as Sherlock said, "I'm sorry, Mr. McBride, but that's enough. Listen to me. Becca's life is what's important, not your wounded feelings. Adam didn't even know Becca until a couple of days ago. He's here to protect her. Now, get a grip on yourself or I'll flip you over my shoulder and lay you out."

Tyler looked like he didn't doubt her for an instant. He turned slowly to face Becca. "I'm sorry," he said. "I didn't mean to hit him, well, I did, but it's just that I'm so scared for you, and this guy shows up pretending to be your cousin and I knew he wasn't. I didn't know what to do. I'm worried about you, Becca, real worried—"

Becca walked to Tyler and slowly stepped against him, clasping her arms loosely around his back. "I know, Tyler, I know. I really appreciate you being here for me, but these folk are all pros. They know what they're doing and there are even more people coming now. We've got to catch this maniac. Now that he's here I can't pick up and run. We've got to get him. He found me, how, I don't know, but don't you see? If I run, he'll just find me again. I've got people here to help me now. Please, Tyler, tell me you understand why I kept quiet about Adam."

He was pressing his cheek against her hair, squeezing her so tightly Adam thought he'd crush her damned ribs. Adam wanted to pull him off and give him one good shot in the jaw.

Becca slowly pulled away. He was afraid for her, she knew that, and she didn't want to hurt him. Her voice was very gentle when she said, "You do understand, don't you, Tyler?"

"Yeah, I do, but I just want to help." Then he lightly traced his fingertips over her cheek. "I've known you for a long time, Becca. I want to help. This is a real creepy business."

"You're telling me." She managed something of a laugh, which was closer to a cry, really.

Tyler said when Savich came back to the entryway, "Thank you for taking care of Sam." He lifted Sam into his arms and squeezed him nearly as hard as he'd squeezed Becca. "Sam, I'm sorry I lost my temper with Adam. I didn't mean to frighten you. You okay?"

Sam nodded. "I heard you yelling."

"I know," Tyler said, kissing Sam's temple. "You're not used to that, are you? Everyone loses his temper sometimes. I'm sorry I did it and sorry you were close by. Now, you and I need to go over to Goose's Hardware and get some washers for the bathroom faucet. Would you like to do that?"

Sam nodded. He looked relieved. Tyler hugged him again.

"What's the name of the street Goose's Hardware is on?" Savich asked as he looked at his wife rubbing her knuckles, an eyebrow arched.

"West Hemlock," Tyler said. "It's the main street."

When Tyler McBride finally left, Adam turned to see Sherlock and Savich speaking quietly. Adam said, "Are you guys going to stay here?"

"That's probably best," Savich said. "First thing, we're going to put a tap on this phone. Sherlock said we should bring our goodies. She's right a lot of the time." Savich picked up what looked like a very small aluminum suitcase. "This is a dual redundant tape. We're going to set it right beside the phone recorder. Now, I'm going to patch it into the phone line via the recorder starting switch. Okay, now let's plug that puppy in between the phone and the outlet in the wall."

"Goodness," Becca said. "That's quite a gadget."

"Yeah," Adam said. "You can get it at RadioShack for about twenty bucks."

"The recorder will start when the phone rings," Savich said.

"Now for the slammer," Sherlock said. She pulled out a small case that looked about the size of a laptop. "See this, Becca? It's an LED—light-emitting diode. When our boy calls his number, the name and address of the person who's registered as the phone owner will appear here on this green screen. It's like the automatic phone display for 911."

"All done, Sherlock?" Savich said, then nodded when she pressed a couple of buttons. "Good. Now I'm going to go meet with the guys, set up a surveillance schedule, tell them about the tap and the trace."

"Fine," said Adam. "I'm coming with you. I want to meet them. I don't want anyone shot by accident. Also, we need to start tracking down our boy. He's somewhere close."

"Three of the guys are already on that. They're checking all the gas stations within fifty miles, all the bed-and-breakfasts, motels, inns. They've already gotten a list of every single guy between the ages of twenty and fifty who arrived in Bangor and Portland within the past three days."

Sherlock yawned. "Becca and I will guard the fort. You guys be careful. Hey, a nap sounds good, what with all the excitement. Is there another usable bedroom in this grandiose monstrosity?"

The men got back to Jacob Marley's house two hours later. It was dark, nearly nine o'clock in the evening. The house was lit up from top to bottom, all the outdoor lights on as well. The newly stained front door both looked and smelled great.

Sherlock was drinking coffee in the living room, studying a file she'd brought with her from Washington. The shades were drawn tight, which was smart. Becca wasn't anywhere around. They'd already checked with Perkins. There had been no phone calls.

Adam found Becca in her bedroom. She was lying flat on her back in the middle of the bed, her hands crossed over her stomach. Her eyes were closed but he knew she wasn't asleep. Her shoulders were locked stiff.

"Becca? You okay?"

"Yeah."

She felt the bed give when he sat down beside her. "What do you want? Go away. I don't want to have to look at your pretty face. Has anyone seen him?"

"I don't have a pretty face. It's Savich who's got the pretty face. No, there's no sign of him yet, just that blood in the woods we found. The guys took samples to be analyzed."

She cracked her left eye open. "Did everything go all right? Were all the men there? Have they found anything out yet?"

"Yes, all six of them are here, each of them well trained. I know four of them, even worked with a couple of them in the past, so that's good. They're all top-notch. It's just a matter of time until we track him down. All of us have favors owed. We'll call them all in if necessary. You know, the reason I was here was to protect you from the cops and the Feebs because we knew they couldn't protect you from the stalker. But things have changed now. The guy's here and there's just no choice. We've got to get him or you'll never be safe."

"Who is this Thomas, Adam? He must be very powerful to be able to have all this guy power up here for one insignificant person, namely me."

"You're not insignificant." He sounded too harsh, too intense, and he clamped his teeth together. "Look, don't worry about Thomas. He's doing what he's got to do. Now, why are you up here, lying down?" He paused a moment. She was dull-eyed, pale again, and it worried him. He looked at his fingernails and said, "But first things first. I'm getting hungry. Any ideas for dinner? It's nearly nine o'clock. It's nearly time to go to bed. Oh yeah, that was a good idea to have all the lights on."

She opened both eyes then and stared up at him. "Sherlock did that. Now let me get this straight. You're worried about food? Now?"

He nodded. He'd distracted her. Her eyes were narrowed on his face, her lips were seamed into a thin line. Good.

"Of course I'm hungry. What about dinner?"

"Well then," she said, rolling to the other side of the bed to stand and streaking her hands through her hair, "let me get my little self downstairs and see what I can whip together."

She stalked out of the bedroom, Adam on her heels, grinning at the back of her head. She was keeping it together. Being pissed was good. He was pleased and inordinately relieved. He was afraid, though, that being an asshole was a bit too easy for him. He noticed again that the tilt of her head was just like her father's.

"So," Sherlock said some thirty minutes later at the kitchen table after she'd chewed a bite of tuna salad that Savich had whipped up, "this Tyler McBride seems hung up on you, Becca, and he's wildly jealous of Adam. Could he be a problem?"

"He already is a problem," Adam said, waving a dill pickle. "The guy attacked me. I wasn't doing a single thing and he attacked me."

"You held back from hurting him," Sherlock said. "That was smart. Mr. McBride is not only very afraid for Becca, he also feels threatened because another male showed up. It's strange. Here he knows that Becca's in trouble. You'd think that the more folks to help, the better."

It was just the way he should have felt the entire time, Adam thought. Bottom line, just like Tyler, he'd felt threatened. And the women knew it.

"I'm glad you didn't hit Savich," Sherlock said, seeing quite clearly what he was thinking. "I would have done more than clip you on the jaw if you had, Adam." She then gave him a sunny smile, raised the plate, and said, "Anyone want another tuna sandwich?"

Becca said, "Or would you prefer raw meat?"

"That's really quite enough, Becca," Adam said, finally annoyed. "I'm going to take another sandwich and go talk to the guys, see how they're doing. The moon's nearly full tonight. It's quiet. Don't worry about the boyfriend being out there to shoot me. I'll take my gun. Oh yeah, if I had attacked Savich, I would have cold-cocked him before you could have hurt me, Sherlock."

He left the kitchen.

Sherlock couldn't help herself; she laughed. Savich looked back and forth between the two women, stood slowly, nabbed a sandwich, then said, "I think it's a little thick in here. See you later, Sherlock. I'm going to go give my mom a call and see how she's faring with our boy."

"Call me when you've got him on the phone," Sherlock said, then took a big bite out of an apple.

Savich walked to the living room, where the only phone in the whole house was. He heard Adam whistling outside.

He hated to lie to his mom when she asked him exactly what he and Sherlock were doing, but he did, and cleanly. "It's a background check on someone very important who's being considered for the Supreme Court. All very hush-hush and that's why Jimmy Maitland asked me and Sherlock to take care of it. Don't worry, Mom, we'll be back in a couple of days. I met a really cute little boy today. It seems his mother abandoned him and his father over a year ago and he hasn't said much since then. Is that Sean gurgling in the background? I'd sure like to speak to him, Mom."

Chapter 16

The phone rang sharply at midnight. Everyone heard it, but Becca was the fastest. She was on her feet, running down the front stairs to the living room by the second ring.

It was him, she knew it, and she wanted to talk to him. There wasn't the need to keep him on for any specified length of time. The slammer was instantaneous, the identification there in a flash.

Her hand shook as she picked up the phone. "Hello?"

"I don't know if I want to be your boyfriend anymore. You shot my dog, Rebecca."

Shot his dog? "That's a lie and you know it. Besides, no animal would have anything to do with you. You're too crazy and sick."

"His name was Gleason. He was very fat and you shot and killed him. I'm really upset, Becca. I'm coming to get you now. Not long. Hey, honey, you want to send flowers to poor Gleason's funeral?"

"Why don't you bury yourself with him, you murdering psycho?"

Adam heard his hitching breath, the flutter of rage. She'd gotten to him. Good.

He saw Savich write down the name and address from the slammer and sit down on the sofa, opening his laptop. He pressed close to Becca.

"You got that big guy there with you, Becca? Listening to me?"

"Yeah, I'm here listening to you, you pathetic piece of shit. Cheer up, you killed the front door, but we're so good we even brought it back to life. It probably looks better than you do."

Becca could feel the black fury in the silence that flooded over the phone line. She could nearly feel the stench of it—hot and rancid, that fury. "I'll kill you for that, you bastard."

"You already tried, didn't you? Not much good, are you?"

"You're a dead man, Carruthers. Soon. Very soon now."

"Hey, where are you holding Gleason's wake? I wanna come. You want me to bring a priest? Or isn't your kind of crazy into religion?"

The breathing speeded up, rough and harsh. "I'm not crazy, you bastard. I'll have Rebecca watch you die. I promise you that. I see you got two more folk there with you. I also know they're FBI. You think they're going to do anything to help? No one can catch me. No one. Hey, Rebbecca, the governor call you yet?"

Adam gave her a cool nod, a thumbs-up sign. She said, "Yeah, he called me. He wants to see me. He told me he loves me, that he wants to sleep with me again. He said his wife is such a bitch, she doesn't understand him, and he wants to leave her for me. The dear man, do you think he's well enough yet for me to tell him where I am?"

Cold, dead silence, then, very gently, they heard the phone line disconnect.

She stared at the phone. The slammer was showing "501-4867, Orlando Cartwright, Rural Route 1456, Blaylock" in black letters on a bright-green screen.

Sherlock said, "Everyone stay still for a moment. Savich will have all the information in just a moment. He sounded healthy enough, didn't he?"

"Yeah," Adam said.

"Then it was only a flesh wound, more's the pity," Sherlock said, and scratched behind her left ear. Her curling red hair was all over her head. She was wearing a sleep shirt that said across the front: *I*

BRAKE FOR ASTEROIDS. Savich had pulled on a pair of jeans. He was bare the rest of the way up. So was Adam.

"That dog bit," Adam said, "it was an excellent ploy on his part. All right, let's head out of here and go get the bastard. You got our directions, Savich?"

"In a second," Savich said.

Adam took Becca in his arms. "You did great, Becca, really great. You rattled him. Now, let's get dressed and go nail that little bastard."

"We're all going," Becca said.

Savich looked up and grinned. "It's a farmhouse some six miles northwest of here, outside a small town called Blaylock. Let me call Tommy the Pipe." He got him quickly on his cell phone.

"Yeah, Tommy, call all the others and head on out there, but don't go in. This guy is very dangerous. Just keep him under wraps until we get there. I'll find out everything I can on the way there. Yeah, on MAX."

While Savich worked in the backseat of Adam's Jeep, Savich kept up a running commentary. "Here we go. The farmhouse belonged to Orlando Cartwright, bought the place back in 1954. He's dead now. Oh yeah, that's good, MAX. He had one daughter, she was with him until he died three weeks ago at Blue Hills Community Hospital. Lung cancer, Alzheimer's. Oh, no, she's still there, alone."

"Shit," Adam said.

"What's her name?" Becca asked, turning in the seat to look at him.

"Linda Cartwright. Just a minute here, okay, good hunting, MAX. She's never been married, age thirty-three, and she's on the heavy side, one hundred and sixty-five pounds, but she's really pretty, even on her DL photo. She's a legal secretary for the Billson Manners law firm in Bangor, been there for eight years. Hold on a

173

second, let me get into her personnel file. Yes, she's got very good evaluations—in 1995 she complained about sexual harassment. Hmmm, the guy was eventually fired. Her work record is clean. Her mother died back in 1985, a drunk driver killed both her and Linda's younger sister. No, MAX, there's no need to go into police files, probably a waste of time."

"She's single and she's alone," Sherlock said. "Not good at all. Hurry, Adam."

"She's alone," Becca said. "She's alone, just like I was."

At one o'clock in the morning, beneath a nearly full, brilliant summer moon, Adam pulled his black Jeep next to a dark-blue Ford Taurus parked on the side of a two-lane blacktop road. They were some fifty yards from the old farmhouse with its peeling white shutters and sagging narrow front porch.

There was no need for introductions.

Two men, both in their thirties, fit, one wearing glasses, the other smoking a pipe, were leaning against the side of the car. Savich said, "The guy in there?"

"The lights are still on, but we haven't seen any movement at all. No one left since we got here. Chuck and Dave are around the back." He took out his walkie-talkie. "You guys see anything?"

The answer was clear and loud. "He hasn't come out this way, Tommy. You and Rollo haven't seen anything?"

"Nothing."

Dave said, "There's no movement in the house that we can see. Chuck wants to go up close and look through the windows."

"Tell Chuck and Dave to stay put," Adam said. "Here's Savich, he'll give you the rundown on what we're facing."

Savich was concise, his voice clipped.

"I don't like this," Tommy said and puffed frantically on his pipe. "Damn, a woman living way out here, all alone, no neighbors for a couple of miles. I'll bet he scoped her out really fast and that he's been here with her. God, this doesn't look good. We've seen nothing of either of them. Maybe she's not here. Maybe MAX is wrong and she was never here."

"Yeah, right, Tommy," Rollo said, and he sounded depressed. He was short, dressed all in black, and he was perfectly bald, his head shining brightly beneath the summer moon.

Tommy the Pipe said, "Maybe he left before we got here. It could be that he took her with him, as a hostage."

Linda Cartwright was a woman alone, and Becca knew he'd been in there, with her.

Damn the bright moon, Adam was thinking, it lit them up as clearly as daylight from the front of the farmhouse. But there were thick pine trees crowding the eastern side of the small farmhouse. Folk grew potatoes in this area, and so much of the land was cleared, open, just occasional random clumps of pines and maples dotted here and there, but no place to hide. There was a big mechanical digger sitting in the middle of an open field. There was a small sagging porch in front of the house, a naked lightbulb burning over the front door.

On the eastern side of the house, he could get to within twenty feet of the structure before the pine trees played out. It would have to be good enough. He pulled out his Delta Elite, thoughtfully rubbed his temple with the barrel. Then he said, a feral gleam in his eyes, "I got a plan. Gather round."

"I don't like it," Savich said after Adam had fallen silent. "Too dangerous."

Adam said, "I was thinking that all of us could go in guns blazing, raising hell, but the woman might still be alive. We can't take the chance he'd pop her then and there and then kill two or three of us, what with all this damned moonlight."

175

"All right," Savich said after a moment, "but I'll go with you."

"Bullshit," said Adam. "I don't care if you're a damned FBI agent and your goal in life is to catch bad guys. You're still married and you've got a kid. What I need from you and everyone else is good cover. I hear you're a pretty good shot, Savich. Prove it."

"I'm coming with you, Adam," Becca said. "I'll cover your back from right behind you."

"No." He held up his hand. "I'm the professional here. Just say some prayers, that's all I ask."

"No," Becca said, and he realized then that if he wanted her to stay put, he'd have to have one of the men tie her down. He didn't like it, but he understood it. It could be dangerous, too dangerous. He just didn't know what to do.

"I'm coming," she said, and he knew she was committed. "I have to, Adam, just have to."

He wished he didn't understand, but he did. He nodded. He heard Savich snort. "Becca will cover me from the woods," he said. "No, no arguments, Becca. That's the deal."

Sherlock took the walkie-talkie and spoke to Chuck and Dave at the back of the house, told them what was going to happen.

Becca's heart was pounding hard and fast. The night was chilly but she was sweating. She felt faint nausea in her stomach. This was real and it was scary and she was terrified, not just for Adam and her, but for that poor woman inside the house, that poor woman she prayed was still alive. Sherlock and the men looked calm, alert, ready. Tommy put his pipe back in his pocket and handed Becca a Kevlar vest. "It's the smallest one, after Sherlock's." He shrugged. "Let me help you with it. You're going to stay under cover in the woods, remember. You'll be out of the line of fire, but hey, it always pays to be careful."

Once she was strapped into the vest, she pulled her Coonan, and checked the clip three times. Adam took one look at her and didn't say a thing, just mouthed at her to stay a bit behind him. Her heart was pounding harder and faster than it had just five minutes before. Her hand was shaking, no good, no good. She stuffed her left hand in her pocket. Keep steady, she thought, as she looked down at her right hand, which held her pistol. She looked over at Sherlock, who was frowning at one of the Velcro fastenings on her Kevlar vest. No one was taking any chances at all.

"Show time," Savich said after he checked his watch. "Go, Adam. Good luck. Becca, you keep down."

Adam, with Becca on his heels, made a wide berth to the east side of the house. He walked slowly, quietly, Becca just as quiet, through the pine trees. When they got to the edge of the woods, Adam pulled up. Twenty feet, he thought, not more than twenty feet. He looked through the window at the other end of those twenty feet, right in front of him. There were curtains, thin, see-through white lace, but they weren't drawn over the single wide window. It was probably a bedroom. He turned to look at Becca, her face as pale as the fat moon overhead. He cupped her neck in his hand and pulled her close. He whispered against her cheek, "I want you to stay right here and keep alert. You stay hidden, do you hear me? You see him, you blow his head off, all right?"

"Yes. Please be careful, Adam. Your vest is on correctly? You're protected?"

"Yeah." He touched his fingertips to her cheek, then dropped his arm. "Stay alert."

It seemed to Adam that it took him damned near an hour to run those twenty feet. Every step was long and heavy and so loud it shook the earth. It seemed to him that every night sound, from owls to crickets, stopped in those moments. Watching, he thought, they were all watching to see what would happen. Nothing from the house, no movement, no sound, not a single quick shadow. He flattened against the side of the house, his pistol held between both hands, then slowly, slowly, he looked around into a bedroom filled with old white rattan furniture with cheap faded red cushions, a dim-watted bulb shining from an old Lava lamp on a nightstand next to a single bed. He saw nothing, no movement, no one. The cover on the twin-size bed barely covered the top of the mattress. He could see that there was nothing beneath the bed except big-time dust balls. No, no one in the room. If anyone was in there, he was in the closet, on the far side, the door closed. He saw that the door to the bedroom was also shut. He quietly tested the window, paused, listened intently. Still nothing. The window wasn't locked. He raised it slowly, the sounds of creaking and scraping against old paint as loud as thunder in his head.

The window was some five feet off the ground. Because he had to, he stuck his pistol in the waistband of his jeans. He'd always hated doing that ever since he'd heard the story some decades back that an agent had stuck his gun in his pants and hit against a car fender in some weird way that pulled the trigger. He shot off the end of his dick. Damn, no, he didn't want to do that. He pulled himself up and eased his leg over the windowsill. He waved back at Becca, motioning for her to stay back and keep hidden. But, of course, she didn't. She trotted right up to the house and stuck out her hand for him to help her through the window.

"Only if you stay hidden in here while I check the rest of the house."

"I promise. Pull me up, hurry. I don't like this, Adam. She was alone here. I know he's done something bad."

A lone owl hooted fifty feet away, from the safety of the woods and a tall tree. The moon glistened down on her face. Adam pulled her over the ledge and she swung her legs to the floor.

She watched him walk toward the closet door, listen intently, then jerk it open. Nothing. Then she watched him walk to the closed bedroom door, staying to the side, never directly facing the door. He slowly turned the knob, then smashed the door open, sending it banging back, and stepped into the hallway, his pistol up. Then he was gone. She stood there shaking, wishing she wasn't, listening to that owl, loud and clear, sounding from the forest.

Where was he? Time passed as slowly as it did in the dentist's office. Maybe even slower.

Finally, she heard him shout, "Becca, go back out the window and tell Savich it's okay for everyone to come in. He's not here."

"No, I want to come out—"

"Out the window, Becca. Please."

When he was sure she was outside, Adam stepped out onto the sagging front porch with its scarred and peeling railing and said, "He's gone. Savich, come here a moment. The rest of you just stay outside and keep watch, okay?"

"Yeah, we'll keep watch, but this is nuts," Tommy said and pulled out his pipe. "No one moved after we got here and we converged on the place not ten minutes after you called, Adam."

Savich said slowly, "Then he knew, of course, that we'd tapped the phone."

"Yes," Adam said. "The bastard knew, all right. In the kitchen, Savich."

"I don't like this," Becca said to Sherlock as she pressed toward the front door. "Why can't we go in the house?"

"Just stay there for the moment, Becca."

Several minutes passed. No one said anything, but one by one the men walked into the farmhouse through the open front door.

Becca didn't know what to do. Sherlock, who was standing on the small front porch, her 9mm SIG drawn, sweeping in a wide arc around her, scanning the perimeter, said, "I'll go check. Becca, why don't you wait out here just a while longer?"

Becca stared at her. "Why?"

"Just wait," she said, her voice suddenly sharp. "That's an order."

Becca heard the men talking, knew all of them but her were in the house. Why didn't they want her in there? She ran around to the back of the house and slipped in behind one of the men who was standing in the middle of the back door. The kitchen was painfully bright with two-hundred-watt bulbs hanging naked from the ceiling. The kitchen was small, the appliances were harsh white, clean, and very old. There was an old wooden table, scarred, a beautiful old vase holding dead roses in the center. It had been pushed against the wall. Two of the chairs were overturned on the floor. The refrigerator was humming loudly, like an old train chugging up a hill.

She slipped around the man in the doorway. He tried to hold her back, but she pulled free. Tommy, Savich, and Sherlock were standing in a near circle staring down at the pale-green linoleum floor. Adam rose slowly.

And suddenly Becca could see her.

Chapter 17

*T*he woman had no face. Her head looked like a bowl filled with smashed bone, flesh, and teeth. He'd struck her hard, viciously, repeatedly. There were two broken teeth on the floor beside the woman's head. There was dried blood everywhere, congealed and black on her face and on the worn linoleum, streaks of blood, like lightning bolts, down the white wall. Her hair was matted to her head, blood-soaked dark clumps falling away onto the floor. And there was dirt mixed in with the dried bloody hair.

"She's young," she heard a man say, his voice low, calm, detached, but underlying that voice was a thick layer of fury. "Jesus, too young. It's Linda Cartwright, isn't it?"

"Yes," Adam said. "He killed her right here in the kitchen."

Linda Cartwright lay on her back on the floor wearing a ratty old chenille bathrobe that had been washed so many times it was nearly white rather than pink, except for the dirt that clung to the robe, dirt everywhere, even on her feet, which were bare, her toe-nails painted a bright, happy red. Becca eased closer. It was real, it was horrifyingly real, in front of her, and the woman was dead. "Oh, God. Oh God, no, no."

She watched Savich bend down and unpin a note that was fastened to the front of Linda Cartwright's bathrobe. She saw for the first time that the woman was heavy, just as Savich had read off her driver's license. "Don't let Becca come in here," he said to Sherlock, not looking up as he read the note. "This is too much. Make sure she stays outside."

"I'm already here," Becca said, swallowing again and again against the nausea in her stomach, the vomit rising in her throat. "What is that note?"

"Becca—"

It was Adam and he was turning toward her. She put up her hands. "What is that note?" she asked again. "Read it, please."

Savich paused, then read slowly, his voice firm and clear:

"Hey, Rebecca, you can call her Gleason. Since she didn't look like a dog, I had to smash her up a bit. Now she does. A dead dog. She's nice and fat, though, just like Gleason, and that's good. You killed her. You and no one else. Give her a good wake. This is all for you, Rebecca. I'll see you soon and it'll be you and me, from then to eternity.

Your Boyfriend.

"He wrote it in black ink, a ballpoint," Savich said, his voice flat, emotionless, as he carefully eased the paper into a plastic bag he pulled out of his pants pocket and closed the zipper. "It's just a plain sheet of paper torn out of a notebook. Nothing at all unique about it."

"Do you think he's out of control?" Sherlock said to no one in particular. Her face was pale, the horror clear in her eyes.

"No," Adam said. "I don't think so. I think he's really enjoying himself. I think at last he's discovering who he really is and what he really likes. I can practically hear him thinking, 'I want to scare Rebecca shitless, prove to her I'm so bad that when I call her again I won't hear any more cockiness from her. No, I'll hear fear in her voice, helplessness. Now, what can I do to really make this happen?'" Adam paused a moment, then said, "And so he decided to kill Linda Cartwright and make her into his fictional dog."

"Yeah," Tommy said, "I think Adam is right. There's nothing but control here. Too damned much of it."

"I need to make some calls," Savich said, but he didn't move, just stared down at the note and at what had been Linda Cartwright.

There was silence in the small, bright kitchen and the harsh breathing of six men and two women, one of them drawing hard on a pipe that wasn't lit. Then Becca broke free, ran out the back door, and fell to her knees, vomiting until her body was jerking and heaving and there was nothing more in her belly. Still she crouched there, holding her arms around herself, shuddering, wanting to die because she'd brought death to Linda Cartwright, just as she had to that poor old woman standing outside the Metropolitan Museum, just as she'd nearly brought death to the governor of New York. She felt him coming up behind her, knew it was Adam.

"Her face—he obliterated her face, Adam, for a sick joke that only he thought was funny. He murdered her and smashed her face so—"

"I know." Adam fell to his knees behind her, pulling her back against his chest. "I know."

She felt him begin to rock her, back and forth. "I know, Becca."

"I'm responsible for her, Adam. If I hadn't shot him, if I hadn't—"

Adam pulled her around to face him. He handed her a handkerchief, waited for her to wipe her mouth, then said, "Now, you will listen up. If you feel any guilt about that poor woman, I'm going to deck you. None of this is your fault. He's the evil one. This guy will do anything to terrorize you, to hear you whimper, beg, plead with him to stop. Anything."

"He's succeeded."

"Yeah, you've got to stop that as well. You can't let him crawl under your skin. That means he wins. That means he's got the control, he's got the power. Do you understand me?"

She pulled away from him and began kneading his arms with her hands, not even realizing what she was doing. "It's hard, Adam. I know he's evil. I know there must be a reason he's doing all this, a reason that makes perfect sense to him, but in my gut, it feels like I smashed in that poor woman's face. Oh, God, if I hadn't fired at him, hit him—"

"Stop it," he said and shook her good. "Now, here's the bottom line. We're going to leave her just as she is in the kitchen and make an anonymous call. No, don't argue." He lightly tapped his fingers against her mouth. "Listen, I know this is very hard to do, given the fact that we're breaking the law and she's not going to get the attention she deserves right away. Even Savich and Sherlock are having a real problem with it.

"Even though they're part of the highest police force in the land, they realize that nothing good would be served if the world suddenly found out that you're here and you're up to your ears in another murder. The cops and the Feds would fight to see who could hold you and question you. On the other hand, you'd be protected, and that's something, but not enough. All of us agree that you would be charged with murder and accessory to murder. It would be a nightmare and it would continue even if they ever let you go. Why? Because he would still be there, just waiting, and it would start all over.

"So, Savich and Sherlock have agreed to keep our connection under wraps for a while. He's getting the woman's phone records right now. We'll find out how long he's been here, holding her prisoner. We'll find out who he called besides you. All the guys are going over the house, top to bottom, right now. They're pros. If there's anything to find, they'll find it. If there are fingerprints, and I'm willing to bet there are, they'll pull those up, too. But it's going to take time because we'll have to clean up after ourselves. The last thing we want is to have the police notice some stray fingerprint powder. So we can't call in her murder for another couple of hours."

"He knew the phone was tapped."

"Oh, yes, he knew, and that's why he had the surprise all ready for you. He can't be far away now. He's close. Real close. It's possible he's watching all of us right this instant, hiding in the pine trees, but I don't think even he is that reckless. We'll get him, Becca. You have to believe that. He'll pay for what he did to Linda Cartwright."

"Oh, God," she said suddenly. "You're right, Adam, he is watching. Maybe he's a goodly distance away and using binoculars, but I don't think so. I'll bet he's just over there, somewhere in those trees, and I think he watched you climb through that window, watched me come out here and puke up my guts. You said he was finally realizing who he is, what he likes, and this is it."

Her eyes went blank, then she said, "He's seen Tyler and Sam. Oh God, he knows I'm close to them and doesn't that make them targets, too? What if he goes after them?"

"He could, but I doubt it and here's why. He knows we're not fools. He knows there are a lot of us. He wants you. He's made his point. I can't see him veering off course to kill Tyler or Sam. Why? He wants to nail me, but I'm with you, staying with you, taunting him. That's why he wants me. Now, Dave and Chuck will start looking around here when they finish in the house."

"He'll be gone by then."

"Probably."

"Do you think he killed her in those short minutes between when he called me and all the men got here?"

Adam hesitated, then shook his head. "No, she'd been dead for several hours, at least."

"But her face, Adam, her face. It looked—fresh, even though all the blood looked dried and clotted."

"He did that after he called you, after he realized the phone was tapped. She was already dead, Becca."

"How did he kill her?"

Adam didn't want to say anything more about it, but he knew she wasn't going to let it go, she couldn't let it go. "He strangled her."

"Why was there dirt all over her? God, it was even on her feet, in her hair."

Oh, shit, he thought. He didn't want to say it but there was no choice. "There was dirt on her because he dug her up to smash her face." There, it was said, and he thought she was going to vomit again. She closed her eyes, her arms fell to her sides, and her head dropped forward against his chest. But she didn't vomit, she cried, making no sound at all, just cried, her hands fists against his Kevlar vest.

"Oh, God, Becca," he said and squeezed her hard. "I swear I'll get him, I swear it."

She said nothing for a very long time. His knees were starting to hurt when she finally whispered against his neck, "Not if I can get him first." She shuddered, then he felt her stiffen and slowly, slowly pull back from him. She said, "He was through with her, probably planning on leaving here, and so he killed her and buried her and then decided it would be fun to play this big joke on me."

"Yeah, that's about the size of it."

"He's still here, Adam. He's close. I can feel him. It's like something very black and heavy crawling over my skin."

He said nothing.

"But why? I just don't understand why he picked me. Why is he doing this to me?"

Again, Adam said nothing, but he thought, *If Krimakov is really dead, then there isn't a motive, and I don't have the foggiest idea, either, why he picked you.*

Becca couldn't get Linda Cartwright out of her mind, she kept picturing her, lying there, her face smashed, and no one to take care of her for hour upon hour.

Sherlock handed her a cup of coffee, steam rising from the mug like cigarette smoke. "You only slept a couple of hours, Becca. Here, drink this."

"None of us slept for more than a couple of hours," Becca said. "Where are Adam and Savich?"

"Adam is out talking to Dave and Chuck. They just took over outside patrol. He's going to get some other people here, some of his own people, to free up these guys."

"Maybe Hatch is coming." At Sherlock's raised eyebrow, Becca added, "I heard Adam talking to him on the phone. Yeah, I was eavesdropping, so Adam had to tell me. He said Hatch speaks six languages, has lots of contacts, is really smart, and smokes. Adam is always trying to get him to stop smoking by threatening to fire him."

Sherlock laughed and lifted her mug to toast Becca's. "I want to meet this guy. If he dares to light up a cigarette, Savich won't threaten to fire him, he'll take his head off."

"So Adam doesn't work for Thomas?"

"No, not now. They've been friends for a very long time. Adam is sort of like a son to Thomas. No, I won't tell you any more about him."

Becca didn't say anything.

"Listen, Becca, it doesn't matter right now. Now, my husband is concerned that the local cops won't be able to do a thing about Linda Cartwright because they're going in completely blind. But we agreed this is the way we'll play it for a while. The cops have been there for a while now, Becca. They're taking care of her. But they won't be able to figure anything out because we're holding back. That really sticks in everyone's craw, probably always will."

"Sherlock, do you know who Krimakov is?"

Sherlock couldn't help it, her eyes gave her away before she could pull down the automatic blinders, and she wanted to kick herself. She shrugged. "Yes, I know. But it would have to be his ghost who killed Linda Cartwright. Evidently, Thomas got information that he was killed in an auto accident just a short time ago in Crete, where he supposedly lived. So it's all academic. If he's dead, then he can't have anything to do with this."

"And Thomas has double-checked that this guy is really dead?"

"I would assume so."

"If this Krimakov were alive, and he were behind this terror, why would he be doing it to me in particular? He's what—Russian? What could he possibly have against me? Why would Thomas think it was him?"

"I don't know," Sherlock said, lying cleanly now because she'd had time to slip her mask into place.

"Who is Thomas, Sherlock? Please, you've got to tell me."

"Just forget him, Becca," she said over her shoulder. "Drop it. Give it time. Now, I want some more coffee. Can I make you some toast or something?"

"No, nothing." *Who was this Thomas person?* Becca wondered. *Why all the secrecy?* It made no sense to her. She looked over at the single telephone. It was nearly nine o'clock on Thursday morning.

Nothing from him. Maybe he was scared now, maybe he knew they were getting close, maybe he would go away. Still, she sat there staring at that damned black phone like it was a snake about to bite her.

The last person any of them wanted to see arrived midmorning.

"The door looks good," Sheriff Gaffney said when Becca opened it. "What with all this mess, I didn't think you'd worry so much about how your front door looked."

Becca said, "You just never know, do you, Sheriff? Would you like to come in? Is there any news about who the skeleton is?"

"Yeah, I'd like to talk to you a moment, Ms. Powell. I believe now that the skeleton that fell out of your basement wall is Melissa Katzen." He rubbed his forehead. "I didn't think old Jacob was that vicious. Bashing a young girl in the face—now that just isn't right."

"Sheriff," Adam said, coming up behind Becca, "I was thinking about that. You said she was supposed to elope. Any leads on her boyfriend?"

"Nope, nobody remembers her ever dating. Isn't that weird? Why would she keep it secret? That doesn't make any sense to me or to my wife, Maude. She thinks that a young girl would be really proud to show off a boyfriend."

"Maybe the boyfriend didn't want her to show him off," Becca said. "Maybe he told her to keep quiet."

"But why?"

"I don't know, Sheriff. I wish I did."

"Rachel Ryan remembers her, said she was really nice, nothing new there. She also said that Melissa didn't ever dress in sexy clothes. She was surprised when I told her about the Calvin Klein jeans and that skimpy pink top. She couldn't remember Melissa ever wearing anything suggestive. Maybe you're right, Ms. Powell. Maybe it was her boyfriend. But you know? I can just see a cute young girl waltzing over into Jacob Marley's yard, him seeing her and getting all het up. Did he smash her?"

Becca said, "Maybe she was off to meet her boyfriend and coming into Jacob Marley's yard was a shortcut."

"Ain't no shortcut to anywhere," said Sheriff Gaffney. "The back of the Marley property trails off into thick woods and finally stops at the ocean."

"Maybe," Sherlock said, "the jeans and top were her cute traveling clothes. Maybe she did intend to elope, maybe she decided at the last minute that she didn't want to and this boy got mad and killed her."

Sheriff Gaffney said slowly, "Who are you?"

"Oh, sorry, Sheriff," Adam said. "Sherlock and Savich here are friends of mine. They just stopped in for a while to visit the town."

"Nice to meet you, ma'am. Now, that's not a bad idea. I guess I'd have to say that for a woman you deduced that real logically, probably better than most other women."

Savich, who heard that, wondered if Sherlock was going to take a flying leap at the sheriff's throat.

"Yeah," Sherlock said thoughtfully, "I'm a lot better than poor Becca here, who can barely find her way to the Food Fort without some guy explaining the poisonous plant streets to her."

"That was sarcasm," Sheriff Gaffney said after a moment. "I know that was sarcasm. I've never believed women should have smart mouths."

Before Sherlock could leap on the sheriff, Adam said, "Are there DNA tests being done?"

The sheriff shook his head. "Still trying to track down her father. No luck yet. Mrs. Ella remembers an aunt, lives in Bangor now. Maybe she read about the skeleton and was the one who made the anonymous call. I've got to track her down." Sheriff

Gaffney sighed and patted the gun at his wide leather belt that was really cutting into his gut today. "But we can't count on the skeleton being Melissa, even though I've made up my mind that it is, so we're looking into other things as well." Sheriff Gaffney leaned his considerable weight back on his heels. "Now, folks, the reason I'm here is to ask about these guys I've seen on and off around Riptide. No, don't lie to me. I know they're with you, Mr. Savich. Would you like to tell me what's going on?"

At that moment, the phone rang.

Tinny, sharp, and too loud, and Becca dropped her coffee cup.

"Becca didn't get much sleep last night," Adam said easily, and picked up the phone. "Hello?"

"Hello, fuckhead. You found my present?"

"Why, yes, I did. Where are you now?"

"I want to speak to Rebecca."

"Sorry, she's not here. It's just me. What do you want?"

The phone went dead.

"It was a salesman," Adam said, all smooth and easy. "The jerk wanted to sell Becca some venetian blinds." He shrugged. "What was it you wanted to know, Sheriff?"

The sheriff had not taken his eyes off Savich. "Those guys around town. Who are they, Mr. Savich?"

"You found me out, Sheriff," Savich said. "Actually, my wife and I are here because we're representing a big resort developer who is seriously interested in this section of the Maine coast. It's true that Adam is a friend of ours and he, well, he gives us some cover. Now, the guys you're seeing around are supposed to be very discreet, which means that you've got a very sharp eye, Sheriff. They're doing all sorts of things, like talking to folk, surveying, checking out soil and other flora and fauna, seeing who owns what and how profitable the businesses are now. This is a lovely section of coastline and Riptide is a real neat little town. A resort not too far away—can you imagine what would happen to your local economy? In any case, we won't be here for much longer, but I would ask you a favor. Could you please keep this under your hat?" Savich said immediately to Sherlock, "I told you the sheriff was too sharp not to catch on to us, honey. I told you he was real smart and he knew everything that went on in his town."

"Yes, Dillon," Sherlock said, "you told me that. I'm sorry I didn't see him as clearly as you did. Yeah, he's pretty smart, all right." She gave the sheriff a brilliant smile.

"So, you want me to keep my mouth shut about this, Mr. Savich?"

"Yes, sir."

"Well, all right, but if any of them cause any trouble, I'll be back. This resort of yours—it wouldn't go spoiling any of the natural beauty around here, would it?"

"No way," Savich said. "That's the prime goal of the group I work with."

Becca eyed Savich after she let the sheriff out the front door, which smelled, he said on his way out, really nice and clean. "You're something, Savich. I really believed you there for a minute. Goodness, I wanted to ask you the name of the planned resort."

Savich said, "The phone call gave me time to come up with a decent story."

"It was him, wasn't it?" Becca said as she turned to Adam, who was still standing by the phone.

"Yes, it was him. He wanted to speak to you but I told him you weren't here. He always calls you Rebecca, not Becca?" At her nod, Adam said, "He was calling from a public phone booth in Rockland. Tommy the Pipe just tracked it down, so there's nothing we can do."

Sherlock said slowly, studying a bruised knuckle she'd gotten when she'd clipped Tyler McBride's jaw, "We've got to get him back. We've got to set up a meeting somehow."

"Next time I'll speak to him," Becca said. "I'll set one up."

"You won't be bait," Adam said, his voice sharp as a knife. "No way."

"Look, Adam, he wants me. If you made yourself the bait, he'd just shoot you and walk away. But not so with me. He wants me up close and personal. Only me. Help me figure out a way to do this, please."

"I don't like it."

Chapter 18

*H*atch, short, built like a young bull, sporting a large mustache, pulled off a tweed Sherlock Holmes hat to show his shaved head. For some reason she couldn't quite fathom, Becca thought he was so impishly cute she wanted to hug him. She thought from the cocky grin on Sherlock's face that she wanted to hug him right along with her.

This guy was potent. He had more charm than a person deserved, she was thinking a few minutes later when Adam held out his hand and said to him, "Give me the pack of cigarettes in your right pocket, Hatch, now, or you're fired."

"Yeah, sure, boss." Hatch obligingly handed Adam a nearly full pack of Marlboros. "Just one, boss, no more, and I didn't inhale much. All I had, just one. I don't want to smoke anywhere near sweet Becca. I wouldn't want to ever take a chance of hurting her lovely lungs. Now, tell me what to do to catch this creep so Becca can go back to writing speeches and smiling a lot." Then he turned those dark-brown twinkling eyes on her and said, "Hi."

Becca grinned and pumped his hand. "Hi, Hatch. Listen, I'm ready. The next time he calls—I'm ready. We're going to set a trap for him. I'm going to be the bait."

"Hmmm. I don't think the boss likes that. His jaw is all knotted up."

Adam unknotted his jaw. "No, I don't like it. It's crazy. I don't want her to take this kind of risk. Ah, shit, I can tell by the look on your face, Becca, that you're going to do it regardless of what I think."

"Look, Adam," Savich said, "if I could think of another way, I'd dive on it, but there are enough of us to keep her protected. Now, Hatch, according to Adam, you have a pretty awesome reputation to maintain. Tell us what you've found out."

Hatch took a slim black book out of his jacket pocket, licked his fingers, and ruffled some pages. "Most of this is from Thomas's guys, who've been working their butts off trying to verify Krimakov's death. Thomas got everyone working on it right away. Now, the CIA has actually spoken to the cop who was the one who poked around his body. Apollo—no shit, that's his name—said Krimakov went over a cliff on the eastern end of Crete, near Agios Nikolaos, died instantly, one would suppose from the injuries. It could have been murder, he allowed, but nobody checked into it all that much for the simple fact that no one really cares. Nothing obvious about it, so they closed the case until our agents flew in and spread out and wanted to see and examine everything."

"So he's really dead," Becca said.

Hatch looked up and gave them a big grin. "Nope, not necessarily. Here's the kicker. Krimakov's body was cremated. You see, for the longest time, our people were stonewalled by the locals, who wouldn't allow them to view the body. It was only after the Greek government got involved that they let it out of the bag that they'd cremated him right away. Why? I don't know, but there was a payoff, somewhere."

No one said a word for a very long time.

"Cremated?" Adam repeated, disbelieving.

"Yes, burned to ashes, poured in an urn. Thing's still sitting on a shelf in the morgue."

Sherlock said, "So there is no definitive proof because there's no body to examine."

"Right," Hatch said. "Now, while we all chew on that, let's go back a bit. Krimakov moved to Crete in the early eighties. Just showed up and stayed. He was into bad things, but not bad enough so anyone would dig and find out exactly who and what he'd been in Russia. Actually, the impression is they never tried really hard to do any nailing. He probably paid everyone off."

"Damn," Adam said. "Okay. Now we've got to search his house, top to bottom and under the basement. If he ever was involved in this, there will be something there."

"Our agents have gone over his house, didn't find anything. No clues, no leads, no references at all to Becca. We heard that he had an apartment somewhere, but we don't know where it is. That might take a little time. There aren't any official records."

Savich said, "If he had an apartment, I'll find it."

"Just you?" Adam said, an eyebrow raised.

"Didn't Thomas tell you I was good?"

Adam snorted, watching Savich plug in MAX.

Hatch said, "More will be coming about his personal activities. But as yet, there isn't anything out of Russia. It seems that way back when, all Krimakov's records were purged. There's little left. Nothing of interest. The KGB probably ordered it done, then helped him go to ground, in Crete. Again, though, they'll continue searching and probing and questioning all their counterparts in Moscow."

"Krimakov isn't dead," Adam said. And he believed it like he'd never believed anything in his life.

Having said that, Adam sat back and closed his eyes. He was getting a headache.

"Well, yeah, we have something else. I was the one who did all the legwork on this." Hatch licked his fingers again and flipped over a couple more pages. "The Albany cops just found a witness not two hours ago who identified the car that ran down Dick Mc-Callum. It's a BMW, black, license number—at least the first three numbers—three-eight-five. A New York plate. I don't have anything on that yet."

"I'll have it run through," Savich said. "It'll be quicker, more complete. I don't want to know how you got that information so quickly."

"I'll just say that she loves my mustache," Hatch said. "Please do call the Bureau, Agent Savich. I didn't have the chance to check back with Thomas and have him do it. Oh yeah, a guy was driving. No clue if it was an old guy or a young guy or in between, really dark windows, like windows on a limo. Fairly unusual for a regular commercial car, and that's probably why he stole that particular car."

Savich was on his cell phone in the next ten seconds, nodded and hung up in three more minutes. "Done. We'll have a list of possibles in about five minutes."

Tommy the Pipe knocked lightly on the front door and came in. "We got a guy buying Exxon supreme at a gas station just eight miles west of Riptide. The attendant, a young boy about eighteen, said when the guy paid for his gas, he saw dirt and blood on the cuff of his shirt. He wouldn't have thought a thing about it except Rollo was canvassing all the gas stations, asking questions about strangers. It's him."

"Oh, yeah," Adam said and jumped to his feet. "Please say it, Tommy. Please tell us that this kid remembers what the guy looks like, that he remembers the kind of car he was driving."

"The guy had on a green hunting hat with flaps, something like mine but with no style. He also wore very dark glasses. He doesn't know if the guy was young or old, sorry, Adam. Hell, anyone over twenty-five would be old to that kid. But he does remember clearly that the guy spoke well, a real educated voice, all smooth and deep. The car—he thought it was a BMW, dark blue or black. Sorry, no idea about the plate. But you know what? The windows were dark-tinted. How about that?"

"Surely he wouldn't have driven the same car up here that he used to kill Dick McCallum in Albany," Sherlock said.

"Why not?" Savich said. "If it isn't dented, if there isn't blood all over it, then why not?"

Savich's cell phone rang. He stood and walked over to the doorway. They heard him talking, saw him nodding as he listened. He hung up and said, "No go. He stole the license plates. No surprise there. He'd have been an idiot to leave on the original plates. However, those heavily tinted windows, I have everyone checking on New York cars stolen within the past two weeks with those sorts of windows."

Savich's cell phone rang again in eight minutes. He listened and wrote rapidly. When he hung up the phone, he said, "This is something. Like Hatch said, few commercial cars—domestic or foreign—are built with dark-tinted windows. Three have been stolen. The people are all over the state, two men and one woman."

Becca said with no hesitation, "It's the woman. He stole her car."

"Possible," Sherlock said. "Let's find out right now."

She called information for Ithaca, New York, and got the phone number for Mrs. Irene Bailey, 112 Huntley Avenue. The phone rang once, twice, three times, then, "Hello?"

"Mrs. Bailey? Mrs. Irene Bailey?"

Silence.

"Are you there? Mrs. Bailey?"

"That's my mother," a woman said. "I'm sorry, but it took me by surprise."

"May I please speak to your mother?"

"You don't know? No, I guess not. My mother was killed two weeks ago."

Sherlock didn't drop the phone, but she felt a great roiling pain through her stomach, up to her throat, and she swallowed convulsively. "Can you give me any details, please?"

"Who are you?"

"I'm Gladys Martin with the Social Security Administration in Washington."

"I know my husband called Social Security. What do you want?"

"We're required to fill out papers, ma'am. Are you her daughter?"

"Yes, I am. What kind of papers?"

"Statistics, nothing more. Is there someone else I can speak to about this? I don't want to upset you."

There was a moment of silence, then, "No, it's all right. Ask the questions. We don't want the government to go away mad."

"Thank you, ma'am. You said your mother was killed? Was this an auto accident?"

"No, someone hit her on the head when she was going out to her car at the shopping mall. He stole her car."

"Oh, dear, I'm so very sorry. Please tell me that the man who did this has been caught?"

The woman's voice hardened up immediately. "No, he wasn't. The cops put out a description of her car, but no one has reported back with anything as yet. They think he painted the car a different color and changed the license plates. He's gone. Even the New York City cops don't know where he is. She was an old woman, too, so who cares?" The bitterness in the daughter's voice was bone-deep, her pain, disbelief, anger still raw.

"Was there anything distinctive about the car the man stole?"

"Yes, the windows were tinted dark because my mother had very sensitive eyes. Too much sunlight really hurt her."

"I see. What was the color of the car?"

"White with gray interior. There was a small dent above the left rear tire."

"I see. Did you say that there were other than just the local cops there?"

"Oh, yes. Of all things, they were from New York City. They should have caught this guy. We don't know why the New York City police are involved. Do you? Is that really why you're calling? You want to pump me for information?"

"No, of course not. This is simply statistical information that we need."

"Are there any more questions, Ms. Martin? I'm sorting through my mother's things and I have to be down at St. Paul's charities in a half hour."

"No, ma'am. I'm very sorry for your loss. I'll take care of everything here." Sherlock turned to see all eyes focused on her. "The killer painted a white car black and stole another license plate. The New York City cops were there. They know. Oh, yeah, the windows are tinted dark because Mrs. Bailey had sensitive eyes."

"Son of a bitch," Hatch said and groped in his pocket for his cigarettes. "How come nobody told me that the cops knew about that damned car?"

Adam just gave him a look and said, "They've got a real lid on that one. My guess is they're keeping it from the Feds, don't want to get aced out. And the victim loses. What the New York cops don't know is that our killer is here in Maine. Shall we tell them?"

Savich said, "Not the New York cops, but I can call Tellie Hawley, the SAC of the office in New York City. He'll see that it gets to where it needs to go."

"Yeah," Adam said, "why not? Anyone think of a good reason why not?"

"How specific should we be?" Becca asked. She was wringing her hands, and Adam frowned.

Savich rolled it around in his brain and said, "Let's just tell him the guy's been seen on the coast. How's that? It's the truth."

"We've got to get him," Becca said. "If we don't, then we have to call this Thomas person who seems to know everyone and direct everything, and tell him to bring in the Marines."

"He hasn't called," Becca said, and took a bite of her hot dog. "Why hasn't he called?"

Adam said as he chewed a potato chip, "I think he's going to lie low for a while. He's not stupid. He's going to dig in somewhere else, give you some time to chew your fingernails, make all of us jumpy as hell, then jump back into the game—his game."

They were all eating hot dogs with relish and mustard, the team of guys outside coming in one at a time. Special Agent Rollo Dempsey said to Adam, "I knew your name but I couldn't remember where I'd heard it. Now I do. You saved Senator Dashworth's life last year when that crazy tried to stick a knife in his ribs."

Adam didn't say a word.

"Yeah, it was you. You saved Senator Dashworth's life. Pretty impressive."

"You shouldn't know about that," Adam said finally, frowning at Rollo. "You really shouldn't."

"Yeah, well, I'm an insider, I can't help it if people tell me every-thing."

"I never heard anything about that," Becca said, her antennae up. "What are you talking about?"

Rollo just grinned at her and said, "Did you find out who tried to off him?"

"You don't know about that, too?"

"Hey, I'm an insider, but the spigot was off when it came to the particulars."

Adam shrugged. "Well, who cares now? The guy who wanted the senator dead was his son-in-law. Irving—that's the guy's name—had sent him threats, all the usual anonymous bullshit. The senator called me. It turned out that Irving had become a heroin addict, didn't have any more money, and wanted the senator's in-heritance. The senator managed to keep it from the media, to pro-tect his daughter, and so we got the guy into a sanatorium, where he belonged, where he's still at. I guess there are only a few insid-ers who know anything at all about it."

"You run some sort of a bodyguard business?" Becca said, frowning at Adam over a spoonful of baked beans. "I thought you did security consulting."

"I like to keep my hand in on a lot of different things," Adam said.

"What I'd like to know," Sherlock said, handing Rollo another hot dog with lots of down-home yellow mustard slathered on it, "is why you didn't find out who it was right away. The guy was an ad-dict? That kind of thing isn't easy to hide."

Adam actually flushed. He played with his fork, didn't meet her eyes. He cleared his throat. "Well, the thing is that the son-in-law wasn't around for those three days I was checking things out. His wife was protecting him, said he had the flu, that he was really contagious, et cetera. She swore to me and to her father that Irving wouldn't even consider doing something like that, no, it had to be a crazy, or a left-wing conspiracy. She was so—well—damned believable."

"Good thing you were there to deflect the guy's knife," Rollo said.

"That's the truth," Adam said.

Rollo sat down at the kitchen table, squeezing in between Savich and Becca. Adam said on a deep sigh, "I just heard that the wife is trying to get the husband out of there. It could start all over again."

"Well, shit," Rollo said. "Not much justice around, is there?"

Then Chuck came in and Rollo, still half a hog dog left, saluted and went back outside.

"It won't be long now," Savich said. "I feel it. Things will happen." He took a last bite of a tofu hot dog, sighed with pleasure, and hugged his wife.

Things didn't happen until later.

They were all in the living room drinking coffee, planning, arguing, brainstorming. There was no activity outside. Everything was buttoned down tight, until at exactly ten o'clock a bullet shattered one of the front windows, glass exploded inward, carrying shreds of curtain with it.

"Down!" Savich yelled.

But it wasn't a simple bullet that came through the window to strike the floor molding on the far side of the living room, it was a tear gas bullet. Thick gray smoke gushed out even before it struck the molding.

"Oh, damn," Adam said. "Back into the kitchen. Now!"

Another tear gas bullet exploded through the window. They were coughing, covering their faces, running toward the back of the house.

They heard men's shouts, sporadic gunfire, sharp and loud in the night. The front door burst open and Tommy the Pipe ran in, his face covered with his jacket. "Out, guys, quick. Through the front door, the back's not covered well enough."

"He shot tear gas bullets," Adam said between choking coughs.

"He's probably using a CAR-15, behind our perimeter. Come on out."

They coughed their heads off, tears streaming down their faces. Savich found himself with Becca's nose pressed into his armpit.

"We've got to get him," Adam shouted, coughing, choking, his eyes streaming tears. "Just another minute to get over this and we'll start scouring."

It took another seven minutes before they headed out in the general direction of where the tear gas bullets must have been shot toward the front windows.

They found tire tracks, nothing else, until Adam called out, "Look here."

Everyone gathered around Adam, who was on his haunches. He held up a shell casing that was four inches long and about an inch and a half in diameter. "Tommy the Pipe was right. He used a CAR-15—that's a compact M16," he added to Becca, "stands for carbine automatic rifle."

Savich found the other shell casing and was tossing it back and forth.

"But how can tear gas come from a gun?" Becca said. "I thought they were canisters or something like that. That's what I've always seen in movies and on TV."

"That's real old-hat now," Adam said. "This smaller M16 is real portable, you could carry it under your trench coat. It's got this telescoping collapsible barrel. The SEALs use this stuff. What you do is simply mount an under-barrel tubular grenade launcher and fire away with your tear gas projectiles. It's wicked."

Sherlock said, "He's obviously connected and very well trained. Got all the latest goodies. And just where would he get all this stuff?"

And Adam thought: *Krimakov.*

No one said anything.

They got back to the house forty-five minutes later. It was late, and everyone was hyped. Adam said, as he shrugged into his jacket, rechecked his pistol, "I'm going to take one of the first watches."

"Get me up at three o'clock," Savich said.

"I'm outta here," Adam said. He looked over at Becca, saw that she was white-faced and couldn't help himself. He walked to her and pulled her tight against him. He said against her hair, "Sleep well and don't worry. We're going to get him."

Becca didn't think she'd be able to slow her heart down enough even to consider sleeping, but she did, deeply and dreamlessly, until she felt a strange jab in her left arm, just above her elbow, like a mosquito bite. She jerked awake, her heart pounding wildly, and she couldn't breathe, just pant and jerk. She was blind, no, it was just dark, very dark, the blinds drawn because nobody wanted him to be able to see into the house. She saw a shadowy figure standing over her, gray, indistinct, and she whispered, "What is this? Is it you, Adam? What did you do—?" But he said nothing, merely leaned closer and finally, when her heart was slowing just a bit, he whispered right against her face, "I came for you, Rebecca, just like I said I would," and he licked her cheek.

"No," she said. "No." Then she fell back, wondering what the silver light was shining just over her face. It seemed to arc toward her, a skinny silver flash, but then it just wasn't important. A small flashlight, she thought as she breathed in very deeply, more deeply than usual for her, and eased into a soft warm blackness that relaxed her mind and body, and she didn't know anything more.

Chapter 19

*H*er heart beat slow, regular strokes, one after the other, easy, steady, no fright registering in her body. She felt calm, relaxed. She opened her eyes. It was black, no shadows, no hint of movement, just relentless, motionless black. She was swamped with the black, but she forced herself to draw in a deep breath. Her heart wasn't pumping out of her chest now. She still felt relaxed, too relaxed, with no fear grinding through her, at least not yet, but she knew she should be afraid. She was in darkness and he was close by. She knew it, but still she breathed steadily, evenly, waiting, but not afraid. Well, perhaps there was just a tincture of fear, indistinct, nibbling at the edges of her mind. She frowned, and it slipped away.

Odd how she remembered perfectly everything that had happened: the jab in her left arm, the instant terror, she remembered all of it—him licking her cheek—with no mental fuzz cloaking the memories.

The nibblings of fear became more focused now, she could nearly grasp it. Her heart speeded up. She blinked, willing herself to know fear, then to control it.

He had gotten her. Somehow he'd gotten into the house, past the guards, and he'd gotten her.

There was suddenly a wispy light, the smell of smoke. He'd lit a candle. He wasn't close by now, he was here, just inches from her. She calmed the building fear, it was hard, probably the hardest thing she'd ever had to do, but she knew she had to. She remembered, very suddenly, her mother telling her once that fear was what hurt you because it froze you. "Don't ever give up," her mother had told her. "Never give up." Then her mother had gripped her shoulders and said it one more time: "Never give up."

It was so clear in her mind in that moment, her mother standing over her telling her this. She could even feel her mother's fingers hard on her shoulders. Odd that she couldn't remember what had happened to make her mother tell her this.

"Where are we?"

Was that her voice, all calm and indifferent? Yes, she'd managed it.

"Hello, Rebecca. I came for you, just like I said I would."

"Please," she said, and then she laughed, choked, "please don't lick my cheek again. That was really creepy."

He was dead silent, affronted, even pissed, she realized, because she was laughing at him.

"You gave me a shot of something. What was it?"

She heard his deep breathing. "Just something I picked up in Turkey. I was told that a side effect is a temporary sense of euphoria. You won't feel like laughing for much longer, Rebecca. The effects will fade, and then you'll be heaving with fear, you'll be so scared of me."

"Yeah, yeah, yeah."

He slapped her. She didn't see his hand, it was just there, connecting sharply against her cheek. She tried to leap at him, but she realized she was tied down, her hands over her head, her wrists tied to the slats of the headboard. So she was lying on a bed. Her legs were free. She was still wearing her nightgown, a white cotton nightgown that came up to her chin and went down to her ankles. He'd smoothed it over her legs.

She said with a sneer in her voice, "Hey, I liked the slap better than you licking me. You're really brave, aren't you? Would you like to let my hands free, just for a minute, and then we'll see how brave you are?"

"Shut up!"

He was standing beside her, leaning down, breathing hard. She couldn't see his hands, but she imagined they were fists, ready to bash her.

She said very quietly, "Why did you kill Linda Cartwright?"

"That fat bitch? She was bothering me, always begging, pleading, whining when she was thirsty or she wanted to pee or she wanted to lie down. I got tired of it."

She said nothing at all, beyond words, wondering what had made him into a madman or had he been born like this? Born evil, nothing to blame but screwed-up genes.

She could hear him tapping his fingers, *tap, tap, tap.* He wanted her to say something, wanted it badly, but she held quiet.

"Did you like my present to you, Rebecca?"

"No."

"I saw you puking your guts out."

"I thought you probably did. God, you're sick. You get off on that?"

"Then I saw that big guy, Adam Carruthers, there with you. He was holding you. Why did you let him hold you like that?"

"I probably would have even leaned against you if I didn't know who you were."

"I'm glad you didn't let him kiss you."

"I had just vomited. That wouldn't be fun for anyone, now would it?"

"No, I guess not."

He didn't sound old, not the age of this Krimakov character. But was he young? She just couldn't tell. "Who are you? Are you Krimakov?"

He was silent but just for a moment. Then he laughed softly, deeply, and it froze her. He lightly ran his palm over her cheek, squeezed just a bit, made her flinch. "I'm your boyfriend, Rebecca. I saw you and I knew that I would have to be closer to you than your skin. I thought about actually getting under your skin, but that would mean I'd have to skin you and then cover myself, and you're just not big enough.

"Then I thought I wanted to be next to your heart, but again, there'd be so much blood, fountains of it. Too many hands ruin the stew, too much blood ruins the clothes. I'm a fastidious man.

"No, don't say it or think it. I'm not crazy, not like that Hannibal character. I just said that to make you so afraid you'd start begging and pleading. Already the drug's wearing off. I can see how afraid you are. All I have to do is talk and you're scared shitless."

He was right about that, but she'd give about anything not to show him, not to let him see that she was boiling white hot inside, nearly burned to ashes with fear. "But then when you're all done talking, you'll strangle me like you did Linda Cartwright?"

"Oh no. She wasn't important. She wasn't anything."

"I'll bet she disagreed with that."

"Probably, but who cares?"

"Why me?"

He laughed, and she bet that if she could see his face, he'd be smirking, so pleased with himself. "Not just yet, Rebecca. You and I have got lots of things to do before you know who I am and why I chose you."

"There's a reason, naturally, at least in your mind. Why won't you tell me?"

"You'll find out soon enough, or not. We'll see. Now, I'm going to give you another little shot and you'll sleep again."

"No," she said. "I have to go to the bathroom. Let me go to the bathroom."

He cursed—American curses mixed with English-sounding curses, and an odd language thrown in that she didn't recognize.

"You try anything and I'll knock you silly. I'll strip the skin off your arm and make it into a pair of gloves. You hear me?"

"Yes, I hear you. I thought you were fastidious."

"I am, about blood. There wouldn't be all those fountains of blood if I just peeled the skin off your arm."

She felt him untie her hands, slowly, and she supposed that the knots must have been complicated. Finally she was free. She brought her arms down and rubbed her wrists. They burned, then eased. She was very stiff. Slowly, she sat up and swung her legs off the bed.

"You try anything and I'll put a knife into your leg, high up on your thigh. I know just the place that won't show much, but the pain will make you wish you were dead it's so bad. There wouldn't be hardly any blood at all. Yeah, forget about skinning your arm. Don't try to see me, Rebecca, or I'll have to kill you right now, and that's the end of it."

She didn't know how she managed to walk, but she did. Then as the strength came back to her feet and legs, she wanted to run, run so fast she'd be a blur and he'd never catch her, never, never.

But she didn't, of course.

The bathroom was just off the bedroom. He'd removed the doorknob. When she was through, she paused to look at herself in the mirror. She looked pale and drawn and gaunt, her hair tangled around her head and down to her shoulders. She looked vague and on the edge, like a woman who had been drugged, knew it, and also realized, at last, that she might very well die.

"Come out now, Rebecca. I know you're through. Come out or you'll regret it."

"I just got here. Give me some time."

There was nothing in the bathroom to use as a weapon, nothing at all. He'd even removed the towel racks, cleared everything from beneath the sink. Nothing.

"Just a moment," she called out. She raced back to the toilet and fell onto her knees. It was old. If the big screw that held the toilet down had ever had a cap on it, it was long gone. She tried to twist it, and to her utter surprise, it actually moved, just a bit. It was thick, the grooves deep and sharp. She was choking, sobbing deep in her throat, praying.

She heard him, just outside the door. Was he touching the door? Was he going to push it inward? Oh, Jesus. "Just a second," she yelled. "I'm not feeling too well. That drug you shot into me, it's making me nauseous. Give me just another minute. I don't want to vomit all over myself." *Turn, damn you, turn.* Finally, finally, it came free in her hand. It was thick, about an inch and a half long, deeply grooved, and those grooves were sharp. What to do with it? Where to hide it?

"I'm coming," she called out as she gently pulled some thread loose in the hem of her nightgown. "I feel a bit better. I just don't want to vomit, particularly if you're going to tie my hands again."

If he'd been standing by the bathroom door, he wasn't now. He was back in the shadows when she came out. She couldn't make out a thing about him. He said, his voice deep, ageless, "Lie back down on the bed."

She did.

He didn't tie her hands over her head.

"Don't move."

She felt the sting in her left arm, right above her elbow again, before she could even react. "Coward," she said, her voice already becoming slurred.

"Filthy coward."

She heard him laugh. And again, he licked her, her ear this time, his tongue slow, lapping, and she wanted to gag, but she didn't because her mind was beginning to float now, and it was easy and smooth and the fear disappeared as she just fell away from herself.

No time, she thought, as what she was and what she thought were slipping away, like grains of sand scattering in a wind. No time, no time to stab him with that screw. No time to ask him again if he was this Krimakov who'd been cremated. No time for anything.

Adam stood there in her open bedroom doorway. She was gone, simply gone. "No," he said, shaking his head. "No. Oh God, no! Savich!"

But she was gone, no sign of her, nothing at all.

It was Sherlock who said as she sipped a cup of black coffee, "He used the tear gas as a diversion. While we were all outside looking for him, he simply slipped into the house and hid in Becca's bedroom closet. Then he probably drugged her. How did he get her out? Our guys were back in position by the time we came back inside. Oh, no, get everyone together! We weren't exactly organized when we were looking for him outside. Dillon, who was assigned to the back of the house?"

"Jesus," Adam said. "No, damnation, no!"

They found Chuck Ainsley in the bushes twenty feet from the back of the house. He wasn't dead. He'd been struck down from behind, bound and gagged. When they peeled the tape off his mouth, he said, "I let him creep up on me. I didn't hear a thing. He was fast, too fast. Oh God, what the hell happened? Is everyone all right?"

Savich said matter-of-factly, "He took Becca. Thank God you're not dead. I wonder why he didn't just slit your throat, Chuck? Why waste time tying you up?"

Sherlock said, as she hunkered down next to Chuck and untied both his wrists and ankles, "He doesn't want the police here yet. He realized that if he killed one of us, that's what would happen. It would force his hand. He would lose control. We're really glad you're okay, Chuck."

Adam said, "He must have knocked you out before he shot tear gas into the house. We came roaring out, everyone trying to find him, and we didn't miss you. There was too much confusion. Damnation."

Sherlock gave Chuck a drink of cold water and a couple of aspirin once they got him into the kitchen. "If you won't have a headache, you should," she told him, then hugged him. "Thank God you're all right. Since you weren't at the back of the house watching for him, he must have just slipped out with Becca over his shoulder."

"We didn't miss you," Adam said slowly. "I can't believe we didn't have the brains to get everyone together and count heads before we settled back into the house for the night. Hell, we didn't even think to search the damned house."

Everyone was rattled as what happened sank in. There was nothing to say, no excuses to make. He'd made fools of them all.

An hour later, Sherlock and Savich found Adam in the kitchen, his head in his hands. Savich lightly laid his hand on his shoulder. "It happened. We've all flagellated ourselves. No thanks to us, Chuck is all right. Now we've got to fix it. Adam, we'll find her."

"I was supposed to keep her safe," Adam said, staring at his clasped hands. "I've got to be the biggest fuckup in this damned world. He's got her, Savich. He's got her and we have no idea where."

"Yes, he's got her," Savich said, "and he's probably going to take her to Washington. That's it, isn't it? He wants her with him when he confronts Thomas? She's his leverage. Thomas would do anything to save her, including giving himself up to this maniac."

"We're talking like Krimakov is alive, like we don't have any doubts about it at all," Sherlock said.

Adam said slowly, "Forget the reports, forget what the operatives said. The body was cremated. That's all I need to know. It's Krimakov. Now, he must not have found out where Thomas is. Thomas owns a house in Chevy Chase, but it's a well-kept secret. The location of his condo in Georgetown is also a secret, but anyone could discover its location if they really wanted to. MAX could probably ferret it out in ten minutes flat. But not the Chevy Chase house. He's very careful. I kid you not, I don't even think the president knows where his house is. So then Krimakov wouldn't know, either. That's why he got Becca. She's his leverage. He'll take her to Washington, to the condo." Adam stopped cold. "We've got to leave now."

Savich said, "I think you should call Thomas first, tell him what's happened. We've put it off long enough, don't you think? He's got to know."

Adam cursed under his breath at the sound of Tyler McBride's angry voice. Tyler came into the kitchen, three agents right behind him, one holding his arm, and yelled, "What the hell is going on here? Every light in the place is on? Who are these guys? Let me go, dammit. Where's Becca?"

"Let him go, Tommy," Savich said, nodding to one of Thomas's men who was guarding the front of the house. "He's a neighbor and a friend of Becca's."

"What the hell is going on here, Adam?"

"He took her," Adam said. "We think he's heading to Washington, D.C., with her. We're going to have to clear out soon."

Tyler paled, then yelled, "You were supposed to protect her, you bastard! You really screwed up big-time, didn't you? I wanted to help but you just kissed me off, I was a civilian, of no use at all. What about you? All these big Fed cops, none of you could protect her. None of you were of any help at all!"

Savich said as he closed his fingers around Tyler's arm, "I understand your anger. But all these accusations aren't going to help anyone, particularly Becca. Believe me, we all know what's at stake here."

"You're damned incompetent bastards," Tyler yelled even louder, "all of you." He jerked away from Savich.

"Tyler," Adam said quietly, "don't go to Sheriff Gaffney. That would be the worst thing you could do."

"Why? How much more could things be fucked up?"

"He might kill her," Adam said. "Don't tell anyone anything."

After Tyler McBride was escorted from the house by three agents, Sherlock said, "Why not tell everyone now?"

Adam shoved his hand through his hair. "Dammit, because if some cop happens to see them, then you know our guy would kill her and take off. We can't take the chance. No, we've got to get to Washington, fast."

"First you've got to call Thomas, Adam."

Adam didn't want to, he really didn't.

Savich and Sherlock listened to Adam flail himself on the speakerphone.

There was silence on the other end. Finally, Thomas said, "Get over it, Adam. We've been dealt new cards now, we'll play them. I'm very relieved that Chuck is all right. His wife would roast me alive if he'd been killed. Now, if this is Krimakov, then he at least knows I'm in Washington, probably knows about the condo. I'll stay here. I'll be ready for him. Get back here as quickly as you can, Adam. Savich? Can you and Sherlock stick with us?"

"Yes, Thomas."

"Now, I've got to get myself ready for Krimakov. It's been so many years. Many times I thought he'd finally given it up, but it appears that he's just been biding his time."

"He could really be dead," Sherlock said.

"No," Thomas said. "Adam, you, Savich, and Sherlock hang around there for a while. Try to get a line on this guy. He's got to be somewhere. He's got to be traceable. Find him. Oh, and Adam?"

"Yes, sir?"

"Stop beating yourself up. Guilt just slows down your brain. I want that brain of yours sharp. Get it together and find my daughter."

They finally rang off. Thomas Matlock looked at the phone for a very long time before he slowly eased it back down. Then he leaned his head back against the soft leather of his chair. He closed his eyes to blot out the feeling of helplessness, for just a moment, an instant, but instead, he felt a deep, soul-corroding fear that a man should never have to feel in his damned life. It was fear for his child, and the knowledge that he was helpless to save her.

It was Krimakov, he knew it, deep in his gut, he knew, and they had cremated the body. No, Krimakov wasn't dead—maybe he'd staged his death, murdered another man who resembled him. He'd somehow found out about Becca and he had begun his reign of terror. There was no doubt at all in Thomas's mind now. Krimakov, a man who had sworn to cut Thomas's heart out even if he had to chase Thomas to hell to do it, had his Becca.

He lowered his face in his hands.

Chapter 20

She was aware of ear-splitting noise—men's and women's voices yelling loudly, car tires screeching, horns blasting, and movement, she could feel the blur of movement everywhere, pounding feet, running fast. She was moving as well, no, she was flying, then she hit hard and the pain ripped through her. She lay on her side, smelling the hot tar of the street, a light overlay of urine, hot and sour, whiffs of food, of too many bodies, feeling the unforgiving cement beneath her. Cement?

People were yelling, coming closer now, and there were men and women shouting, "Stay back! Let us through!"

She tried to open her eyes, but her muscles were too weak, wouldn't obey her, and the pain was boiling up inside her. She was so very tired, nearly blown under with it. Then she felt a hideously sharp stab of pain somewhere in her body, fierce, unrelenting, and she knew tears were leaking out of her eyes.

"Miss! Can you hear me?"

She felt his hand on her shoulder, felt the sun beating down on her, hot on her bare skin—what bare skin? Her legs were bare, that was it. But he was over her, a shadow blocking the sun.

"Miss? Can you hear me? Are you conscious?"

She opened her eyes then because he sounded so very afraid. "Yes," she whispered, "I can hear you. I can see you. Not clearly, but I can see you."

"My God, it's her! It's that Matlock woman!"

More shouting, yelling, some curses, and so much heat, the press of bodies, the running thuds of shoes and boots.

A woman lightly tapped her cheek. "Open your eyes for me. Yes, that's right. Do you know who you are?"

She looked up into Letitia Gordon's grim, incredulous face.

Maybe there was also a touch of worry in those unforgiving eyes. Becca whispered to that hard face over her, "You're the cop who hates me. How can you be here, right over me, speaking to me? You're in New York, aren't you?"

"Yes, and so are you."

"No, that's not possible. I was in Riptide. You know, I never could figure out why you hated me and believed I was a liar."

The woman's face contorted. Into anger? What?

"He drugged me," she whispered, her mouth so dry she nearly swallowed her tongue. "He drugged me. I hurt so much but I just can't tell where."

"All right. You'll be all right. Hey, Dobbson, is the ambulance here yet? Get off your butt, usher them through. Now!"

Letitia Gordon's face was really close to hers now, her breath minty on her cheek. "We'll find out what's happening here, Ms. Matlock. You just rest now."

She felt hands pulling cloth down over her legs. Why were her legs bare? She realized then that there was pain in her legs. But it wasn't as bad as the other pain. Where was she? In New York? But that made no sense. Nothing made sense. Her brain nestled back into the shadows. The pain faded away. Becca sighed deeply and closed down.

She heard them speaking, soft, quiet voices not four feet away from her, talking, talking. Then they were closer, much closer, talking above her, which meant what? She opened her eyes. Blinked. She was flat on her back. The people speaking were on the left, and one of the people was Adam.

She wet her lips with her tongue. "Adam?"

He whirled around so fast he nearly lost his balance. Then he was at her side and he lifted her hand and held it hard between his two large ones. She felt the calluses on his palms.

"What's going on? Where are we? I dreamed I saw Detective Gordon, you know, that cop who hates me?"

"Yes, I know. She left just a little while ago. She'll be back, but later, when you've got it together again. You're going to be all right, Becca. There's nothing to worry about. Just take it easy and breathe nice shallow, light breaths. That's right. Does your head hurt?"

She thought about that. "No, not really, it's just that I'm all fuzzy. Even you're kind of fuzzy, Adam. I'm so glad to see you. I thought I was going to die, that I'd never see you again. I couldn't bear it. Where are we?"

He lightly touched his fingertip to her cheek. "You're at New York University Hospital. The guy who took you from your bed in Jacob Marley's house, the guy who was holding you, he shoved you out of his car right in front of One Police Plaza."

"It was Krimakov?"

"We believe so. At least it's a strong possibility."

She said, "I asked him if he was Krimakov but he wouldn't answer me. We're in New York City?"

"Yes. You did see Detective Gordon. She was one of the cops who came running. It was early in the afternoon, bunches of people around, lots of cops heading out for lunch. Detective Gordon was there because she had some meetings with the Narcotics Division."

"My lucky day," Becca said.

"Damn, I'm sorry, Becca, so sorry. I really fucked up and just look what happened."

She heard the awful guilt in his voice, the fear, and finally, overlaying all of it, the relief that she was alive. He couldn't be as relieved as she was. "It's okay, Adam, really."

"Hi, Becca."

She smiled up at Sherlock and Savich, one on either side of her hospital bed. "We're sure glad to see you."

"Me, too. I thought you were in Riptide."

"We can move quickly when we have to," Sherlock said, lightly patting Becca's shoulder. "Dillon got a call from Tellie Hawley, the SAC at the New York City office. Tellie told him what happened. We got here three hours later."

"What happened to him? Did they get him?"

Sherlock said, "Unfortunately, no. There was mass confusion. He shoved you out of the car, then jumped out while the car was still rolling and disappeared into the crowd. The car hit three other people before it smashed into a fire hydrant and drenched another fifty people. It was a zoo. We've gotten some descriptions, but no one agrees with anyone else so far."

He was still out there, free. She felt flattened. "So he got away again," she said, and wanted to shriek with the helplessness that flooded her.

Adam was clearing his throat. "We'll get him, Becca. You've got to believe that. Now, there's someone here for you to meet."

Her head came up, fast. "Please, no doctors, Adam. I hate doctors. Oh, God, so did my mother." And she started crying. She didn't know where all the tears came from, but they were there, swamping her, and she was sobbing, tears streaming down her face, and she wanted her mother desperately. "My mom died in a hospital, Adam. She hated it, then she just didn't care because she was in a coma. No one could do anything. She died in a hospital just like this one." The tears kept coming, she couldn't stop them.

Then suddenly someone was holding her, drawing her close, and a man's dark, smooth voice said next to her ear, "It's all right, my darling girl. It's all right."

And she stilled. Strong arms were around her. She felt his heart pounding rhythmically, powerful and steady against her cheek. "I'm sorry, I don't mean to carry on like this. I miss my mother. I loved her so much and she died. There isn't anyone else for me."

"I miss your mother, too, Becca. It's going to be all right. I swear it to you."

She pulled back just a bit and looked up at an older man who looked oddly familiar to her, but that was impossible, wasn't it? She was sure she'd never seen him before in her life. The drugs were still affecting her, holding her brain back, scrambling things, making her cry. "I'm nobody's darling girl," she whispered, and raised her hand to lightly touch her fingers to the man's cheek. He was so handsome, his face lean, his nose thin, straight, his eyes a soft light blue, dreamy eyes. Now that was strange. Her mother had told her that she had dreamy eyes, summer dreamy eyes. "I don't understand," she said, frowning up at the man's face. "Who are you?"

The man looked as if he would cry with her, but he swallowed, several times, and cleared his throat. "I'm your father, Becca. I'm Thomas Matlock. I can't bring your mother back, but I'm here now, and I'll stay."

"You're Thomas? You're the man Adam and Savich are working for?"

"Well, let's say they're helping me out."

She didn't say anything then, just frowned a bit, trying to assemble things in her mind, in her memory, to make some sense of

225

them, realizing suddenly that she recognized his eyes because he'd given them to her, realizing— "When he slipped the needle into my arm that second time," she whispered, looking directly into his eyes, "just before I went under, he said right against my ear, 'Tell your daddy hello for me.'"

His face paled and he grew vague, indistinct, his arms loosening. She grabbed his shirt with her fist, trying to pull him closer. "No, don't leave me, please."

"Oh, God, I won't." Thomas looked up at Adam. "I guess that says it all."

"Yes," Adam said. "At least now we know for bloody sure."

"Amen to that," Sherlock said. Then she added, "Why don't we all go out to get a cup of coffee while Thomas gets to know Becca a bit better?"

When she was alone with the man who'd said he was her father, she looked up at him and said, "Why did you leave us? I don't even remember what you looked like I was so young when you left. There is this old photograph of you and Mom, and you looked so young and so handsome. Carefree. It's a wonderful picture."

He held her very close for a long time, then slowly he said, "You were all of three years old when it happened. I was a CIA operative, Becca, and I was very good. There was this other KGB spy—"

"Krimakov."

"Yes. I was sent over to what is now Belarus, to stop him from killing a visiting German industrialist. Krimakov had brought his wife, as if they were there on some sort of vacation. It was in the mountains. There was a gunfight and she tried to save him. I hadn't seen her, hadn't even known she was there." He paused a moment, memory stark and alive in his eyes. He said simply, "I shot her in the head and killed her. Krimakov promised me he would kill not only me but my family. He vowed it. I believed him.

"He managed to escape me. I decided that I would have to kill him to protect you. When I tried, I found out that he'd simply disappeared. There was no trace of him. The KGB helped him, obviously, and he stayed buried until very recently, when I was told he was killed in an auto accident in Crete. You know the rest."

"You left us to protect us?"

"Yes. Your mother and I discussed it. Matlock is a common name. She took you and moved to New York. I saw her four, maybe five times a year. We were always very, very careful. We couldn't tell you. We couldn't put you in danger. It was the hardest thing I've ever had to do in my life, Becca. Believe me."

All of a sudden she had a father. She stared at his face, seeing herself in him, seeing also a stranger. It was too much. She heard him say something, heard Adam arguing with someone just inside the door, sharp and loud, then she didn't hear anything at all. That was a good thing, she thought as she slipped away, back where there were no dreams, just seamless darkness, without *him,* no worries or voices to tear her apart. Her father was dead, dead since she was very young. It was impossible that he was here, there was just no way. Maybe she was dead, too, and had seen what she wanted to see. Dead. It wasn't bad, truly it wasn't. She heard a sound, like a wounded animal. It had come from her, she realized, but then there was nothing at all.

When she awoke, it was dark in her room except for a small bedside lamp that was turned to its lowest setting. The small hospital room was filled with shadows and quiet voices. There were needles in both of her arms connected to bags of liquid beside both sides of her bed. There were two men sitting in chairs next to the window, in low conversation. One was Adam. The other was her father—oh yes, she believed him now, perhaps even understood a bit—and he'd called her his darling girl. She blinked several times. He didn't fade back into her mind. He remained exactly where he was. She saw him very clearly now, and she could do nothing but stare, breathe him in, settle his face, his features, his expressions, into her mind. He used his hands while he spoke to Adam, just like she did when she was trying to make a point, to convince someone to come around to her way of thinking. He was her father.

She cleared her throat and said, "I know I'm not dead because I would kill for some water. And I don't believe that if someone is dead, she's particularly thirsty. May I please have some water?"

Adam was on his feet in an instant. When he bent the straw into her mouth, she closed her eyes in bliss. She drank nearly the entire glass. She was panting when she finished. "Oh goodness, that was delicious."

He didn't straighten, just placed one large hand on either side of her face on that hard hospital pillow. He was studying her face, her eyes. "You okay?"

"Yes. I realize I'm not dead, so you must be real. I remember you told me that he threw me out of the car. Is there anything bad wrong with me?"

"No, nothing bad. When he shoved you out of the car yesterday right there at Police Plaza, you were still wearing your nightgown. You got a lot of scrapes, a bruised elbow, but that's it. Now it's just a matter of getting the drug out of your system. They pumped your stomach. Nobody seems to know what the drug was, but it was potent. You should be just about clear of it now." He had to close his eyes a moment. He'd never been so afraid in his life, never. But she would live. She would be fine. He said, "Do the scrapes hurt? Would you like a couple of aspirin?"

"No, I'm all right." She licked her lips, looked over into the shadows, clutched his hand, and whispered, "Adam, he really is my father, isn't he? That story he told me, it's the truth? It happened that way?"

"Yes, all of it is true. His name is Thomas Matlock. He never died, Becca. There is probably a whole lot more to tell you—"

"Yes," Thomas said, "a lot more. So many stories to tell you about your mother, Becca."

"My mom said I had dreamy eyes. You do, too. I have your eyes."

Thomas smiled and his eyes twinkled. "Yes, I guess maybe you do have my eyes."

Adam said, stroking his chin, "I'm not sure about that. The thing is, Becca, I've never before looked at his eyes in quite the same way I look at yours."

Suddenly, all her attention was on Adam. She said, "Why not?"

"Because—" Adam stopped dead in his tracks. She was actually coming on to him, teasing him. He loved it. He cleared his throat. "Now's not the time. We'll talk about that later, you can count on it. Now, are you up to telling us about this guy who took you?"

"You mean Krimakov."

"Yes."

"Just a moment, Adam. Sir, you sent Adam to protect me, didn't you?"

"Yes, he did, but I screwed up, big-time."

Becca said, "Sorry, Adam, but you can't take all the credit. What that monster did was very clever. None of us would have ever guessed that he came back to the house while we were out looking for him. How'd he get me out of the house without being seen?"

"Sherlock figured that one out really fast. Also he knocked out Chuck and tied him up. That's how he escaped with you." He saw the worry in her eyes and quickly added, "He's okay—just a headache for a while. I'm sorry, Becca, so sorry. Did he hurt you?" God, it hurt to say it, but he did: "Did he rape you?"

"No. He licked my face. I told him not to do it again because it was creepy. That made him really mad, but you see, that drug he shot into me, it also calmed me, made me all loose, so when I woke up that first time I wasn't afraid of him. I don't think I was afraid of anything. It was a side effect of the drug, he said, and he didn't like it. He wanted me to be real afraid, he wanted me to beg and plead, just like Linda Cartwright did." She shuddered as she said the name. "He said she didn't matter. She was just his present to me."

"Did he tell you his name?"

She shook her head. She said to her father, "I can't even describe him. He never let me see him. When he had me tied down to a bed, he always stood in the shadows, just beyond what I could make out. I don't think he was old, but I can't be one hundred percent certain. Was he young? I just don't know. But when he cursed, he used a mixture, some American, some British, and some in a language I didn't recognize. Isn't that strange?"

"Yes, but we'll figure it out."

Thomas was standing beside her bed, opposite Adam. He was wearing a dark suit, the dark-red tie loosened. He looked tired and worried and, oddly enough, happy. Because of her? Evidently so, and that pleased her very much. He picked up her left hand and held it. His hand was strong, lightly tanned. He was wearing a wedding ring. She stared at that ring, just stared and stared, touched her fingers to it, then said finally, "My mother gave you that ring?"

"Yes, when we got married. I wore it all our married lives. I plan to wear it until it finally dissolves off my finger sometime in the distant future. I loved your mother very much, Becca. Like I said, I had to leave both of you so you wouldn't be killed. I know it's all still very confusing. There are lots of facts and details, but the bottom line is exactly what I already told you. I accidentally killed a man's wife and he swore he would kill my family, and then he would kill me, but only after I saw, firsthand, how he had killed everyone I loved. I had no choice. I had to leave my family in order to protect them."

Adam said, "We believe this man who is stalking you, who murdered that old bag lady, who shot the governor, we believe it's Krimakov and somehow he found you and began terrorizing you." He paused for a moment, nodding to Thomas.

Thomas was looking down at this lovely young woman who was his only child. It took him a moment before he said, "Vasili Krimakov was one of the KGB's top agents back in the seventies, as I was for the CIA. Again, there's a whole lot more, but it can wait for a while. Right now, what's important is that we find him, that we neutralize him once and for all."

"You're sure it's Krimakov."

He smiled then. "Oh yes, I'm very sure, particularly after what he told you."

" 'Say hello to your daddy.' "

"Yes. No one else would know that."

"My mom wore a ring just like yours. When she died—" She couldn't speak, the tears clogged her throat, burned her eyes. He said nothing at all, just held her hand, squeezed it a bit more tightly. She swallowed, looked away from him toward the window. It was black out there, no sign of stars from her vantage point. "—I wanted desperately to have something to connect me to her and I almost took that ring, but then I remembered how much she loved you, and I just couldn't take it from her.

"Sometimes when she spoke to me of you, she would start

crying and I hated you for leaving us, for leaving her, for dying. I remember when I was a teenager I told her she should get married again, that I would be going off to college, and she needed to put you in the past. She needed to find someone else. She was so young and beautiful, I didn't want her to be alone. I remember she'd only smile at me and say she was just fine." Then, suddenly, Becca said, "Oh God, he came after me so he could get to you."

"Yes," Adam said. "That's exactly right. But he didn't know where Thomas was, so he came up with a way to flush Thomas out. He dumped you right in front of One Police Plaza."

"What I don't understand," Thomas said, "is why he didn't simply announce all over the media that he had her, threaten to kill her if I didn't show myself in Times Square. He must have known that I would be there. But he didn't."

Adam said, "Who knows? Maybe a cop saw him, saw an unconscious woman in the backseat, and he was forced to dump Becca in order to escape. However, it's far more likely that he planned this down to the exact spot he'd leave her. I think it's gamesmanship. He wants to prove he's better than you, smarter than all of us, and he wants you to suffer big-time in the process."

"He's succeeded admirably," Thomas said. "He has flushed me out. I guess maybe that's why he didn't let you see him, Becca. He wants to keep playing this insane game. He wants to terrorize you and now he can continue the terror, with me squarely in the game with you."

"And only he knows the rules," Becca said.

"Yes," Adam said. "I wonder if he's been living on Crete all this time."

"Probably so," Thomas said.

"Wait," Becca said, chewing on her bottom lip. "Now I recognize those curses—they were Greek."

"That settles that," Thomas said. "We've got all the proof we need that the ashes in that urn in the Greek morgue aren't Krimakov's."

He leaned down and kissed Becca's forehead. "I won't leave you again. Now we'll find Krimakov, and then you and I have a lot of catching up to do."

"I'd like that," she said. Then she smiled over at Adam, but she didn't say anything.

Chapter 21

*D*etective Letitia Gordon and Detective Hector Morales of the NYPD looked over at the woman who lay in that skinny hospital bed, looking pale and wrung-out, IV lines running obscenely into her arms, her eyes shiny with tears.

Detective Gordon cleared her throat and said to the room at large, "Excuse me," and flashed her badge, as did Hector Morales, "but we need to speak to Ms. Matlock. The doctor said it was all right. Everyone out."

Thomas straightened and looked at them, assessing them, quickly, easily, and smiled even as he walked forward, blocking their view of his daughter. "I'm her father, Thomas Matlock, detectives. Now, what can I do for you?"

"We need to speak to her now, Mr. Matlock," Letitia Gordon said, "before the Feds get here and try to big-foot us."

"I am the Feds, Detective Gordon," Thomas said.

"Damn. Er, a pleasure to meet you, sir." Detective Gordon cleared her throat. "It's important, sir. There was a murder committed here in New York, on our turf. It's our case, not yours, and your daughter is involved." Why had she said all that? Because he was a big federal cheese, and that's why she'd tried to excuse herself, tried to justify herself. What was he going to do?

Detective Morales smiled and shook Thomas's outstretched hand. "Hector Morales, Mr. Matlock. And this is Detective Gordon. We didn't realize she had any relatives other than her mother."

"Yes, she does, detectives," Thomas said. "There's still some drug in her system, so she's not really completely back yet, but if you would like to speak to her for a couple of minutes, that probably wouldn't hurt. But you need to keep it low-key. I don't want her upset."

"Look, sir," Detective Gordon said, pumping herself up, knowing that she should be the one giving the orders here, not this man, this stranger who was with the government. "Ms. Matlock ran away. Everyone was looking for her. She is wanted as a material witness in the shooting of Governor Bledsoe of New York."

Thomas Matlock merely arched a very patrician brow at her and looked intimidatingly forbearing. "Fancy that," he said mildly. "I can't imagine why she would ever want to leave New York what with all the protection you offered her."

"Now see here, sir," Detective Gordon said, and tried to shake off Hector Morales's hand on her arm, but he didn't let go, and she looked yet again into that man's face, and she shut up. There were words bubbling inside her, but she wasn't about to say them. He was a Big Feeb, and she saw the power in his eyes, something that flashed red warning lights to her brain, an ineffable something that shouted power, more power than she could imagine, and so she kept her mouth shut.

"There is a lot we do not understand, Mr. Matlock," Detective Morales said, his voice stiff, with a slight accent. "May we please speak to your daughter? Ask her a few questions? She does look very ill. We won't take long."

The thing of it was, Letitia Gordon thought as she walked to the bed where the young woman lay staring at her with dread, her dyed hair tangled and dirty about her face, she wanted to stand very straight in front of that man, perhaps salute and then do exactly what he told her to do. And here was Hector, acting so deferential, like this guy was the president or, more important, the police commissioner. Whatever he was, this man wore power like a second skin.

"Ms. Matlock, in case you don't remember, I'm Detective Gordon and this is Detective Morales."

"I remember both of you very clearly," Becca said, and concentrated on clearing the sheen of tears out of her eyes. These people couldn't hurt her now, Adam and her father wouldn't let them. And she wouldn't, either. She'd been through enough now that a couple of hard-assed cops couldn't intimidate her.

"Good," Detective Gordon said, then she caught herself looking over at Mr. Matlock, as if for approval of her approach. She cleared her throat. "Your father said we could ask you a couple of questions."

"All right."

"Why did you run, Ms. Matlock?"

"After my mother died and I'd buried her, there was no reason for me to stay. He found me at the hotel where I was hiding, and I knew he would get me. None of you believed me, and so I didn't think I had a choice. I ran."

"Look, Ms. Matlock," Detective Gordon said, coming closer, "we still aren't certain there was a man after you, calling you, threatening you."

Adam said mildly, knowing until he and Thomas had discussed it, Krimakov's probable identity would remain under wraps to the NYPD, "Then who do you think kicked her out of a moving car at One Police Plaza? A damned ghost?"

"Maybe it was her accomplice," Detective Gordon said, whirling on Adam, "you know, the guy who shot Governor Bledsoe."

Becca didn't say anything. Thomas saw she was pulling away, even though she hadn't moved a finger, trying to draw into herself. She looked unutterably tired.

"Also," Detective Gordon added, not looking at Mr. Matlock, "our psychiatrist reported that he believed you have big problems, Ms. Matlock, lots of unresolved issues."

Adam raised an eyebrow. "Unresolved issues? I love shrink talk, Detective. Do tell us what that means."

"He believes that she was obsessed with Governor Bledsoe, that she had to have his attention, and that was why she made up these stories about this guy calling her and stalking her, threatening to kill the governor if she didn't stop sleeping with him."

Adam laughed. He actually laughed. "Jesus," he said. "That's amazing."

"I'm sure that old woman who was blown up in front of the Metropolitan Museum didn't think it was funny," Detective Gordon said, her jaw out, not ready to give an inch.

"Let me get this straight," Adam said mildly. "You now think she blew up that old woman to get the governor's attention?"

"I told you the truth," Becca said, cutting in before Letitia Gordon could blast Adam. "I told you that he phoned me and told me to look out my window, which happens to face the park and the museum. He killed that poor old woman, and you didn't do anything about it."

"Of course we did," Detective Morales said, his voice soothing and low. "It's just that there were a lot of conflicting stories coming in."

"Yes," Becca said. "Like the ones Dick McCallum told the cops in Albany that made all of you disbelieve me. This guy probably paid off Dick McCallum to lie about me, and then he murdered him, too. I don't understand why it isn't clear to you now."

Detective Gordon said, "Because you ran, Ms. Matlock. You wouldn't come in and speak to us, you just called Detective Morales from wherever you were hiding. You're at the center of all this. You, only you. Tell us what's going on, Ms. Matlock."

"I believe that's enough for the time being," Thomas said, and calmly moved to stand between the two New York detectives and his daughter. "I am very disappointed in both of you. Neither of you is listening. You are not using your brains. Now, let's get this perfectly clear: Since you're having difficulties logically integrating all the facts, I want you to focus on catching the man who kidnapped my daughter and shoved her out of his car right in front of cop headquarters. I trust you people have been trying to find witnesses? Questioning them? Trying to get some sort of composite on this guy?"

"Yes, sir, of course," Detective Morales said. As for Detective Gordon, she wanted to tell him to go hire his damned daughter a fancy lawyer, that Dick McCallum had been murdered, that she could have had something to do with that, too, maybe revenge, since McCallum had blown the whistle on her. She opened her mouth, all worked up, but Thomas Matlock said quietly, "Actually, detectives, I am a director with the CIA. I am now terminating this conversation. You may leave."

Both detectives were out of there in under five seconds, Detective Gordon leading the way, Morales on her heels, looking both apologetic and scared.

Becca just shook her head, back and forth, back and forth. "They didn't even want to know anything about him. Don't they have to believe me now that Dick McCallum was murdered, too?"

"One would think," Adam said, his eyes narrowed, still looking at the now-empty doorway. "New York's finest aren't shining in this particular instance. Now, not to worry, Becca."

"I think Detective Gordon needs to be pulled off this case," Thomas said. "For whatever reason, she made up her mind about you early on and is now refusing to be objective. I'll make a call."

"I want to leave this place, Adam. I want to go far away, forever."

"I'm sorry, Becca, but there's not going to be any forever yet," Thomas said. "Krimakov got what he wanted. I'm out in the open now. The problem is that you still are, too. Now I'm going to make that call." Thomas walked out of the hospital room, his head down, deep in thought, as he pulled out his cell phone.

The Feds arrived forty-five minutes later.

The first man into the room came to a fast stop and stared. He cleared his throat. He straightened his dark blue tie. He looked as if he wished his wing tips were shinier. "Mr. Matlock, sir, we didn't know you were involved, we had no idea, didn't know she was related to you—"

"No, of course you didn't, Mr. Hawley. Do come in, gentlemen, and meet my daughter."

He leaned over her and lightly touched his fingertips to her cheek. "Becca, here are two guys who want to talk to you, not batter you like the NYPD detectives, just talk a bit. You tell them when you're tired and don't want to talk anymore, okay?"

"Yes," she said, her voice so thin Adam swore she was fading away right before his eyes. If he hadn't been worried sick, Adam would have enjoyed watching Thomas turn his power onto the FBI guys, but he didn't. Now Adam wondered how Thomas knew Tellie Hawley, a longtime FBI guy who had a reputation for eating crooks for breakfast. He never cut anyone any slack. He was sometimes very scary, sometimes a rogue, admired by his contemporaries and occasionally distressing to his superiors.

"Hey, Adam," Hawley said. "I guess I'll find out soon enough why you're here. Where's Savich?"

"He and Sherlock will be in a bit later." Adam nodded then to Scratch Cobb, a tough-looking little man who wore elevator shoes that brought him up to Adam's chin. He got his nickname years before, when it was said that he scratched and scratched until he found the answers in a high-profile case. "Scratch, good to see you again. How's tricks?"

"Tricks is good, Adam. How's it going, my boy?"

"I'm surviving." Adam took Becca's hand and lightly squeezed it. He leaned close and whispered in her ear, "The guy standing to the left has hemorrhoids. The big one with the mean eyes, Hawley, will want to cross the line, but he doesn't dare try it, not with your dad here. Actually, he has five dogs and they rule his house. Now, go get 'em, tiger."

If she were a tiger, she thought, she was a very pathetic one, not worthy of the name, but still— She smiled, she actually smiled. "Hello, gentlemen," she said, and her voice wasn't as paper-thin now. "You wanted to speak to me?"

"Yes," Hawley said, stepping forward. Adam didn't move, just smiled a feral smile at him that could make a person's teeth fall out.

"Adam, I'm not going to bite her. I'm a good guy. I work for the U-nited States government. You don't have to stand guard."

"I'm supposed to be protecting the lady, Tellie. The thing is, I screwed up, and the bad guy got her, drugged her, and dumped her right in front of One Police Plaza."

Hawley nodded, then said, "Okay, so you're not going to budge." Hawley continued smoothly, coming one step closer, watching Adam from the corner of his eye. "This guy who kid-napped you and drugged you and put you out of his car, who is he?"

"I don't know, Mr. Hawley. If I did, I would have announced it to the world via CNN. You know that I reported his stalking me, calling me, threatening to kill the governor. It started in Albany and he followed me to New York. Then he killed that old woman in front of the Metropolitan Museum."

"Yes," Tellie Hawley said, and he shifted from his left foot to his right. "But what we want to know is who this guy is, why he tried to kill the governor. We need to know why and how you're involved in all this—"

Adam said very quietly, "The governor was shot, just like the guy threatened to do, and then the aide to Governor Bledsoe turned out to be the one who told the cops that Becca was an obsessed liar. He was murdered. Did you know that, Tellie? Did you know that the guy who killed him ran him down in a car he'd stolen in Ithaca, after he'd murdered the owner? Did you know that the cops have impounded that car with its dark-tinted windows so no one would be able to identify him when he ran down Dick McCallum? Hey, do you and your fed techs realize that you can go crawl all over it right now?"

"Yeah, okay, we know all that."

"Then why are you pretending it didn't happen?"

"We're not pretending it didn't happen," Hawley said, his hands fisted, anger creeping up over his shirt collar to redden his neck. "But there's no damned reason for him to have picked Ms. Matlock out of the blue, that he targeted someone as unlikely as she is. It only makes sense that she must know something, that she must be aware of his identity, have some idea who he is and why he's doing this. This is big, bad stuff, Adam, and she's slap-dab in the middle of it. I hear there's all sorts of doings in the CIA, but I can't find out what's going on. I've heard that it involves this case, but no one will tell me anything, even my bosses. Let me tell you that it burns my ass to be kept on the outside. Now back off, Adam, or I'll burn your ass before they get mine."

Thomas stepped up. "I wanted to avoid this but now I don't see a choice. I believe it's time for official talks. You people haven't been let in on what's going on here, and it's time."

Thomas raised his hand when all of the men would speak at once. "No more hotdogging, Adam. Mr. Hawley, if you like, you and Mr. Cobb here can come to Washington. We're going to be meeting with the director of the FBI and the director of the CIA, that is, if I can manage to get the two of them in the same room without bloodshed. I'll have to pick a meeting place where neither of them will get his nose out of joint."

Hawley gaped at him. "Both the CIA and the FBI? But why? I don't understand, Mr. Matlock."

"You will," Thomas said. "Now, go make arrangements to come to Washington, if your bosses want you to stay involved."

"We're New York FBI, Mr. Matlock," said Tellie Hawley. "Of course we'll stay involved. We're the primary players. I've heard that there's some really, really deep shit going down and Cobb and I want to be part of it."

"Just call the director's office in a while and find out when and where."

After the FBI guys had left, champing at the bit to find out what was going down, Thomas closed the hospital door and turned to Becca. "No way will they be allowed to come to Washington, but at least we got rid of them for a while. Now it's time to play with both the big boys, not just Gaylan Woodhouse. I'm hoping he'll see reason and get Bushman at the FBI to work on it. Everyone needs to know what's going on now."

"First thing," Adam said, "is for Savich to find that apartment Krimakov rented. Then we send our own people over to Crete and take the place apart."

"Agreed," Thomas said. "Let's do it. Now, Becca, Tommy the Pipe, Chuck, and Dave will all be here to protect you until we get back."

"No," Becca said, coming up on her elbows. "I'm coming with you."

"You can barely walk," Adam said. "Lie back and calm down. No way our people will let him get near you again."

"No more orders, Adam. Now, sir, there's no way you're going to face this alone." Becca calmly pulled the IV lines from her arms. She pushed back the hospital sheets and swung her legs over the side of the bed. "Give me another drink of water, ask Sherlock to buy me some clothes, and we're out of here. An hour. That's all I need."

"I think," Thomas said slowly, stroking his long fingers over his chin, "that there is perhaps a bit too much of me in you."

Becca grinned at him. "That's what Mom told me, many times."

"Then I'd best clear your leaving town with our local cops," Thomas said, and wanted to pat her cheek, but didn't because she wasn't a little girl anymore and she barely knew him. The thought of that made him clear his throat.

Washington, D.C.

The Eagle Has Landed

There weren't any leaks. None of them could believe it. Their short flight to Washington, then the drive to Georgetown to a small restaurant called The Eagle Has Landed didn't raise any curious eyebrows. There wasn't a single TV van in front of the restaurant, not a single reporter from *The Washington Post*.

"I don't believe it," Thomas said as he ushered Becca into the foyer of the small British pub. "No flashbulbs."

"Glory be," said Adam.

Andrew Bushman, appointed director of the FBI six months previously after the unexpected retirement of the former director, stood tall even with his rounded shoulders, his gray hair tonsured like a medieval monk's, and beautifully suited, when Thomas walked to the small circular table at the back of the restaurant. Bushman raised an eyebrow. "Mr. Matlock, I presume? You have pulled me away from some very important matters. I came because Gaylan Woodhouse asked me to, told me it had to do with the attempted assassination of the governor of New York. My people are directly involved in this. I will be interested to hear how the CIA could possibly be involved, what they could possibly know that's pertinent."

Gaylan Woodhouse eased around the back of a shoji screen. He was a slight man of sixty-three who had come up through the ranks of the CIA and had been known in the old days as the best spy in the world because no one—absolutely no one—ever noticed him, and still he was paranoid, staying in the shadows until there was no choice but to come out. He had been the director of the CIA for four years now. Thank God, Thomas thought, Gaylan had a long memory and a flexible mind.

"Thank you," Thomas said and shook first the FBI hand and then the CIA hand. "Now, this is my daughter, Becca, who is very closely tied to this matter, and my associate, Adam Carruthers. Gaylan, thank you for putting in a good word for me with Mr. Bushman."

Gaylan Woodhouse merely shrugged. "I know you, Thomas. If

you say something is critical, then it's critical. I hope by that you think it's time to bring the FBI up to speed on this thing."

"Yes, it's time," Thomas said.

The two directors eyed each other and managed affable smiles and civil greetings. Andrew Bushman cleared his throat. "Mr. Hawley and Mr. Cobb won't be joining us today, but I suspect you knew they wouldn't. I will have any information needed by them sent to New York when and if it's appropriate. Now, I need a martini. Then we can nail this thing down."

Becca would have killed for a glass of wine, but she was taking medications that didn't allow it. She would even have accepted Adam's beer. She suffered through approximately four and a half minutes of small talk. Then Gaylan Woodhouse said, "What have you got that's definitive on Krimakov, Thomas?"

Mr. Bushman's eyebrow shot up. "Does this have to do with the attempted assassination of the governor?"

"Indeed it does," Gaylan said. "Thomas?"

Thomas launched into the story of a CIA agent, namely himself, who was playing cat and mouse with a Russian agent in the mid-1970s and accidentally killed that agent's wife. And that Russian agent had promised that he would get revenge, that he would kill both Thomas and his family. As Thomas spoke, Becca thought about what her life, her mother's life would have been like if her father hadn't been in that godforsaken place, trying to get the best of a Russian agent named Vasili Krimakov. "Of course, Gaylan knows all of this already. The reason the FBI needs to be involved is because we are trying to prove whether or not Krimakov is still alive and thus was the one who tried to assassinate the governor of New York. Actually, now we're very certain that it's him."

FBI Director Bushman was lounged back in his seat, holding the nearly empty martini glass in his hand. "But this guy is after you. Why would he shoot the governor of New York? I'm not getting something here. Oh my God, Matlock—you're the Rebecca Matlock, the young woman who escaped the police and went into hiding?"

"Yes, sir, I am."

Andrew Bushman sat forward, his drink forgotten. "All right, Thomas, tell me everything, even stuff that Gaylan doesn't know. I need to have a leg up on him somewhere."

"Krimakov wanted to flush me out. Somehow he found out that I have a daughter—Becca. We don't know how he found out about her, but it appears that he did and he came after her. That's why he's been terrorizing her, that's why he kicked her out of his car in front of One Police Plaza in New York."

"To get you out in the open."

"Yes, that's it exactly. It's not so complicated when you cut right to the chase. He wants to kill me and he wants to kill my daughter. All the rest is window dressing, it's drama, giving him the spotlight, showing the world how brilliant he is, how he's the one in control here." And Thomas thought, *He can't kill Allison because she's dead already, and I wasn't there with her.*

It was Adam who ended things, saying, "So that's it, gentlemen. We found out that Krimakov was cremated, thus leaving doubt that it was indeed he who was killed. However, the man who kidnapped Ms. Matlock whispered in her ear before he shot a drug into her—"

Becca interrupted. " 'Say hello to your daddy.' "

"So now there's simply no doubt," Thomas said. "The man cremated wasn't Krimakov."

Gaylan said, "We've been spending hundreds of hours on this because there was the possibility that it could be Vasili Krimakov. Now that we know it's him, you need to stick your oar in, Andrew. Get all those talented people of yours involved in finding this maniac."

"I've got a man trying to track down an apartment we understand Krimakov owns somewhere in Crete, in addition to his house. When we find it, we want agents to go over it."

Gaylan nodded. "As soon as we know, I've got a woman in Athens who can fly down and check it out for us. She's good. She's also got contacts among the local Greek cops. She won't get any problems from them."

"It's Dillon Savich who's finding the apartment," Thomas said.

Andrew Bushman raised an eyebrow. "Why am I not surprised? Savich is one of the best. I gather you're telling me now so that I can cool down before I bust his balls?"

"That's right," Thomas said. "I knew Savich's father, Buck. I asked the son for help. He and Sherlock have been in the thick of things."

Andrew Bushman sighed and took the last sip of his martini. "All right. Now, I've got lots of stuff to do, meetings to hold, people to assign to get this off and running. What about the NYPD?"

Thomas said, "Hell, why not tell the world? Have Hawley in New York interface with the local cops."

Bushman said, "Hawley is good, very good. He's tough and he deals well with the locals. Talk about bigfoot. He's a Mack truck when he needs to be. All right, gentlemen, we now tell the world."

"Well, then—" Gaylan Woodhouse broke off as his stomach growled. "We forgot to order lunch. I want a hamburger, lots of red meat, something my wife, bless her heart, doesn't allow."

Andrew said even as he was reading the menu, "I want everything to clear through the FBI before it goes to the media. We want our spin on things."

"For sure," Becca said.

Chapter 22

*T*he black government car moved smoothly onto the Beltway. It was still too early for rush-hour traffic to gnarl things to the screaming point. It didn't help, though, that the temperature was hovering at about ninety degrees. Inside the big car it was thankfully very cool. Their driver had said nothing at all since picking them up at The Eagle Has Landed. There was still no sign of the media. So far so good, Thomas had said. There would be a media release soon now.

Adam was humming as he flipped off his cell phone. "Thomas, the photo you asked Gaylan Woodhouse to dig out for you is coming over right away. He's sorry that he couldn't immediately put his finger on it."

Thomas turned from studying his daughter's profile to look at Adam. "I'm glad they finally located it. I was afraid I would have to use an artist and re-create him."

Adam said to Becca, "It's a photo of Krimakov from over twenty years ago. We'll age it and both can go to the media to plaster everywhere."

"Sir," Becca said, "are you really a CIA director?"

"That's not my title. I just used it because it would be familiar to the New York detectives. Actually, I run an adjunct agency that's connected to the CIA. We do many of the same things we did during the Cold War. I'm based here now, though, and don't travel much abroad anymore to the hot spots."

"This photo of Krimakov," Becca said after nodding to her father, "I want to see it, study it. Maybe I'll see something that could help. Did he speak English, sir?"

If Thomas noticed that she hadn't called him Father or Dad, he didn't let on. He had, after all, been a dead memory that had suddenly come alive and was now in her face. He'd also brought terror into her life. He also hadn't been around when her mother was dying, when her mother died. She'd been alone to handle all of it. The pain was sharp and so bitter he thought he'd choke on it. Soon he would tell her how he and her mother had e-mailed each other every day for years. Instead, he managed to say, "Yes, he did. He was quite fluent, educated in England. He even attended Oxford. Quite the *bon vivant* in his younger days." He paused a moment, then added, "How he despised us, the self-indulgent children of the West. That's what he called us. I always enjoyed locking horns with him, outwitting him, at least until that last time when he brought his wife with him to Belarus. The fool was using her as cover—picnics, hikes, pretending it was a vacation, when all the time he planned to kill the West German industrialist Reinhold Kemper."

"Krimakov," she said, as if saying his name aloud would help her remember more clearly, picture him standing in the shadows, "he had a very light sort of English accent, more so on some words than on others. He was fluent in English. I don't think he sounded particularly old, but I just can't be certain. Krimakov is your age?"

"A bit older, perhaps five years."

"I wish I could say for certain that he was that old but I just can't. I'm sorry."

Thomas sighed. "I've always thought it unfair that nothing's easy in this life. He's had years to plan this, years to think through every move, every countermove. He knows me, probably now he knows me better than I knew him back then. When he finally found you—my child—then he was in business."

"I wonder where he is," Becca said. "Do you truly believe he's still in New York?"

"Oh yes," Adam said, no doubt at all in his voice. "He's in New York, planning how he's going to get to you in the hospital. He's licking his chops, absolutely certain that you'll be there with her, Thomas. He's got to believe that he's trapped you now. He's flushed you out and now he's got his best chance to kill both of you."

"It was an excellent idea, Adam," Thomas said, "to let everyone in the media believe that Becca is still at NYU Hospital, recovering from internal injuries and under close guard. I pray he disguises himself and tries to get in."

"I have no doubt he'll want to. I just hope he doesn't smell a trap. He's smart, Thomas, you know that. He might have figured we'd do exactly what we have, in fact, done."

"I'm worried about the people at the hospital who are playing us," Becca said. "He's—" She paused a moment, trying to find the right words. "He's not normal. There's something very scary about him."

"Don't be worried about the agents," Adam said. "They're professionals to their toes. They're trained, and their collective experience probably exceeds the age of the world. They know what they're doing. They'll be ready for him to make a move. Another smart thing done—the FBI has installed security cameras to record everyone who goes in and out of that room. They've scheduled doctors and nurses to go in there at given hours. Our guys will stay alert. Our undercover agent who's playing you, Becca, Ms. Marlane, won't take any chances if he does show up. She's got a 9mm Sig Sauer under her pillow."

Thomas said, "Then there'll be that black government car

pulling up and a guy who looks remarkably like me getting out and going into the hospital."

Adam said, "Yep. Twice a day. I hope Krimakov does try to get in. Wouldn't that be something if it all ended there, in the hospital, in New York? That would be a hell of a thing."

Becca said, "He managed to down Chuck with no one the wiser. So far he hasn't failed at anything he's tried."

"She's right, Adam," Thomas said. "Like I said, Vasili is smart; he improvises well. If there aren't any leaks, it's possible he'll sniff out the trap. But even if he's fooled into thinking she's there, perhaps believing that I'm there with her, under guard, for just twenty-four hours, it'll give us time to try to come up with some sort of strategy."

Adam nodded and said, "If he doesn't go down in New York, then he'll go down here." He sighed. "Strategy is all well and good, Thomas, but I can't think of anything at the moment that isn't already being done."

Thomas said, "I keep wondering if the agents playing our parts should be told that it's a former KGB agent who might come there. Maybe it would make them sharper."

"No, knowing that a killer is coming is all they need," Adam said. "Besides, they'll know who they're dealing with quick enough. I believe that Krimakov will make a move real soon now. Maybe he'll even make a mistake." Adam looked at Becca, whose hands were fisted in her lap. She was too pale and he didn't like it, but there was nothing he could do about it.

She said, more to herself than to either of them, "If they don't get him, then how do you come up with a strategy to catch a shadow?"

Thirty minutes later, their driver pulled up in front of a white two-story colonial house, set back from the street on a gently sloping grass-covered yard, right in the middle of Bricker Road in the heart of Chevy Chase. It looked like many of its neighbors in this upper-middle-class neighborhood, lots of surrounding land, lots of oak and elm trees, and beautifully landscaped lawns.

"Your house, sir. No one followed us."

"Thank you, Mr. Simms. You took excellent evasive action."

"Yes, sir."

Thomas turned to Becca, who was staring out the car window. He took her hand. "I've lived here for many years. Adam probably told you no one knows about this house. It's a closely guarded secret to protect me. Given Krimakov's actions, he hasn't discovered this house. Don't worry. We'll be safe here." Thomas looked over at the oak tree just to the side of the house. He and Allison had planted it sixteen years before. It was now twenty feet taller than the house, its branches full and laden with green leaves.

"It's lovely," Becca said. "I hope it does all end in New York. I don't ever want him to find out where you live. I don't want him to hurt this house."

"No, I would prefer that he didn't, either," Thomas said. He gently took her hand to help her out of the car.

"Mom and I always lived in an apartment or condo," she said, walking beside her father up the redbrick steps to the wide front porch. "She never wanted a house. I know there was enough money, but she'd always just shake her head."

"When your mother and I were able to meet, she usually came here. This was her house, Becca. You'll see her touch everywhere, and I'm sure you'll recognize it as hers."

His voice was low, so filled with pain, with regret, that Adam turned away to focus on the rosebushes that were blooming wildly beside the brick stairs up to the front porch. He saw two agents in a car half a block down the street. He wondered if Thomas would tell his daughter that this house might look like just a home-sweet-home, but the security in and around the place was state-of-the-art.

"It'll be dark in about three hours," Adam said, looking up from his watch. "Let's make our phone calls, talk to the guys in New York, get the status on everything, make sure they stay alert. I have this gut feeling that Krimakov is going to try to get into NYU Hospital soon. Now we can tell them exactly who they're up against. As you said, Thomas, there are always leaks. Detective Gordon, for example. I can see her telling everyone in sight. If he doesn't act in the next twenty-four hours, then he won't, because he'll know it's a trap."

Adam looked down at Becca, who was staring intently at the house. He knew she was trying to visualize her mother there, perhaps standing next to her father, smiling at him, laughing. Only she wasn't there, had never been a part of the two of them. He said, "Get rid of that ridiculous hair dye, will you, Becca?"

Thomas turned at his words. "That's right. Your hair is very blond, just like your mother's."

"Mom's was more blond than mine," she said. "But all right, Adam, but I'll have to go to the store. Who wants to go with me?"

"Me and about three other guys," Adam said. The look on her face had changed, lightened, and he was pleased.

At seven o'clock that evening, Savich and Sherlock, Tommy the Pipe, and Hatch arrived at Thomas's house for pizza and strategy, pizza first. Adam doubted there would be much helpful strategy, but it was good to have everyone together. Who knew what ideas might pop out after hot, cheese-dripping pizza?

Savich was carrying a baby draped over his right shoulder. The kid was wearing only diapers and a little white T-shirt. Adam looked at Savich, checked out the baby's feet, and said, "You're this little guy's father?"

"Don't act so surprised, Adam." He lightly rubbed his hand over his son's back. "Hey, Sean, you still awake enough to punch this guy in his pretty face?"

The baby sucked his fingers furiously and poked out his butt, making Savich grin.

"He's nearly down for the count," Sherlock said, lightly touching the baby's head, covered with his father's black hair. "He sucks his fingers when he doesn't want to be disturbed and he knows you're talking about him."

"What do you think, Adam? Six-ounce free weights for my boy?"

Adam stared at the big man holding his kid who was madly sucking his fingers, then threw his head back and laughed. "This is not good. Jesus, I can nearly see him lifting three envelopes in each hand." And he laughed and laughed. "Maybe he can even handle a stamp on each envelope."

There were ten pizzas spread around Thomas Matlock's living room an hour later. Hatch was hovering over the large pepperoni pizza, his shaved head glittering beneath a halogen floor lamp, talking even as he stuffed a big bite into his mouth. "Yipes, this sucker's really hot. Oh boy, delicious. But hot, real hot."

"I hope you burned your tongue," Adam said as he pulled the hot cheese free of a slice of pizza from another box that was closer to him than to anyone else, and reverently lifted it up. "Serves you right for being a pig. God, I love artichokes and olives."

"Nah, my tongue isn't burned. It's just a bit of a sting," Hatch said, and pulled up another piece. After he took another big bite, he said, "Now, just to make sure everyone's on the same page. All federal agencies are up to date on Krimakov. The New York Bureau guys are going over the car the guy dumped you out of, Becca, with every high-tech scan, every piece of sophisticated equipment they have. Haven't found anything yet. I was really hoping they would find something, but this guy Krimakov is careful, real anal, one of the techs said. He didn't leave anything helpful. Rollo and Dave, who just left Riptide yesterday, sent the FBI all the fingerprints we got in Linda Cartwright's house, all the fibers we bagged. No word yet. The woman he killed in Ithaca, and stole her car—they've combed the hills for witnesses but came up empty. All that boils down to nada, nothing, zippo." And then he cursed in some language Becca didn't recognize. She lifted her eyebrow at him. Hatch said, flushing a bit, "That was just a bit of Latvian. A nice set of words, full-bodied and pungent, covers a lot of the hind end of a horse and what one could do with it."

There was laughter, lots of it, and it felt so good that Becca just looked around at all the people she hadn't even known existed until very recently. People who were friends now. People who would probably remain friends for the rest of her life. She looked over at the baby lying in his carryall, sound asleep, a light-blue blanket tucked over him. He was the image of his father except for his mother's blue, blue eyes.

She looked at Thomas Matlock, who was also looking at the baby and smiling. Her father, who hadn't eaten much pizza because, she knew, he was so worried. About her.

My father.

It still felt so very strange. He was real, he was her father, and her brain recognized and accepted it, but it was still too new to accept all the way to the deepest part of her that had no memories, no knowledge of him, nothing tangible, just a couple of photos taken when he and her mother were young, some when they were even younger than she was now, and stories her mother had told her, many, many stories. The stories were secondhand memories, she realized now. Her mother had given them to her, again and again, hoping that she would remember them and, through them, love the father she'd believed was dead.

Her father, alive, always alive, and her mother hadn't told her. Just stories, stupid stories. Her mother had memories, scores of them, and she had stories. *But she kept quiet to protect me*, Becca thought, but the sense of betrayal, the fury of it, roiled deep inside her. They could have told her when she was eighteen or when she was twenty-one. How about when she was twenty-five? Wasn't that adult enough for them? She was an adult, a real live independent adult, for God's sake, and yet they'd never said a thing, and now it was too late. Her mother was dead. Her mother had died without telling her a thing. She could have told her before she fell into that coma. She would never see them together now. She wanted to kill both of them.

She remembered many of those times when her mother had left her for maybe three, four days at a time. Three or four times a year she'd stayed with one of her mother's very good friends and her three children. She'd enjoyed those visits so much she'd never really ever wondered where her mother went, just accepting that it was some sort of business trip or an obligation to a friend, or whatever.

She sighed. She still wanted to kill both of them. She wished they were both here so she could hug them and never let them go.

Savich said, "I've got the latest on Krimakov. A CIA operative told me about this computer system in Athens that's pretty top-secret and that maybe MAX could get into. Well, MAX did invite himself to visit the computer system in Athens that keeps data on the whereabouts and business pursuits of all noncitizens residing in Greece. It is top-secret because it also has lists of all Greek agents who are acting clandestinely throughout the world.

"Now, as you can imagine, this includes a lot of rather shady characters that they try to keep tabs on. Remember, there was nothing left in Moscow because the KGB purged everything on Krimakov. But they didn't have anything to do with the Greek records. This is what they had on Krimakov. Now, recognize that we've already learned most of this, that it was pretty common knowledge. However, in this context, it leads to very interesting conclusions." Savich pulled three pages from his jacket pocket and read: "Vasili Krimakov has lived in Agios Nikolaos for eighteen years. He married a Cretan woman in 1983. She died in a swimming accident in 1996. She had two children by a former marriage. Her children are dead. The oldest boy, sixteen, was mountain-climbing when he fell off a cliff. A girl, fifteen, ran into a tree on her motorcycle. They had one child, a boy, eight years old. He was badly burned in some sort of trash fire and is currently in a special burn rehabilitation facility near Lucerne, Switzerland. He's still not out of the woods, but at least he's alive." Savich looked up at all of them in turn. "We've had reports on some of this, but not all of it presented together. Also, they had drawn conclusions, and that's what was really interesting. I know there was more, probably about their plans to act against Krimakov, but I couldn't find any more. What do you think?"

"You mean you have those programs encoded so well you couldn't get in?" Thomas asked.

"No. I mean that someone who knew what he was doing expunged the records. Only the information I just told you was left, nothing more. The wipe was done recently, just a little over six months ago."

"How the hell do you know that?" Adam said. "I thought it

would be like fingerprints. They'd be there but there was no clue when they were made."

"Nope. I don't know how the Greeks got ahold of it, but this system, the Sentech Y-2002, is first-rate, state-of-the-art. What it does is hard-register and bullet-code every deletion made on any data entered and tagged in preselected programs. It's known as the 'catcher,' and it's favored by high-tech industries because it pinpoints when something unexpected and unwelcome is done to relevant data, and who did it and when."

"How does this hard register and bullet code work?" Becca said.

Savich said, "What the system does is swoop in and retrieve all data that the person is trying to delete before it can be deleted. It's funneled through a trapdoor into a disappearing 'secret room.' That means, then, that the data isn't really lost. However, the person who did this was able to do what we call a 'spot burn' on the information he deleted, and so, unfortunately, it's really gone. In other words, there was no opportunity to funnel the deleted data to safety.

"Now, the person who supposedly wiped out the bulk of Krimakov's entries was a middle-level person who would have had no reason to delete anything of this nature, much less even access it. So either someone got to him and paid him to do it or someone stole his password and made him the sacrificial goat in case someone discovered what he had done."

"How long will it take you to find out this person's name, Savich?" Thomas asked.

"Well, MAX already did that. The guy was a thirty-four-year-old computer programmer who was in an accident four months ago. He's dead. Chances are very good that he was set up as the goat. Chances are also good that he knew the person who stole his password. I wouldn't be surprised if the guy talked about what he did to someone who took it to Krimakov, who then acted."

"And just what kind of accident befell this one?" Thomas asked.

"The guy lived in Athens, but he'd gone to Crete on vacation, which is where Krimakov lived. You know the Minoan ruins of Knossos some five miles out of Iráklion? It was reported that he somehow lost his footing and fell headfirst over a low wall into a storage chamber some twelve feet below where he was standing. He broke his neck when his head struck one of the big pots that held olive oil way back when."

"Well, damn," Adam said. "I don't suppose Krimakov's former bosses in Moscow have any information at all on this?"

"Not that MAX can discover," Savich said. "If they have any more, and that's quite possible, they're holding it for a trade, since they know we want everything they've got on Krimakov. You know what I think? They've got nothing else useful. There hasn't been a peep out of them in the way of exploratory questions."

"You found out quite a lot, Savich," Thomas said. "All those accidents. Doesn't seem possible, does it? Or very likely."

"Oh, no," Savich said. "Not possible at all. That was the conclusion their agents drew. Krimakov murdered all of them. Hey, wait a minute, when you knew him, there weren't any computers."

"There wasn't much beyond great big suckers, like the IBM mainframes," Thomas said.

Sherlock said, "I wouldn't even want to try to figure out the odds of all those people in one family dying in accidents. They are astronomical, though."

"Krimakov killed all those people," Becca said, then shook her head. "He must have, but how could he kill his own wife, his two stepchildren? Good grief, he burned his own little boy? No, that would truly make him a monster. What is going on here?"

"He didn't kill his own child," Adam said.

"No, he didn't," Sherlock said. "But the kid won't ever lead any kind of normal life if he survives all the skin grafts and the infections. Was his getting burned an accident?"

Thomas said, "Listen, all of this makes sense, but it's still supposition."

Savich said, "I've put Krimakov's aged photo into the Facial Recognition Algorithm program that's in place now at the Bureau. It matches photos or even drawings to convicted felons. It compares, for example, the length of the nose, its shape, the exact distance between facial bones, the length of the eyes. You get the drift. It'll spit out if there's anyone resembling him who's committed crimes either in Europe or in the United States. The database isn't all that complete yet, but it can't hurt."

"He was a spy," Sherlock said. "Maybe he was a convicted felon, too. It's just possible he's done bad stuff other places and got nabbed. If that's so, then there'll be a match and just maybe there'll be more information available on Krimakov."

"It's a long shot, but what the hell," Adam said. "Good work, you guys." Adam paused a moment, then cleared his throat. "Maybe it wasn't such a lame idea for Thomas to bring you guys on board. Hey, you've even got a cute kid."

The tension eased when they heard Sean sucking his fingers. Sherlock said as she lightly rubbed her son's back, "Hey, Becca, I like your hair back to its natural color."

"I don't think it's quite the right color," Adam said, stroking his fingers thoughtfully over his chin. "It still looks a little fake, a bit on the brassy side."

Becca got him in the belly with her fist, not hard, since he'd eaten at least four slices of pizza covered with olives and artichokes. Of course he was right and she just laughed now. "It will grow out. At least it's not a muddy brown anymore."

Thomas thought she looked beautiful, her hair, just like Allison's, straight and shiny to her shoulders, held back from her face with two gold clips.

Becca cleared her throat and said in a short lull in the conversation, "Does anyone know how Krimakov found me?"

The chewing continued, but she could nearly feel the strength of all that IQ power, all that experience, turned to her question.

Her father took a drink of Pellegrino, then set the bottle down on the Japanese coaster at his elbow. "I can't be certain," he said. "But you're more in the public view now, Becca, what with your speech writing for Governor Bledsoe. I remember several articles about you. Maybe Krimakov read the articles. Naturally he knows the name Matlock very well. He must have checked into it, found out about your mother, seen her travel plans to Washington. He's a very smart man, very focused when he wants to be."

"It makes sense," Sherlock said. "I don't have another more likely scenario."

Sherlock was looking very serious, but one eye was on her small son. Becca remembered Adam saying something about Sherlock taking down an insane psychopath in some sort of maze. It was hard to imagine until she remembered Sherlock clipping Tyler on the jaw with no fuss at all.

"No matter how he finally managed to find out who she was," Adam said, "he did find out and then he set up this elaborate scheme."

"Krimakov was always so straightforward," Thomas said, "back then. No deep, murky games for him." Then he sighed. "People change. It's frightening in this case. He's taken more turns than a byzantine maze."

Hatch, just a bit of mozzarella cheese clinging to his chin, rose and said, "I'm going to go out and see what our guys are doing. They were eating their way through three large pizzas the last time

I saw them." His pepperoni pizza box was empty, not even a cold thread of cheese left.

"If you smoke out there, Hatch, I'll smell it on you and I'll fire your butt. I don't care what you've found out, your butt's on the line here."

"No, Adam, I swear I won't smoke." Then Hatch sighed and sat down again.

Adam, satisfied, turned to Becca. "As for you, Becca, eat. Here's my last piece of pizza. I even left three olives on it. I didn't want to, but I looked at your skinny little neck and restrained myself. Eat."

She took the pizza slice and sat there holding it, even as the cheese cooled and hardened. She picked off an olive.

Savich said, smiling at everyone, perhaps preening a bit, "Oh, yeah, I've got something that's not supposition. MAX found Krimakov's apartment. It's just a small place in Iráklion. Mr. Woodhouse knows about it. He's sent agents in."

Everyone stared at him a moment, gape-mouthed.

Savich laughed. He was still laughing when the phone rang minutes later. "That's on my public line," Thomas said as he rose. "The tape recorder will automatically kick on and it will tell me who's calling." He saw Becca blink and smiled. "Just habit," he said as he picked up the phone.

He didn't say a word, just stood there, listening. He was pale as death when he nodded and said to the person on the other end of the line, "Thank you for calling." Becca jumped to her feet to go to him. He held up a hand and said in a very low, contained voice, "The two agents guarding Becca's room are dead. Agent Marlane is dead. The agent posing as me is dead, shot through the head, three times. I shot Krimakov's wife through the head," he added unemotionally. "The security cameras are smashed. There's pandemonium at the hospital. He got away."

Chapter 23

*A*dam came into Becca's bedroom at just after midnight to see her sitting up in bed, her arms wrapped around her knees, staring blankly at the wall. A single lamp was turned on and in the dim light he could see that she was pale, her face strained. She looked over at him and said, guilt weighing her down, heavy in her voice, "I still can't believe it, Adam. Four people dead and it's because of me."

He quietly closed the bedroom door and leaned back against it, his arms crossed over his chest. Her feelings weren't unexpected but it still made him angry. "Don't be a damned fool, Becca. I'm the one who carries most of the blame because it was my fucking plan in the first place. What no one can figure out is how the bastard managed to walk right up to the guards outside the room, close enough to see the color of their eyes, and shoot them. Of course he used a silencer. Then he waltzed into the hospital room and kills the other two agents before they can react. To top it all off, he shot out the security camera. And poof—he's gone, escaped, and no one can figure it out.

"Jesus, everyone knew he was coming, it was a trap, contingencies all covered, and sure enough he walked right into it, only it didn't stop him. We lost. Whatever his disguise, it must have been something. My God, four people are dead." He snapped his fingers. "Just like that, they're gone. Damn him, how did he do it? What did he look like to make them lower their guard?"

She shook her head numbly. "Tellie Hawley still doesn't know anything?"

Adam shook his head. "They've been studying all the security cameras all over the damned hospital, and they've spotted some men who might be possibles. I told him that didn't make sense. Track down the little old ladies, track the folk on the cameras who no one in their right mind would take for Krimakov." He moved away from the door and walked to the side of her bed. He leaned over and lightly touched his fingers to her cheek. "I came to check on you. I imagined you would be blaming yourself, and I was right. Stop it, Becca, just stop it. It was a good plan, a solid plan. Any fault for its failure comes right to my door, not yours."

She turned her face into the palm of his hand. She whispered against his skin, "He doesn't seem human, does he?"

"Oh, he's human enough. I want him very badly, Becca. I want to kill him with my bare hands."

"So does my father. I've never seen anyone so enraged, and yet his voice remained calm and controlled. But it was so cold, so deadly. I wanted to shriek and yell and put my fist through a wall, but he didn't."

"Control is very important to your father. It's saved his life on several occasions and other people's lives as well. He's learned not to let emotion cloud his thinking." He cupped her face in his hand. "I haven't learned it yet, but I'm trying. A terrible thing happened, Becca, but please believe me, it wasn't your fault. We'll catch him. We have to catch him. We've both got to get some sleep." He kissed her mouth, then immediately straightened. It was hard because he wanted to kiss her again, and not stop. He wanted to ease her back down and pull up that virginal nightgown of hers and get his mouth on every bit of her he could get naked. He wanted to make both of them forget the horror, for just a little while. But he knew he couldn't. He took a step away from the bed. "Good night, Becca. Try to get some sleep, all right?"

She nodded mutely. The pain in her eyes, the god-awful guilt that was still burrowed deep inside her—he just couldn't stand it. He kissed her again, hard and fast, and before he lost his head, he was out of her bedroom in a flash.

In the hallway, he was frowning, wondering how the hell to do that when he was supposed to protect her, rage at Krimakov roiling away in his belly, when he walked straight into Thomas, who was just standing there, watching him, a thick dark brow arched.

Adam came to a dead stop. "Dammit, I didn't touch her."

"No, of course not. I never thought you did. You were in there to ease her guilt, weren't you?"

"Yes, but I doubt I was successful."

"There's enough guilt for all of us to wallow in," Thomas said. "I'm going downstairs for a while. I've got some more thinking to do."

"There isn't any more thinking to do, there's just worrying and second-guessing, all sorts of worthless shit like that. Wait a second—it just occurred to me that he's got to be pissed, rattled. After all, he was expecting to find both you and Becca in that hospital room, but you weren't there. He has to doubt himself now, his judgment, his take on things. He's been meticulous up until now, but this time he wasn't able to be thorough enough. He screwed up big-time. He was wrong. I don't know what he's going to do next, but whatever it is, he might make another mistake. He's also got to contend with the fallout of his cold-blooded murder of four federal agents. They'll mount the biggest manhunt in a decade. He can't believe he's so good he can just walk away from this, that he's somehow immune from capture. We're not alone in this anymore. Everyone and his aunt knows about him and what he is."

"I know that, Adam." Thomas shoved his long fingers through his hair. "You know how quick he is, how clever. Look at how he flushed all of you out of that house in Riptide and then snuck in and hid in Becca's closet. That took balls and cunning. And luck. It is possible that you could have missed Chuck when you were all scouring the area for him, possible that you would have found Chuck tied up and gagged, but you didn't. He was lucky there and he got her.

"I hate to say this, but I firmly believe he'll evade capture. He knows I'll be at the center of things, trying to figure out how to get him. He'll come to Washington. He's going to try to find Becca and me. He's got nothing else to do."

"I still can't figure out why he threw Becca out of his car in New York. He had her. He could have announced it and had you knocking on his door to try to save her. But he let her go. Why? Shit, I'm making myself crazy. But if he's as smart as you say he is, he won't come down here, at least not yet, not until things cool down a bit."

"There's one thing I am sure about now, Adam. I'm his reason for living, probably his only reason now. That's why he's leaving a trail of death. He doesn't care about himself anymore. He just wants me dead. And Becca, too. I'm thinking that Becca should head out to Seattle or maybe even Honolulu."

"Yeah, right. You be the one to convince her of that, okay? She's just found you. You believe for a single second that she'd just pull out now, be willing to say *sayonara* to the father she just met?"

"Probably not." Thomas sighed. "She's still so wary of me. It's like she can't make up her mind whether to hug me or shoot me for leaving her and her mother."

"I'm thinking she wants to do both. At least now you two are together. The rest will come, Thomas, just be patient. For God's sake, she's known you for twenty-four hours."

"You're right, of course. But—never mind. Jesus, Krimakov just went right in there and killed everyone," Thomas said. "Everyone, without hesitation. To flush me out that first time, he released Becca. I can't imagine what he'd do to her now that she's with me. Well, yes I can. He'd kill her with no more remorse than when he killed all the others. And yes, there's no doubt in my mind that he believes she's with me now. Damnation, he had a silencer on the gun, Adam."

"Yes."

"Agent Marlane had six shots pumped into her. He saw that the male agent wasn't me, knew he'd been set up, and went berserk. Dell Carson, the agent playing me, had his gun out, but he didn't have time to fire. Neither did Agent Marlane."

"Yes. I know."

"How the hell did he get away? Hawley had undercover folk stationed all over that floor and the exits."

Adam shook his head. "His disguise must have been something else. Maybe he even dolled himself up as a woman. Who knows? Do you remember if Krimakov did disguises back then?"

Thomas leaned against the corridor wall, his arms crossed over his chest. "No. But it's been so many years, Adam, too many. What troubles me, and I know I can't let it, is that Becca just can't be sure that the guy who took her, the guy on the phone to her, was older." Thomas shook his head. "Another thing. Vasili was fluent in English, but I've read the transcripts of the conversations he had with Becca. It sounds so unlike him. And what he wrote, what he said to her, what he did. Calling himself her boyfriend, murdering Linda Cartwright, then digging her up, smashing her face, all as a sick joke to drive Becca over the edge. That's the behavior of a psychopath, Adam. Krimakov wasn't a psychopath. He was supremely arrogant, but as sane as I was."

"Whatever Krimakov was back then, he's changed," Adam said. "Who knows what's happened to him during the past twenty years? Don't forget all those killings: a second wife, two children, the guy whose password he used to get into the computer system to expunge all his personal data, killing someone to fake his own accidental death in that car accident. How many more we don't know about? And that brings up another question. You said that you believe you're now his only focus, his purpose for living. What about his son? He's in that burn clinic in Switzerland. He doesn't care about him anymore? Or maybe that wasn't an accident, either, and he tried to kill him, too?"

"I don't know."

Adam said, "Hell, maybe he was always over the top and he's just gotten more so, and maybe that goes to explain why he appears not to be worrying about his son. No, Thomas, don't argue with me. He's now here—in a foreign country to him—no longer in Crete. He's on our turf, and he probably hasn't been here for all that long."

"Listen, Adam, we don't know that. Officially, Vasili Krimakov hasn't come into this country in the past fifteen years. He was here once back in the mid-eighties, checking around, trying to sniff me out. That was when he killed that assistant of mine simply because he'd seen her with me and decided that she was my mistress. But I got away that time and he left, returned to Crete. We've learned he went to England a number of times, but he hasn't gone back there recently. Unofficially, he could have bounced in and out of the United States with a dozen different phony passports. Who in Greece would catch on to that? Or if they did, even care?"

"Still, we have to assume that he was in Crete most of the time. For God's sake, he was married. He eventually had a kid with this woman. So he simply can't know his way around here all that well."

Thomas said, "Becca is right. He's a monster, no matter the excuses I make for the man I knew more than twenty years ago. Of course I didn't really know him. He was just a target to me, always on the opposite side, the black king to checkmate. Now we're forced to wait, to gnaw our elbows. Krimakov will find us, count on it.

"Oh yeah, Tellie Hawley and Scratch Cobb are coming tomorrow morning to speak to Becca. Maybe that'll be good. I think she liked them both when she met them in New York. Maybe she'll remember more talking to them. They're pretty desperate, as you can well imagine. Hawley is eating himself alive with guilt. They were his agents, all four of them, and now they're dead."

"Yes," Adam said, and streaked his fingers through his hair, sending it on end. "Since Savich found Krimakov's apartment in Iráklion, our people will go in. Just maybe they'll find something."

Becca leaned her forehead against the closed door, listening to their voices as they moved off down the hall. She turned then and leaned back against the door, her arms crossed over her chest, just as Adam had done when he'd first come into her room. She closed her eyes.

He'd murdered four more people. Like Thomas, she knew Krimakov would find them. It was as if he were somehow programmed to find Thomas and kill him. And her, too, of course. He would do anything, go anywhere, kill anyone in his way, to gain his objective.

How could he have killed his wife and her two children, his stepchildren? And his own son was in a burn hospital in Switzerland. Had that one truly been an accident? No, there were no accidents when it came to Krimakov. It was beyond terrifying.

She returned to her bed, curled up, hugging her arms around her knees. It was warm, very warm, but she was cold all the way to her bone marrow. Suddenly, she heard her mother's voice, sharp with impatience, telling her that if she even considered going out with Tim Hardaway—that juvenile delinquent—she would lock her in a closet for a month. Now she smiled with the memory; then, at sixteen, she had believed her life was over. She wondered what her mother would think of Adam. She smiled, then shivered a bit, remembering that hard, fast kiss. Her mother, she thought, would love Adam.

Suddenly, she heard a whispery sound. She jerked up in bed, her heart pounding, and looked toward the window. Again, that whispery brushing sound. Her heart pumping fast and faster now, she walked over and forced herself to look outside. There was an oak tree there, the end of one leaf-laden branch lightly brushing its leaves over the windowpane.

But he was close, she knew that. On her way back to bed, she kept looking over her shoulder out the bedroom window. She didn't want to speak to any more agents. Oh God, just how close was he?

How close?

Now everyone in the world knew about Krimakov. Adam watched the old photograph of him flash on CNN and all the major networks. Then it was set beside the photograph the CIA artist had aged, showing what Krimakov would probably look like today. It was a fine job. With luck, it matched enough so he could be recognized. Becca hadn't remembered anything more, however, when she'd looked at the photos.

Everyone wanted to interview Becca Matlock, but no one knew where she was.

The New York cops wanted to talk to her, but this time, she didn't have to put up with Letitia Gordon. The FBI had told them to stuff it after the murder of the four FBI agents in NYU Hospital. There was a lot of name-calling, a lot of rancor, but at least she wasn't in the middle of it now. She'd been lost in the shuffle. She was safe.

As for Thomas Matlock, his identity had leaked quickly enough, but at least no one knew where he was, either. If there had been a leak, they knew media vans would be parked in the yard and microphones would be sticking through the windows of the house.

As it was, everything was quiet. The agents posted all around the house and the neighborhood checked in regularly, reporting nothing suspicious.

Ex-KGB agent Vasili Krimakov—who he was exactly, where he was at present, what his motives were, anything and everything that could possibly be tied to him—was discussed fully, exhaustively, on every news show, every talking-head show. Ex–CIA operatives, ex–FBI antiterrorist agents, and three former presidential aides spoke authoritatively about him with Sam Donaldson and Cokie Roberts, Tim Russert, and William Safire. The question was: Why did he want Thomas Matlock so badly? The question remained unanswered until there was some sort of anonymous release from Berlin about how Thomas Matlock had saved Kemper's life and in the process accidentally killed the wife of the Soviet agent, Vasili Krimakov, who'd been sent to present-day Belarus to assassinate Kemper. The press went wild. Larry King interviewed a former aide to President Carter who remembered perfectly and in great detail the incident when CIA Operative Thomas Matlock had a face-off with Krimakov in the faraway land, killed his wife by accident, and the resulting brouhaha with the Russians. No one else could seem to recall any of it, including President Carter himself, and everyone knew that President Carter remembered everything, including the number of rubber bands in his Oval Office desk drawer.

An ex–United States Marine who had served with Thomas Matlock back in the seventies spoke authoritatively about how Thomas had refused to be intimidated by the enemy. Which enemy? Didn't matter, Thomas would go to hell and back before he'd ever break. This wasn't at all relevant, but nobody really cared. The bottom line was that all the folk interviewed were ex- or former somethings. The current FBI and CIA directors had put a seal on everything. The president and his staff weren't saying a word, at least officially. Everything was working as it had always worked. Speculation was rife, theories were rampant, but nothing could be proved.

As for Rebecca Matlock, the governor of New York was quoted as saying, "She was an excellent speech writer with a flair for humor and irony. We miss her." And then he'd rubbed his neck where Krimakov had shot him.

NYPD continued with their "No comment" when there was any question from the press about her. There was no more talk about her being an accomplice to the shooting of Governor Bledsoe. Thank God, Becca thought, that no one had found out about Letitia Gordon. She'd bet Detective Gordon would be glad to trash-talk her.

Every murder Krimakov had committed was brought out and examined publicly and exhaustively. There was public outrage.

But no one knew where Rebecca Matlock was.

No one knew where or really who Thomas Matlock was, but the world was coming to believe that he was a dashing, quite romantic James Bond sort of guy who had kept the world safe from the Russians and was now being hunted by a former KGB agent who didn't hesitate to murder people to draw him out.

Becca wondered aloud later to Adam about what the United States Marine had said about Thomas on TV. Adam, who was cleaning his Delta Elite at the kitchen table, said, "It means that this ass got paid maybe five hundred bucks to say something so the ratings would spike."

"The guy said Thomas would never break. What does that mean?"

Adam shrugged. "Who cares? I just hope that Krimakov is watching. Talk about misdirection. Maybe he'll come to believe that Thomas is invincible." Adam snorted, then buffed the handle of his pistol. "We couldn't do it better if we scripted it ourselves."

"I wonder if Detective Gordon still thinks I'm somehow responsible for all of it."

"I think once she makes up her mind, it'd take an avalanche to change it. Yeah, she still thinks you're a big part of it. I spoke to Detective Morales. I could see him shaking his head over the phone. He's depressed, but glad you're safe now."

"It was the murder of Linda Cartwright that got everybody going."

"Yes. She was an innocent. A very nice middle-class woman. Everyone wants him to fry for what he did to her. Don't forget that older woman in Ithaca. Another innocent. Krimakov has a lot to answer for."

"Does anyone know yet how Dick McCallum was involved with him?"

"Yeah. Hatch found out that McCallum's mother had an extra fifty thousand bucks in a checking account."

"That doesn't seem like so much money if you have to die to get it. Did she tell the police or Hatch if Dick told her anything?"

Adam shook his head, lifted his gun, looked at a face that needed a shave in the reflection of the barrel. "Nope. She was upset about it, but he wouldn't tell her anything, except to keep the money quiet, which she did until Hatch tracked her down and got her to talk."

"The FBI are coming soon."

"Yeah. Don't worry, both Thomas and I will be there."

She smiled at him. "That's nice, Adam, but unnecessary. I'm not a child or helpless, you know. And I do know Mr. Cobb, and poor Mr. Hawley, who's got hemorrhoids."

He grinned up at her. "Nope, it's Cobb with the hemorrhoids. Now, you were helpless, don't try to rewrite the past, and I don't care what you say, I'll be there."

"I should probably go dig out my Coonan and buff it."

"I'd just as soon never see that pistol anywhere near you again."

"Scared you but good, didn't I?"

Thomas appeared in the kitchen doorway, frowning. "This is odd, but a man named Tyler McBride called Gaylan Woodhouse's office with the message that you, Becca, were to call him immediately. Nothing more, just that instruction."

"I don't understand," Becca said, "but of course I'll call him. What's going on?"

Adam was on his feet in an instant. "I don't like this. Why the hell would McBride call the director of the CIA?"

"I'll find out, Adam. He's probably really worried and wants to make sure I'm okay."

Adam said, "I don't want you to call Tyler McBride. I don't want him anywhere near you. I'll call him, find out what the hell he wants. If he wants reassurance, I'll give it to him."

"Look, Adam, you told me he was really scared for me. He just wants to hear my voice. I'm not going to tell him where I am. Now, I'm calling him. Let it go."

"Why don't you two stop bickering?" Thomas said. "Call the man, Becca. If something's wrong, Adam, she'll tell us."

"I still don't like it. Another thing: I've been thinking that maybe you would be safer at my house. At least you could stay there some of the time."

Her left eyebrow went up. "Where do you live, Mr. Carruthers?"

"About three miles down the road."

She stared at him. "Then why are you staying here? Why aren't you going home at all?"

"I'm needed here," he said, studiously rubbing the barrel of his Delta Elite to an even higher shine. "Besides, I do go home. Where do you think I get clean clothes?"

"Get over it, Adam," she said, and went to get her small address book.

"Use my private line," Thomas said. "It's untraceable. Adam, your gun looks good."

"You'll like my house," Adam called after her. "It's a showcase, it's the prettiest place you've ever seen. Plants don't like me, but everything else does. I have a housekeeper come in twice a week and she even makes me casseroles."

Becca turned to face him. "What kind?"

"Tuna, ham and sweet potato, whatever. Do you like casseroles?"

"You bet," she said.

He heard her laugh as she walked away.

He wanted to hear what she said to Tyler McBride, he really did, but he didn't move. Neither did Thomas, who stood there leaning against the refrigerator, his arms crossed over his chest.

"I'm giving her privacy," Adam said. "It's tough."

"Yeah, and you want her to think about your house, don't you?"

"It's a very nice house—an old Georgian brick two-story, lovely yard that I pay a big chunk to keep looking good. Remember I told you how my mom talked me into buying the property some four years before, told me it was a good investment. She was right."

Thomas said, "Parents usually are."

Adam grunted and looked at his reflection in the gun barrel. "McBride wants her, that's why he's called. He wants her to know that he's still laying claim. Damn, I don't trust him, Thomas. He'll use Sam if he has to. He can't have her."

Thomas said, grinning now, "I can see your scowl on your face in the barrel of the gun. No, more than a scowl."

Adam grunted. "How about seriously pissed off?"

What the hell was she saying to Tyler McBride? Worse, what was he saying to her?

Chapter 24

In her father's study, the door closed, Becca was leaning on the big mahogany desk, so pale, so off balance that she felt transparent. She knew that if she looked in a mirror, she wouldn't see anything at all. "No, Tyler," she said again. "I can't believe this."

"No, Becca, it's happened. Sam is gone. Gone from his bed when I looked in on him this morning. There was this note pinned to his blanket that said I had to call you, that I could get to you by calling the office of the CIA director. So I did. And now you've called."

"No, Sam can't be gone," Becca said, but she knew that he was, she just knew it.

"He wrote in the note that I wasn't to say a word to anyone, not the local cops, not anyone, just you. He wrote that he'd kill Sam if I said anything."

She heard his breathing hitch before he said, "Thank God you called, Becca. Jesus, what am I going to do?"

Becca heard the awful deadening fear in his voice, the anger, the helplessness.

"Don't call Sheriff Gaffney, Tyler. Don't. Let me think."

He nearly yelled, "Of course I won't call Sheriff Gaffney. Do you think I'm nuts?" Then he added, more calmly now, "He wrote that you had to come to Riptide."

Oh, God, she thought, and said, "Just a second, Tyler, let me get Adam."

"No!" She nearly dropped the phone he'd yelled so loud. Then she heard him draw a deep breath. "No, Becca, please, not yet. He says if you tell anyone—including your father—he'll kill Sam. Dammit, I didn't even know you had a father until the media went nuts over you and him. Jesus, Becca, the guy's just murdered four more people. He's got Sam. Do you hear me? That maniac's got Sam!"

"I know, I know. Read me the entire note, Tyler."

"Oh God, all right." He was breathing hard, and she knew he was trying to get control. Finally, his voice more steady, he read: "'Mr. McBride, you will speak as soon as possible to Rebecca Matlock. To find her, call the office of the director of the CIA. Tell them to inform her that she is to call you immediately, that a life is at stake. Then you will tell her to come to Riptide. You will tell her not to tell anyone, including her father, or else your son is dead. You don't want him to end up like Linda Cartwright. You have twenty-four hours.'"

"How did he sign it?"

"He didn't sign any name at all. Just what I read to you, that's it. Oh God, Becca, what am I to do? You know what he did to Linda Cartwright, what he's done to all those other people. Look at what he did to you. All of Maine is up in arms about Cartwright's murder." He waited a beat, then yelled, "Aren't you listening to me? A fucking Russian agent has got my son!"

"I wonder why he doesn't want my father to come? It's my father he's after. It just doesn't make any sense."

"I've listened to everything on the news," Tyler said, calmer now. "It doesn't make any sense to me, either. Please, Becca, you've got to come. If you hadn't called me, I don't know what I'd have done."

"If I come, he'll hold me to get my father. Then he'll kill both of us." She didn't add that he would also kill Sam. Why wouldn't he? She was afraid that Sam was already dead, but she wasn't about to say it aloud. Just the thought nearly brought her to her knees. Not Sam, not that precious little boy. No, she couldn't fall apart. Think. There had to be something she could do.

"Oh shit, I know he'd try to kill both of you. Yes, I know that. What are we going to do?"

"I don't know, Tyler."

"Please don't tell that Adam character or your father, please."

"All right. Not yet, anyway. If I do decide to tell them, I'll call you first, warn you. I'll get back to you in three hours, Tyler. Oh God, I'm so sorry. It's all my fault. I should never have come to Riptide. The man's crazy, obsessed."

He didn't disagree with her, on any of it. "Three hours, Becca. Please, you've got to come. Maybe you and I together can trap him. Somehow."

When Adam came into Thomas's study five minutes later, he saw her standing at the front window, staring out over the fine green lawn. She was rubbing the bridge of her nose with her fingers, her shoulders slumped. She looked defeated, beaten down. He frowned.

"What's going on? Why did McBride have to speak to you?"

She shrugged. "It was just as you thought. He was worried about me, very worried, what with all the stuff on TV."

"I don't believe that's all, is it?"

Then she turned slowly to face him. "Of course it is. The FBI people have just pulled up." The car was black, the two men were wearing black, their hair was cut short. And Krimakov had taken Sam. He moved fast, too fast, faster than any of them could have imagined. What to do?

"What's wrong, Becca? You look white around the gills."

"Not a thing, Adam. It's Agent Hawley and Agent Cobb. Let's see what they have to say. I suppose they're sworn to secrecy about where they've come from?"

Adam said as he walked toward the front door, "They would be drawn and quartered if they ever opened their mouths."

Adam shook the two men's hands and stepped back. Tellie Hawley said, "It's good to see you again, Adam. Mr. Matlock, Ms. Matlock. Bet you're wondering how we got ourselves assigned to this."

"It did cross my mind," Thomas said, as he waved them toward the living room.

"Boy, it's hot out there," Scratch Cobb said, gave Becca a big smile, and unbuttoned his black suit coat one button. "A very nice house," Scratch added to Thomas as he walked beside him into the living room. He was looking at a particularly lovely old Tabriz carpet.

"Thank you, Agent Cobb," Thomas said. "Won't you be seated?"

After everyone was settled, Agent Hawley said, "Since we were the ones who initially spoke to Ms. Matlock in the hospital, and since I knew you, sir, Mr. Bushman decided we should stay on as the leads. Of course Savich and Sherlock are on it as well, and he approves of that. It doesn't mean, of course, that the folk here at FBI headquarters are sitting on their hands. They're not."

Thomas nodded. "No, they never do. I'm very sorry about the agents Krimakov murdered in New York, Hawley. It's got to be an awful blow."

Tellie Hawley turned pale, then just as suddenly he flushed red with anger. "The bastard killed four more people in cold blood. He just waltzed into the hospital—God knows how he was disguised—and he killed the two agents guarding her room, then went inside and put six shots in Agent Marlane and three more shots in Del's head. How did he get away? We don't know. Damnation, it's driving everyone nuts. His aged photo is plastered everywhere. We've got dozens of agents walking around a mile radius of NYU Hospital showing everyone his photo. Nothing yet." He stopped and Becca could feel the pain, the guilt, the rage, radiating from him, spilling out in waves. He'd been the one in charge, the one giving orders. She wouldn't want to be in his shoes. She felt guilty enough in her own shoes.

Sam. Oh God, Sam. What to do?

She watched Tellie Hawley get himself together. He cleared his throat, looked directly at her, and said, "Now, Ms. Matlock, we're here to speak to you in detail about your time with him."

"I'm very sorry, Agent Hawley, but I've told you everything I know. I wish there were more but I just can't come up with anything else, even irrelevant."

Agent Hawley sat forward in his chair, his hands dangling between his legs. "The mind is a marvelous instrument, Ms. Matlock. It takes in stuff you're not even aware of. We're betting you do know more about Krimakov. You just don't remember it on a conscious level. We're hoping it's lurking in your subconscious. Ah, Agent Cobb here is an expert hypnotist. He'd like to take you under, really get at what this guy was like, maybe even what he looked like. You know, stuff you've blocked out or you're not even aware that you know, stuff you just can't bring up to a conscious level."

Agent Cobb handed her the old photo of Krimakov. "You've seen this?"

"Yes, of course. My father showed it to me immediately, the aged photo as well. I've studied and studied it. I'm sorry, but I just don't know if it's him. I never saw him. He was always in the shadows."

"Look again at the aged photo."

She took it, studied it yet again. She still saw an older man, whose face was lean and deeply tanned from years of living on the

Mediterranean. His hair had receded, leaving two deep slashes of tanned scalp on either side of a spear of gray hair. His eyes were dark, his features Slavic, wide, flat cheekbones. He looked like he could be a very nice grandfather. And she wondered: Is that you? Are you the one who took me from Jacob Marley's house? Did you lick my cheek? She handed Agent Cobb back the photo. "I have thought and thought. I really don't consciously remember anything more. I'm willing to go under."

"Are you sure, Becca? You don't have to."

She glanced toward her father, who was standing behind a chair, looking at her intently. She didn't know that very handsome man with all those expressions on his face that she didn't understand, but then, she realized that she did know him; on a very deep level, she knew him quite well. It was a very strange feeling. "Yes, sir"— her voice was steady—"I'm sure."

"All right, then," Agent Cobb said, looking directly at her. "There's nothing to be concerned about. I don't go for the couch thing. I prefer the traditional face-to-face method.

"Now, there are also many different ways to hypnotize someone. I use the fixation object method." He pulled a shiny pocket watch out of his vest pocket. For a moment he looked embarrassed, then shrugged. "It belonged to my grandfather. I've always worn it, just discovered a couple of years ago that it was the perfect object for me to use to relax people. Now, I want you to sit back and look at this watch, Becca. Just listen to the sound of my voice." He started talking, nonsense really, his voice low and smooth and never rising, never falling, always the same. She stared at the watch that was swinging gently back and forth, back and forth. "You will find that your eyelids have a tendency to get heavy," he said in that singsong soft voice. "That's right, just look at the watch. See how it's moving so slowly right before your eyes?"

Agent Cobb continued reciting a familiar litany to everyone in the room. His voice stayed low and smooth and very intimate. That damned watch kept swinging back and forth, shiny, gold, swinging. Adam had to shake his head and look away. He was getting drawn under.

Five minutes later, Becca was still staring at the shiny gold pocket watch, listening to Agent Cobb's voice telling her about how her eyes were going to close now, how she felt good, and comfortable, how she could just let herself drift. But she didn't. She tried desperately to relax, to get with the program, but she couldn't. All she could see was Sam, that sweet little boy, holding out his arms to her, smiling but hardly ever saying anything. Krimakov had him. He would kill him, kill him without hesitation, without a qualm of regret, if she didn't do something. An innocent child, it didn't matter to him, any more than Linda Cartwright had mattered. She had to—

Agent Cobb knew it wasn't working, but he kept swinging the watch as he said calmly, in an easy, deep voice, "You were sound asleep, right, Becca, the night he took you?"

"Yes, I was," she said, her voice slow, mimicking his. "I remember knowing that I wasn't dreaming, a very good thing. Then I felt this prick in my arm and I jerked awake. It was him."

"But you couldn't make out his features? Could you make out anything? Surmise anything from the way he was standing, the way he held his arms? His body?"

She shook her head. "No, I'm sorry."

"You're not going under, Becca." Scratch sighed. He lowered the beautiful gold watch, slipping it easily back into his vest pocket. "I don't know why it's not working. Usually someone very intelligent, very creative, like you are, goes under right away. But you didn't."

285

She knew why. She couldn't tell him, couldn't tell anyone.

He said in that same easy voice, hitting it right on target, "Something's holding you back. Perhaps you know what it is?" When she didn't say anything, he looked over at Thomas Matlock. "No go. For whatever reason."

Tellie Hawley nodded. "Okay, then, we ask questions and you answer as best you can."

She nodded and talked. And there wasn't anything at all new or earth-shattering. Except—

"Adam, did anyone find anything in the hem of my nightgown?"

He shook his head.

"Then he must have found it," she said. "He let me go to the bathroom. I knew I had to do something. I managed to unscrew one of those enamel bolts that hold the toilet to the floor. I pulled open the hem in my nightgown and worked it in. He must have found it."

"Yes," said Hawley, "he found it. He left the toilet bolt in the room, on Agent Marlane's bed. The techs found it and I read it on the collected evidence sheet—'one toilet bolt'—and I just forgot about it in all the chaos. Actually when the techs found it, they thought some nurse's aide had dropped it and they were laughing about it. Well, it wasn't any joke. That proves conclusively it was the same guy." He shook his head. "A toilet bolt, a damned toilet bolt."

"He was taunting us," Thomas said. He got to his feet and began pacing the long living room. "I wish to God I knew where he was. I'd just put an end to it. Face him, just the two of us."

Becca said, her voice overloud, too sharp, "No." And everyone stared at her. "I will not let you face him alone, Father. No way."

They took a break in the kitchen, drinking coffee. Then Thomas took them to his office to see some of his high-tech goodies. Then they went back to the living room. It was then that Agent Cobb said to Becca, "May we try one more time to put you under?"

She agreed. What else could she do?

This time, though, Agent Cobb handed her a small white pill. "It's a Valium, to help relax you, to keep you from focusing on something else that might be holding you back. Nothing more than that. You game?"

She took the Valium.

And ten minutes later, when Agent Cobb said, "Are you completely relaxed now, Becca?" she answered in an easy, light voice, "Yes, I am."

"You're aware of everything going on here?"

"Yes, Adam is over there staring at me as if he'd like to wrap me into a very small package and hide me inside his coat pocket."

"What is your father doing?"

"It's still hard for me to think of him as my father. He was dead for so very long, you know."

"Yes, I know. But he's here now, with you."

"Yes. He's sitting there wondering if he should let you continue with this. He's afraid for me. I don't know why. This can't hurt me."

"No, it can't."

"She's right," Thomas said. "But I'll deal with it. Continue, Agent Cobb."

Agent Cobb smiled and patted her hand. "Now, Becca, let's go back to that night when you awoke to that prick in your arm."

She moaned, then jerked.

"It's all right," Agent Cobb said quickly. "Listen to me now. He's not here. It's okay, you're safe."

"No, it's not okay. He'll kill him. I know he'll kill him. What am I going to do? It's all my fault. He'll kill him!"

Just a slight pause, then Agent Cobb said, "You mean that he'll kill you, Becca? You're afraid that he injected some long-waiting poison in your arm?"

"Oh no. He'll kill him. I've got to do something. Oh God."

"Do you mean he'll kill your father?"

"No, no. It's Sam. He's got Sam." And then she started crying, deep, tearing sobs that jerked her wide awake. "Oh, no," she said, staring at all the appalled faces. "Oh, no."

"It's all right, Becca," Agent Cobb said. "You'll be just fine now."

Thomas said very slowly, "So that's what McBride had to say to you. Krimakov kidnapped Sam and had McBride call the director to find you and have you call him."

"No," she said. "No. I don't know what you're talking about."

Valium, she thought. She'd just killed Sam, just killed her father, God knew who else, all because of one damned Valium.

Adam was on his feet. "Where's your address book? I'm going to call McBride, find out what the hell's going on here."

"No," she said, jumping up to grab his arm. "No, you can't, Adam."

"Why the hell not?"

Chapter 25

*T*he room was dead silent.

"No, you can't have my address book."

"Fine. I'll call information." Adam walked toward the phone. "We've got to know exactly what's going on here."

Becca didn't say another word. She ran out of the living room, grabbed her purse from the table in the entryway, and made for the front door.

"Becca! Dammit, come back here!"

She heard Adam yelling but didn't pay any attention. She heard her father's voice, then Special Agent Cobb's voice. She didn't slow. She was out on the narrow front porch before Adam reached the entryway.

She heard all of them shouting at her, running after her, but she knew she had to get away. No one else was going to die. Not Sam. Not her father. She had to stop it. She didn't know how she was going to do it yet, but she would think of something. She should have thought of something before—maybe even been a bit on the subtle side. Yes, you fool, you should have just calmly left the living room, pretending to go upstairs or go to the bathroom, whatever. But no, she'd lost it—here she was running away with people chasing her, FBI agents everywhere. But that didn't matter, either. She had no choice. If she could prevent it, no one else was going to die. She ran.

There were no sidewalks in this very nice neighborhood, just big lawns, thick curbs, and the road. She hit the road. She was fast, always had been since she was on the track team in high school. She put her head down, turned off all the voices, and ran. She felt the breath pumping in and out of her lungs, felt herself filling with energy, with power, expanding, moving faster, faster. Her feet in Nikes were unbeatable.

She ran right into Sherlock. Both women went down.

Becca was on her feet in an instant. "Sorry, but I've got to go."

"Stop her!"

Sherlock grabbed her ankle and pulled. Becca went down on the edge of a lawn, hitting her hip on the curb. A shaft of sharp pain went through her, but she ignored it. She was ready to fight, ready to do whatever she had to, but Sherlock had somehow managed to straddle her, how she didn't know, but she'd been fast, too fast, and now she was holding her arms down. How could she be so strong when she was so small, hardly anything to her at all? How did she get her in this position so quickly? Sherlock was leaning over her, her curly red hair bouncing against Becca's face. "What's going on here, Becca?"

"Get off me, Sherlock. Please, you've got to let me go. I don't want to hurt you."

"You can't hurt me, so don't even try. Tell me what's happened."

Becca started struggling, but then it just didn't matter, and she stilled because Adam was there, not even panting hard, standing over them, staring down at her, his hands on his hips. "Thanks for bringing her down, Sherlock. That wasn't very smart, Becca."

Sherlock didn't like this one bit. She looked at all the men running to the scene, even the two dark-suited FBI guys who'd been parked discreetly down the street. "What's going on, Adam? Oh yeah, given that I could have hurt Becca dragging her down, I'd really better like the answer." She pulled herself off Becca and slowly got to her feet. She held out her hand.

Becca looked at that slender white hand that was surely too strong, but she didn't move. She just rolled over away from them, grabbed her purse, and was off again. A sharp pain went through her hip but she ignored it.

She got at least ten feet before two arms went around her waist and she was picked up, twirled around, and thrown over a man's shoulder. She hit her chin against his back, damn him. "Hold still," he said, and his voice was calm and quiet. Too calm, too quiet.

Sherlock was one thing. Having a big guy haul her over his shoulder was another. It was humiliating. "Bullshit," she yelled, and jerked and pulled and kicked. "All right," he said, and pulled her down. He brought her back up against him, wrapped his arms around her, and held on tight. No matter what she did, she couldn't get free. He'd pinned her arms to her sides but good.

Three hours, she thought. Time was running out. "Oh God, what time is it?"

"I'll tell you after you promise not to run away again."

She leaned down and bit his hand, hard. He didn't make a single sound, just jerked her around to face him and said, "I'm sorry, Becca," and lightly tapped his fist against her jaw. It was the strangest feeling. It didn't really hurt, but she saw a whole skyful of white lights, popping all over her brain, then it was as if someone switched off the lights. Just nothing. She slumped against him.

"She's a fighter," he said to Sherlock, who was standing beside him as he picked Becca up in his arms. He looked at the back of his hand. At least he wasn't bleeding, but he could see the row of even teeth marks. That had been close, too close. But now he had her, thank God. She was too thin, he thought, as he carried her back.

She didn't weigh enough; well, he'd see to that. He'd force food down her gullet if he had to. He frowned as he realized she was a fast runner, very fast. He wasn't certain if he could have caught her if Sherlock hadn't been there. He didn't like that thought, not one bit. He saw Thomas striding toward him, looking frantic.

"What's going on here, Adam?" Suddenly Sherlock was right in his face, and she wasn't going to move. He couldn't very well clip her on the chin. She'd probably flatten him. Since she was married to Savich, he wouldn't be surprised if she had a black belt, maybe two.

He said, "Krimakov kidnapped Sam McBride. Come on back to the house and we'll let everyone know what's happening. Hell, she promised McBride that she wouldn't tell anyone. However, when Agent Cobb gave her some Valium to relax her so he could hypnotize her, she inadvertently spilled the beans. She did go under. Then it all came out."

"This is insane," said Sherlock. "That maniac kidnapped Sam? Let me get ahold of Savich. I can't believe this. Is that guy everywhere?" She stepped away and pulled the cell phone out of her purse.

The agents who'd been watching the house were now standing next to Thomas and agents Hawley and Cobb.

They parted from his path and Adam carried Becca back into the house, not saying another word. He hoped no neighbors in this lovely neighborhood had seen this bizarre action and called the cops.

"I hope you didn't hurt her," Thomas said, right on his heels.

"She nearly bit my hand off," Adam said.

"Yeah, but you brought her down."

"No, that was Sherlock. I just clamped my arms around her."

"You weren't gentle enough."

"Damn, Thomas, what did you want me to do, lie down and let her stomp on me before she ran another four-minute mile?"

"Yeah, Adam," Agent Hawley said. "She got you good, but it's not bleeding. Good straight teeth. Put her down on the couch."

Thomas covered her with an afghan Allison had given him some seven years before. He didn't realize it was quite hot, since they'd left the front door wide open and all the cold air had seeped out.

"I was careful," Adam said, but he was sitting beside her, lightly touching her jaw where he'd hit her. "She shouldn't even bruise. Listen, Thomas, she was going to run and run until we brought her down. She would have fought me until I might have hurt her by accident. She wasn't thinking."

"Yeah, I guess I understand." Thomas raised his eyes to Hawley and Cobb. "We're in deep trouble now."

Becca moaned and opened her eyes. She lurched up only to have two hands push her back down, and Adam's voice close to her face saying, "If you try anything again, I'm going to lock you in your room. If you bite me again, I'll lock you in your closet and feed you moldy bread and water."

Her hair was hanging in her face, her jaw felt swollen and sore, and she was so mad she wanted to spit. More than that, she was desperate. She was tired of failing. All she'd done since Krimakov had come into her life was fail. She raised her head and looked him squarely in the eye. "That wasn't funny. Go to hell."

"No, I won't do that. What I want to do is help you if you'll just let me."

The three hours were up, she knew it. She had to do something. She had to do something right this minute. But it didn't matter. It was too late. All of them knew now. She said, trying to control her misery, her deadening fear, "I've got to call Tyler. I promised to call him in three hours. If I don't, I don't know what he'll do, probably go to the media. Don't you understand? Krimakov has Sam. He wants me to come to Riptide, doesn't want me to tell you or Dad. Tyler is desperate."

Adam came down on his knees in front of her. "Becca, look at me."

"I was looking at you. You're trying to lighten things up. You can't. You can't help me. Only I can do something here. I don't want to look at you. Just because you're stronger, well, never mind what you are, Sherlock got me first. It doesn't matter. I've got to call Tyler. You can't help."

"All right." He rose and offered her his hand. A big hand, she thought, a strong hand, and she wished she could take it and bite it again, then flip him over the back of the sofa.

"You all right, sweetheart?" Thomas said, handing her a cup of tea.

Sweetheart? He'd called her sweetheart and it seemed to have come out naturally, not a fake endearment. It nearly made her cry. No one had ever called her sweetheart before. Her mom had always called her honey, or when she was a little girl she'd been Muffin.

She didn't let it touch her. She couldn't, not now at any rate. "I've got to call Tyler, tell him that I'm coming right away to Riptide and that none of you are coming with me. Do you understand? Sam dies if anyone comes with me. No, Adam, just shut up. I will not let that little boy die."

"But that doesn't make any sense," Thomas said slowly. "He wants you, that's true, but he wants me more. Why doesn't he want both of us to come to Riptide? The package deal he always wanted? What's he up to now?"

Becca said, "I don't know. I agree that it doesn't make any sense at all, but that's what he wrote in his note to Tyler. He told Tyler how to contact me, and then when I did call, Tyler was to tell me to come to Riptide alone. Not to tell either of you or Sam would die."

"Note?" Sherlock said. "What note?"

"The kidnapping note," Becca said. "Krimakov left it on Sam's bed after he took him. Told him exactly what to do, told him that if I didn't come, he'd kill Sam, just like Linda Cartwright."

"It might not even matter now," Sherlock said, "but if we can get the note, I'll give it to our handwriting experts. Also, they can compare the handwriting to other documents that you have, Thomas, with Krimakov's handwriting on them."

Thomas said, "There are some samples of his handwriting, yes, but what good would it do to analyze it? You're right, it probably doesn't even matter now. We're coming down to the endgame here." Thomas sighed and streaked his fingers through his hair. "I wish to God I knew what kind of gambit Krimakov was playing."

Sherlock said, "I do, too, but since we don't, we have to keep using the tools we've got. If he gives us the time, if he continues with his delaying tactics, and more distractions, I can get the two samples of his handwriting compared. Maybe they could tell us how far over the edge he's gone, or maybe prove that all he's done is cold manipulation and butchery, and he's as sane as you and I. Our people are good, trust me. There's no reason not to do it."

"I've got to talk to Tyler," Becca said, rising, throwing off the afghan. "Reassure him. Tell him what's going on here."

Sherlock said, "At the very least, if there's still time, the analysis and comparison will let us know what we're up against. Trust me on this. Get that note from Tyler, Becca."

"Yes, she will," Thomas said. "Go make your call, Becca."

Becca nodded and walked to the phone, pulling the small address book out of her purse as she walked. She looked up Tyler McBride's number. She dialed.

After three rings, Tyler answered, his voice frantic. "Becca? Is that you?"

"Yes, Tyler."

"Thank God. Where are you? What are you doing? What's happening?"

"Okay, Tyler, just listen to me. Here's the plan. It's the only way to handle this, so don't yell at me. We're all coming up to Riptide, but not together. No, just be quiet and listen. We're all going to trickle in. He'll never know there's anyone else but me in Riptide. I'll come directly to your house, we'll speak, he'll see me, then I'll go to Jacob Marley's house. He'll come for me there. You know it. I know it." She drew a deep breath. "He has no reason to kill Sam. He'll have me, so he can keep his word and release him."

"The others will be hiding in Jacob Marley's house?"

"No, but they'll be close by. It will work, Tyler."

She was aware that all of them were staring at her, but she just shook her head at them. It was the only way to go, and all of them knew it. There'd been no reason to flail about and discuss any number of options into the ground. She had to go and she knew no one would let her go alone. Fine. They had a chance now. "Oh yes, Tyler, I need you to give me Krimakov's note. Sherlock wants it. Now, just go about your business. Don't say a word to anyone. We'll be there in under four hours."

Slowly, she lowered the phone into its cradle. She looked up. "Sam's not going to die."

"No," Adam said, walking to her, "no, he won't." Then he just couldn't stand it. He pulled her against him and held her there, his hand tight across her back, his other hand fisted in her hair. He felt her heart beating against his chest, hard, fast strokes. He brought her closer. He looked up to see Thomas staring at him, and slowly, he loosened his fingers in her hair, smoothing it down, but he didn't want to let her go.

Thomas said, "Agent Hawley and Agent Cobb, this kidnapping

will stay amongst us. It doesn't go to anyone else in the FBI. All right?"

"No problem," said Tellie Hawley. "Hell, we're in this thing to the end. That bastard butchered four of my people. I want him as much as you do. If Savich and Sherlock aren't saying anything to the higher-ups, why should we?"

"Let's get rolling," Sherlock said once Thomas had given her several papers with Krimakov's handwriting. "We'll meet at Reagan in an hour?"

"No," Thomas said. "We'll go over to Andrews Air Force Base. I'll have a plane ready for us."

They were nearly out the door when Thomas's private phone rang. He looked undecided, then said, "Hold on. It's got to be important if it's on that phone."

Slowly, because she didn't really want to, Becca forced herself to pull away from Adam. "I'm all right," she said.

"I'm not," he said, and smiled at her. "We'll get through this."

They all followed Thomas back to his study, watched him pick up the phone on the edge of the mahogany desk.

"Yes? . . . Hello, Gaylan."

It was Gaylan Woodhouse, the CIA director. They all watched Thomas's face stiffen, then slowly turn pale and set. "Oh no," he said, his voice bleak. "You're absolutely certain of all this?"

They watched him lower the phone and stare over at them. He looked shaken, dazed. "This is just too much," he said. "Just too much."

"What the hell is it?" Adam was at Thomas's side in but a moment.

Thomas shook his head, his eyes dazed. There was a fine tremor in his hands. "You're not going to believe this. CIA Agent Elizabeth Pirounakis was blown up when she went into Vasili Krimakov's apartment in Iráklion. Krimakov must have worked there, left notes there, evidence of his plans.

"The whole building blew up. It's now rubble. Agent Pirounakis is dead, the two other Greek agents with her dead as well. Gaylan isn't certain yet, but given the time of the explosion, thankfully very few people were in the apartment building."

"He did this before he left Crete," Agent Hawley said. "It's not something he's just done."

Adam said, "At least now there has to be an inquiry about the guy they buried. Surely now they can't hang on to the fiction that the man in the car accident was Vasili Krimakov?"

Thomas looked at Adam. "It doesn't much matter now. There's hell to pay over there, but that doesn't help us."

"Time," Adam said. "It's what he hasn't given us."

Thomas nodded, then paused another moment and looked over at his daughter. "You're right. Let's go."

She gave him a smile filled with rage and said, "Yes. Lock and load."

Chapter 26

It was hot that day in Maine, even by the water. Lobster boats bobbed up and down in the inlets, fishermen, their hats pushed back on their heads, lay in the shade of the awnings on their boats, if they were lucky enough to have awnings.

The white spires of the Riptide churches shone beneath the bright afternoon sun. There wasn't much movement anywhere. It was just too hot. The tourists weren't wandering around taking photos of the quaint Maine town, they were holed up in air-conditioned pubs.

The hot weather didn't bother the birds. Osprey dove for fish off the spruce-covered points. Gulls squawked and whirled over the lobster boats. The smell of dead fish left too long in the heat sent out odors that meant you had to take shallow breaths to survive. Cumulus clouds in fantastic shapes dotted the steel-blue sky. There was no breeze at all. Still, hot air blanketed the land.

Becca was so scared that all the beauty of the land and ocean, the sound of the birds, the incredible blue of the sky—none of it penetrated her brain. She felt frozen in the near hundred-degree heat.

She'd driven herself in a rented white Toyota from a private airfield near Camden. It had taken her nearly an hour to negotiate the tourist traffic on Highway 1 south to Riptide, just below Rockland. Her hands were clammy, her heart slowly thudding in her chest. She tried to think of all that could go wrong, but her mind just wouldn't slip into gear.

When a mosquito bit her as she was pumping gas, she was pleased that she felt it. She wasn't even aware of being pissed off that the rental agency hadn't filled her car before renting it to her.

When she arrived in Riptide at three o'clock in the afternoon, she drove directly to Tyler's house on Gum Shoe Lane. He was standing in the yard, waiting for her. He was quite alone.

Tyler held her very close, as if she were a lifeline, and so she stood there, his arms locked tightly around her. Finally, she eased back and looked up at him. "Any word at all?"

"Another note from Krimakov."

"Let me see it."

"This is all a huge mess, Becca."

"Yes, I know, and I'm so sorry for it, Tyler. It's all my fault. If I could go back into the past, make the decision not to come here, I swear I would. I'm so sorry. I swear that Sam will be all right. I swear it to you."

He looked at her for a very long time, but he didn't say anything, to either agree or disagree.

"Show me the new note. Then I'll take both of them with me, okay?"

The note was handwritten, big strokes, black ballpoint: *The boy will be all right for another eight hours. If Rebecca isn't here, he's dead.*

She folded both notes, put them in the pocket of her sundress, and left for Jacob Marley's house twenty minutes later. Undoubtedly Krimakov was watching Tyler's house, at least he should be. She would call in another half hour just in case Krimakov hadn't been watching. For sure he'd have a trace on Tyler's phone.

She unlocked the front door of Jacob Marley's house. It was so still and hot inside, so very silent, nothing moving at all, not a single sound, not even a floorboard. She opened all the windows and switched on the overhead fans. The hot air stirred, nothing more, until fresh air began creeping in. The curtains billowed ever so slightly.

So quiet. It was so very quiet in the house. She went into the kitchen and put on water to boil. She'd make iced tea, there were still bags in the cabinet. She opened the refrigerator, saw that it had been cleaned out, and wondered who had done it. Probably Rachel Ryan, she thought. It was a nice thing for her to do. She had to go to the Food Fort. Good, he could see her driving around, know that she was here, know that she was alone. She hoped she wouldn't see Sheriff Gaffney because surely he'd want to talk to her.

When she got into the Toyota, she pulled out the small button on her wristband and said, "I'm heading out to Food Fort now. The cupboard's bare. I'll be back in under an hour. I want to make sure he knows I'm here. I'll leave the notes on the front seat of the car at Food Fort." Then she pushed the button back in.

She was greeted at Food Fort like she was a celebrity. Everyone knew who she was, impossible for them not to now, what with her photo and her story on every news station in the United States. People peered around corners to look at her, even stare at her, but they really didn't want to get close enough to speak to her. She smiled, nothing more, and put stuff in her shopping cart.

When she was checking out, a woman behind her said, "Well, finally I get to see you. Sheriff Gaffney told me all about you, what a pretty girl you are, how there was this big fellow there at Jacob Marley's house who really wasn't your cousin. He didn't buy that one for a minute. You really lied to him, didn't you, and he couldn't do anything about it. But now everyone knows who you are."

"But I don't know who you are, ma'am."

"I'm Mrs. Ella, his chief assistant."

It was the Mrs. Ella who'd kept her from getting hysterical when she'd called the sheriff's office to report the skeleton falling out of the wall in the basement by telling her about all her dogs, every last one of them. Mrs. Ella, who also shopped at Sherry's Lingerie Boutique. She was a big woman, muscular, with a corded neck and a mustache shadowing her upper lip.

"You're a liar, Miss Powell. No, you're Miss Matlock. You made up that name when you came here."

"I had to lie. So nice to speak to you, ma'am."

"Ha, I'll just bet. Why are you back here?"

Becca smiled. "I'm a tourist now, ma'am. I'm going to go out on a lobster boat." And she hefted her two grocery bags and left Food Fort.

"The sheriff will want to speak to you," Mrs. Ella yelled after her. "It's a pity he had to drive to Augusta on O-fficial Business."

She heard Mrs. Ella say behind her, as she was supposed to, "She's back here to do more bad things, you mark my words, Mrs. Peterson. Here she was all nice and hysterical when she found Melissa Katzen's skeleton in her basement wall, but it was all a lie. If the skeleton hadn't been so old, I would have bet she'd done it."

Becca turned slowly in the half-open door, her arms aching with the heavy bags, and said, "Melissa Katzen was murdered, ma'am, and not by me. That isn't a lie. Does anyone know anything yet?"

"No," called out Mrs. Peterson, the cashier, who had bright red dyed hair. "We're not even one hundred percent sure that it is Melissa Katzen. The DNA tests haven't come back yet. It takes weeks, Sheriff Gaffney said."

"No, I'm the one who told you that," Mrs. Ella said. "Sheriff Gaffney doesn't keep track of DNA sorts of stuff, I do. As for you, Ms. Matlock, I'm going to tell the sheriff that you're here again just as soon as I can raise him on his cell phone, which he usually doesn't carry because he hates technology."

When Becca got back to the car, the notes in Krimakov's handwriting were gone. She hoped the sheriff wouldn't get to her anytime soon. She hoped that her little trip to Food Fort wouldn't backfire. Surely Krimakov knew she was here now, surely.

Riptide, she thought as she got into the Toyota, her haven once upon a time, with its Food Fort on Poison Oak Circle and Goose's Hardware on West Hemlock. She drove slowly along Poison Ivy Lane, then turned onto Foxglove Avenue, down two blocks to her street, Belladonna Drive. She turned yet again on Gum Shoe Lane, drove past Tyler's house, then turned back onto Belladonna Drive to Jacob Marley's house. It was getting a bit cooler, thank God, even though the sun was still high in the summer sky. Maine gave you the earliest sunrise and latest sunset.

She was still wearing the light-blue cotton sundress that Sherlock had brought back to New York with her, and she wished she had a sweater. Fear seemed to leach the heat right out of her.

The house was cooler. She made iced tea, put together a tuna salad sandwich, and sat out on the wide veranda, watching night slowly fall. She wondered if anyone would slip into Jacob Marley's house. The wristband was one-way.

Odd, but she didn't think about Krimakov. She thought about Adam, his face now clear in her mind.

He'd snuck up on her, just as, she supposed, she'd snuck up on him. She smiled. He was a good man, sexy as hell, which she wouldn't tell him just yet, and he had a streak of honor a mile wide. Even when she'd bitten his hand and cursed him, wanted to kick him into the dirt, she'd known that honor of his was real and wouldn't ever change to suit the circumstance.

And Adam knew her father a lot better than she did. And he'd never said a word. What did that say about this mile-wide honor of his? She'd have to think about that.

She took the last bite of her sandwich and wadded up the napkin. It was nearly dark now. Surely Krimakov would do something soon. Her Coonan was in the pocket of her sundress. She hadn't told anyone about the gun, but she suspected that Adam knew she had it. He'd kept his mouth shut, a smart move, or else she might have bitten him again.

She hadn't seen a soul, at least not a soul who was here especially for her. It would be soon, she felt it. Krimakov was close. Everyone else was close, too. She wasn't alone in this. And she thought of Sam and of Krimakov's note.

She waited and looked up at the sliver of moon in the dark sky. She prayed that Sheriff Gaffney had decided not to come see her tonight. Finally, she walked into the house, shut and locked the front door. She closed and locked all the windows. She didn't want to go upstairs to the bedroom where he'd hidden in her closet and stuck a needle in her arm.

She was on the stairs when the phone rang. Her fingers clutched at the oak railing so tightly they turned white. The phone rang again. It had to be Krimakov.

It was. She pushed the small button on the wristband and pressed her wrist close to the phone receiver.

"Hello, Rebecca. It's your boyfriend." His voice was playful, filled with crazy fun. It scared her to death. "Hey, I hope I didn't hurt you too badly when I threw you out of the car in New York?" His voice was still mischievous, but now he'd pitched it lower, maybe even put a handkerchief over the mouthpiece. She wondered if her father would recognize his voice after twenty years.

"No, you didn't hurt me too badly, but you already know that, don't you? You killed four people in NYU Hospital to get to me and my father, but we weren't there. You failed, you murdering butcher. Where the hell is Sam? Don't you dare hurt that little boy."

"Why not? He's worth nothing except that he did get you here for me. I'll just bet the CIA director got ahold of you really fast. Now you're here and you're alone, I see. You followed my instructions. Hard to believe they let you come here all by yourself, all unprotected."

"I ran away. I'm waiting for you, you bastard. Come here and bring Sam."

"Now, now, there's no rush, is there?"

He was playing with her, nothing new in that. She drew a deep breath, tried to be calm. "I don't understand why you didn't want my father to come with me. It's him you want to kill, isn't that right?"

"Your father is a very bad man, Rebecca, very bad, indeed. You have no idea what he's done, how many innocent people he's destroyed."

"I know that he shot your wife by accident a long time ago, and that you swore to get revenge. All the rest of it, it's a fabrication of your own crazy mind. I don't think anyone has killed more people than you have. Listen to me, please. Why not just stop it all now? My father was devastated when he accidentally shot your wife. He told me you had brought her with you, faking a vacation when you were really there to assassinate that visiting German industrialist. Why did you use your wife like that?"

"You know nothing about it. Shut up."

"Why won't you tell me? Did you really believe that she wouldn't be in any danger if you took her with you?"

"I told you to shut up, Rebecca. Hearing you talk about that wonderful woman dirties her memory. You're from his seed, and that makes you as filthy as he is."

"All right, fine. I'm filthy. Now, why didn't you want my father to come here with me? Don't you still want to kill him?"

"I will, never fear. How and when I do it is up to me, isn't it, Rebecca? Everything is always up to me."

"What am I doing here alone? Why did you take Sam if you just wanted me to come here to Riptide?"

"It got you here quickly, didn't it? You'll find out everything in time. Your father was smart. He hid you and your mother very well. It took me a very long time to find you two. Actually, it was you I found first, Rebecca. There was an article about you in the Albany newspaper that was picked up in syndication. It talked about you. I saw your name and got interested. I found out about your mother, your supposedly dead father, and then I learned about your mother's travels each year. It was then I knew. Most of her trips were to Washington, D.C."

He laughed. Her skin crawled. "Hey, I'm real sorry about your mother, Rebecca. I had hoped to get to know her really well, but then she had to go so quickly into the hospital. I suppose I could have gotten into Lenox Hill easily enough and killed her, but why not let the cancer do it? More painful that way. At least I hoped it would be. But as it turned out, your mother didn't have a lick of pain, that's what a nice nurse told me. Then she patted my arm in sympathy. She just went away in her mind and stayed there. No pain at all. Even if I had come to her, she wouldn't have known it, so why bother?

"But you're different, Rebecca. I have you now and I will have your father, also. I will kill that bloody murderer." She heard the rage now in his voice, low and bubbling, and it would build and build. She heard his breathing, harsh but more controlled now, and he said finally, "I want you to get in your car and drive to the gym on Night Shade Alley. Do it now, Rebecca. That little boy is depending on you."

"Wait! What do I do when I get there?"

"You'll know what to do. I've missed you. You have a lovely body. I touched you with my hands, ran my tongue all over you. Did you know I left that toilet bolt on that woman's bed at NYU Hospital? It was for you, Rebecca, so that you would know that I was all over you, looking at you, feeling you, rubbing you. You hoped when you unscrewed that bolt that you could smash it in my eye, didn't you?"

She was shaking with fear and rage, each so powerful alone, but mixed together they quaked through her, making her light headed.

"You're an old man," she said. "You're a filthy old man. The thought of you even near me makes me want to vomit."

He laughed, a deep laugh that was terrifying. "I'll see you very soon now, Rebecca. And then I'll have a surprise for you. Never forget, this is my game and you will always play by my rules."

He hung up. She knew in her gut that wherever he was hiding this time, there wouldn't have been any way to trace the call, no matter how sophisticated the equipment. All the others knew it, too.

She depressed the button. They'd heard everything. They knew exactly what she knew now.

She didn't take anything with her, except her Coonan. When she got into the Toyota, she again pressed the small button, then started the car. "I'm leaving for the gym now."

Her precious mother, she thought. She'd escaped him by falling into the coma. He'd been in the hospital, asking about her. It was too much, just too much.

She drove to Klondike's Gym in just over eight minutes. It sat right at the very end of Night Shade Alley, a big concrete parking lot in front, trees crowding in all around the rest of the two-story building. There were windows all across the front, lights filling all of them. There were at least two dozen cars in the big concrete lot.

She'd been here once with Tyler. That had been in the middle of the day. Not nearly the number of cars there then. Perhaps since it was so hot during the day, the Mainers waited until the evening cool to work out. She drove in, picked a place that had no cars near it, turned off the engine, and sat there. Five minutes passed. Nothing. No sign of Krimakov, no sign of anyone at all.

She depressed the button on the wristband. "I don't see him. I don't see anything out of the ordinary. There are lots of people here."

Everyone should be here by now. They were ready. They all wanted Krimakov. They would do absolutely nothing until they had Krimakov. Everyone had agreed on that.

There was nothing to worry about. "I'm going in now." She got out of the car and walked into the gym. There was a bright-faced young man at the counter, looking like he'd just worked out hard. His clothes were sweated through. "Hi," he said, and looked at her.

She wasn't wearing workout clothes.

She smiled. "I was here once before and I rented a locker in the women's locker room. My clothes are there. I need to pick them up."

"I know you. You've been on TV, on every channel."

"Yes. May I please come in now?"

"That'll be ten dollars. What are you doing here?"

She opened her wallet and pulled out a twenty. "I'm here to pick up my workout clothes." He didn't even look up. She watched him for what seemed like forever as he got her a ten in change. He pressed a buzzer and she went through the turnstile.

The room was large, filled with machines and free weights and mirrors. The lights were very bright, nearly blinding. A radio played loud rock, booming out from the overhead speakers. There were lots of young people here tonight, thus the raucous music.

There were at least thirty people throughout the big room. Upstairs were all the aerobic machines. She heard talk, music, groans,
the harsh movement of the machines, nothing else.

What was she to do?

She walked back to the women's locker room. There were three
women inside, in various stages of undress. No one paid her any attention. Nothing there.

She walked out of the dressing room, and this time she walked
slowly, roaming through the big room, looking at all the men.
Many of them were young, but there were some older ones as well,
all of them different one from the other—fat, thin, in shape,
paunchy. So many different sorts of men, all there on this night,
working away. Not one of them approached her.

What to do?

A couple of young guys were horsing around, doing fake hits,
laughing, insulting each other. One of them accidentally backed
into the arm of an old chest machine. The big weighted arms
weren't clicked in to a setting. When the young guy hit it, it swung
out and hit her squarely on her upper right arm. She stumbled into
a big Nautilus machine and lost her balance. She went down.

"Oh shit. I'm sorry. You all right?"

He was helping her up, rubbing her shoulder, her arm, looking
at her now with a young male's natural sexual interest. "Hey, talk to
me. You okay?"

"Yes, I'm fine, don't worry."

"I haven't seen you here before. You new in town?"

"Yes, sort of."

He was lightly touching her arm now, as if assuring himself that
she was okay, and she tried to smile at him, assure him that she was
just fine. The other young man came up on the other side, vying
with the first for her attention.

"Hey, I'm Troy. Would you like to go have a drink with me? I figure I owe you since I knocked you on your butt."

"Or maybe you'd like to go with both of us? I'm Steve."

"No, thank you, guys. I absolve you of all guilt. I have to leave now."

She finally managed to get away from them. She turned once and saw them looking after her, smiling, waving, looking really pleased with themselves now that she'd looked back at them.

Neither of them was more than twenty-five, she thought. Well-built boys. She was twenty-seven. She felt ancient.

Finally, because she couldn't think of anything else to do, she went through the turnstile at the front of the gym. The young guy who'd let her in wasn't there. No one was there. She felt a ripple of alarm. Where had the kid gone? Maybe a shower. Yeah, that was it. He'd really been sweating.

She thought she saw a shadow just outside the front door. It was one of the good guys, she thought, it had to be.

Where was Krimakov? He'd said she'd know what to do. He was wrong.

She walked slowly back to the Toyota. The lights weren't bright in this part of the lot and that was why she'd elected to park here. She hadn't wanted to park close by other cars, hadn't wanted to take the risk of Krimakov hurting anyone else. Now she wished she hadn't because no one seemed to be about.

She reached out her hand to the door handle. Suddenly, without warning, she felt a sharp sting in the back of her left shoulder. She gasped, whirled around, but there was nothing, no one. Just the dim light from the lights overhead. No movement. Nothing. She felt herself slipping. That was odd—she was falling, but slowly, just sort of sliding down against the door of her car.

Chapter 27

*N*o," she said into her wristband. "Nobody move. I'm all right. I don't see him. Don't move. Something struck me in the left shoulder, but I'm okay. Stay where you are until he comes out."

She sat on the concrete, the unforgiving hard roughness against her bare legs. She put her head back, listened to her heart pounding, did nothing, unable to do anything. She wanted to cry out but she didn't, she couldn't, Sam's life was at stake, and if she did cry out, she knew Adam would come running. She couldn't allow that. What had he done to her? What kind of drug had he shot into her back? Had he killed her? Would she die here in the concrete parking lot at the gym?

Now she felt only light pain in her shoulder. She pressed back against the door and felt something sharp dig into her flesh. Something was sticking out of her shoulder. She said quietly, because she didn't know if Krimakov was near, "No, don't move. He shot me with something, and now I can feel some sort of dart sticking out of my back. Don't move. I'm all right. There's still no sign of Krimakov." She reached both arms back and managed to grip the narrow shaft. What was going on here? Slowly, because it seemed the only thing to do, she pulled on the shaft. It slipped right out, sliding easily through her flesh, not deep at all, just barely piercing the skin. She leaned over, suddenly light headed. She believed she would faint but she didn't. "I'm all right. Stay hidden. It's some kind of small dart. Just a moment."

She looked at the shaft she'd pulled out of her shoulder. There was something rolled tightly around it. Paper. She pulled it off, unrolled it. Her fingers were clumsy, slow.

She was still alone, still sitting by her car. No one had come out of the gym.

She managed to make out the black printing on the unrolled piece of paper in the dim light. It was in all caps:

GO HOME. YOU'LL FIND THE BOY.
YOUR BOYFRIEND

"It says that Sam's at home. Nothing more. He signed it 'Your Boyfriend.'"

What was going on here? She didn't understand, and doubted that any of the others did, either. She wanted to drive like a bat out of hell to get back to Jacob Marley's house, to find Sam, but she couldn't, she was too dizzy. Waves of light headedness came over her at odd moments. She drove home slowly, watching for other cars, headlights behind her. But nothing seemed out of the ordinary. She knew they had to stay low. No one wanted to risk Sam's life by showing themselves too soon.

She was clearheaded by the time she reached Jacob Marley's house. She turned off the engine, sat there a minute, staring at the house. Everything was silent. The sliver of moon shone nearly directly overhead now.

There were lights on only downstairs. She remembered she hadn't even gone upstairs, hadn't wanted to, and then the phone had rung.

Had Sam been locked in her closet upstairs all this time where Krimakov had hidden himself waiting for her to get into bed?

She was into the house in under three seconds, racing up the stairs, picturing Sam tied up, stuffed in the back of her closet, perhaps unconscious, perhaps even dead. She yelled at the wristband, "Is everyone still there? Oh God, of course you are! I think you'd better still stay out of sight. I don't know what he's up to. You don't, either. Stay hidden. I'll find Sam if he's here."

She dashed into her bedroom and switched on the light. The room was still, stuffy, closed up for too long. She pulled open the closet door. No Sam. She knew they could hear her footsteps pounding up the stairs, hear her harsh breathing, hear her curse when she didn't find Sam.

She went into every room, opened every closet, searched every bathroom on the second floor.

"No Sam yet. I'm looking."

She called out to him again and again until she was nearly hoarse.

She was in the kitchen, pacing, when she saw the door to the basement. Oh, Jesus, she thought, and pulled it open. She flipped on the single light switch. The naked hundred-watt bulb flickered, then strengthened.

"Sam!"

He was sitting on the concrete floor, propped against a wall, bound hand and foot, a gag in his mouth. His eyes were wide, dilated with terror. How long had the bastard left him sitting in the dark?

"Sam!" She was on her knees next to him, working the gag loose. "It's all right, honey. I'll have you loose in just another second." She got the gag off him. "You okay?"

"Becca?"

A thin little voice, barely there, and she nearly wept. "It's all right," she said again. "Let me get you untied, then we'll go upstairs and I'll make you some hot chocolate and wrap you up in a real warm blanket."

He didn't say anything more, not that she expected him to. She got his ankles and wrists untied and lifted him in her arms. When she got back into the kitchen, she sat down with him and began rubbing the feeling back into his wrists and ankles. "It will be all right now, Sam. Do you hurt anywhere else?"

He shook his head. Then he said, "I was scared, Becca, real scared."

"I know, baby, I know. But you're with me now. I'm not going to let you out of my sight." She carried him into the living room and wrapped him in an afghan. Then she went back to the kitchen, sat him down in a chair, the blanket firmly wrapped around him. "Now some hot chocolate. You hungry, Sam?"

He shook his head. "I want Rachel. My tummy feels weird. She knows what to do."

"Mine would, too, if I'd been through what you have. I'll tell your dad that you want Rachel." While the water heated, she poured the cocoa mix into a cup. Then she held Sam close again, telling him how brave he was, how everything was all right now, how she would call his father. While Sam was drinking the chocolate, Becca, not taking her eyes off him, pulled out her cell phone and called Tyler. "I've got him. He's safe."

"Thank God. Where are you?"

"At home. Krimakov put him in the basement. He's all right, Tyler."

"I'll be right there."

Obviously they'd all heard her but had waited to see if Krimakov was going to show himself. But no longer. Sam was safe. Still, there wasn't a sign of Krimakov. She'd forgotten to tell Tyler to get Rachel.

Adam came through the back door like an avenging angel. Then he saw Sam's white face, saw that the little kid was all wrapped up in a pale-green afghan. He wanted to kill Krimakov with his bare hands.

He slowed down, pinned a big smile on his face. He came down

314

on his haunches beside him. "Hi, Sam. You're the youngest hero I've ever known."

Sam stared at him for a minute, then he smiled, a really big smile. "Really?"

Adam was surprised to hear even that one short word out of him. "Really. The youngest. Boy, am I impressed. Do you think you could tell Becca and me what happened?"

Tyler came running through the front door. He stopped cold when he saw the three of them, but his eyes were on Becca first, then slowly he looked at his son.

He didn't say another word, just scooped up Sam in his arms and sat down with him. He rocked him back and forth. Becca thought the contact was more for Tyler than to comfort his son. Finally, he raised his head and said quietly, "Tell me what happened."

Becca told him, short, stripped sentences, no emotion in them, stark facts, no details.

"But why did this Krimakov take Sam when all he did was get you here then tell you he was here in the house?"

"I don't know. Adam, did any of you see him? Did you see anything at all?"

Adam shook his head. "We've been looking, behind every damned tree."

She wished then that she hadn't reminded Tyler that Adam was here. His eyes narrowed, he hugged Sam more tightly to him. "You bastard, this is all your fault."

"Get a grip, McBride. Your son is all right. Now, if you don't mind, let's see if Sam can tell us anything about the guy who took him. You know it's important. You don't want Krimakov to get Becca again, do you?"

Tyler said, "Sam rarely says anything, you know that."

"He had a thick sock over his head. I never saw him. He gave me potato chips to eat. I was real hungry, but he told me to be quiet, that Becca would come for me soon enough."

Everyone stared at Sam. He looked quite pleased with himself. He grinned at Becca.

"Sam, that's great." Becca came down on her knees beside him. "I did come for you, didn't I? That's right, sweetie. Take another drink of your hot chocolate. It's good, isn't it? Now, tell us what you were doing when he got you."

But Sam didn't say anything more. He looked once at his father, yawned, and shut down. It was the strangest thing she'd ever seen. Sam just shut his eyes and went to sleep, slumping against Tyler's chest. One minute smiling, then just gone.

"He's a very brave little kid," Adam said, rising. "If it's okay with you, McBride, can we speak to him in the morning? At least try?"

Tyler looked like he wanted to shoot all of them, but in the end, he slowly nodded. "I'm taking him home now."

Adam looked at Becca, then said, "Nah, forget about us talking to him again. Sam probably doesn't have all that much more to tell us that would be useful. It's done and over. Please don't tell the sheriff about it. We're leaving right now. I guess whatever it was Krimakov wanted, he got."

"But what the hell did he want?"

"I don't know, Tyler," Becca said. She kissed Sam's cheek. "He's a very brave little boy."

"Will you come back to see him again?"

"Yes," she said. "I will. I promise. We just have to get all this business resolved first."

When Tyler was out the front door, Adam said suddenly, "Hold it right there, Becca. Your back. With all the excitement, I forgot about your back. He shot you with something. Let me see."

But there wasn't much to see. A bit of blood, a small hole, nothing more. "Why did he do this?"

"I don't know," Becca said to him over her shoulder, "but I promise I feel just fine. Here's the dart he shot into my shoulder. You see the rolled paper around it."

Adam unrolled the paper, frowned as he read it. "The bastard. What is he thinking? What is his plan? I hate this. He's controlling us. All we're doing is reacting to what he initiates. Damnation."

"I know. But we'll turn it around. Come on, Adam, let's get out of here. I'm very relieved that Sheriff Gaffney hasn't found his way here yet. Where is my father? Sherlock and Savich?"

"Sherlock went back to Washington with the handwriting samples. Your father, Savich, Hawley, and Cobb are waiting for us. I'll tell them to meet us at the airport; we're out of here."

They were driving away in her rented Toyota when she thought she saw Sheriff Gaffney's car in the distance. She stomped down on the gas.

She looked over at Adam's profile. He looked pissed and very tired. Not physically tired, but a defeated tired. She understood because she felt the same way.

Nothing made any sense. He'd gotten her here, he'd shot her with a dart in the shoulder, and delivered Sam. Nothing else.

Where was Krimakov? What in God's name was he planning to do now?

Dr. Ned Breaker, a physician whose son Savich had gotten back safely after a kidnapping some years before, was waiting at Thomas's house when they arrived.

All the men shook hands, Savich thanking him for coming. "She refused to go to a hospital."

"No one you work with ever does," Dr. Breaker said.

"This is Becca, Thomas's daughter. She's your patient, Ned."

"Dr. Breaker," she said, "I'm really okay, nothing's wrong. Adam already checked me out."

Adam said, "And now it's time for the real doctor to step up and have a look at the wound in your shoulder. We have no idea what was on that shaft that Krimakov shot into you. Be quiet, Becca, and do as you're told, for once."

She'd honestly forgotten about her shoulder. It didn't hurt. Adam had washed it with soap and water and put a Band-Aid over it. She was frowning when Thomas said, "Please, Becca."

"All right then." She took off her sweater and lifted her hair out of the way.

"Come into the light," Dr. Breaker said. She felt his fingers on the wound, gently pressing, pushing the flesh together, perhaps to see if any liquid or poison or God knew what came out. Finally, he said, "This is very strange. You were actually shot with this dart in the parking lot of a gym?"

"That's it."

She felt his fingers probe the area again, then he stepped away. "I'm going to take some blood, make sure there's nothing bad going on inside you. It looks fine, just a shallow puncture wound. Why'd he do it?"

"I think it might have just been to deliver a note to us," Savich said. "There was a note wrapped around the shaft."

"I see. Interesting mail delivery service this guy has. Well, better to be careful." He took a sample of her blood, then left, saying that he'd have results for them in two hours.

"A very good man to have as a friend," Savich said. "I wonder, though, how many more favors he'll believe he owes me."

Thomas said to Savich, but his eyes were on his daughter, "You got his kid back for him. He'll believe he owes you forever."

It was nearly one o'clock in the morning when Dr. Breaker called. Thomas took the call, looked very relieved as he listened. He was smiling when he turned to Becca and Adam. "Everything's okay. Nothing there but your beautiful normal stuff, Becca. He said not to worry."

Becca had rather hoped there might be something, nothing terminal, naturally, but something. Otherwise, they still had not a single clue about anything. Krimakov had kidnapped Sam to get her back to Riptide. Then he'd shot her in the shoulder to deliver that ridiculous note. In the gym parking lot. Nothing made sense.

That night Adam came to her. It was very dark in her room. She was lying there, unable to sleep even though it was very late, staring toward the window, looking at the slice of white moon just above the maple treetops. The trees were silhouetted stark and silent against the night, and they were perfectly still, no breeze at all. Thank God the house was air-conditioned. It was cool in her bedroom.

Her door opened, then closed quietly. His voice was soft, pitched low. "Don't be afraid. It's just me. And I'm not here to jump you, Becca."

She looked over at him, standing with his back against her closed door.

"Why not?"

He laughed, a painful sound, and walked toward her, tall, strong, and she wanted him.

He said, stopping beside her bed, looking down at her, "You never say what I expect. I want to jump you, at least a dozen times an hour, but no, this is your father's house. One doesn't do that under the parental roof when one isn't married. But don't get me wrong. If I could strip that nightgown off you, I would have it gone in a second flat. But I can't. Not here. I just wanted to see how you were doing. Oh hell, that's a big lie. I'm here because I want to kiss you until we're both stupid with pleasure."

He was beside her then, drawing her up and against his chest, and he kissed her, lightly, then with more pressure, and she opened her mouth and didn't want him to stop. His breath was hot and sweet, his scent rich, dark, and that mouth of his was delicious, and she let herself enjoy him fully. She wanted more and more. It was Adam who pushed her gently back after what seemed like only an instant.

"You're beautiful," he said and streaked his fingers through her hair, pushing it behind her ears. "Even with your hair still a bit brassy."

"I'm not stupid with pleasure yet, Adam."

"I'm not, either, but we've got to stop." He was breathing hard, his hands flexing and unflexing against her back.

"Maybe we could kiss just a little bit more?"

"Listen, if we don't stop right now, I'll start crying because I know that sooner or later we'd have to stop. We'll stop now before it kills me."

"All right, then. You be strong and let me mess with you just a bit." She kissed his chin once, then again. She touched her fingers to his cheeks, his nose, his brows, lightly traced over his mouth. She looked at his mouth as she said, "I haven't told you this before, Adam. So much has happened. We haven't known each other all that long, and nothing we've done together has been remotely normal or predictable. But here goes: You're very, very sexy."

He stared at her in the dim light as if he hadn't understood her. "What did you say? You think I'm sexy?"

"Oh, yes, the sexiest man I've ever seen. And finally I've gotten to kiss you. I like it, very much. I kissed your chin because it's sexy, too."

He looked inordinately pleased with himself, and with her. "I guess being sexy is okay. Is that all you think of me, Becca? I'm just a sexy hunk? Isn't there anything else, maybe, that you'd like to say to me?"

"What else should I say? Your ego is big enough without my saying more." Then she looked up at him beneath her lashes, a provocative thing to do, and she knew it. For the first time in so very long, actually, longer than she could remember, she allowed herself to enjoy what was happening here.

He didn't say anything, then suddenly he pulled her tightly against him again. He was rubbing his big hands up and down her back. His breathing was sharp, ragged. "I was scared to death when you were in that damned gym parking lot. When he shot that dart at you, Savich had to just about sit on me. I knew I shouldn't move, shouldn't yell like a banshee, but it was hard just staying still, watching you, damned hard. In fact, it was about the hardest thing I've ever had to do in my blessed life."

He pressed his forehead to hers, holding her loosely now.

His warm breath feathered over her skin. "Oh, yeah, I was married once. It was a long time ago. Her name was Vivie. Everything was okay for a while, then it just wasn't. She didn't want kids and I did. But I'm not serious about anyone else. It's just you, Becca. Just you."

"That's nice," she said and yawned against his shoulder. Then she bit his neck, then kissed where she'd bitten him. "I wish you were naked." To his immense credit, he didn't do anything other than shake a bit. "This is very close, Becca. My fingers are actually itching they want to touch you so much. But this is your father's house. We can't. Hey, how would you like to go out in the backyard, maybe we could take a couple of blankets?"

"Out from under the parental roof?"

"That's it. Oh yeah, for sure we could wave to the FBI agents that are scattered around." He sighed deeply, kissed her ear, and sighed again. "My molecules are even horny."

Becca sighed and rested her hand on his chest. His heart was pounding hard and fast beneath her palm. She arched up and kissed his throat, then eased back in the circle of his arms. "Not fair at all. I mean, the shirt you're wearing is nice but I would love to kiss your chest, maybe even run my hands down over your belly."

He shuddered, drew quickly away from her, and rose. "I've been feeling your breasts against me and it's driving me nuts. Now, since we can't be wicked the way I would like, I've got to get out of here. I just can't take any more. I'd like to try but I know it wouldn't work. Good night. I'll see you in the morning. I might be a bit late. I've got to go home and do some stuff." And he was gone. Her bedroom door closed very quietly behind him.

She sat there on her bed, hugging her knees. So suddenly her life had changed. And in all this nightmare, she'd found herself a man she hadn't believed could even exist. His first wife, Vivie, had had peas for brains. She hoped that Vivie—silly name—lived as far away as Saint Petersburg, Russia. It was a good enough distance away.

Soon enough, of course, Krimakov intruded. She wanted to shoot him, just point a gun at his chest and fire. She wanted him gone, into oblivion, so he couldn't ever hurt anyone again.

The next day, at precisely noon, when Governor Bledsoe of New York was walking his dog, Jabbers, in his protected garden, a sniper shooting from a distance of at least fifteen hundred feet nailed his dog right through the folds of his neck. Jabbers was rushed to the vet and it looked like he would survive, just like his master had.

Thomas turned slowly to his daughter, the two of them alone in the house. "This is over the top. It's just too much. Damnation, he shot the dog in the neck. Unbelievable. At least the sick bastard isn't here."

"But why did he do it?" Becca said. "Why?"

"To laugh at us," Thomas said. "To make this big joke. He wants us to know just how invincible he is, how he can do anything he wants to and get away with it. How he's here and then he's there, and we'll never get him. Yes, he's laughing his head off."

Chapter 28

*G*aylan Woodhouse sat at an angle across from Thomas's desk with his face in the shadows, as was his wont, and said, "I don't want you to worry about your daughter, Thomas. Your whereabouts will not be leaked. As you know, the media is still in a frenzy over the shooting of poor Jabbers. The country is primarily amused at his audacity, titillated, glued to their TVs. Everyone wants to know about Krimakov, this man who swore to kill you twenty-some years ago. By shooting that damned dog, he's turned up the heat. He wants the media to find you for him and then he'll come after you."

"No," Thomas said slowly, shaking his head. "I don't think that was his motive at all. You see, Gaylan, he had me in Riptide. He had to know I would never allow Becca to go up there alone. He could have easily shot me. He proved he was an excellent distance shooter when he shot the governor of New York. From that kind of distance, he could have nailed me with little effort. But he didn't force anything after he kidnapped Sam McBride, except to shoot Becca in the shoulder with a dart that had a piece of paper rolled around the shaft. No, Gaylan, he shot the governor's dog because he wanted to give me the finger, show me again that it was his decision not to kill me and Becca in Riptide. He wants to show me that he doesn't have to do anything until he decides he wants to do it. He wants to prove to me over and over that he's superior to me, that he's the one in control here, that he's the one calling all the shots. It's a cat-and-mouse game and he's proving again and again that he's the cat. Damnation, he is the cat. Adam's right. During all of this, we've only been able to react to what he does."

Gaylan said slowly, "One of my people pointed out that Krimakov certainly managed to get from one place to the next with no difficulty at all, suggested that maybe he has a private plane stashed somewhere. What do you think?"

Thomas said, "Makes you wonder, doesn't it? Heaven knows you can't have much faith in the commercial airlines. But you know, Gaylan, shooting that dog wasn't on a set timetable. You can check it out, but I doubt it."

Gaylan sighed. "We still don't have any leads in New York. His disguise must have been something. The security tapes showed old folk, pregnant women, children—do we track all of them down to question? Still no witnesses. Damnation, four good agents dead because of that maniac."

Thomas said, "I've been thinking about that. I'm coming to believe that Krimakov wants Becca and me together, to torment us together, prolong our deaths. But yet he went right to New York University Hospital, shot everyone, then ran. What if Krimakov somehow found out it was a trap? What if he still did it, in fact made a big production of it, all to tell us that he knew about our plan and it didn't matter. Yes, he knew, and he thumbed his nose at us."

"You're making him sound wilier than the Devil," Gaylan said, a brow arched. "More evil, too."

"I would say certifiably insane," Thomas said. "But it doesn't make him stupid. It doesn't really matter what the truth of his motives was, four agents are still dead. Yet it fits into all the things he's done since then. Over the top, frightening as hell."

"Yes," Gaylan said. He looked toward Thomas's bookshelves for a moment. He seemed to shake himself, then took a sip of his coffee. He carefully set the cup back into the saucer. He crossed his legs, then said, "There's another reason I came here, Thomas. The fact is that the president isn't going to sit still much longer. He called me over, paced in front of me for ten minutes, told me that all this mess had to come to a close, that the media are totally focused on it to the detriment of what he's trying to accomplish. He's got this new tax increase he's trying to sell to the country, only the media is ignoring him in favor of this. He said he'd even tried to make a joke, but the media was still talking about Jabbers and his sore neck."

"Tell the president that if he wants me to go public, challenge Krimakov at high noon, I'll do it."

"No," Gaylan said, "you won't. I won't allow that. He could take you out easily—his shot at the governor was from a distance of at least fifteen hundred feet. You yourself pointed that out to me. He's better than good, Thomas, he's one of the best." He held up his hand when Thomas would have said something. "No, let me finish. All I'm saying is that we've got to come up with something else. Somehow, we've got to make him dance to our tune."

"A lot of very good minds are working on this, as you know, since some of those minds work for you."

Gaylan nodded, picked up a pen from Thomas's desk, and began rhythmically tapping it against his knee. "Yes, I know. But for now, your whereabouts stays unknown. I'll tell the president that everything will be resolved in a couple more days. Think it's possible?"

"Sure, why not?" And he thought, *How the hell am I supposed to make that come about?*

"All right. We continue the silence. What about that incident with Krimakov in Riptide?"

Thomas said, "Evidently, the media doesn't know about her visit there yet. And Tyler McBride—you know, the man whose son

Krimakov kidnapped in Riptide—he isn't saying anything to any-one about Becca. I think he's in love with her and that's why he won't explode sky-high with all this. Becca, however, as much as she cares for his little boy, isn't headed his way." He paused a mo-ment, looking down at the onyx pen set that Allison had given him some five Christmases before. "It's Adam," he said, smiling briefly as he looked at his old friend. "Isn't that nice?"

Gaylan Woodhouse grunted. "I'm too old," he said, then sighed again. "Krimakov won't find you, Thomas. Don't worry. I'll deal with the president. Let's say forty-eight hours, then we'll reassess. Okay?"

"Again, Gaylan, maybe Krimakov needs to find me. Forget the president's political agenda. Just maybe Krimakov's reign of terror will continue until he knows where I am. Maybe we should let him know, somehow."

"We'll all think about that, but not just yet. Forty-eight hours. Jesus, next the guy might try to shoot off the mayor's wig." Gaylan Woodhouse rose, dropped the pen back on top of the desk, shook Thomas's hand, and stepped back through the door, where the shadows were thicker. Three dark-suited men fell in beside and be-hind him as he left Thomas's house.

Thomas stared after him. Shadows surrounded him. Thomas un-derstood shadows very well. He'd lived in the shadows himself for so long he could see them even as they gathered around him, and won-dered if after a while anyone would actually see him or just the shad-ows.

Forget shadows, Thomas thought. Now wasn't the time to wax philosophical. He thought about the meeting. Gaylan was a good friend. He'd hold out against the president's whining about losing the limelight for as long as he could. Forty-eight hours—that was the deal. It wasn't a lot of time and yet it was an eternity. Only Krimakov knew which.

The next evening, Sherlock and Savich arrived with thick folders of papers, MAX, and Sean, who reared up on Savich's shoulder, staring about sleepily at everyone, a graham cracker clutched in his hand.

Sherlock looked at everyone in the living room. She didn't look happy as she said, "I'm really sorry here, guys, but our handwriting experts turned up something we didn't expect."

"What have you got, Sherlock?" Adam asked, rising slowly, his eyes never leaving her face.

"We were hoping to learn whether or not Krimakov's mental state had deteriorated, at least determine where he was sitting presently on the sanity scale, in order to give us a better chance of dealing with him, predicting what he might do, that sort of thing. That's off now. We have no idea, you see, because the two new samples of handwriting Becca gave me aren't Krimakov's."

Thomas looked like someone had slapped him. He said slowly, "No, that's not possible. Admittedly I just looked at the ones from Riptide briefly, but they looked the same to me. You're sure about this, Sherlock? Absolutely?"

"Oh, yes, completely sure. We're dealing with a very different person here, and this person's mind isn't like yours or mine."

"You mean he's not sane," Thomas said.

"It's difficult to say with absolute certainty, but it's possible he's so far over the edge he's holding on by his fingernails. We could throw around labels—psychopath comes readily to mind—but that's just a start. The only thing we're completely certain about—

he's obsessed with you, Thomas. He wants to prove to you that you're nowhere near his league, that he's a god and you're dirt. He sees himself as an avenger, the man who will balance the scales of justice, the man who will be your executioner.

"It's been his goal for a very long time; it could at this point even be his only reason for living. He's rather like a missile that's been programmed for one thing and one thing only. He won't stop, ever, until either he's killed you or you've killed him."

"So it was never Krimakov," Adam said slowly. "He really was killed in that auto accident in Crete."

"Probably so. Now, not all of this is from our experts' analysis. Profiling had a hand in it, as well." Sherlock turned back to Thomas. "Like you said, the two different sets of handwriting look close to a layman's eye, which probably means that this guy knew Krimakov, or at least he'd seen his handwriting a goodly number of times. A friend, a former or present colleague, someone like that."

"We're sorry, guys," Savich said. "I know that Krimakov's former associates have been checked backwards and forwards, but I guess we're going to have to try to do more. I've already got MAX doing more sniffing around Krimakov's neighbors, business associates, friends in Crete and on mainland Greece, as well. We already know that he had a couple of side businesses in Athens. We'll see where that leads."

"No, all that has already been checked," Thomas said.

Savich just shook his head. "We'll have to do more, try anything."

Sherlock said, "We've also inputted everything we know into the PAP to see what comes out. Remember, the computer can analyze more alternatives more quickly than we can. We'll see."

Thomas said, "All right. What exactly did the profilers have to say, Sherlock?"

"Back to a label. He is psychotic. He has absolutely no remorse, no empathy for any of the people he's killed. None of them mean anything to him. They were detritus to be swept out of his way."

"I wonder why he didn't kill Sam," Becca said.

"We don't know," Savich said. "That's a good question."

"It just doesn't seem possible," Adam said. "Just not possible. Why would a colleague or some bloody friend—no matter how close to Krimakov—go on this rampage? Even if he is a psychopath, always has been a psychopath, why wait more than twenty years after the fact? Why take over Krimakov's mission as his own?"

No one had an answer to that.

Adam said, "Now we've got to find out who would follow up on Krimakov's vendetta once Krimakov himself was dead. What's his motivation, for God's sake?"

"We don't know," Sherlock said, and she began rubbing Sean's back with her palm. He was cooing against his father's shoulder, the graham cracker very wet but still clutched tightly in his hand.

"There are graham cracker crumbs all over the house," Savich said absently.

Becca didn't say anything. There were few things she'd ever been absolutely sure were true in her life. This was one of them. It simply had to be Krimakov. No matter how infallible the handwriting experts usually were, they were wrong on this one.

But what if they weren't wrong? A psychopath obsessed with finding and killing her father? He'd called himself her boyfriend. He'd blown up that poor old bag lady in front of the Metropolitan Museum. He'd dug up Linda Cartwright and bashed in her face. No empathy, no remorse, people were detritus, nothing more. God, it was unthinkable.

She looked over at Adam. He was looking toward Savich, but she didn't think he really saw him. Adam was really looking inward, ah, but his eyes—they were cold and hard and she wouldn't want to have to tangle with him. She heard her father in the other room, speaking to Gaylan Woodhouse on the phone.

Sherlock and Savich left a few minutes later, leaving Adam and Becca in the living room, looking at each other. He said, his hands jiggling change in his pockets, "I've got stuff to do at my house. I want you to stay here with Thomas, under wraps. Don't go anywhere. I'll be back tomorrow."

"Yeah, I want to do some stuff, too," she said, rising. "I'm coming with you."

"No, you'll stay here. It's safe here."

And he was gone.

Her father appeared in the doorway. She said, "I'll see you later, sir. I'm going with Adam." She picked up her purse and ran after him. He was nearly to the road when she caught up with him. "Where are you going?"

"Becca, go back. It's safer here. Go back."

"No. You don't believe any more than I do that some colleague or friend of Krimakov's from the good old days is wreaking all this havoc. I think we're missing something here, something that's been there all the time, staring us in the face."

"What do you mean?" he said slowly. She saw the agents in the car down the street slowly get out and stand, both of them completely alert.

"I mean nothing makes sense unless it's Krimakov. But just say that it isn't. That means we're missing something. Let's go do your stuff together, Adam, and really plug in our brains."

He eyed her a moment, looked around, then waved at the agents. "We've got to walk. It's three miles. You up for it?"

"I'd love to race you. Whatcha say?"

"You're on."

"You're dead meat, boy."

Since they were both wearing sneakers, they could run until they dropped. He grinned at her, felt energy pulse through him. He wanted to run, to race the wind, and he imagined that she wanted to as well. "All right, we're going to my house. I have all my files there, all my notes, everything. I want to scour them. If it is some-one who knew Krimakov, then there's got to be a hint of him in there somewhere. Yes, there must be something."

"Let's go."

She nearly had his endurance, but not quite. He slowed in the third mile.

"You're good, Becca," he said, and waved his hand. "This is my house."

She loved it. The house wasn't as large as her father's, but it sat right in the middle of a huge hunk of wooded land, two stories, a white colonial with four thick Doric columns lined up like soldiers along the front. It looked solid, like it would last forever. She cleared her throat. "This is very nice, Adam."

"Thanks. It's about a hundred and fifty years old. It's got three bedrooms upstairs, two bathrooms—I added one. Downstairs is all the regular stuff, including a library, which I use for a study, and a modern kitchen." He cleared his throat. "I had the kitchen redone a couple years ago. My mom told me no woman would marry me un-less the stove would light without having to hold a match to a burner."

She smiled. She nearly had her breathing back to normal.

"I had one of the two upstairs bathrooms redone, too," he said, looking straight ahead. They climbed the three deep steps to walk across the narrow veranda to the large white front door. He stuck a key in the lock and turned it. "My mom said that no woman wanted to bathe in a claw-footed tub that was so old rust was peeling off the toes."

"That does sound pretty gross. Oh my, Adam, it's lovely."

They stood together in a large entryway, with a ceiling that soared two stories, a chandelier hanging down over their heads and a lovely buffed oak floor. "I know, you redid the floors. Your mom told you no woman would marry you if she had to be carried into a house across a mess of old ratty linoleum."

"How did you know?"

He'd preserved all the original charm of the house—the deeply carved, rich moldings, the high ceilings, the lovely cherry wood carved fireplaces, the incredible set-in windows.

They prepared to hunker down in the library, a light-filled room with built-in bookshelves, beautiful oak floors, a big mahogany desk, and lots of red leather. She looked around at the bookshelves stuffed with all kinds of books—nonfiction, fiction, hardcovers, paperbacks—stuck in indiscriminately.

Adam said as he handed her two folders, "My mom also told me that women liked to read all cozied up in deep chairs. It was just men, she said, who preferred to read in the bathroom."

"You've even got women's fiction here."

"Yeah, it seems a man can never stack the deck too much in his favor."

"I want to meet your mama," Becca said.

"Undoubtedly you will, real soon." Then he couldn't stand it. He walked to her and pulled her tightly against him. She looked up at him and said, "I want to forget Krimakov for just a minute."

"All right."

"Have I told you lately that I think you're really sexy?"

He smiled slowly and kissed her lightly on the mouth. "Not since last night." She wrapped her arms around his neck, stood on her tiptoes, and kissed him back, thoroughly.

"I don't want you to forget it," she said after several minutes had passed. "You've gotten me a bit breathless. I really like it, Adam."

"We're in my house now," he said, and this time he kissed her, really kissed her, no holding back, letting himself crash and burn, letting himself burrow into her. He brought her tightly against him, feeling all of her against him, and he wanted to jerk down her jeans, he wanted to devour her, take her until both of them shattered with the pleasure of it. He wanted to kiss her breasts, touch and kiss every inch of her, and not stop until he was unconscious. And then there was her mouth. Jesus, he was making himself crazy. It was so good he really didn't want to stop, and why should they stop?

His hands were on the buttons of her jeans when he felt the change not only in himself but in her. It was Krimakov and he was there, just over their shoulders. Waiting. He was close, too close. Krimakov was out there, only it wasn't really Krimakov now. Whoever he was, he was a madman. Adam sighed, kissed her once more, then once again, and said, "I want you very much, but now, at this moment, we've got to solve this thing, Becca."

"I know," she said when she could speak. "I'm getting myself back together. I'm getting myself focused now. You're quite a distraction, Adam, it's hard." She pulled away from him, stiffened her legs. "Okay, I'm ready to think again."

"I promise there'll be more," he said, grabbing her and giving her one last kiss. "How about a lifetime full of more?"

She gave him a dazzling smile. "Given that gorgeous modern kitchen and how I believe, without a doubt, that you're about the best kisser in the whole world, I think bunches of years might be a wonderful thing." Then she looked at his groin and he nearly expired on the spot.

"Good," he said finally, just a slight shiver in his voice, and she loved the way those dark eyes of his were brilliant with pleasure in the afternoon light shining in through the windows. "Now, let's do it."

Two hours, three cups of coffee, a demolished plate of Wheat Thins and cheddar cheese later, Adam looked up. "I was going over my notes on Krimakov's travel out of Greece over the years. It's been here all the time, just staring up at me, and I didn't see it until now." He gave her a mad grin, jumped up, and gathered her beneath her arms and lifted her, then swung her in a circle. He kissed her once, then again, and set her back down. He rubbed his hands together. "Hot damn, Becca, I think I've got the answer."

She was laughing, stroking her hands over his arms, so excited she couldn't hold still. "Come on, Adam. What is it? Spill the beans."

"Krimakov went to England six times. His trips to England stopped about five years ago."

"And?"

"I never stopped to wonder why the hell he went to England all those times, until now. Becca, think about it. Why did he go? To see a former colleague, to see a friend from the good old days? Not a woman, he'd remarried, so no, I don't think so."

She said slowly, "When he moved to Crete, he was alone. No relatives with him. Nobody."

"Yeah, but his files had been purged. Remember, there wasn't even anything about his first wife. It was like she never existed, but she did. So why did the KGB purge her?"

Becca said slowly, "Because she was important, because—" Suddenly, her eyes gleamed. "Oh my God. Sherlock is right. It isn't Krimakov, but neither is it a friend or a former colleague. It's someone a whole lot closer to him."

"Yep. Somebody so close he's nearly wearing his skin. We're nearly there, Becca. The timing of his visits—they're in the early fall or very late spring. Every one of them."

"Like the beginning or the ending of school terms," Becca said slowly. "And then they stop like there's no more school." Then she remembered what had happened in the gym in Riptide, and it all fell together.

When they got back to Thomas's house, only Thomas and Hatch were there, their conversation desultory, both of them looking so depressed that Adam nearly told Hatch to go smoke a cigarette. Becca heard Hatch cursing. It sounded like Paul Hogan and his sexy Aussie accent.

"Cheer up, everyone," Adam said. "Becca and I have a surprise for you. One that will get you dancing on the ceiling. All we've got to do now is have Savich turn on MAX and send him to England. Now we've got a chance." He bent down and kissed Becca, right in front of Thomas. She raised her hand and lightly touched her fingertips to his cheek. "Yes, we do," she said.

The doorbell rang, making everyone suddenly very alert and very focused. It was Dr. Breaker. "Hello, Savich." He nodded to everyone else. "We've found something none of you is going to believe." And he told them about the very slight abnormalities in Becca's blood that a tech had caught. Then he checked Becca's shoulder, and finally he checked her upper arm. It wasn't long before he looked up and said, "I feel something, right here, just beneath her skin. It's small, flexible."

Adam nodded. "The visit to Riptide makes sense now. You know what's in your arm, don't you, Becca?"

"Yes," she said. "Now all of us know." She raised her hand when her father would have begun arguments. "No, I'm not leaving. No more people are going to die in my place, like Agent Marlane. No one is going to be bait in my stead. No, no arguments. I stay here with you. Hey, I've got my Coonan."

For the first time in more nights than she could count, Becca wanted to stay awake, stay alert, keep watch. He was close. She wanted to see him with clear eyes and a clear mind and her Coonan in her hand. She wanted to shoot him between the eyes. And she wanted to know why he was doing this. Was he really mad? Psychotic?

Oh damn, she didn't think she'd be able to hang on. She was nearly light headed she was so tired. She'd been so hyped up the past couple of nights, she'd just lain there and blinked at the rising moon outside the bedroom window.

Adam had insisted on tucking her in. She wanted him to stay just a little longer, but she knew he couldn't. He kissed her, just a nibble on her earlobe, and said against her ear, "No, I don't want another cold shower. But dream of me, Becca, okay? I've got the first watch. It starts soon."

"Be careful, Adam."

"I will, everyone will. Try to sleep, sweetheart. He knows the house. He knows which room is Thomas's. We've got Thomas well guarded." He kissed her once again and rose. "Get some sleep."

She didn't want to. After he eased out of her bedroom door, closing it quietly behind him, she sat up in bed, thinking, remembering, analyzing. She was asleep in under six minutes. She dreamed, but not of the terror that was very close now, not of Adam.

She found herself in a hospital, walking down long, empty corridors. White, so much white, unending, going on and on, forever. She was looking for her mother. She smelled ether fumes, sweet and heavy, the ammonia scent of urine, the stench of vomit. She opened each white door along the corridor. All the beds were empty, the white sheets stretched military tight. No one. Where were the patients?

So long, the hallway just went on and on and there were moans coming from behind all those doors, people in pain, but there were no nurses, no doctors, no one at all. She knew the rooms were empty, she'd looked into all of them, yet the moans grew louder and louder.

Where was her mother? She called out for her, then she started running down the corridor, screaming her mother's name. The moans from those empty rooms grew louder and louder until—

"Hello, Rebecca."

Chapter 29

*B*ecca lurched up in bed, sweaty, breathing hard, her heart pounding. No, it wasn't her mother, no, it was someone else.

Finally he was here. He'd come to her first, not to her father. A surprise, but not a big one, at least to her. She lay very still, gathering herself, her control, her focus.

"Hello, Rebecca," he said again, this time he was even closer to her face, nearly touching her.

"You can't be here," she said aloud. He'd gotten past everyone, but again, that didn't overly surprise her. She wouldn't be surprised if he'd gotten both the house plans and the security system plans. And now he wasn't even six inches from her.

"Of course I can be here. I can be anywhere I want. I'm a cloud of smoke, a sliding shadow, a glimmer of light. I like how frightened you are. Just listen to you, your voice is even trembling with fear. Yes, I like that. Now, you even try to move and I will, very simply, cut your skinny little throat."

She felt the razor-sharp blade against the front of her neck, pressing in ever so slightly.

"We knew you would come," she said.

He laughed quietly, now not even an inch from her ear. She felt his hot breath touch her skin. "Of course you knew I'd find you. I can do anything. Your father is so stupid, Rebecca. I've always known it, always, and now I've proved it the final time. I figured out how to find his lair, and poof—like shimmering smoke—I'm here.

You and your bastard father lose now. Soon, you and I are going down the hall to his bedroom. I want him to wake up with me standing over him, you in front of me, a knife digging into your neck. Even with those hot shot FBI guards he's got positioned all around this house, I got through with little effort. There's this great big oak tree that comes almost to the roof of the house. Just a little jump, not more than six feet, and I was on the roof, and then it was easy to pry open that trapdoor into the attic. I took care of the security alarm up there, cut it off for all of the upstairs. No one saw me. It's nice and dark tonight. Stupid, all of you are stupid. Now, get up."

She did as he said. She felt calm. He kept her very close, the knife across her neck as he opened her bedroom door and eased her out into the hallway. "The last door down on the right," he said. "Just keep walking and keep quiet, Rebecca."

It was nearly one o'clock in the morning; Becca saw the time on the old grandfather clock that sat in its niche in the corridor.

"Open the door," he said against her ear, "slowly, quietly. That's right."

Her father's bedroom door opened without a sound. There was a night light on in the connecting bathroom off to the left. All the draperies were open, beams of the scant moonlight coming in through the balcony windows. There was no movement on the bed.

"Wake up, you butchering bastard," he said, one eye on the balcony windows.

There was still no movement on the bed.

She heard his breathing quicken, felt the knife move slightly against her neck. "No, you don't move, Rebecca. Just one little slice and your blood will spew like a fountain all over the floor." Suddenly, he said, nearly a yell, "Thomas Matlock! Where are you?"

"I'm right here, Krimakov."

He whirled Becca around, facing Thomas, who was standing,

fully dressed, in the lighted doorway of the bathroom, his arms crossed over his chest.

"It's about time you got here," Thomas said easily, his eyes on the knife that was pressing into Becca's neck. "Don't hurt her. We've been waiting for you. I was starting to believe you'd lost your nerve, that you'd gotten too scared, that you'd finally run away."

"What do you mean? Of course I got here quickly, at least as quickly as I wanted to. As I told Rebecca, your defenses are laughable."

"Get that knife away from her neck. Let her go. You've got me. Let her go."

"No, not yet. Don't try anything stupid or I'll cut her throat. But I don't want her dead just yet."

Thomas saw that he was dressed in black from the ski mask that covered both his face and his head to the black gloves on his hands. "You're the one who's lost," Thomas said, and he saluted him. "There's really no need for you to wear that black mask over your head anymore. We all know who you are. As I said, we've been waiting fourteen hours for you to finally show up."

Adam spoke quietly into the wristband. "He can't see me. I'm only a shadow at the corner of the balcony door. I can't get him. He's got Becca plastered against the front of him, a knife against her throat. I can't take the risk, even this close. They'll keep him talking. Thomas is good. He'll keep control."

And he prayed with everything that was in him that it would be so.

"Just keep alert," Gaylan Woodhouse said. "The minute he makes a move toward Thomas, he'll ease up on her. Then you take him down."

"Damn," Adam said, "now the bastard's pulled a gun out of his jacket pocket. It's small, looks like a Colt, the Compact .45. He's pointed it straight at Thomas. Oh God." And he concentrated, readied himself, saying over and over, *Let Becca go, you crazy fuck. Just twitch.*

"Turn on the bedside light, Matlock."

Thomas walked slowly into the bedroom, leaned over, and switched on the light. He straightened.

"Now, don't move. Those draperies are open. There's probably a sniper out there, and I don't want the bastard to have a clean shot. He'll get you, Rebecca, if he pulls the trigger."

Thomas said, "I wanted very much for you to be my old enemy, but you aren't. You're something far more deadly than Vasili, something deadly and monstrous that he spawned. Perhaps after he brainwashed you, he realized what he'd produced, realized that he'd unleashed uncontrolled, unrelenting evil, and that's why he kept you away from his new family. He didn't want the evil he'd spawned and nurtured to live in his own house, to be close to all those innocent, pure lives. Pull off the mask, Mikhail, we know who you are."

Stone-dead silence, then, "Damn you, you can't know, you can't! No one knows anything about me. I don't exist. No records show me as Vasili Krimakov's son. I've covered everything. It isn't possible."

"Oh yes, we know. Even though the KGB tried to erase you, to protect you, we found out all about you."

"Damn you, pull those draperies closed, now!"

Thomas pulled them closed, knowing that now Adam was blind to what was going on in the room. He turned and said slowly,

"Take off the mask, Mikhail. It really looks rather silly, like a little boy playing hoodlum."

Slowly, his movements jerky, furious, he pulled off the black mask. Then he shoved Becca over toward the bed. Thomas caught her, held her close to his side. But she moved away from him. She sat down on the bed, drew her legs up.

Thomas stared at Vasili Krimakov's son, Mikhail. There was some resemblance to his father in the high, sharp cheekbones, the wide-set eyes, the whiplash-lean body, but the dark, mad eyes, those were surely his mother's eyes. Thomas could still see her eyes, wide, staring up at him.

Becca knew Mikhail had wanted shock, but it was denied him when he realized they knew who he was. Still, he threw back his head and said, "I am my father's son. He loved me. He molded me to be like him. I am here, his avenger."

His dramatic moment got nothing except a laugh from Becca.

"Hi, Troy," she said, giving him a small wave. "Cute, preppy name. Tell me, what if I'd decided to go out with you that night after you planted that little micro homing chip in my upper arm? How would you have gotten out of it?" She said to her father, "I told you how he managed to have the arm of that big old chest machine swing into me as I was walking by, and then he was right there, patting me, making sure I was okay, flirting with me. That was when you planted that little chip in my arm, isn't it, Troy? You were good. I didn't feel a thing, just the sting from that machine arm hitting me. It hurt a little longer than it should have, but who would really notice?"

"No," he said, shaking his head back and forth. "This isn't possible. You couldn't have found that chip. It's plastic mixed with biochemical adhesives, almost immediately becomes one with your skin. After just a few minutes, no one could even tell it was

345

there, least of all you. No, you weren't even aware of it. You and everyone else were just worried about that dart in your shoulder. I fooled you, I fooled all of you. You were all so worried about that ridiculous dart in her shoulder, about that stupid note I wrapped around it."

"For a while, that's right," Thomas said. "But actually, it was an analysis of handwriting by some very smart FBI agents that started your downfall. I had samples of your father's handwriting. They compared yours to his. Remember the notes you wrote to Mr. McBride in Riptide? There was no comparison, of course, so it couldn't be Vasili.

"Then Adam remembered that your father had traveled to England quite a number of times. He wondered why, particularly since the visits were always at the beginning of the school term or at the end. He knew your father had remarried, so it probably wasn't a woman he was visiting. He'd purged files, even your mother's name, and we wondered why he would do that. After all, who cared if he had a wife, now dead, or any children?

"It wasn't tough then to track you down, the son whose father had sent him to England to be educated, so that one day he could avenge the murder of his dearest mother. You were at that private boys' school at Sundowns."

Thomas continued, "Your father molded you, taught you to hate me, to hate everything I stood for, programmed you for this."

"I was not programmed. I do this all of my own free will. I am brilliant. I have won. Even though you found out about me, it is I who am standing here in control. It is I who run this show."

Thomas said, "Fine. You run the show. Now tell us how you got into NYU Hospital without being stopped by the FBI agents."

He laughed, preened. "I was a young boy, so sorry-looking in my slouchy clothes, my pants halfway to my knees, and my baseball cap, holding my broken arm, and everyone wanted to help me, to send me here, to send me there, and I came up to those stupid agents, crying about my arm, and then I shot them both. So easy, all of it. In the room when I saw neither of you were there, I just killed them, too, but with the woman, it was very close, too close. But I escaped. I was out of there before anyone realized what had happened."

Thomas said, "Why, Mikhail? What did your father tell you to make you want to do this? What?"

"He didn't make me do anything. He simply told me how you butchered my poor mother, went through her to get to him. You shot her in the head and laughed as my father held her until she died. Then you tried to kill him but he managed to get away. He told me that, and he began teaching me to prepare myself to avenge her. And I'm here now. I'll kill you just as you killed my mother."

"You killed your stepmother, didn't you, and her children?" Becca said.

He laughed, actually laughed. "Yes, I hated her as much as she hated me. She didn't want me ever to come back during my vacations. And her spawn—they weren't all that surprised when I killed them because they had guessed that I hated them. As for her, she pleaded just like her pathetic daughter."

Becca said, "And your own little brother? Your father's other son?"

"I tried to kill him, burn him out of existence, just to leave ashes, but he survived. My father sent him to Switzerland, to this clinic that specializes in burns. He knew then what I'd done. I called him a coward, told him he'd let that wretched woman, those children, distract him from killing the man who butchered my mother. You know what he said? He said it over and over, tears in his eyes, wringing his goddamned hands—it had been an accident, he'd lied

347

to me all those years. I didn't believe him. He wanted it soft and easy—a woman in his bed, children around him—but I wasn't going to let him forget my mother, just erase her memory, and turn away like you would turn away.

"Now I've got you both and I'm going to kill you, just as you killed my mother. It's justice. It's retribution." He smiled as he raised his gun, aiming right at Thomas.

"No!" Becca yelled. "I won't let you!" She hurled herself in front of her father.

Mikhail Krimakov gave a scream of rage when Thomas shoved Becca to the floor. But he didn't have time to cover her with his own body. Mikhail shot him in the chest, knocking him backward.

Mikhail dropped to the floor, grabbed Becca's ankle, and jerked her hard toward him. He slammed his arm around her neck, and pressed the gun against her ear even as the balcony glass door shattered inward and Adam leapt through the billowing draperies and the broken glass into the bedroom. He stopped dead in his tracks.

Mikhail smiled at him. "You try to kill me and the little bitch is dead. You got that?"

Chapter 30

Mikhail said, the gun pointed in Becca's left ear, "That bastard shot my mother in the head. He's paid for it. You move and I'll blow her head off. You won't even recognize what's left."

Adam couldn't believe it, just didn't want to accept what he was seeing. "I should never have let you stay here. Damn me, I should have drugged you, Becca, and hidden you away."

But Becca didn't hear him. Mikhail's arm had tightened until she couldn't breathe, until everything turned black and she heard voices in the distance, but they didn't reach her, not really.

Mikhail eased up on Becca's neck as he waved his gun at Adam. "Drop that gun and do it slowly and very carefully."

Adam let the gun fall to the floor. It came to a stop, he saw, about thirteen inches beyond his left foot.

"I dropped the gun. You've killed Thomas. No one else is near. Let her go, damn you, you've already choked her unconscious."

"Yeah, right, you asshole."

Thomas felt as if his chest was frozen, a good thing, he knew, because soon enough he would be in such pain he probably wouldn't be able to think, much less move. Krimakov's son was pressing a gun against Becca's throat. Adam stood not four feet away, helpless, frozen in place, shattered glass all around him. Thomas knew he was trying desperately to figure out what to do. Becca's eyes were closed, Mikhail's hold against her throat was too strong, far too strong. She'd passed out. He had to do something, anything.

He couldn't let her die, not like this, not after she'd hurled herself in front of him, to save him, to take the bullet herself. He felt the pain pulsing deep in his chest, but with it, he felt such an intense surge of love for her that gave him a burst of strength. He managed to ease his hand down to his pants pocket, to the small derringer. Just a bit more strength, that's all he needed, strength.

Mikhail saw the slight movement from the corner of his eye. "Damn you, you're supposed to be dead. Don't move!" His hold against her throat lightened and almost immediately he saw that Becca was coming out of it. He clouted her hard on the side of the head, and shoved her away from him. He leaped to his feet, pulled a Zippo lighter from his pocket and set it to the bedding. In an instant, the blanket and sheets burst into flame.

Thomas fired the derringer. Mikhail yelled and grabbed his arm as the bullet punched him backward. He hit the wall but didn't fall. Adam dove for his gun. Thomas fired again, but Mikhail had twisted low and the bullet just grazed the side of his head.

Thomas fell back, the derringer falling from his hand. Adam twisted about, his gun raised, but Mikhail was out of the bedroom, and when Adam fired, the bullet hit the door frame. Mikhail slammed the door behind him and the flames gushed higher with the sudden rush of air, igniting the pillows, the thick brocade drapes that were ripped from Adam's run into the bedroom.

"Damnation," Adam shouted. "Becca, are you all right?" He leaned over and slapped her face. "Come on, we've got to get out of here. Damn, the drapes are on fire now." He scrambled on his knees to where Thomas lay on his back. He shook him. "Thomas, open your eyes. That's it. Now, can you make it?"

Thomas just smiled at him. "No, unfortunately not, Adam. I think this is the end of the line for me. Get Becca out of here. Tell her I love her."

"Don't be a jackass," Adam said. "We're all getting out of here. Come on, you can do it." He wrapped an arm around Thomas and jerked to his feet, pulling Thomas with him. He started to lift him over his shoulder.

"No, not yet," Thomas said, the pain flooding over him now, drawing at his brain, making everything darken, darken. "No, dammit, we'll get out of here. Becca, get yourself together! I'm not going to lose you now."

Becca was sitting now, shaking her head, trying to breathe. She heard agents yelling outside, prayed they wouldn't try to come into the burning room, prayed they'd be ready to pump a hundred bullets into Mikhail when he came out of the house. She said, "I'm okay. Just give me a second, just a moment." She stared at her father. "Mother left me. There's no way you're going to leave me now. I'll help you, Adam." Together, one of them on each side of him, they managed to get the door open and drag Thomas into the hallway. The flames were whooshing up high behind them, thick, incredibly hot, smoke gushing out of the room. No time, Adam thought, just no bloody time to put it out.

All of them were coughing now from the smoke. "Let's move," Adam said. He pulled the bedroom door closed after him, but it was too late. The fire was already eating away at the hallway carpeting.

"If he isn't dead yet," Adam said, "they'll get him the instant he gets out of the house."

Becca was panting with effort and coughing at the same time. "I had my gun strapped to my leg, but it didn't matter," she said, coughing. "Are you all right, Daddy? Don't you dare talk about dying again. Do you hear me?"

"I hear you, Becca," Thomas said, and his chest was on fire, just as the fire raged around them, it raged inside him. He knew he couldn't last much longer. He didn't want to leave her, not yet, please God, not yet.

"Just a little farther."

They heard a whoosh of flames behind them. The smoke was dense and black now. "We've got to hurry," Adam said. He didn't ask, just picked up Thomas and eased him over his shoulder. "Becca, get downstairs. I'm right behind you."

A shot rang out in the thick smoke. Adam felt the punch in his arm, sharp, hard. He didn't loosen his hold. "Jesus, Becca, get down, crawl. I don't want him to shoot you."

But Becca had her Coonan in her hand. She stepped behind Adam and fired back through the smoke in the direction of the shot. There were three more shots. Then silence.

"He must be back near the bedroom, Adam." And she fired off another shot. "That'll keep him away. Get my father out of here. Oh God, the walls are on fire. It's bad, Adam. Hurry! Save my father!"

Adam felt his arm pulsing with raw pain, weakening as he carried Thomas down the front stairs. He felt an instant of dizziness, then shook his head, coughed, and kept moving. He felt a strange pulling in his back, weird, but nothing really. Thomas was now unconscious. He prayed he wasn't dead. He heard another shot, then another, but nothing all that close.

"I'm right behind you, Adam. Go, quickly!"

He didn't realize Becca wasn't with him until he was out the front door and two agents had lifted Thomas from his shoulder. "Jesus, a chest wound. Get the the paramedics over here!"

"The fire department is on the way," Gaylan Woodhouse said, running up, his gun still at the ready. "My God, you're shot, too, Adam. Hey, Hawley, get over here. We need some help." Adam stood there holding his arm, his teeth gritted. And now, of all things, that pulling in his back, it was bringing him down.

"Where the hell is Krimakov?" Savich shouted.

"Becca," Adam said, looking around wildly. "Becca?"

"Jesus," Hatch said, running to Adam. "He got you in the back, boss. Did you know you got shot in the back? Oh God, hurry, let's get him down."

"Becca," Adam said, frantic now, and he knew he was barely hanging on. "Where's Becca?" He saw the flames billowing out of the upstairs windows. The beautiful ivy that nearly covered that side of the house was on fire.

"Thomas shot Krimakov," Adam said to Gaylan Woodhouse and Hawley, who were bending over him. "He's got to still be inside. Maybe he's unconscious or dead. Jesus, where's Becca? Please, you've got to find her."

The walkie-talkie boomed out, "No one has tried to come out of any windows or the back of the house."

"Get Krimakov," Gaylan shouted. "Dammit. GET HIM!"

Becca, oh God, where was Becca? He wanted to go back into that house to find her. He had to, had to, but he just couldn't move. The fire wasn't only in the house now, it was inside him and it was eating its way out. The pain in his back held him utterly locked in place. He couldn't move.

"Oh my God," an agent shouted. "Up there!"

"It's Becca," Gaylan Woodhouse whispered. "Oh, no."

Adam did move, suddenly, with a spurt of strength he didn't know he had. He roared to his feet. He followed everyone's eyes to the roof of the house and felt his heart drop to his feet. No, please Jesus, no. But it was Becca, on the roof of the burning house.

"Becca!"

There were at least a dozen people standing in the front yard, looking upward. Then everyone was silent, still.

There, highlighted in flames, stood Becca, in her white nightgown, her bare feet spread, holding the Coonan between her hands.

"Becca," Adam shouted, "shoot the fucker!"

But she didn't. She just stood there, pointing the Coonan at Mikhail Krimakov. He was holding his arm, blood dripping through his fingers. Blood also dripped down his cheek from a head wound. He was leaning over, as it was nearly beyond him to straighten. What had happened to his gun? Oh God, Adam couldn't believe what he was seeing, would have given five years of his life if he could have changed it, if he could even have moved, at least tried to save her. But there was nothing he could do. He saw an agent raise a rifle. "No," he said, "don't try it. He's off at an angle. Don't take the chance of hitting her. Where are the firemen?"

Flames had caught the roof on fire now, licking out of the balcony off Thomas's bedroom. It wouldn't be long now until the flames ate the roof and sent it crashing into the house, until it was too hot on the roof for her to stand there, barefoot.

He heard her then, speaking loudly, very clearly.

"It's over," Becca said to the young man not eight feet from her. "Finally, it's over. You lost, Mikhail, but the cost was too high. You killed eight people, just because they were there."

"Oh no, I killed many more than that," he said, raising his head, panting with the pain. "They didn't count, any of them. I used them, then of what possible use were they to me?"

"Why didn't you stop when your father died in that car accident?"

He laughed, he actually laughed at her. "It wasn't an accident, you stupid bitch. I killed him. He wanted me to stop this, said I'd already done enough, that this was just too much. He'd turned soft, he'd become a coward. I killed him because he'd become a weakling. He wasn't worthy any longer. He betrayed my beloved mother's memory. Yes, I clouted him on the side of the head and drove him in his car over a cliff."

There wasn't a sound from anyone standing below. Then, the sound of sirens in the distance. The flames were licking up over the edge of the roof now. She had to get out of there. Adam stood there, impotent. *Becca, please, please. Get the hell out of there.*

Becca said, her voice still strong, still clear and loud, "It ends here, Mikhail. Since I knew you'd try to escape back through that roof trapdoor, you had to know I wouldn't let you get away. It ends here."

"Yes," he said. "It ends here. I killed the bastard who murdered my mother—your beloved father. I've done what I promised to do. And I took pleasure along the way, cleaning out the vermin that had invaded my life."

He was standing very still, this handsome young man she'd spoken to in the gym in Riptide. He was slowly straightening now, standing tall.

"My father isn't dead, Mikhail. He'll survive. You failed."

"The roof is going to collapse beneath us, Rebecca. It's getting hotter. You're barefoot. It's got to be burning your feet now, isn't it?"

Fire trucks pulled up to the curb, men jumping out, going into action. Becca heard a man yelling, "We've got a two-story residential fully involved structure fire! Jesus, what's going on here?"

"Oh shit, there are people standing on the roof! That woman has a gun!"

"We can't ladder the building, it's too late. Get the life net!"

Becca heard them, felt her feet now, the heat burning them, wondered if the roof would collapse under her. "We're going down, Mikhail," she said. "Look, they're bringing one of those safety nets. We'll jump."

"No," he said. "No." Then he pulled the lighter out of his jacket again and lit his sleeve. He rubbed it on his shirt, his pants, even while she watched, so horrified she froze. Then he smiled at her, nearly ablaze now, and ran at her, yelling, "Come away with your boyfriend. Come, let's fly together, Rebecca!"

She pulled the trigger, once, and still he came, a ball of flame now, running toward her, nearly at her, his arms outstretched. She fired again, then again and again, fired until the Coonan was empty.

He fell forward, nearly into her, but she jerked away just in time and he rolled over and over, a flaming ball of fire, off the roof to the ground below.

She heard people yelling. A jet of flame caught the sleeve of her nightgown. She ran quickly to the side of the roof, stood there for just an instant, slapping down the flames on her arm even as the fire inched closer and closer, and at last the firemen had the safety net in place.

Adam yelled, "Jump, Becca!"

And she did, without hesitation, her nightgown billowing out around her, her long legs bare, the white sleeve of her nightgown smoking. She hit the white safety net, her nightgown tangling around her. It closed over her for just an instant, and then a fireman yelled, "We've got her. She's okay!"

He watched her scramble out of the confines of the safety net, shake off the firemen. She ran toward him, and he saw the shock in her face, the blindness in her eyes, but he couldn't think of anything to say to her. Then there was simply nothing. He collapsed where he stood. The last thing he heard before the blackness closed over him was the huge roar of the collapsing roof and Becca's voice, saying his name over and over.

Chapter 31

*H*e was buried in pain, so deep he wondered if he'd ever climb out, but he knew he could deal with it, even appreciate it, because it meant he was still alive. Finally, after what seemed like beyond forever, he managed to gain a bit of control and forced his eyes to open. He looked up at Becca's smiling face. Ah, but the worry in her eyes, her pallor, it scared him. Was he going to die after all? He felt her fingers lightly touch the line of his eyebrow, his cheek, his chin. Then she leaned down and kissed where her fingers had touched him. Her breath was sweet and warm. His own mouth felt like he'd dived mouth-first into a box of dried manure.

"Hello, Adam. You'll be just fine. I'll bet you're really thirsty, the nurse said you would be. Here's some water to drink. Take it slow, that's it."

He drank. It was the best water he'd ever tasted in his life. He managed to say, "Thomas?"

"He'll live. He told me so himself when he came out of surgery. The doctors say it looks good. He's in great shape, so that's a big help."

"Your arm?"

"My arm is okay. Just a bit of a burn, nothing serious. We all survived. Except for Mikhail Krimakov. He's very dead. He'll never terrorize anyone again or kill another person. I know you're in bad pain, the bullet went through your back, broke a rib. The other bullet went right through your arm. You'll be okay, thank God."

He closed his eyes and said, "It nearly killed me watching you on the roof with him. The flames kept getting closer and closer, the wind whipping your nightgown around your legs, whipping the flames higher. I wanted to do something, but I just stood there yelling at you and I nearly lost what sanity I had left."

"I'm sorry, but I had to go after him, Adam. That's how he got into Thomas's house, from the end of a very long oak branch; then he jumped onto the roof and managed to get the trapdoor open and made it into the attic. When I saw him going down to the end of the hall where those pull-down steps to the attic are, I knew he would escape. I just couldn't let him do it. He got in that way, the chances were he'd get out. I had to stop him." She paused a moment, looking inward. "Then he wanted to die. And he wanted me to die with him. But I didn't. We won." She kissed him again, and this time he managed to smile just a bit through the god-awful pain.

"Now, no more about it. I've done nothing but answer question after question for the FBI. Mr. Woodhouse keeps coming back again and again, but it's mainly to see Dad, not for any more questions. Do you know what Savich is doing? He's sitting in the waiting room, checking out churches on MAX to find one for us to get married in. He said he did that for another FBI agent who'd been shot, and sure enough, the other agent got married on the date and in the church that Savich picked. He said it was a special calling of his."

"My folks?" Adam said. The pain was getting worse, that damned broken rib was digging into him like a sword, dragging him under, and he wanted to howl with it. The novelty of having himself distracted was losing its touch and wearing thin. But he knew he had to hold on, just a bit longer. He wanted to look at Becca, just look at her, hear her voice, perhaps have her kiss him again. He wanted her to kiss him all over, that would be very nice. He tried to smile up at her but it was a pathetic effort. Thank God she was safe. He wanted to lie very quietly and keep knowing that she was safe and she was here and that was her hand on his face.

"But Becca, I have to ask you to marry me before Savich can find a church. What if you say no?"

"You already sort of asked me when we were at your house. But I want the real words now. Ask me, Adam, and see what I say."

"I hurt real bad but will you marry me? I love you, you know."

"Yes, of course I will. I love you, too, more than even I can imagine. Now, Savich has already spoken to both your mother and your father. In fact, the last time I checked in, they were sitting on either side of him. Ah, I like them, Adam, very much. There are brothers and sisters and all sorts of second and third cousins coming in and out. They seem to be on some sort of rotation schedule. Oh yes, everyone is sticking his oar in about church locations and dates. I didn't know you had such a large family."

"Too large. They refuse to mind their own business. Always underfoot." He coughed and it hurt his rib so badly he thought he'd expire on the spot. He couldn't control it any longer. The pain in his rib and in his arm was slicing right through him, pulling him down and down. He was going to sink under and never come up. Then he heard the nurse say, "I'm going to give him some morphine. He'll be okay in just a moment. I guess he forgot it was there. Then he needs to rest." He hadn't forgotten, he just knew he wouldn't have been able even to push down the button because he was just too bloody weak. His arms were limp at his sides. He hated needles and there were two of them sticking out of his arms. Jesus, he was a mess but he'd be okay. Becca loved him. He said, his voice slurred, "I'm glad you love me. That makes two of us now."

He thought he heard her laugh. He knew he felt her palm against his cheek.

And then he drifted away, the pain pulling back, like a monster's fangs pulling out of his flesh, and it felt blessedly wonderful. Then he was asleep again, deeply asleep, and it was black and dreamless and there was nothing there to hurt him and that was a very good thing.

Becca slowly straightened over him.

The nurse smiled at her from the other side of his bed. "He's doing great. Please don't worry, we're taking really good care of him. I hope he'll sleep now. He should, since the pain has lightened up. You need to get some rest, too, Ms. Matlock."

Becca gave Adam one last long look, a last kiss on his mouth, then walked out of his room, down the corridor to the small sitting room with two windows looking onto the parking lot, pale yellow walls dotted with Impressionist prints. That small room was filled with the latest batch of relatives. There was Adam's mom, Georgia, playing with Sean, while Sherlock and Savich were laughing, taking turns announcing yet another church and yet another possible date for Becca and Adam's wedding, only to have a boo from one relative who had to go salmon fishing in Alaska, or another who had to go to Italy on business, or yet another who had an appointment with her lawyer to cut her husband out of her will. On and on it went.

Becca said from the doorway, "I'm happy to announce that Adam asked me to marry him and I accepted. However, he was hurting a lot. Maybe he won't remember when he wakes up. If he doesn't, why, I'll just have to ask him."

"My boy will remember," his father said, a man Adam resembled closely. He grinned at her. "One of the first things Adam told us when he could talk was that he is going to have that second bathroom on the top floor of his house redone so you wouldn't turn him down due to ugly green tile on the counters."

"Well, that certainly shows commitment," she said. "Tell you what, I'll pick out the new tile and then we'll see how fast I can get him to the altar."

She left them laughing, a very nice sound, and now they could do it more easily since their son would be all right. They seemed to like her, which was a relief. His mom was something else. She owned a Volvo dealership in Alexandria and was an auctioneer on the side. His father, she'd been told by one of Adam's older brothers, owned and operated a stud farm in Virginia.

Well, *her* father was alive, but that was all he needed to be, thank you very much. Actually, she wasn't at all certain what he did for a living, but who cared? She thought briefly of his house, where her mother had spent time. Now it was gone, just a shell left. It didn't matter. Her father was alive.

She took the elevator up to the sixth floor, to the ICU. She could make that trip in her sleep, she'd gone back and forth so many times now.

Thank God the hospital administration had managed to keep the media away from this area. The doctors and nurses nodded to her. She walked into the huge room with its hissing machines, its ever-present mixture of smells that was overlaid with a sharp antiseptic odor that reminded her of the dentist's office, and the occasional groan from a patient.

An FBI agent sat by her father's cubicle.

"Hello, Agent Austin. Everything all right?"

"No problem," he said and a grin kicked in that was positively evil. "You'll like this. One enterprising reporter managed to get this far, and then I nabbed him. I decked him, stripped him naked, and the nurses and doctors tossed him in a laundry cart and wheeled him down to the emergency room, where they left him, his hands and feet tied with surgical tape, his mouth gagged. Ah, since then, no one else has tried it."

"I just heard about that," she said, rolling her eyes. "One of the doctors told me he'd never before been surrounded with such laughter in the emergency room. Well done, Agent. Remind me to stay on your good side."

He was still chuckling when she eased around the light curtain surrounding her father's bed and sat down in the single chair. He was asleep, not unexpected, and it didn't matter. He was on powerful medications and even when he was awake, his mind couldn't focus. "Hello," she said, watching him breathe slowly, in and out through the oxygen tubes in his nostrils. "You're looking wonderful, very handsome. I might have to give your hair a trim though, maybe in a couple of days. Adam will be all right as well, but maybe he's not quite as good-looking as you are. He's sleeping right now. Oh yes, I'm sure you'll be pleased to know that we're going to get married. But you won't be surprised, will you?" White bandages covered his chest. Tubes stuck out of him, and like Adam, he seemed to have a score of needles in his arms. He lay perfectly still, but he was breathing evenly, steady and deep.

"Now, let me tell you again what happened. Mikhail shot you in the chest. You have a collapsed lung. They did what's called a thoracotomy. They cracked open your chest to stop the bleeding and put a chest tube in between your ribs. It's hooked up to suction. That thing's called a pleuravac and you'll hear bubbles in the background. Now, when you wake up the tube will hurt a bit. There are two IV's in place and you'll have this oxygen tube in your nose for a while longer. Other than that, you're just fine."

He was breathing slowly, smoothly. The bubbles sounded in the background. "The house is gone and I'm very sorry about that," she said. "They couldn't save anything. I'm sorry, Dad, but we're alive, and that's what's really important. I just realized that not everything is gone, though. After Mom died, I put all of her things in a storage facility in the Bronx. There are photos there, and a lot of her things. Maybe there are even letters. I don't know, because I couldn't take the time to go through her papers. We'll have those. It's a start."

Did his breathing quicken a bit?

She wasn't sure.

What was important was that he was alive. He would get well.

She laid her cheek against his shoulder. She stayed there for a very long time, listening to the steady sound of his heart beating against her face.

She got the call at the hospital at eight o'clock that evening. She'd just left her father and was going back downstairs to be with Adam when a nurse called out, "Ms. Matlock, telephone for you."

She was surprised. It was the first call she'd gotten, or rather, it was the first call they had put through to her.

It was Tyler and he was talking even before she could say hello. "You're all right. Thank God it's all over, Becca. Jesus, I've been frantic. They had footage of your father's burning house, for God's sake, with this huge safety net in the front yard. They said you'd nearly died, up there on that roof with that maniac, that you shot him finally. Are you truly all right?"

"I'm fine, Tyler. Don't worry. I'm spending all my time at the hospital. Both my father and Adam Carruthers were shot, but they'll both survive. The media is outside, waiting, but it will be a long wait. Sherlock is bringing me clothes and stuff so I don't have to try to sneak out of here and take the chance the media might nab me. How's Sam doing?"

There was a bit of silence, then, "He misses you dreadfully. He's really quiet now, won't say a word. I'm worried, Becca, really worried. I keep trying to get him to talk about the man who kidnapped him, to tell me a little bit about him and what he said, but Sam just shakes his head. He won't say a word. The TV said that man was dead, that he set himself on fire and hurled himself at you. Is that true?"

"Very true. I think you should take Sam to a child psychiatrist, Tyler."

"Those flimflam bloodsuckers? They'll start psychoanalyzing me, claiming I'm not a fit father, tell me I need to lie on a couch for at least six years and pay them big bucks. They'll say it's about me, not Sam. No way, Becca. No, he just wants to see you."

"I'm sorry, but I can't leave here for another week, at least."

Then she heard a little boy's wail, "Becca!"

It was Sam and he sounded like he was dying. She didn't know what to do. It was her fault that Sam was having problems, all her fault. "Put Sam on the phone, Tyler. Let me try to talk to him."

He did, but there was only silence. Sam wouldn't say a word. Tyler said, "It's bad, Becca, really bad."

"Please take him to a child shrink, Tyler. You need help."

"Come back, Becca. You must."

"I will as soon as I can," she said finally, and hung up the phone.

"Problem?" a nurse asked, a thick black brow arched.

"Nothing but," Becca said, and lightly touched her fingers to her right arm. The burns were healing and were itching a bit now.

"Problems are like that," the nurse said. "It rains problems, and then, all of a sudden, it's a sunny day, and the problems have just evaporated away."

"I hope you're right," Becca said.

The next day, Adam was much improved, even managed to joke with his nurse, who patted his butt, and her father came down with pneumonia and nearly died.

"It's nuts," Becca said to Agent Austin. "He survives a bullet to the heart and gets pneumonia."

"There's got to be some irony in that," Agent Austin said, shaking his head, "but no matter, it still sucks."

"He'll pull through," the doctor said over and over again to Becca, taking her hands in his. Maybe the doctor didn't like the irony, either, Becca thought, lightly touching her father's shoulder. It was odd, when she touched him—settled her hand on his arm, laid her hand over his, lightly touched his shoulder—his breathing calmed, his whole body seemed to relax, to ease.

And when he was finally awake, his mind alert, and she touched him, he smiled at her, and she saw the pleasure in his eyes, deep and abiding. And when she whispered, "I love you, Dad," he closed his eyes briefly, and she knew she didn't want to see his tears. "I love you," she said again, for good measure, and kissed his cheek. "We're together now. I know you love Adam like a son, but I'm very pleased that he isn't your son. If he were, then I couldn't marry him. Now you'll get him anyway."

"If he ever makes you cry, I'll kill him," said her father.

"Nah, I'll do it."

"Becca, thank you for telling me about all your mother's things safely in storage in New York."

He'd heard her, actually heard her speaking to him. And since he'd heard her speaking to him, just maybe her mother had heard her as well, maybe she did have a final connection with her. "You're welcome. As I said then, it's a start."

"Yes," Thomas said, smiling up at his daughter. "It's a very good start."

Adam was now walking up and down the corridor, ill-tempered, his back throbbing, his arm throbbing, feeling useless, wanting to hit someone because he felt so damned helpless. At least the damned catheter was out.

He was carping and carrying on when Becca laughed and said, "All right, you've finally driven me away. My father is doing fine, the pneumonia is kicked, and I'm going to Riptide to see Sam."

"No," he said, leaning against the hospital corridor wall, utterly appalled. He wanted to grab her and tuck her under his arm. "I don't want you going there alone. I don't trust McBride. I don't want you out of my sight. I'd really like it if you would sleep in my bed with me and I could hold on to you all night."

She realized she'd rather like that as well, but she said, "There's no danger, Adam. How could there be? I'm not going to see Tyler. I'm going to see what's going on with Sam. Don't forget, Adam, it's my fault that Krimakov even took him, my fault that Sam got traumatized. I've got to fix it. Tyler has nothing to do with it."

"Dammit, it was Krimakov's fault. Give it another couple of days, Becca, and I'll go with you."

"Adam, you can barely get to the bathroom by yourself now. You'll stay here and just concentrate on getting well. Spend time with my father. And maybe you could work on all those church dates as well. None of your family can come to an agreement."

"Well, are you still going to marry me?"

"Is that your final offer?"

He looked both pissed and chagrined. Suddenly he laughed. "I swear I'll change that green tile. Do you mind moving from New York, living down here? We're really close to your dad. Is he going to rebuild?"

"We haven't discussed it yet. Yes, Adam, I'll marry you, particularly if you change that bathroom tile. Consider it a done deal. I have no real ties to Albany. Goodness, there are so many folk around here who need good speechwriters. I'll make a fortune.

Now, you can't flirt with any of the hospital staff anymore, you got that? I'm considering that we're now officially engaged.

"Ah, good, here's Hatch. Is that cigarette smoke I smell, Hatch? Adam won't like that. He'll probably take a good strip off you for that, maybe hit you with his walker."

She watched the two men argue, smiling. Sherlock came up behind her and said, "Everything nearly back to normal, I see. Let's watch CNN. Gaylan Woodhouse is going to be on in about a minute. He's speaking for the president, and you're going to love this spin."

Good grief, she thought, watching the TV, she was now a heroine. Someone, she had no idea who, had somehow taken a photo, very grainy, showing her facing Krimakov on that burning roof, her white nightgown blowing around her legs, her Coonan held in front of her in both hands, pointed straight at Krimakov. Gaylan Woodhouse wouldn't shut up. "Oh dear," Becca said. "Oh dear."

"It's been a long haul, and you came through," Sherlock said, and hugged her tightly. "I'm really glad to have met you, Becca Matlock, and I like your being a heroine. I have this feeling that you, Adam, and your father will be coming to lots of barbecues over at our house, beginning when they get out of this joint. Did I tell you that Savich is a vegetarian? When we barbecue, he eats roasted corn on the cob. We won't know about Sean and his preferences for a while yet. Have you agreed to the date and that marvelous Presbyterian Church your in-laws have been members of for years and years?"

"Not yet," Becca said. "Hey, I'm so famous maybe I'll ask if the churches want to place bids for our ceremony."

"You're a writer, you could write a book, make a gazillion bucks."

"She'll have to make it fast," Savich said, coming up and squeezing his wife against his chest, "fame is fleeting nowadays. Another week, Becca, and you'll be a last-page footnote in *People* magazine."

The next day, Becca flew to Portland, Maine, rented a Ford Escort, and drove up to Riptide. It was cooler this trip, the breeze sharp off the ocean. The first person she saw was Sheriff Gaffney, and he was frowning at her, his thumbs hooked in his wide leather belt.

"Ms. Matlock," he said, and gave her his best intimidating cop look.

"Hi, Sheriff," she said, grinned at him, and went up on her tiptoes. She gave him a big kiss on the cheek. "I'm famous, at least for a week, that's what I was told. Be nice to me."

For the life of him, Sheriff Gaffney couldn't think of a thing to say except "Humph," which he did. "I'll want to speak to you about that skeleton," he called after her. "I'll come to Jacob Marley's house this evening. Will you be there?"

"Certainly, Sheriff, I'll be there."

Then she ran into Bernie Bradstreet, the owner and editor of *The Riptide Independent.* He looked very tired, as if he'd been ill. "My wife's been sick," he said, then he tried to smile at her. "At least all your troubles are over, Ms. Matlock." He didn't mention how she'd lied to him that long-ago night when Tyler had taken her out to dinner at Errol Flynn's Barbecue on Foxglove Avenue. He was a good man, bless him.

And then she was knocking on Tyler's front door just as the sun was setting. The insects were beginning their evening songs. She heard a dog bark from a house farther down on Gum Shoe Lane. She wished she'd brought a cardigan. She shivered, rang the bell again.

Tyler's car wasn't in the driveway.

Where was he? Where was Sam?

She didn't understand it. She'd told him when she'd be here and she was only ten minutes off. She got back in her rental car and cut over to Belladonna, to Jacob Marley's house. She'd paid the rent through the end of the month, so the place was still hers. She planned to use this time to pack up the rest of her things, have the place cleaned, and return the keys to Rachel Ryan. Surely Rachel was spending a lot of time with Sam, helping him. She hoped Rachel was also trying to convince Tyler to take Sam to a child shrink.

She turned the key in the lock and shoved the door open.

"Hello, Becca."

It was Tyler, standing there, Sam in his arms, smiling really big. "We decided to wait for you here. I left the car just down the road. We wanted to surprise you. I've got champagne for us and some lemonade for Sam. I even bought a carrot cake; I remembered that you liked it. Come in." He set Sam down, and Sam stood there staring at her.

Tyler walked to her and wrapped his arms around her back. He kissed the top of her head. "I like your hair. It's natural again. God, you're beautiful, Becca." He kissed her again, pulled her more tightly against him. "I thought you were beautiful in college, but you're even more beautiful now."

She tried to ease away from him, but he didn't let her go.

He gently pushed her chin up with his thumb and kissed her. It was a deep kiss, and he wanted to make it deeper, he wanted her to open her mouth. Sam was standing there saying nothing, just looking at them.

"No, Tyler, please, no." She shoved hard against his chest and he quickly stepped back.

He was still smiling, breathing hard, his eyes bright with excitement, with sex, lust. "You're right. Sam is standing right here. He's four, not a baby anymore. We shouldn't do this in front of him." He turned to smile down at his son. "Well, Sam, here's Becca. What do you have to say to her?"

Sam didn't have anything to say. He just stood there, his small face blank of all expression. It scared her to her toes. She walked slowly to him and went down on her knees in front of him. "Hello, Sam," she said, and lightly touched her fingertips to his cheek. "How are you, sweetie? I want you to listen to me now. And believe me because I wouldn't lie to you. That bad man who kidnapped you, who tied you up and put you in the basement, I swear to you that he's gone now, forever. He'll never come back, ever, I can promise you that. I took care of him."

Sam didn't say anything, just suffered her touching his face. Slowly, she brought him against her even though his small body was stiff, resistant.

"I've missed you, Sam. I would have come sooner, but my father and Adam—you remember Adam, don't you?—they were both hurt and I had to stay with them in the hospital. But now I'm here."

"Adam."

One word, but it was enough. "Yes," she said, delighted, "Adam."

She turned her head when she heard Tyler say something, but he shook his head at her. "Sam's okay, Becca. I also brought some barbecue from Errol Flynn's for our dinner. All the fixings, too. Would you like to have dinner now?"

And so they drank champagne, Sam drank his lemonade, and everyone ate barbecue pork ribs, baked beans, and coleslaw in Jacob Marley's kitchen. The carrot cake from Myrtle's Sweet Tooth on Venus Fly Trap Boulevard stood on the kitchen counter.

After she'd answered countless questions about Krimakov, she said, "What about the skeleton, Tyler? Have the DNA results come in yet? Is it Melissa Katzen?"

Tyler shrugged. "No word yet that I know of. Everyone believes it is. But that's not important now. What's important is us. When do you want to move up here, Becca?"

Becca was handing Sam another rib. Her hand stilled. "Move back here? No, Tyler. I'm here to see Sam and pack up my things."

He nodded and tore meat off the rib he was holding. He chewed, then said, "Well, that's all right. You've just reconnected with your dad, so you need to make sure he's okay, get to know him and all that, but we need to set our wedding date before you go back to see him. Do you think he'll want to move up to be near you after we're married?"

She set down her fork near the coleslaw. Something had gone terribly wrong. She didn't want this, but there was no hiding from it now. She said it slowly, calmly, aware that Sam was now very still again, not eating, listening, but she had no choice. She said, "I'm truly sorry if you've misunderstood, Tyler. You and Sam are my very dear friends. I care about both of you quite a lot. I've appreciated all you've done for me, the support you've given me, the confidence you've had in me, but I can't be your wife. I'm very sorry, but I just don't feel about you the way you want me to."

Sam continued to sit there on two thick phone books, still and silent, the half-chewed pork rib clutched in his small fingers.

She forced a smile. "We should probably have this talk after Sam's gone to bed, don't you think?"

"Why? It concerns him. He wants you for his mother, Becca. I told him that was why you were coming back. I told him you were going to fix everything and you'd be here for him forever."

"We should speak of this later, Tyler. This is between us. Please."

Sam looked down at his plate, his small face drawn, pale in the dim kitchen light.

"All right then," Tyler said. "I'm going to put Sam down with a blanket in the living room, on that real comfortable sofa. What do you think, Sam?"

Sam didn't tell them what he thought.

"I'll be right back, Becca."

He scooped Sam up off his phone books and carried him out of the kitchen. She shivered. The house felt uncomfortably cool. She hoped Sam would be warm enough with just one blanket. She hoped Sam had gotten enough to eat. She wished Tyler had wiped Sam's fingers off better.

What was she going to do? Was she the one off base here? Had she given Tyler the wrong impression? She'd known he was jealous of Adam, and that's when she had pulled back from him, even cooling her friendship toward him. But still he'd misunderstood, still he'd come to believe that she wanted to be his wife. How could it be possible? She'd said nothing, done nothing, to give him that idea. And he was using Sam, which was despicable of him.

Sam. What was she going to do? There was something very wrong, triggered, she supposed, by Krimakov's kidnapping of him. She heard Tyler walking back toward the kitchen. She had to clear this up, quickly and cleanly. She had to think what she could do to help Sam.

She'd gotten the name of a really good child psychologist in Bangor from Sherlock. She would start there.

But she didn't have a chance to start anything because Tyler said from the doorway, "I love you, Becca."

Chapter 32

*N*o, Tyler, no."

Tyler just smiled at her, an intimate smile that chilled her to the bone. "I've loved you from that first time I saw you in Hadley's freshman dorm at Dartmouth. You were looking lost, wondering where to find a bathroom."

She smiled at that, no recollection at all of that meeting. "You didn't love me, Tyler. You dated lots of girls in college. You married Sam's mother, Ann. You loved her."

He came into the kitchen and sat down across from her. "Sure I loved her for a while, but she left me, Becca. She left me and she didn't plan to come back. She was even going to take Sam, but I didn't let her."

What was he talking about? Of course things couldn't have been smooth between them, since Ann had ended up leaving him. They'd faced off about it? There'd been a confrontation? But that didn't concern her now. She said, "I'm really sorry if you've gotten the wrong idea, Tyler. Please believe me. I am your friend and I hope I always will be. I would like to see Sam grow up."

"Since you're going to be his mother, of course you'll see him grow up. You'll make him well again, Becca. He's been silent and withdrawn ever since his mother left."

"Would you like some coffee?"

"Sure, if you're going to make some." He watched her measure the coffee into the machine, then pour in the water. He watched her press the switch, watched it turn red.

"Tell me about Ann," she said, wanting him to remember the woman he'd loved, distract him from her. Why had Ann left him? Had there been another man? Why hadn't she taken Sam with her? So what if Tyler had tried to fight for custody? Sam was still her child, not his. But she had just run away without him.

Tyler was still watching the coffeemaker. She watched him breathe in the aroma. Finally, he said, "She was beautiful. She'd been married to a guy who left her the minute he found out she was pregnant. We hooked up kind of by accident. She couldn't get the gasoline cap off her car. I helped her. Then we went to Pollyanna's Restaurant." He shrugged. "We got married a couple months later."

"What happened?"

He said nothing for a very long time. "The coffee's ready."

She poured each of them a cup.

He took a drink, then shrugged. "She was happy and then she wasn't. She left. Nothing more, Becca. Listen, I swear I'll make you happy. You won't ever want to leave. We can have more kids, yours and mine. Sam was Ann's kid anyway."

"I'm going to marry Adam."

He threw the coffee at her. He roared to his feet, sending the wooden chair crashing against the wall, and shouted, "No, you're not going to marry that goddamned bastard! You're mine, do you hear me? You're mine, you damned bitch!"

The coffee wasn't scalding anymore, thank God, but it hurt, splashing on her neck, on the front of her shirt, soaking through to her skin.

He leapt toward her, his hands out.

"No, Tyler." She ran, but he was blocking any escape out the back door. There was no place to go except down to the basement. But she'd be trapped down there. No, wait, there was another small entry on the far side of the basement where long-ago Marleys had had their winter cords of wood dumped. She saw it all in a flash, and ran to the basement door, jerked it open, then pulled it closed behind her. She locked it, flipped on the light, saw the naked bulb dangling from the ceiling by a thin wire, even as she heard him pulling on the knob on the other side, yelling, calling her horrible names, telling her that he would get her, that she wouldn't leave him, not ever.

She ran down the wooden stairs. She looked at the wall where she'd found Sam propped up, bound and gagged, then at the far wall that still gaped open from when the skeleton had fallen out of it after that storm.

She heard the basement door splinter. Then he was on the stairs. She pulled and jerked at the rusted latch that held the small trap-door down. It was about chest high. *Move, move,* but she was shrieking it in her mind, not out loud. What the hell was going on with him? It had happened so quickly. He had snapped, just snapped, and turned into a wild man. Oh God, a crazy man.

She heard his feet clattering to the bottom steps. The latch wouldn't give. She was trapped. She turned to see him running across the concrete floor. He came to a stop. He was panting. Then he smiled at her.

"I nailed that trapdoor shut last week. It was dangerous. I didn't think we should take the chance that a kid could open it and fall through. Maybe hurt himself. Maybe even kill himself."

"Tyler," she said. *Be calm, be calm.* "What's going on here? Why are you acting like this? Why this rage? At me? Why?"

He said, all calm and serious, and he actually waved his finger at her, like a lecturing teacher, "You're like the others, Becca. I hoped you would be different, I would have wagered everything that you were different, that you weren't like Ann, that faithless bitch who wanted to leave me, wanted to take Sam and go far away from me."

"Why did she want to leave you, Tyler?"

He shrugged. "She thought I was smothering her, but that was just in her mind, of course. I loved her, wanted to make her and Sam happy, but she started pulling back. She didn't need all those other friends of hers, they just wasted her time, took her away from me. Then she told me that night that she had to leave me, that she couldn't stand it anymore."

"Stand what?"

"I don't know. I tried to give her everything she wanted, both her and Sam. I just wanted her for myself, wanted her to commit herself only to me, and all I asked was that she stay close to me, that she look to me for everything. And she did for a while, and then she didn't want to anymore."

"She left?"

In that instant, Becca knew that Ann McBride hadn't gone anywhere. She was still here in Riptide.

"Where did you bury her, Tyler?"

"In Jacob Marley's backyard, right under that old elm tree that was around when World War One began. I dug her deep so no animals would dig her up. I even gave her a nice service. She didn't deserve anything, but I gave her all the religious trappings, the sweet and hopeful words. After all, she was my wife." He laughed, remembering now and said with a smirk, "Old Jacob had been dead by then nearly three years so I didn't worry about getting rid of him that time."

He started laughing then. "I killed that ridiculous old dog of his—Miranda—a long time ago. The bitch didn't like me, always growled when I came near. The old man never knew, never."

She remembered the sheriff telling her how much Jacob Marley had loved that dog, how she'd just up and died one day. Her heart was pounding, slowly, painfully. Somehow she had to reach him. She had to try. "Listen to me, Tyler. I didn't betray you. I would never betray you. I came here to Riptide because of what you'd told me about it. I was here to hide out. This was sanctuary for me. You helped me, so very much. You don't know how much I appreciate that." Were his eyes calmer now? Maybe, but he frowned and she tried to still her fear, said quickly, "That madman was trying to kill both me and my father. The last thing I wanted to think about was falling in love with anyone. I never meant for you to believe there was more to it than friendship."

His eyes were darker now, a barely leashed wildness that scared her to her soul. He said, his voice sarcastic, "You didn't want to fall in love, Becca? Then why are you marrying that bastard Carruthers?"

For a moment, her brain refused to work. He was right, oh God, he was right. She had to think, she had to do something. She was alone in the basement with a man who wasn't sane, a man who was somehow twisted, a man who had murdered his wife and buried her in Jacob Marley's backyard. Sheriff Gaffney had been certain that Tyler had murdered his wife. Everyone believed that the skeleton that fell out of the basement wall had been Ann McBride. But it wasn't.

She couldn't bear it, just couldn't. She had to know, all of it. "Tyler, the girl in the wall. Was it Melissa Katzen?"

He said, his voice indifferent, bored, "Yes, of course it was."

"But she was young, not more than eighteen when someone killed her. That was more than twelve years ago. Did you kill her, Tyler?"

He shrugged. "Another faithless bitch, little Melissa. Everyone thought she was so sweet, so giving, so yielding. And she was with me, at first. I gave her attention, small presents—lots of them, all clever, imaginative. I told her how pretty she was and she soaked it up until one day she turned down my latest gift to her. It was a Barbie, all dressed to travel, ready to elope.

"She didn't want to tell anyone about us, and that was okay by me. I was going to laugh my head off when we came back married. She called me that night, asked me to meet her. She gave me back the Barbie, then told me she didn't want to run away with me after all. She whined that she was too young, that her parents would be hurt if she ran off with me. I told her that she had to marry me, that no one else would, that I was the only one who really loved her." He shook his head then, frowning at something he was remembering, at what he was seeing. He said slowly, "She became afraid of me. She tried to get away from me, but I caught her."

She could see him with Melissa in her Calvin Klein white jeans, the cute little pink tank top, see him, hear him trying to convince her, then screaming at her, then killing her. She knew she had to keep him talking. She couldn't let him stop now. When he stopped talking, he would kill her. She didn't want to die. She remembered then that Sheriff Gaffney was coming over, at least he'd told her he was. Sometime during the evening. Dammit, it was evening, right in the middle of evening. Where was he? What if he just left when no one answered the door? She was so afraid, she stuttered. "B-but Jacob Marley was here, wasn't he?"

"True enough." He shrugged. "I put her in the shed out back, and then the next day, I got Jacob Marley out of the house with a phone call. He had a very old sister who lived in Bangor. I called and told him she was dying and asking for him, begging him to come to her. The old jerk left and I dug out the wall and put Melissa behind it. Then I bricked it back up. My dad was in construction before he fell off a building and he taught me a whole lot. I knew all about bricklaying. Then I left. You want to know something funny? Jacob Marley's ancient sister died the very day he showed up at the old folks' home in Bangor. He never even realized that it had been a fake call."

"Tyler, why did you bury Melissa in the basement wall? Why Jacob Marley's house?"

He laughed, and that laugh chilled her. "I was thinking maybe I'd call in an anonymous tip, tell everyone I saw Jacob Marley kill Melissa, then saw him with cement and bricks."

"But you didn't."

"No. Maybe I'd left fingerprints somehow on her. I couldn't take the chance." Then he slashed his hand through the air. His voice lowered, his eyes darkened, became as intense as a preacher's in a revival tent. "I wanted you to marry me, Becca. I would have taken care of you all your life. I would have loved you, protected you, kept you close forever. You could have been Sam's mother. But once you were with me, you wouldn't have spent all that much time with him. Sam would have understood that you were mine first, that he really had no claim on you, not like I did."

She was cold, so cold her teeth would soon be chattering. This lovely man who'd seemed so kind, so gentle—he was crazy, probably he'd been born crazy.

"Melissa was only eighteen, Tyler. Both of you were too young to run off."

"No," he said. "I was ready. I believed she was. She was faithless. She would have left me, just like Ann did."

How many other women had he believed to be faithless? How many others had he killed, then hidden their bodies? Becca looked around for some sort of weapon, anything, but there was nothing. No, she was wrong. There were about half a dozen bricks stacked against the gaping open wall, about six feet away from her.

She took a step sideways.

He said thoughtfully now, "I think I'll bury you close to Ann. Out under that elm tree. But you don't deserve a nice service, Becca, not like the one I did for Ann. She was Sam's mother, after all."

"I don't want to be buried there," she said and took another step. "I don't want to die, Tyler. I haven't done anything to you. I came here to be safe, but I wasn't ever safe, was I? It was all an illusion. You were just waiting, waiting for another woman to love, to possess, to imprison so she'd want out and then you could kill her, do it all over again and again. You need help, Tyler. Let me call someone." She took another step toward the bricks.

He began walking toward her. "I would rather have held you close, Becca. If only—"

There was the sound of a car pulling up outside.

"The sheriff's here," Becca said quickly. "Just listen. It's over, Tyler. The sheriff won't let you hurt me now." She took another quick step to the side. Three feet, just another three feet. Tyler looked up and frowned when he heard a car door slam. He cursed even as he ran toward her, his hands outstretched, his fingers curved inward.

Becca leapt toward the pile of bricks, went down on her knees, and grabbed one. He was on her then, his hands around her neck, and she slammed the brick against his shoulder. His fingers tightened, tightened, and his face was blurring above her. She raised the brick again, brought it upward slowly, and he twisted just as she heaved it toward him. It struck his face and he howled with agony, and his fingers loosened for just a moment. She gulped in air and struck again. He sent his fist against her head, and she saw blinding flashes of light, felt the pain sear through her head, knew she couldn't hold on. She was losing and she would die because she wasn't strong enough. She tried to raise the brick again but she just couldn't.

"You faithless bitch, you're just like all the rest of them!" His fingers tightened around her neck.

Sheriff Gaffney yelled, "Let her go, Tyler! Let her go!"

Tyler was heaving now, his fingers strong, so strong, tighter and tighter now and she knew she would die.

Then there was a shot. Tyler jerked over her. His hands fell away. She blinked and saw him turn slowly to face Sheriff Gaffney, standing in a cop's stance, his Ruger P85 pistol held tightly between his hands. "Get away from her, Tyler. Now! MOVE!"

"No," Tyler said and lunged for her again. Another shot rang out. Tyler fell on top of her, his face beside her head. Dead weight, oh God, he was now dead weight.

"Hold on, Ms. Matlock, and I'll get him off you."

Sheriff Gaffney pulled Tyler away. He'd shot him once in the head and once in the back. He gave Becca a hand up. "You okay?"

She was shaking, her teeth chattering, her throat burning, Tyler's blood all over her, and the healing burn on her arm was throbbing fiercely. She smiled up at him. "I think you're the most wonderful man in the whole world," she said. "Thank you for coming in the house. I prayed and prayed that you would see all the lights on and come in."

"I heard little Sam crying," Sheriff Gaffney said.

"Hello?"

A small, thin voice. It was Sam and he was standing at the top of the basement stairs.

"Oh, no," Becca said. "Oh, no."

"I told him to wait in the kitchen for me. Damn. Okay, I'll get

Rachel over here. Can you pull yourself together, Ms. Matlock? We'll go upstairs and you can take care of little Sam until Rachel comes. He loves Rachel a whole lot, you'll see. Just keep hanging in there, ma'am." He shook his head, then said, "Jesus, I knew Tyler killed his wife, just knew it in my lawman's gut, you know? But he also killed poor little Melissa twelve years ago. I wonder how many other women he's killed who rejected him."

Becca didn't want to know.

Adam was stretched out on the sofa in his living room, a soft pillow under his head, a light afghan pulled to his waist, so relieved that Becca was back safe and sound, staying in his house, her stuff scattered around, all at home now, that all he could do was grin. He didn't want her to leave, not ever. He heard her moving about in his wonderful, fully equipped, very modern kitchen, making him a healthy snack, she'd said.

The house was cool since he'd had the good sense to install central air conditioning when he'd moved in. Soon, he thought, he'd get that ugly green tile out of that second-floor bathroom. Another four days and his energy would come roaring back and he'd head right down to the tile store. The master bedroom was sort of stark though, with just a big black lacquer bed and a matching black lacquer dresser, a couple of comfortable black and white chairs, and a good-sized closet, nearly walk-in, he'd said to her, lots of room for both of their clothes.

He'd had big plans for the bed the night before, about two hours after she'd gotten back from Riptide, and even though he couldn't move a whole lot and his flexibility was nearly nil, and he'd tended to moan from pain as well as pleasure, it hadn't mattered. She'd simply taken charge. He nearly shook the afghan off now just thinking of how she'd looked astride him, her head thrown back when she'd screamed out his name. And then she'd just fallen over on him and the pain had nearly made him yell again. But he'd just lain there, silent, holding her against him as best he could, stroking her smooth back, and then she'd slowly straightened, frowned at the sight of his rib, all yellow and green now, and said, "I nearly killed you, didn't I? I'm sorry."

"Kill me again," he'd said, and she laughed and kissed him and kissed him again and again, and loved him until he'd yelled again, this time not from any pain in his damned ribs.

He felt good. He had plans for that bed again today, maybe in just about an hour from now. He was stronger today, maybe he'd be able to do a bit more moving around. He hadn't been able to get his hands and mouth everywhere he'd wanted to last night. Ah, but today. His fingers itched, his mouth sort of tingled. And what about tomorrow and the next day? Maybe he'd just keep her in the bedroom until they had to leave for the church to get married, then right back here again. It sounded really fine to him. He wondered what Becca thought about mirrors everywhere.

She brought him some iced tea and a plate of celery stuffed with cream cheese. She sat beside him and fed him between kisses.

He realized suddenly that there was something different about her, something he couldn't quite put his finger on. Then he realized what it was—she was hiding something from him. And her eyes, something different there—he realized, finally, that it was shock. Well, he supposed that nearly burning to death on the roof of her father's house would leave its mark. Or realizing that a man she'd really liked was in actuality a madman. Or just maybe, he thought, his mouth tightening, that madman, Tyler McBride, had, in fact, hurt her or tried to, and she hadn't seen fit to tell him.

He ate another celery stick, eyeing her, then said, his voice all suspicious, his brows lowered, "You swear you didn't lie to me? You swear that there was no real trouble up in Riptide?"

She lightly stroked her fingers over his cheek. She loved to touch him. She particularly liked him naked so she could touch all of him, kiss all of him. She leaned down now and kissed his mouth, then straightened again. She said, all easy and blasé, "Nothing that couldn't be handled. Sam's all right. I can't tell you how wonderful Rachel is with him. I knew they were close, but when she came running into the house, Sam left me in a flash and went right to her. I thought she would fall apart, she was so relieved that Sam was all right. Sheriff Gaffney told me that since there are no relatives, Rachel and her husband would very likely adopt Sam. I called up this morning, and she's already got him an appointment with that child psychologist Sherlock recommended up in Bangor. Oh yeah, I also told Rachel she was probably a very conscientious great real estate agent, but I would never ever rent another house from her again." His frown was still in place. "Rachel laughed." The frown lightened.

Adam said, "Yeah, I'm relieved about Sam, too. But wait a minute, Becca. Back up here. You're telling me that McBride didn't try to hurt you when you told him you didn't love him?"

She stuffed another celery stick in his mouth and kissed him all over his face as he chewed. She whispered in his ear before he could talk again, "Nothing to worry about, really, Adam. It's all over and done with. Hey, you do like the celery sticks?"

"Yeah, they're good. All three dozen that you've stuffed down me. Now, tell me about how Sheriff Gaffney had to shoot Tyler once he knew the skeleton was that girl Melissa Katzen. I'm not really all that clear on any of it. I want every little detail, Becca. No, no more celery sticks. Yeah, a kiss is all right, but hold off now. You're not going to distract me anymore."

But she just kept kissing him until he was nearly heaving himself off the sofa. She said against his ear, "I used low-fat cream cheese, better for your arteries."

"Becca." He grabbed a fist of her hair and pulled her close to his face. "Tell me the truth. What the hell happened up there?"

"Adam, it wasn't all that big a deal. Really, nothing worth mentioning except that Sheriff Gaffney really came through. He was the hero. I've probably forgotten lots of it because it just wasn't that memorable. Really, the sheriff had everything under control. I didn't even count. I wasn't even important. Would you please stop your worrying and just forget it? I'm home now." He felt her hand on his belly and he nearly lost it, but he didn't. He let her go but his frown deepened. Before he could say anything, Becca smiled and said as she got up from the sofa, "Oh, my, just look at the time. Not enough time for me to have my way with you. But I do have a couple of minutes. Do you want me to give you a nice rubdown before I go to the hospital to see Dad?"

He thought about her hand on his belly, moving south, and he nearly went *en pointe*. He said on a big sigh, "No, but how about an apple, Becca? I love apples."

She knew exactly what he was thinking. "I love you, Adam. Maybe when I get back from the hospital, we can play a game of Monopoly, or something, okay? But that means you've got to rest while I'm gone. Now, you just sit tight and I'll get you that apple."

The phone rang. Adam stared after Becca, then picked it up. "Hello."

"Is this Mr. Carruthers?"

"It is."

"This is Sheriff Gaffney, from Riptide."

"Hello, Sheriff. What can I do for you?"

"I just wanted to speak to Ms. Matlock, make sure she was all right."

"Well," Adam said slowly, staring toward the door, "there's still some shock, you know, from what happened."

The sheriff sighed. "Understandable, of course, poor girl. I don't mind telling you that it was pretty hairy there for a while, Mr. Carruthers. I'm sure it's made your hair stand on end, hearing about her lying on the basement floor with McBride straddling her, choking the life out of her. She was hitting him with a brick, but it wasn't working, she was getting too weak. The guy was strong, really strong. As you know, I had to shoot him, but even that didn't stop him. He was over the top, completely whacked out, as my boys say, and all he wanted to do was kill her. I had to shoot him again and the guy fell right on top of her, covered her with blood. But it's over now. All the questions answered. Ms. Matlock didn't get hysterical, thank the good Lord. She's a strong girl. As a man of the law doing my duty, I really appreciated that. And now she's home, and I hear the two of you are going to get married. You're a lucky man."

"Yes, Sheriff. Thank you."

"Anytime. Well, do give my best to Ms. Matlock."

"You can be sure that I will, Sheriff." Adam heard her breathing. She was on the line in the kitchen. She'd listened in, heard everything, hadn't said a word. His heart was pounding slow, heavy strokes. He was so furious he couldn't think of anything to say. Then he opened his mouth and shouted into the receiver at the top of his lungs, "BECCA!"

She cleared her throat. "Ah, Adam, I've got to go to the hospital now."

He breathed deeply, got hold of himself, and said, "Not just yet. Bring me my apple. I'll even give you a bite before I wash your mouth out with soap for those whoppers you told me."

"Sorry, Adam, the apples aren't ripe enough. You know Sheriff Gaffney, he exaggerates, really, he—"

"After I wash your mouth out, I'm going to maybe shave your head. Then if I'm still pissed off, I'm going to make you change that green tile in the bathroom, then—"

"I'm outta here, Adam. I love you. Er, I'll buy ripe apples while I'm out."

She hung up the phone.

"BECCA!"